Quake

Quake

Philia Players Book Three

Giuliana Victoria

Copyright © 2024 by Giuliana Victoria. All rights reserved.

No portion of this book may be reproduced in any form without written permission from the publisher or author except as permitted by U.S. copyright law.

No part of this book may be reproduced in any form by any electronic or mechanical means, including information storage and retrieval systems, without explicit written permission from the author, except for the use of brief quotations in a book review.

This is a work of fiction. Names, characters, places, businesses, organizations, events, and incidents are either the product of the author's imagination or used fictitiously. Any resemblance to actual persons, living or deceased, is unintentional and merely coincidental.

Editing by Steph White (Kat's Literary Services)

Proofreading by Louise Murphy (Kat's Literary Services)

Illustrated cover and chapter headers by Sonia (artbysoniagx on Instagram)

Typography and hardcover design by Disturbed Valkyrie Designs

French Translation confirmation by Alexa (abookybrunette on Instagram)

Contents

Also by	IX
Content Warning	X
Table of Cocktents	XI
Playlist	XII
De Laurentiis Family Tree	XV
Signature Fragrance	XVI
Excerpt from Harmony	XVII
Dedication	XVIII
Foreword	XIX
Prologue: Gianni	1
1. Gianni	5
2. Gianni	15
3. Lark	21
4. Gianni	25
5. Gianni	27
6. Lark	33
7. Gianni	41
8. Lark	47

9.	Lark	55
10.	Lark	65
11.	Gianni	73
12.	Lark	79
13.	Lark	85
14.	Lark	91
15.	Gianni	101
16.	Lark	107
17.	Gianni	111
18.	Lark	113
19.	Lark	119
20.	Gianni	123
21.	Lark	127
22.	Gianni	133
23.	Lark	145
24.	Gianni	149
25.	Lark	153
26.	Lark	159
27.	Gianni	165
28.	Lark	167
29.	Gianni	187
30.	Gianni	193
31.	Lark	199

32. Gianni	203
33. Gianni	205
34. Lark	209
35. Lark	217
36. Gianni	221
37. Lark	227
38. Gianni	231
39. Lark	235
40. Gianni	241
41. Lark	251
42. Lark	255
43. Gianni	257
44. Lark	261
45. Gianni	267
46. Gianni	271
47. Lark	275
48. Lark	281
49. Gianni	295
50. Lark	301
51. Gianni	305
52. Lark	309
53. Gianni	317
54. Lark	321

55. Gianni	329
56. Lark	331
57. Gianni	333
58. Lark	335
59. Gianni	337
60. Gianni	339
Epilogue: Part One - Gianni	353
Epilogue: Part Two - Lark	361
Epilogue: Part Two - Gianni	365
Bonus Scene: Gianni	367
Afterword	369
Acknowledgments	370
About the Author	372
Books & Book Clubs Mentioned In Quake:	373

Also by

Philia Players Series
Quiver
Tremble
Quake
Book #4 in the Philia Players Series: Coming Soon!
Sign up for my newsletter for a sneak peek at Luca and Samara's story.
Ps. Did you find the title hidden in Quake?

Secret Trials Series
Professional rugby (rugby thighs and hoochie daddy shorts? Sign me up!) x Female college soccer series COMING SOON!

Rosa Ranch Series
Western romance with cowboys and a lot of Latin influence COMING SOON!

Standalones & Novellas
Mistletoe Misconduct[1]

---

1. Read Mistletoe Misconduct

Content Warning

There are mentions of death, graphic on-page motor vehicle accident caused by a drunk driver, parental death, parental abandonment, depression, anxiety, bipolar disorder, a hypoglycemic episode, discussion of a transphobic experience had by a side character, exploration of kinks, and mention of past suicidal ideation, as well as explicit language. Chronic illness and mental health representation are a few main themes in *Quake* and will be in each of my books in some capacity. Please keep that in mind and protect your mental health. <3

Table of Cocktents

For anyone who wants to jump straight to the spice, know how far ahead the "good stuff" is, or wants to skip it entirely.

Chapter 6: Intrusive Thoughts
Chapter 26: Private Practice
Chapter 28: Big Bad Wolf
Chapter 31: Breakfast For Two
Chapter 37: Carnival Chaos
Chapter 40: Gearshifts & 'Gasms
Chapter 48: Ghosted
Chapter 51: Good Boy
Chapter 52: A Smacking Good Time

Playlist

Teenage Dirtbag – Wheatus
Dance, Dance – Fall Out Boy
Pain – Three Days Grace
Out of My League – Fitz and The Tantrums
Heart-Shaped Box – Nirvana
I'm Not Okay (I Promise) – My Chemical Romance
I Am Machine — Three Days Grace
Misery Business – Paramore
I Will Not Bow — Breaking Benjamin
Animal – Neon Trees
Drive – Incubus
One Step Closer – Linkin Park
Zombie – BadWolves
golden hour – JVKE
Use Somebody – Kings of Leon
Cupid's Chokehold – Gym Class Heroes
Tear in My Heart – Twenty One Pilots
What You Need – The Weeknd

The Kill – Thirty Seconds To Mars
All The Small Things – blink-182
R U Mine? – Arctic Monkey
All My Life – Foo Fighters
Tongue Tied – GROUPLOVE
Sweater Weather – The Neighbourhood
Dirty Little Secret – The All-American Rejects
Whore – In This Moment
Animal I Have Become — Three Days Grace
Welcome to the Black Parade – My Chemical Romance
I Found — Amber Run
Fuck it I love you – Lana Del Ray
Leave a Light On (Talk Away The Dark) — Papa Roach feat. Carrie Underwood
I Write Sins Not Tragedies – Panic! At The Disco
Sugar, We're Goin Down – Fall Out Boy
Ocean Avenue – Yellowcard
bitches broken hearts – Billie Eilish
Still into You – Paramore
1985 – Bowling For Soup
Somebody Told Me – The Killers
The Pretender – Foo Fighters
Best of You – Foo Fighters
The Middle – Jimmy Eat World
Afraid – The Neighbourhood
Say It Ain't So – Weezer
Chasing Cars – Snow Patrol
Breakeven – The Script
I Hate Everything About You – Three Days Grace
Papercut – Linkin Park
Can't Stop – Red Hot Chili Peppers

Kryptonite – 3 Doors Down
Mr. Brightside — The Killers
Bring Me To Life – Remastered 2023 — Evanescence

De Laurentiis Family Tree

Gloria: Mother
Angelo: Father
Alessandro (Ale pronounced Ah-lay): Oldest Brother
Luca: Second Oldest Brother
Dante: Oldest Adopted Brother
Arielle: Dante's Wife
Sammy, Benny, & Lily: Dante & Arielle's Children
Gianni (Gi): Youngest Adopted Brother
Charlene (Charlie): Youngest & Only Adopted Sister
Rose: Charlie's Wife
Arlo & Sofia: Charlie & Rose's Daughters

Signature Fragrance

Lark Hughes:
Voce Viva Eau de Parfum by Valentino
Gianni Amato-De Laurentiis:
Y Eau de Parfum Intense by Yves Saint Laurent

*"if you ever get the chance to love a person who knows grief,
do not let them go.
you see, the thing about grief
is that it's not exclusive
it consumes life
it taints everything a little gray.
it won't hesitate to remind you
that everyone and everything you love
will disappear someday.
but i've found that the people who carry grief
love with a fierceness that no one else knows.
they understand what's at stake
because they've had to let someone go.
so they remember the little things
and they show up when it counts
they know that life is rare
you won't have to spell it out.
so don't take for granted
the people who know loss
for they know more about love
because they know what it costs.
healing requires visiting versions of your past self and
treating them with kindness."*

—Whitney Hanson

For my husband, whose ability to love me unconditionally and manage to put me first in every way never ceases to amaze me. Every. Single. Day. This one's for you. <3

I've never been quite as proud of anyone in my life as I am of you, and I hope the strength you've exuded throughout your battle with depression is something that my readers can feel as they read about Gianni. He was created in your likeness, with many of your talents and struggles in mind. Every day, you continue to surprise me in the most amazing ways.

Foreword

While this book is a work of fiction, and was written as a love letter to my husband, who spent his entire life believing everyone felt the way he did at baseline and has worked through this with the help of therapy and lifesaving medication, I wrote the first draft of Quake during my own struggle with depression and anxiety.

I felt like I wasn't good enough for any of this. Not good enough to be an author or a physician assistant, a career I've dedicated my entire adult life to, and then some. I was under an immense amount of pressure, struggling with constant change from being thrown around between preceptors, clinical rotations, and a few extremely abusive preceptors, at that. It was also winter, which is a time of year that I have difficulty with, as many people do.

During this time, I contemplated ending my life on multiple occasions. The emotions written in this book are real and raw. They're transparent and will be difficult to read for many of you. If you need to DNF this book for the sake of your mental well-being, I'll never judge you for that.

A major fear of mine is losing my husband in any capacity, but specifically in a motor-vehicle accident. I have an unnerving amount of anxiety about it every day, even with very little reason for this thought to consume so much of my life. I'd like to think that by writing this story the way I have, it's been healing in a way. I'm unsure of whether that's true or not. I guess that's between me and my therapist, but I hope this story finds you at the right time and is able to help in some capacity.

For anyone considering ending their life, or who's finding it difficult to rationalize against their inherently irrational thoughts, please ask for help. I've included resources at the back of this book, because you never know what you can overcome if you don't stick around to find out.

I'm not really sure whether I'd be here today if it weren't for the support of my friends, family, professors, advisor, program director, and of course, my incredible husband. But what I *can* say for certain is this: I would've never known how unbelievably amazing the rest of this year had turned out if I hadn't stuck around, and I sincerely hope you do too.

***

I wanted to quickly note that while many people living with diabetes who have a diabetes alert dog will have them with them everywhere, as many service animals are expected to, not all do. This is for many reasons, including the fact that it just doesn't always make sense to do so, especially when in a situation where you have a working continuous glucose monitor and others around you who would be able to provide emergency medical attention if needed.

This will not be the experience of everyone with diabetes, but I wanted to mention it for anyone who had questions about it. I'd also like to mention that having a dog around constantly in a spicy book is, well, not ideal.

Prologue: Gianni

Friday, September 13, 2024

"Come on, Alex, it's too late for this shit. We can just call him an Uber or something. The guy doesn't even *like* you. Why would he ask you in the first place?" I ask my best friend, confusion and frustration lacing my words and a grimace firm on my face.

He looks at me with his light brows pulled taut and that small pout he knows I can't say no to. "Gi, does it matter *why* he texted me? Maybe the guy has no one else, and if he hates me as much as he tries to make you believe..." His choice of words strikes me as odd. Make *me* believe? Not *us*? But before I can ask, he's already moving on. "Isn't that even more reason to help him out? Because it means he must be really, *truly* alone in this world." He pleads with me to change my mind, though I know he's going anyway. And if he's going, so am I. That's how it's always been.

I groan, grab the keys off the kitchen counter, and head to the door. "Fine, but we get him, dump him at his place, and *leave*. Nothing more, got it?" I ask.

Alex jumps up and down, clapping his hands together before heading to toss on a pair of sneakers. "You're the best, Gi!" he shouts.

"Yeah, yeah, yeah, let's make this quick."

***

"Please remind me why we're picking up a grown-ass man from a fucking party?" I groan, making a right onto the road Alex just told me to turn onto.

I can feel, rather than see, him roll his eyes at me playfully. "*Because,* Gi, he asked for our help, so we're doing this."

One of these days, Alex is going to *help* the wrong fucking person, and it's gonna get him in trouble.

"Okay, now make a left onto Swanberry," he instructs, pointing across the road. I stop at the red light, waiting as Alex messes with the Bluetooth, swapping the song from "Teenage Dirtbag"[1] to "Dance, Dance."[2]

The light turns green, so I pull out, making the left onto the one-way street within the small community.

Seconds later, a massive white truck comes flying around the corner of the road ahead, turning left instead of right and heading straight at us. Their headlights nearly blind me as I try to swerve off to the side of the road.

My heart is pounding, my mind going fuzzy as my tires skid through the wet grass and into a tree. It makes direct contact with Alex's side of the car, and when we're finally stopped, my gaze swings straight to him.

He braces his hands against the dashboard, his head hanging between his shoulders. "Alex," I breathe out, my throat constricting with worry.

---

1. **Teenage Dirtbag – Wheatus**

2. **Dance, Dance – Fall Out Boy**

He slowly lifts his gaze to mine, and those bright eyes of his are now glossy and dull. "Call nine-one-one," he chokes out, each word leaving him looking more and more pained.

My vision blurs with hot tears as I scramble in my seat, reaching for my phone, but before I can pull it out of my pocket, red and blue lights are pulling beside us. My stomach drops to my toes, bile climbing my throat.

This can't be happening.

Alex reaches his hand out to grip my thigh, and it's at this moment that I know *I'm about to lose him.*

Chapter One

Gianni

Sunday, February 9, 2025

I wake up to a dark room, the blackout curtains preventing me from telling what time it is. My head is pounding already, which doesn't bode well for the day. Soccer practice starts up again in a couple of weeks, and I have no idea how I'm going to manage this time around. Every day, it gets harder and harder to care about my career, or anything else, for that matter.

Alex's death is the single worst thing to have ever happened to me. And yet, I feel mostly *numb*.[1]

I toss my legs over the side of the bed, righting myself and grabbing for my phone. I check the time.

2:37 p.m.

---

1. **Pain – Three Days Grace**

Shit. I didn't fall asleep until after three this morning, but I didn't think I'd sleep in this late. I have two hours to get my shit together and head to my parents' house for Sunday dinner.

I flick on my lamp, illuminating my studio apartment, which looks like I live with thirty unruly house guests and not just the golden retriever mix I adopted at Pawsitively Purrfect. Thankfully, Pickles is with Kat and Ale this weekend because they requested a playdate at their apartment. Something about their pit bull, Tank, bonding with Pickles or something. I'm not really sure. I miss the damn dog though. Some days, she seems to be the only reason I bother waking up *at all.*

Taking another look around the apartment, I cringe with self-loathing. *Who fucking lives like this?* I need to hire someone to come clean this mess up. These days, I just have no will to do anything. It's already a chore to get up, feed myself, work out, and make sure Pickles gets taken care of. Cleaning my apartment is just entirely too much work right now.

I get up, stopping at my dresser to grab a set of clean clothes and head to the shower to get washed up before hopping in the car to stop for some items my mom requested. She said she needed some WD-40 for her wheelchair because the wheels were sticking again.

An hour and a half later, I'm approaching the large brownstone home that I grew up in. I make my way inside, greeting everyone as I pass through, heading over to find Mom in the kitchen. When she sees me, she wheels over. "There's my handsome boy," she says solemnly. "Come give your momma a hug." I do as I'm told, realizing by the tone of her voice that I let my mask slip. Righting myself, I plaster a fake smile across my face, but the knowing look she gives me confirms that it never meets my eyes.

"Hey, Mom, I got the grease for your wheels so you can continue running over unsuspecting bystanders." I grab the WD-40 from the bag and kneel beside her, spraying the hinges and coating each one.

"Thank you, sweet boy. Now, what's got you so down today?" She's unlikely to let it go unless I give her an explanation. She probably won't believe anything I say, rightfully so, but I have to attempt to appease her anyway. If not for her, then for whatever's left of my sanity.

"I just missed Pickles this weekend while she's been with Ale and Kat, and training starts up in a couple of weeks, and I'm not super excited to have Damien on our team this year." None of that was a lie, but it isn't the reason for my perpetual shit moods.

"Ah, Damien is a real piece of work, but your teammates have your back. Don't let it get to you," she says in a reassuring tone, reaching out to squeeze my hand. Mom smiles sweetly at me in that gentle way that reminds me just how fragile she thinks I am.

I give her a nod, standing and putting the cap on the WD-40, placing it under the sink for her to use next time she needs it. Before she can continue to pry, I head out of the kitchen as quickly as I can, looking to hide out on the back patio despite the frigid temperatures outside.

On my way to the back, I see Dante sprawled out on the couch watching some children's show while he holds Lily across his chest. He looks up at me and quietly says, "Hey, kid, the boys missed you at their game last week."

My face automatically contorts. I know he doesn't mean to make me feel bad. He's just letting me know they care, but it makes me feel like shit all the same. I *wish* I could have been there too, but I just couldn't drag myself out of bed, let alone my apartment. The entire week—hell, the last month—has been a royal shit show. I give him a noncommittal grunt. "Yeah, I wish I could've made it too. Next time though," I say, but we both know I'm lying.

It's getting more and more difficult to hide how fucking exhausted I am all the damn time.

No amount of sleep seems to improve the bone-deep exhaustion that's settled into my soul since losing Alex, and that thought alone has an uncomfortable weight settling in the pit of my stomach.

"The boys are with Arielle at the grocery store. Charlie and Rose will be here shortly, and Kat and Ale are headed over with Pickles and Tank," Dante tells me as I make a move to head outside.

"Cool, I'll be out back if anyone needs me." *God, I hope no one needs me.*

The cool air hits my face, and a chill quakes through my body, making me shiver. I love the cold. It helps clear my head, and the crisp air makes it easier to breathe, but there's no denying that emotionally, I feel worse in the winter months.

I take a seat in the old metal chair with the chipped white paint and rust forming. I'm facing away from the house, overlooking the fenced-in yard, as I pull out my phone, pop my earbuds in, and press play on my audiobook. The book's about someone who gets trapped in a dystopian video game, and while none of it makes any sense, it's enough chaos to act as a distraction.

I allow myself to get lost in the chasm of this new world being built by the author, and about thirty minutes later, the sliding door behind me opens, letting a rush of heat burst out. I hear children shouting in the background, which means Alessandro and Kat have just arrived. The kids love Ale. He's clearly their favorite uncle, and I can't fault them. Luca is an ass, and I'm just a downer. I'd pick Ale over me too.

"Hey there." Kat's cheerful voice greets me as I turn my head toward her. "I've got a cute little lady ready to see you."

I hear a high-pitched whine and see Pickles trying to make her way through Kat's legs before she finally opens the door wide and lets her out to tackle me. She's a big girl, but she doesn't know it. Pickles hops directly in my lap, giving me kisses before spinning and plopping down on my legs.

My fingers twine into her soft fur, and I focus my attention behind her ears, giving her scratches in her favorite spot. I bend to kiss the top of her head, my mouth stretching with the first, albeit small, but genuine smile I've had in weeks. "Hi, pretty girl. Did you miss your daddy?"

She perks up, licking at my face again to confirm that she has missed me. I turn to Kat, who's now seated in the chair beside me with her knees tucked under her chin.

"Thanks for socializing her. What'd you guys do while she was there?" I ask because I really do care, but also because Kat is one of the kindest people you'll ever meet, and she's also the only one who doesn't look at me with pity.

"We took them to the dog park. She got covered in mud, though, and I'm pretty sure icicles were literally forming on her fur," Kat says, letting out a little snort. "So we took her to Pet Kingdom to get groomed, which is where she got that super cute bandana she's wearing." Kat points to Pickles, where a pink bandana with little dancing pickles is tied around her neck. "Oh, they also did a couple of feeding puzzles and..." She trails off, looking away sheepishly, and the guilty look in her eyes has my stomach fluttering with butterflies. "So..." she says, dragging out the word. "I went down an internet rabbit hole and found that there's a place called 'Rocket Dog' that offers classes like rally, rodeo, and agility. So I signed Pickles and Tank up for a tricks-for-treats class."

My eyes widen with alarm, but again, she continues. "Don't worry, though, it was super cheap." *That wasn't my concern at all.* "And I already have it worked out with Kas for him to take Pickles if you can't make it. He really doesn't mind," she promises, wrapping her arms around her drawn-up knees and clasping her hands together. "I would've waited to confirm with you, but there were only two spots available in the class, and I didn't want it to sell out!" She sucks in a breath for what seems like the first time since she started speaking.

She's cute enough to get away with murder, so I don't particularly mind the rambling, but the content of her thoughts is a tad disconcerting.

I look away from her for a moment, closing my eyes briefly and sucking in a deep breath. I blow it out slowly, focusing on calming my pounding heart before answering her. "Thanks for taking such good care of Pickles. I'm sure she'll really like the classes."

She gives me a small smile that crinkles the edges of her honey-brown eyes.

As the silence stretches, my heart begins to hammer against my ribs. I try to focus on anything other than that feeling.

I glance over and take note of her outfit, providing my racing thoughts with something less ominous to focus on.

Kat's wearing a cherry-red turtleneck and black denim pants, her hands turning white from the freezing weather.

"Gi," she finally says, her tone hushed. "I know you're not a fan of talking about your feelings." She pauses, her cheeks heating with embarrassment as she takes another moment to make sure it's okay if she keeps going. I work on a swallow, my jaw grinding together, but I give her a nod so she can get it out and we can get this over with. "I'm sorry if this is overstepping, but I care about you. We all do. And it isn't really any of my business, but Ale's shared some of what happened to your parents with me, and I can sort of relate. You know, because of everything with mine." She and her brother had their own horror show to live through as kids, and when that information got leaked to the press, they made it their mission to spread every detail of that tragic day to anyone who'd listen. "And Alex was a really great guy. I'm just sorry I hadn't gotten to know him better."

My heart sinks. Alex really liked Kat, and even hearing his name still stings.

"All that to say, I don't know what you're going through or how you're feeling." That admittance is exactly why I like Kat so much. She's capable of showing empathy without making me feel pitied like I do by every other well-meaning person in my life. "But if you ever need someone to talk to, I'm always here. And I mean that, Gi. I won't tell Ale or anyone else anything you want to share with me," she tells me with sincerity in her tone. "I won't dissect what you tell me or try to psychoanalyze you." Of course, as someone who lives with anxiety, she would know that that's one of my biggest fears. "I can just be a listening ear, but there's also absolutely nothing wrong with seeking professional help. You might think you hide it well, but every time I see you, your eyes lose just a bit more light." She trails off before catching herself, eyes suddenly brimming with tears.

My heart is lodged in my throat, and I feel bare and raw as she speaks so freely of the things I fear so much.

"It's okay to ask for help. It's *okay* to take medication for a chemical imbalance that's causing you to be so unhappy. It's *okay* to speak with a therapist. You're never alone in this, okay?" she asks me, and I give her a noncommittal nod. I know she's right, but the thought of seeing a therapist makes me want to vomit.

She grips the arms of her chair, pushing herself up and out before smiling at me and heading back inside. I should go in, too, but my head is spinning with thoughts. I always hear, "Mental health *is* health," and I agree, especially as someone who hasn't felt well in as long as I can remember. But seeing a therapist? That scares the shit out of me. I don't want to relive my trauma. I don't *want* to talk about it. And I definitely don't want the press meddling in my life and sharing all the sordid details of my childhood with the world when someone snaps a photo of me walking into or out of a psychiatric office.

The door slides open behind me. Luca's leaning through the doorway with one hand on the door and another on the wall beside him. "Come on, Eeyore, get inside. Mom won't let us eat until your sad ass is at the table with us." Luca's the only one who doesn't tiptoe around my shitty moods, and sometimes I wonder if it's because he feels the same or at least something similar. Like a shared cloud of sadness and anxiety looming over us both, but he's better at hiding it.

"I'm coming," I tell him, not having it in me to joke with him tonight. I lean down, whispering to Pickles, "Come on, pretty girl, you've gotta get up. We need to eat dinner." She lifts her head, her eyes finally opening as she stands, stretching her long spine with her front paws on the ground and her back ones still in my lap. She climbs down, sniffing around the back patio as she waits for me to peel myself out of this chair.

I get up, and she follows me inside, taking her place on the floor beside me at my end of the table.

Dinner goes as expected. The kids fight at their table in between giggling at one another and throwing food around like tiny piglets. Everyone pesters me and Luca about when we're going to bring someone home for them to meet, and then they rag on Ale for not having proposed to Kat yet. It's a lot of the same stuff we talk about every week at Sunday dinner. That's not to say these dinners are boring. That couldn't be further from the truth, but it's just familiar.

After dinner, we all help clean up. Ale and Kat put the kids to bed for their Sunday night sleepover.

Ale has always slept over at our parents' house on Sunday nights when he didn't have a game the next day. He does a much better job at spending time with our nephews and nieces than I ever have, and I envy his ability to give so much of himself to others.

Not that I'd expected it to, but even after he started dating, this routine hasn't changed much. Now Kat just stays over, too, treating our family as if it were her own, and truthfully, it feels like we always have been.

Dante and Arielle sneak back to their house, same as Charlie and Rose, who take this one night a week to have some alone time, knowing their children are in excellent hands. Once they're gone and Luca has sufficiently given us an Irish goodbye, leaving without saying a word, I leash up Pickles and start heading home, kissing Mom on the cheek and getting a hug from Dad.

I drive for the next twenty minutes before pulling up outside of my apartment. I park and, instead of heading inside, take Pickles on a walk around the block. There's a small park with a few black metal benches directly across the street from where we live. The trees are decorated with twinkling lights year round, so it's pretty well lit, even for a late-night stroll.

I start my audiobook again, feeling confident that the area is nice enough to not be in any danger. Pickles trots ahead of me, her tan tail wagging and the bells on her collar jingling with each step. When I first adopted her, I had trouble finding her in the apartment because she liked to flatten herself into a pancake and army crawl under the furniture or anywhere she could make herself fit. I got her a collar with tiny jingle bells so I'd hear her and know where she was. Eventually, I got used to them and haven't had the heart to do away with them.

We do a couple of laps around the park before I stop by a trash can, tossing my gum out. Just as I'm steering us back home, I hear a squawk and see a flash of black wings pass by us. This park is filled with crows, even at night. I read that crows don't see well at night, but with the constant artificial light here, you see them at night a lot more frequently than you would otherwise.

I feel Pickles tug on her leash, jolting forward toward something on the ground. She's got it in her mouth, and she's chomping. My lips pinch, and my eyebrows pull taut when I realize the damn crow dropped a fucking chicken bone for her! I quickly crouch down beside her, working to pry her mouth open and grabbing for the bone, but she panics and swallows it, looking at me with wide, guilt-ridden eyes. "Ah fuck, Picks, now we've gotta go to the vet," I tell her, running my hand through my hair, tugging on my roots in frustration.

"Come on, pretty girl, let's get in the car." I direct her over to the SUV, open the trunk and let her jump in. I've got a hot-pink dog bed back there with a blanket and her favorite stuffy. The dog is obsessed with things that happen to be pink, so I have an embarrassing amount of pink items in my possession. I really need to learn to stop letting her pick out her own beds, toys, and blankets because it's always *pink*. Dogs can't even *see* shades of red, but somehow, she always wants the pink toy, blanket, bed or whatever else.

She snuggles up in the back, suckling on her stuffy as I close the trunk and round over to the driver's side. I hoist myself into the SUV and start the heater for her before searching for the nearest emergency vet. It's almost midnight, so my options are limited because even the emergency clinics are mostly closed by now. It takes a few minutes, but I find a place that says it's open twenty-four hours, and it's only twenty-six minutes from here. I call them and let them know what happened so they know I'm on my way and can add me to their queue.

Chapter Two

Gianni

Monday, February 10, 2025

We have to take a lot of back roads once we get out of the perimeter of the city. After about a half hour of driving, we pull up to a gravel road with cottage-style homes on the right and a one-story building with glass walls directly ahead of us. Leafless cherry trees are to the left, and a stone-paved walkway leads from the parking lot to the front door.

I open the trunk, and based on the look on her face, I made the right decision by taking my poor, sweet girl to get help. Her tummy looks like it might be a bit distended already, and her eyelids look heavy. She's got a bit of drool hanging from her jowls, and it's clear she's not feeling well. "Come on, pretty girl, let's get you inside so you can feel better, okay?" I coo to her, keeping my voice gentle. She lifts her head, acting as pitiful as possible, and a wave of anxiety hits me. God, please don't let anything happen to this damn dog.

I lean over her, picking her up as gently as I can, grabbing her blanket to cover her as the snow starts falling in thicker sheets around us. I'm about to close the trunk when I hear her whimper, her eyes glued to the trunk as she gazes over her shoulder. And, of course, she's looking at her fucking stuffy. I shake my head at her, grabbing her stuffy and tucking it under my armpit as I support her giant body with one arm, closing the trunk and locking the Jeep Wrangler.

As we approach the doors, a short woman with a straight black bob comes rushing toward us, swinging the door out and holding it open. "Hi! You must be Gianni." Her eyes land on Pickles curled up in my arms, and she gushes over her. "Oh my gosh, and this little bundle of love must be Pickles! Oh goodness, Pickles, you don't look so good, but we're gonna have you feeling better in no time!" Her voice is high-pitched, and I internally cringe, having the same reaction to the way she speaks as I would to nails on a chalkboard. I know she's just being nice, and I imagine that kind of baby talk comes with the territory of working with animals all day, so I give her a small smile before heading to the counter to check in.

"I'll be with you in just a sec," the young blonde at the counter says without looking up at me. The woman who opened the door for me comes around the desk, whispering in the blonde's ear so quickly that I can't make out what she's saying. The blonde's head pops up from whatever she is doing, her eyes wide with surprise, before she quickly recovers, plastering a grin on her face. She gives me a slow perusal, visibly ogling me, and it makes my skin crawl. I'm officially losing my patience.

"What can I do for you, handsome?" she drawls, continuing to eye fuck me.

I huff with frustration. "I called about thirty minutes ago. Pickles ate a chicken bone, and she needs to be seen."

Her eyes dance with laughter, her cheek twitching. "Oh yeah, I remember your call. A *crow* dropped a chicken bone in front of your dog's face for her to eat?" she says with disbelief and amusement. "When did this happen exactly?"

"Just before I called," I tell her, refraining from rolling my eyes at her blatant mockery.

"Crows aren't nocturnal. Everyone knows that. If you gave your dog a chicken bone, you can just say that, silly. You don't need to *lie*; we all make mistakes," she tells me. I hope this isn't her failed attempt at flirting because she's going to be single for a long time if so.

I bristle regardless. "I didn't feed her a fucking chicken bone." My temper has officially flared, my patience worn so thin that I let the next words fly out of my mouth with little regard for the regret I'm bound to feel later. I'll let the guilt consume me as I try and fail to sleep tonight. "Do your damn job and check her in so she can see someone who can actually help her instead of eye fucking me and wasting my goddamn time."

The room, once filled with chatter and the occasional yipping dog, goes silent. Those in the waiting area with pets are holding their breath, shocked that I'd speak to someone like that. Frankly, I'm shocked too.

The blonde's dark brows shoot up her forehead in surprise before she sputters, "I... I wasn't, um, I wasn't doing that. I'll, uh, get you checked in." Then she mutters, regaining some of her earlier bravado, "You don't have to be such a dick though."

"Oh, shut up, Valerie. You should be able to get arrested for the way you were molesting this poor man with your eyes. And he's right, do your *damn job for once*," the black-haired woman from earlier says.

It's my turn to be shocked. Her voice is far less annoying to me now. I meet her dark eyes with my own, giving her the warmest and most genuine smile I can muster before saying, "Thank you. I'm sorry for causing a scene." My eyes cast downward toward the giant lump of fur in my arms. "I just want my pretty girl to get help, and I wasn't expecting to be accosted when I checked in." I'm not about to pussyfoot around the fact that this Valerie woman was being inappropriate.

"I completely understand. There's absolutely no need to apologize, and Val here was just heading out, weren't you, Valerie?" she asks the blonde with a now-harsh quality to her voice.

Valerie is clearly still stunned. Stammering, she grabs her things and makes her way around the counter.

The other woman leans across the desk to offer her hand. "I'm Betty. I've got Pickles all checked in, and Dr. Hughes will be with you guys as soon as she can." I shake her outstretched hand, thanking her again before taking Pickles to sit down.

The waiting room has been a revolving door of new people and new animals, and an hour later, I hear someone call for Pickles. I stand up abruptly, carrying her toward the person who called for her. "Hi, I'm Ryan. I'll take you and Pickles back to an exam room." She heads back, so I follow the petite brunette. Her white Crocs catch my eye, the jibbles in them almost making me laugh. I can't make out what all of them are, but as I enter the room, I take a seat on the blue bench. Still holding Pickles, I get a better look and see that there are otters, dogs, and dinosaurs on her shoes. The absurdity makes me chuckle, and I guess that's probably the purpose behind her strange attire. To bring some light to a place that is sometimes filled with grief as much as it is joy.

"So, Pickles, I hear a little birdy dropped a bone off for you. Poor thing. I've just gotta get some info from your daddy, and then Dr. Hughes will be right back to help you feel all better, okay?" She coos at her as she crouches down, squeezing Pickles's cheeks regardless of the drool she's now letting fall down her face in rivulets of slime.

She goes over some basic health history with me and then steps out to grab the doctor. A few minutes later, there's a gentle knock at the door before a woman, who I assume is Dr. Hughes, steps into the room.

My mouth is agape, and it'll take a forklift to pick it up off the floor. Dr. Hughes isn't some wrinkly older lady with graying hair. She's the most gorgeous woman I've ever laid eyes on. She's short, maybe five foot two, and her skin is a creamy porcelain, with light freckles dusting her cheeks. Her crimped waves of glossy, fiery auburn hair cascade down her chest.

When I finally raise my eyes to meet hers, she's looking at me with wide hazel eyes that look like a churning pot of emerald green, honey, and rust.

I realize I've been staring for longer than what would be considered socially acceptable, my mouth snapping closed before I recover. "Hi, sorry, it's um, it's just really late, so I'm tired. Social skills are a bit off at this hour," I tell her with an awkward chuckle that sounds foreign coming from my mouth. "I'm Gianni, and this pretty girl is Pickles." I gesture at the melted pile of fur, who's now peering up at me from my lap.

"Hi, Gianni. I'm Dr. Hughes, but you can call me Lark." She gives me a genuine smile that starts melting the edges of my ice-encased heart. My chest is heating, my stomach filling with what might be butterflies, but who knows? It's the shit you hear people describe in movies, but for all I know, it might just be anxiety. Or heartburn? I'm about to be thirty-one next month. Thirty-one-year-olds get heartburn, right? We had red sauce for dinner, so it's probably just that, and I'm overanalyzing this feeling.

She's standing so close to me, petting Pickles as she lifts her lips, inspecting her gums and palpating as she works her way down her body to her abdomen. Her scent is intoxicating, like an orange cream isicle or something equally as sweet and delectable as she looks. The closer she gets, the more foggy my mind becomes. *What the hell is happening to me?*

"Okay, sweet girl, your daddy is gonna have to plop you on this table for me so I can get a better look at you." I stand obediently, and Dr. Hughes takes the pink blanket and stuffy from me, placing it on the metal table in front of us. I place Pickles on top, and she groans.

Leaning down, I kiss her soft head and whisper to her, "You're gonna be okay, pretty girl. The pretty lady doctor is gonna make you feel all better." I'm rubbing her velvety ears when I finally look to my side and see Dr. Hughes staring at me with an inscrutable expression.

Chapter Three
Lark

Did he just call me pretty while whispering to his sweet golden baby? The most gorgeous man on the planet, whose home games I used to attend every chance I got, just called me *pretty*. I was admittedly a tad shell-shocked when I stepped in the room, especially with how he was staring at me like he wanted to eat me, but now? *Is it hot in here?* I fight the urge to wave my hand like a fan to cool off. I'm burning up.

Back to business though. I'm sure I'll thoroughly dissect this entire encounter later. "I'd like to do an abdominal ultrasound on her to see if there's any free fluid that might indicate bleeding from a bone fragment, and I'll need to get some X-rays as well to better visualize it and determine what our next steps should be. I'd usually induce vomiting since it hasn't been too long since she's eaten, but being that she's already looking sick, I don't want to risk her puking up sharp fragments and causing more harm. Is it okay if I bring her back for those tests?"

He gives me a nod before asking, "Can I actually carry her back? I'll stay out of your way, but she just likes to be held, and I don't want anyone breaking their back trying to lug around her hundred-pound bulk." I can tell he's worried, and aside from when he's on the field, he doesn't strike me as someone who gets in people's way.

"Yeah, of course. You'll just have to step out when we do the X-rays." I lead him back to the room where we do all of our tests and get started setting up the ultrasound. A while later, we've done all the necessary tests, and we've discussed a treatment plan.

"So I'm going to give her a shot of an anti-nausea medication to calm her tummy. It treats nausea and should help her keep fluids down. Then I'm gonna give her a few pieces of white bread coated in a couple of capfuls of mineral oil. The white bread will form around the chicken bone, and the mineral oil will act as a lubricant and laxative in her gut, so not only will she get it out sooner, but it'll prevent some of that friction as it comes out. That way, she doesn't have to deal with any unnecessary discomfort. If she doesn't pass it in the next forty-eight hours, or if she looks worse, which means if you see her drooling more, panting, acting lethargic, or anything abnormal for her, just call and head over." I ensure he understands the plan and is okay with everything before giving her the shot.

"Alright, pretty girl, you should be feeling better soon, sweetie pie," I say, speaking softly to her as I rub her ears. They're really just the softest ears ever. "Call if you have any questions or concerns, okay?" I smile at them, turning to leave just as Gianni wraps his large, warm hand around my arm. His hand is so large it completely dwarfs me, nearly covering my entire forearm.

I turn back to face him. His eyes are bright despite the late hour, and he's wearing the smallest of smiles, and yet, it lights his entire face up, his dimples making me sway a little. He looks down at his hand on my arm, shocked by his own behavior. He drops it, and the loss of warmth causes my body to *quake* as the chill of the room settles into my skin. "Sorry, I didn't mean to grab you like that. I was just wondering if you'd like to go out with me," he rushes, and the shock must be written all over my face as he continues. "On a date, I mean. I know that's really forward." His cheeks flame red, and he no longer meets my eyes as he continues rambling. "I never ask anyone out, but I'm afraid I won't see you again, so I'm pushing myself to just take the leap," he admits, and it makes me feel warm and fuzzy for a second before I squash that feeling.

I'm sure he doesn't have any trouble getting dates, which is why he never has to ask. People probably flock to him, though the media has been less than kind to Gianni. They're always picking apart his expressions, making comments about how sorrowful he is, and one reporter even described his eyes as "lifeless." Looking at me right now, they look gentle and warm. Like a clear pool on a sunny summer day that I could float away from all of my problems in. But all the warm and gooey feelings I have burn to ash when I'm hit with a wave of nausea.

"I'm sorry, Gianni," I say, my mouth dry as I piece together the right words. "I actually have a boyfriend, so I'll have to decline, but it's very sweet of you to ask. I hope you and Pickles get home safely." This time, I successfully leave the room, and I immediately run into Betty, practically bouncing off her scrubs-clad back. Her eyes are wide, but she recovers quickly, grabbing hold of my arms and pulling me into one of the empty rooms.

"Lark, I know Valerie is your cousin, but you need to fire her once and for all," she huffs out, hands on her hips in frustration.

I groan. "What'd she do now?" I ask, rolling my eyes. It's always something with her. I really, really can't stand her. She has a piss-poor attitude, and I'm not sure she even likes animals, but my dad helps fund this place, and his brother practically begged him to get her a job here.

"She was hitting on Mr. De Laurentiis and then made accusations about him having been the one to knowingly feed Pickles chicken bones," she angry whispers, her hands flailing in front of her face as she speaks. "Valerie can't seem to do her job, and she's driving me up a damn wall." She takes a deep breath. "I hate to do this to you, but it's getting to where it's me or her, honey. I can't keep working with her."

My heart sinks. She's frustrated, and I understand, but Betty is one of my favorite people on the planet, and she's the most hardworking employee I've got.

"Okay, I'll figure it out. What do you think about maybe switching her position instead? She could scan paperwork, or I could even open up the office for bathing and tell her she's in charge of cleaning all the kennels out. Maybe she'd just quit at that point." This is something I've thought about before, but I agree, it's time. She's gotta go, and that's not just my sudden surge of protectiveness over Gianni.

"You'll figure it out," she says, squeezing my shoulder reassuringly. "Maybe just speak with your dad. I think he'll understand." She seems so sure of that, and frankly, neither of us has any reason not to. *My dad is the best.*

Chapter Four

Gianni

It's nearly three in the morning by the time we're done at the vet, and my pretty girl seems to be doing better already, though she still refuses to walk. That's not really anything new though. She's always loved to be held, and I can't say I blame her. *I'd like to be held sometimes too.*

I approach the checkout counter, getting ready to pay for what I imagine will inevitably be a couple-thousand-dollar visit, when I see Betty hurrying around the desk to her seat. "Hi, Mr. De Laurentiis. I'm happy to see things are okay with Pickles." She beams at me, holding a finger up as she says, "Give me just one second while I pull up the bill."

"Not a problem. Take your time," I tell her.

"Okay, so your bill will be two hundred and thirty-three dollars. Cash or card?"

My brows pinch, and I finally stammer, "Are you sure that's the right price? We did X-rays, too, and gave her a shot for nausea. Could you just double-check the bill, please?" There's literally no way that's right, but it's late, so she probably just hadn't input it yet.

She smiles at me sheepishly. "The price is correct. We don't overcharge like the other emergency vets. It's important that pets receive quality care, especially in emergencies, so we pride ourselves in offering those services at an affordable price."

I'm honestly taken aback by that. I've never left a standard veterinary clinic without paying at least three hundred dollars just for vaccines, let alone an emergency appointment. It's nice to know that whoever owns this place has their heart in it. I could tell that based on who works here. Betty and Dr. Hughes have been really great.

I look around the waiting room, seeing several people with their sick pets waiting to be seen before turning back to look at her. "Um, okay. Well, I was expecting to pay at least two thousand, so let me pay you that anyway, and you can put the excess toward covering the costs for anyone else you guys see here tonight. Is that okay? I don't want to overcomplicate anything for you." It's the least I can do. I have the money, and you never know what someone else is going through. Pickles has become my whole world these last few months, and without her, I'm not sure I'd bother waking up at all. If there's something I can do to make it even a little easier for someone in here to take care of their furry family, I'm more than willing to.

Her eyes widen slightly as her mouth pops open. "That's so generous of you," she rushes to say, waving a hand in my face. "And it's not complicated at all, thank you."

I nod at her. My social battery is officially drained. I just want to pay and take Pickles home to sleep for the next twelve hours. I hand her my card, approve the payment, and give her the best smile I can manage before thanking her and heading out into the cool air.

Chapter Five

Gianni

Saturday, February 15, 2025

I wake up to a wet nose pressed against my cheek and a high-pitched whining sound. It takes me a moment to come out of my nightmare-induced daze, but finally, I realize it's Pickles asking to go out.

God, what time is it? I reach for my cell phone and notice six missed texts from Kat and a voicemail from Alessandro.

I'm wracking my brain for any reason they'd be trying to get ahold of me when I suddenly remember that damn tricks-for-treats class Kat signed Pickles up for!

I hop out of bed, running around the apartment like a chicken with my head cut off. I change, brush my teeth, and splash some water on my face before leashing Pickles and running us downstairs to get in the car and drive to the address Kat sent me days ago.

Thankfully, Pickles does her business quickly before we head out.

For my sake, I fully plan to delete that voicemail without bothering to listen to it. My brother is the kindest man in the world, but he can turn into an absolute creature from the dark lagoon where Kat's concerned. I have no interest in having my ass reamed out for disappointing her.

Luckily, I haven't missed the class yet, but I'm cutting it close. I swear, if this were for anyone else, and if Ale wouldn't kick my ass for it, I wouldn't be out of my house yet. Hell, I wouldn't even be awake, let alone dressed.

Kat was right though; this place was really close. It's only a three-minute drive, so I honestly could have walked had I known beforehand. I'll try to remember that for next time.

I pull up to a small white building with a blue-and-purple sign out front that reads, "Rocket Dog."

Well, we must be in the right place.

I park and turn off the engine, run around to the trunk, and grab Pickles before sprinting with her to the front door of the facility, where I now see Kat's glossy eyes and pink cheeks standing with Tank's elderly self. He really is an ancient dog, and I'm not sure the shock will ever wear off from how far he's come. When Ale first adopted him, it was a surprise that he liked him at all. He was told that Tank was hesitant and not a fan of men. We think he may have been abused by a previous male owner in the past.

Ale and Kat have shown him so much care and attention, being sure to socialize him constantly. I guess a little love and attention really go a long way, even with an old, broken, and battered guy like Tank.

When she sees me, her eyes light up, and a grin spreads across her pretty face. Tank's ears perk, and Pickles nearly drags me to the door, beelining straight for her favorite friend.

"Good morning, Gi! I'm so glad you made it." She's beaming at me, so I return the smile, if not a little less enthusiastically.

My chin dips to my chest, and my throat feels thick. "Sorry, Kat. I forgot to set an alarm. I'll be earlier next time," I promise her, even though I shouldn't.

"Don't worry about it." She waves a dismissive hand. "You're here now. Class doesn't start for a couple of minutes, so let's just head in and get them set up," she tells me, easing some of my anxiety before it ratchets up again when I realize we're going to be in a large open space, chairs turned inward. I know it's so we can all watch each dog as they complete whatever tasks they're going to be taught today, but it adds a bit of pressure that I don't look forward to. *I'll get over it.* I have on the field, and I will here too. Kat says this is low stakes, so I'll try to treat it as such.

"Come on, let's sit over here." She guides us to two plastic folding chairs toward the back of the room, and she lays out a blanket on either side of the chairs. I glance around the room, and I'm instantly filled with the familiar low hum of dread. Everyone in here has blankets and dog beds for their canine companions to sit on, and I didn't even think about it. Not only did I not consider this or even ask Kat what I needed, but she just assumed I wouldn't and brought it herself. I feel bile begin to climb up my throat, remorse and self-loathing not far behind.

"Gi, take a seat." She smiles at me nervously, realizing I'm having an internal freak-out. Kat has dealt with more than her fair share of mental illness in her life, and I think it's why we get along so well. Same recognizes same. She sees the broken mess that I am and aims to calm me down. Meanwhile, I act as a buffer for her, always one notch more sad and broken than she ever showed anyone, so the attention stays off her and on me. I hate it, but I can't change it, and she deserves happiness, so it's a weight I'll bear.

I take a seat next to her, and Pickles immediately lies down on the baby-pink Sherpa blanket Kat brought her.

I pat her head, giving her scratches behind her ears, and focus on how soft her fur is beneath my fingertips until class starts. Moments after the instructor introduces herself to the class, the doors burst open, and a black-and-white Great Dane sprints across the linoleum floors to greet everyone as a flash of red hair is tugged behind him.

"Tiny, calm down!"

My eyes widen at the realization of who it is. I'd recognize those glossy red waves just about anywhere, and somehow, it comes as no surprise that she's the one being dragged behind that bulldozer of a dog.

"Hi, everyone. So sorry I'm late!" Dr. Hughes pants, keeled over with her hands on her knees, trying to suck in a breath. "I had to see a kitten with a hairball," she says with a chuckle, her face a bright pink, and somehow, she still looks gorgeous. "Yeah, I know, literally a hairball!" she exclaims loudly and out of breath. She turns around, greeting each owner and their dog, which seems on brand for her given her occupation. She must come here regularly, and that knowledge has my gut twisting in knots. [1]

Her eyes continue sweeping over the room, looking for an empty seat. She looks past me, but I recognize the exact moment my face registers in her mind because her eyes widen, returning to mine, and her mouth just barely pops open in surprise. It only takes her a moment to collect herself before she greets me with a tight smile. "Mr. De Laurentiis, I'm glad to see Pickles is doing better!" she tells me without pretense, sounding genuine.

Of course, the one time I get up the nerve to ask someone out, convinced that Alex would've pushed me to do it, it backfires. At least she doesn't seem to feel too awkward around me, which helps settle my restless thoughts the smallest bit.

I smile at her, my ears heating, and an unfamiliar thump reverberating in my chest. "Good morning, Dr. Hughes. I'm glad to see I'm not the only one who's late." I keep the smile on my face as hers falls a bit. I didn't mean to sound like a dick. That was my failed attempt at flirting with her. Emphasis on *failed*. Again, she catches herself quickly, returning my smile and taking her seat.

And for good reason, I remind myself. *She has a boyfriend, you idiot.*

---

1. **Out of My League – Fitz and The Tantrums**

Kat nudges my knee with her own, drawing my attention to her. She leans over to me to whisper in my ear, "Who was that?" Her eyebrows raise, and a knowing grin adds to my discomfort. I don't like how she reads the situation so well. For someone oblivious enough to not know her twin brother and her best friend had been madly in love for years, she has her moments of enlightenment.

"She's the veterinarian I brought Pickles to the other day when she ate the chicken bone on our walk." She wears a mask of obvious disappointment that reflects how I felt when she told me she was in a relationship. I've thought about that every day, hoping on one hand that it's true and not just her way of saying she's uninterested. Then, on the other hand, I sort of wish it wasn't true so I could somehow convince myself I might still have a shot at wooing her if I were ever to get my head out of my ass and find some piece of my personality that isn't a complete fucking dumpster fire. *Who the hell are you kidding, Gi? You aren't capable of wooing anyone.*

The class starts, and thankfully, it goes by pretty quickly. The trainer has a fluffy, overly hyper Australian shepherd with bright-blue eyes, which she calls her "demo dog." Before we practice a trick, she uses the demo dog named Pixie to demonstrate the trick and how to get our own dogs to replicate them.

We all take turns teaching our dogs a series of tricks that we need to complete for the novice tricks certificate. I have no desire to file that paperwork, but watching Pickles crawl under a pool noodle or a balance beam, search for treats in boxes, and walk across a wooden beam is worth the time this class took from my day. It's hard to get out of bed most days, but I haven't felt this unfamiliar happiness in months. My chest feels warm as I work with Pickles, giving her entirely too many treats as slobber pools out of her wide mouth.

That same sort of low-level joy ratchets up when I look over to see Lark's small frame wrestling with her massive dog. I learned that she ironically named her dog "Tiny." I steal glances at her, noting her fur-covered scrubs with purple and pink cartoon dogs and cats on them and a bit of mascara smeared under her eyes. She must have come here straight from work, and it pulls at something in my chest that she probably hasn't slept.

When class is over, I wave at her retreating form, watching as she stops by the front to speak with the trainer.

Kat bounces on the balls of her feet, pulling me out of my thoughts. "That was fun, wasn't it?" she asks.

"Yeah," I say with a nod, doing my best to keep my voice light. "It actually was." I cough into my fist, trying to cover the croak that just left my throat. "It looked like Tank and Pickles were thrilled too. Same time next week, then?" I ask her because now, more than ever, I'm *almost* excited about coming to this class. Truly, it's for selfish reasons, most of which include the first feelings of anything besides pure dread or numbness that seeing Dr. Hughes elicits in me.

I walk her out to her car, helping Tank in the backseat before giving Kat a tight hug and a kiss on either cheek.

Chapter Six
Lark

Oh my god, what a dick! I'm fuming as I leave Rocket Dog, an unnatural grimace pulling at my lips.

I can't believe that asshole had the *nerve* to act all sweet and reserved, pretending he was shy. I bet he does this kind of shit all the time, but even that thought doesn't dull the shock that some people can behave this way while in a relationship.

Tyler and I have our problems, plenty of them, in fact, but I'm pretty confident he'd never cheat on me.

An ache settles in the center of my chest. That gorgeous woman Gianni was with genuinely seemed to have not a single clue that her partner, someone she's supposed to be able to trust, has been betraying her.

Obviously, I wouldn't have said yes to him because I have a boyfriend, one I'm convinced will propose soon, but *still*. Just because I said no doesn't mean someone else won't accept his offer!

And now I have to attend these classes every week, knowing that he was planning on cheating on her if given the opportunity. Who does he think he is? Has he *seen* her? She's stunning! Golden skin, honey-colored eyes, and long, dark waves.

To add insult to injury, she seemed so nice, and I want to be her friend already, *which I can't stand*. She was so loving with that handsome old dog, Tank, she brought in.

***

Tiny and I trot home, my eyes feeling heavier with every step we take. We're almost home when a dark cloud moves overhead, and it starts sprinkling around us.

My skin feels sticky and cold as we finish our trek home, nearly getting run over by some asshole in a sports car who blares his horn at us as we sprint across the wet crosswalk. Thankfully, we don't live far from Rocket Dog, so these classes aren't usually too difficult to make it to on weekends, regardless of how exhausted I am.

Our pets are like children. They rely on us to take care of all of their needs, and that includes emotional ones too. This means that even when I've been working overnight, and I want nothing more than to take a hot shower and crawl under the covers, I still have a responsibility to ensure Tiny and Rex are being properly stimulated.

We get home just before noon, and I let myself into the dingy apartment I've been sharing with Tyler for a little over a year now. The door makes an annoying creaking sound that grates at my mind. Tyler said he'd fix that *two weeks ago*. Before we step inside, I clench my eyes shut for just a second, dragging in a deep breath to center myself. *It's not a big deal, Lark. He works too.*

I shake myself out and head inside, setting my keys on the unbalanced entryway table before unleashing Tiny and hanging my coat in the small closet.[1]

Loud yapping greets me as Rex, my Chihuahua-shih tzu mix, comes sprinting down the hall from his normal seat in the old, peeling leather recliner.

I bend down, picking him up and planting a kiss atop his wiry head. "Hi, my handsome little man. How were you for Daddy while I was gone with your brother?" I ask him, my voice a high pitch that causes his ears to perk up, but of course, it isn't Rex's answering voice that I hear.

"Lark, stop talking to that damn dog like he's a human being. I'm not his 'daddy,' and Tiny is not his 'brother.' Have you seen that dog? There's no way they'd have come from the same womb." He grunts from where he's standing in the kitchen, setting his dirty coffee mug on the *side* of the kitchen sink. *Why can't he put the dish in the sink?*

When I don't answer, he rolls his eyes, leaning back against the counter with his narrowed eyes set on me. He changes the subject when I continue to stare at him, too exhausted to hide the contempt I'm feeling. "How was work?" Tyler asks, pushing off the counter to invade my space. Instinctually, I turn my body to the side, pretending to inspect something on my pants, scratching at a random spot with my nail. He doesn't take the hint, wrapping his arms around me from behind and nuzzling his face into my hair. My shoulders tense as his hands travel down toward my navel.

"It was good, but I haven't showered yet," I say as if that'll somehow explain away the way my skin crawls when his hands are on me. I take his hands in mine, moving them off me and stepping out of his grasp. "Obviously." I chuckle nervously, realizing I just got home, so he's already

---

1. **Heart-Shaped Box – Nirvana**

aware that I haven't showered. "I'm gonna take one real quick and then head to bed."

His face is unreadable as he scrutinizes me before deciding to let whatever was on his mind go. "Yeah, okay," he says, blowing out a resigned breath before he breaks into the mischievous grin I used to be fond of. Recently, though, it's just riddled me with anxiety. "Mind if I join you in the shower?"

My mind is a chaotic mess of emotions. *Why don't I want him to shower with me? When was the last time we were even intimate?*

I used to love showering together, but these days, I just work so much, and the clinic can't run itself. Ever since I got Toute la Famille up and running, I've been running myself ragged. It's just so hard to find reliable staff I can trust those babies with, and it makes me anxious to think about. I put so much pressure on myself to succeed so I can prove to *myself* that I can be independent regardless of the fact that it's my dad's money that funds the clinic.

"Uh, maybe later," I say with a tight-lipped smile. "I'm just so tired," I tell him, ignoring the anger etched into his features as I lean in to kiss his cheek before practically sprinting down the hall to shower and head to bed for the foreseeable future.

I turn the water to warm and opt to toss a lavender and eucalyptus shower steamer in for a more luxurious experience. Betty had gotten them for me in a cute gift basket she made me when I seemed particularly worn out last month. She's right. I really need to unwind. *I deserve to relax.*

I lock the door to the bathroom to ensure total privacy and get in the shower, wetting my hair first. I lather my roots, applying pressure and giving myself a half-decent scalp massage before rinsing and coating my ends in conditioner.

The calming floral scent wraps around me, and I feel the tension slowly leeching from my shoulders as I let the warm water run down my body.

I let my conditioner sit for a while, pumping some body wash into my hands and skating them over my body, cleansing the day away. As my fingers glide over my glucose monitor, it serves as my daily reminder that as well-controlled as my diabetes usually is, I'm still reliant on this little device.

Now that I actually have time to think, my mind decides to wander to a place I'm not fully prepared for.

Thoughts of Tyler and our relationship start to flood in, unease settling into my chest with each passing thought. I'm realizing that much of our time together hasn't been positive, and that's only become more apparent over the last few months.

It feels like every day, we drift further and further apart.

But I love him, don't I?

I mean, we've been together for years. He makes me feel… safe? Content? *I'm not so sure anymore.*

Maybe it's the lack of intimacy. He never wants to just cuddle anymore, and as someone who deeply values physical touch as a love language, I *want* to be held without the expectation that it'll lead to something else.

With Tyler, he always expects it to go beyond cuddling, and I just can't deal with his disappointment. He doesn't seem to understand that I'm fucking *exhausted*.

I love what I do, but it's draining, and the hours I've made for myself aren't great. I have three new veterinarians who recently started, so there's a light at the end of the tunnel. Soon, I hope to be able to work three days a week and have the opportunity to see my friends more than just at our once-monthly book club.

Maybe if I actually made an effort to have sex, he'd be more than willing to just cuddle and relax together. *Stop it.* Sex isn't going to fix our relationship, and if we're at this point, maybe it's time to start considering a different future for myself.

Besides, Tyler hasn't satisfied me in years. He refuses to do anything other than missionary, and for someone who makes me feel like crap for "holding out on him," he sure is a prude.

He's never been open to a single position or kink I've wanted to explore. I'm not asking for anything totally out of left field, but just *anything* other than missionary. Why can't he seem to understand that our sex life is awfully freaking *boring*?

As if I weren't already down a needlessly upsetting rabbit hole, my mind lands on the one person it has absolutely no business thinking about.

I *tried* to ignore Gianni today, but my skin felt like it was on fire the entire time, prickling periodically as if I had some sixth sense to tell me when his eyes were on me.

I've done my best to repress the feelings flowing through my body since having his eyes on me again.

I rinse my body, a pang of desire shooting to my deprived clit as my hand gently glides over the sensitive skin. Maybe this is the answer? It's scientifically proven that masturbation is healthy and increases libido the more regularly you have an orgasm.

Hopefully, if I remind myself what it's like to feel pleasure, I'll actually *want* to have sex again. Besides, I deserve to come whenever and however I want, without guilt for not involving Tyler.

I brace my right hand against the tile wall, holding the shower head in my dominant hand and changing the setting to a thick stream instead of the more dispersed rainfall I use when rinsing my body. Leaning my forehead against the cool wall, I hold the stream directly over my clit, letting the pressure ease the ache in my core.

My thoughts drift to sex, but as I picture myself riding the thick, veiny dick I want inside me, my mind flashes with images of Gianni's face as his body tenses.

My eyes burst open, a chill rippling through my body as guilt weaves its way inside my chest.

I take a deep, steadying breath, pushing the thought away, but when I close my eyes again, all I see is *him*.

I picture Gianni going still as my body lights on fire, sparks of pleasure flying straight to my clit.

A moan creeps up my throat, and I cry out, heat rushing to my cheeks. I'm already too close to the orgasm I desperately need, and I can't make myself stop.

The pressure is too much; my skin is on fire, but a chill quakes through me. My breasts ache to be touched, and my abdominal muscles clench tightly as I near my release.

My breathing becomes shallow, and I know I shouldn't be picturing this man or his toned, tan arms, eyes I want to swim in, and rough, calloused hands wrapping around my throat. *He has a girlfriend, and I'm taken.*

The reminder does nothing to quell the storm brewing in my core. I've gone too far, and my orgasm has taken hold of me. It tears through me. My legs turn to jelly as I fight to keep my arm locked in position, holding pressure to my clit.

Blinding pleasure tingles down my limbs, spreading throughout me as I whimper, my throat feeling thick.

My back arches as I pant, coming back down from the high of the first satisfying orgasm I've had in what's probably been *three years*.

A flush creeps across my cheeks, and I swallow thickly as embarrassment takes a firm hold of me. The haze has worn off, and I know I *should* be ashamed of who I was just picturing. Somehow, I can't bring myself to regret it despite knowing how hypocritical I'm being.

Chapter Seven

Gianni

Sunday, February 16, 2025

Pickles drags me around the neighborhood on our walk before we head to my parents' place for Sunday dinner.

I pull up to the brownstone and grab Pickles from the trunk bed, heading inside.

The entryway hall feels particularly dark today. I drag my eyes up the wall, noting the way the ancient wallpaper is peeling at the seams before my eyes land on the intricate lamp. *A bulb is blown out.* I'll have to remember to fix that before I leave.

My dad claps a hand over my shoulder, squeezing it in greeting as I pass through the kitchen and into the living room.

My eyes land on Kat sitting out on the patio. I head out there with Pickles, and Tank is hot on our heels.

Her dark hair is pulled up into a messy bun on the top of her head, and dark circles line her light-brown eyes. She looks up at me from over her shoulder and plasters a small, closed-lip smile on her face. It doesn't meet her eyes like it normally would, and my heart starts to sink as worry rears its ugly head.

My gaze flicks to Pickles and Tank, who streak through the yard, blissfully unaware of the somber mood we're both in.

I pull out a rusty patio chair from beside her, the metal legs scraping against the concrete and sending chills down my spine.

Kat shoves her hand in her back pocket, pulling out a coin and setting it down on the table. "Penny for your thoughts, Gi?" she asks as her lips turn up in a little grin that does nothing to tame my anxiety.

I shake my head, having no interest in talking about myself. Especially not when she's clearly dealing with something. "You first. Looks like you've got more on your mind than I do today."

She lets out a long sigh, propping her feet up on the chair beside her and leaning back. She closes her eyes and places her hands in her lap, fiddling with the thin gold chain of her bracelet. "There isn't really anything wrong. The week just wore me down, and I'm finding it hard to repress the anxiety today," she answers honestly.

I nod. "You wanna talk about your week? Maybe get it off your chest?" I ask her, sounding like Dante for a moment.

"If you don't mind," she says, glancing at me quickly before closing her eyes again.

"Not at all," I tell her, and that's all it takes. We sit there for a half hour, the sun setting and the air growing more frigid with every passing minute. She recounts her week, every patient she lost, all the anxiety she's been feeling, and how her therapist is out of the office for vacation, but she didn't want to bother Dante about it. I'm glad she felt she could trust me with this information, and her shoulders seem to carry a little less after she's gotten it off her chest.

"Your turn," she says to me, her eyes a little brighter than they had been when I first sat down.

My head jerks back, my eyes wide. *Absolutely not.*

I don't tend to tell people about my problems or feelings. It's not that I think no one would care; that isn't the case. It's actually the opposite. *I know* my family cares desperately, and that alone is so damn overwhelming. I'm blessed to have a family who loves me unconditionally and makes it their mission in life to show it day in and day out, but that just makes the reality of being so fucking sad all the time even more grim. It's as if I'm not only carrying my own grief and frustrations but pieces of theirs as well.

And as Kat just said, she's got a lot going on. I'd feel guilty adding to that.

"I'm fine, Kat. Thanks though," I say, giving her a tight-lipped smile and swallowing down the lump forming in my throat.

She shakes her head slowly as she stares out into the yard at the dogs now lying in the soggy, cold mud, panting.

"Do you know what *fine* stands for?" she asks, her eyes challenging as they narrow, pinning me to my seat. I shake my head in denial, my stomach rolling at the inflection of her words.

She stares straight at me as if looking directly into the deepest, most well-hidden pieces of my soul. The next words to leave her mouth have me reeling. My head spins as nausea claws up my throat. "Freaked out. Insecure. Neurotic. And emotional." She pauses with each word, enunciating every syllable so they have time to seat themselves in my brain.

I feel like the breath has been stolen from my lungs as I stare back at her, my eyes trained down the barrel of a loaded gun. "So, Gi, are you *fine*?"

And the hits just keep on coming.

I stand abruptly, the legs of the metal chair scraping under me as I move frantically, turning to the sliding glass door. I wrench it open and call for Pickles to follow me in. Kat grabs my wrist, releasing me quickly, but tells me in a hushed tone, "I'm sorry I pushed you too far, Gi, but please, talk to someone. I'm worried." Her eyes are brimming with tears, and I feel like I've got a frog in my throat to accompany the ten-ton elephant sitting on my chest. I give her a tight nod and head inside, fleeing to the bathroom.

***

My knuckles are white as I grip the edge of the sink, my head sagging against my chest while I work to calm my ragged breathing.

A light knock raps against the door. I straighten my spine, dragging a deep, steadying breath in. I open it, finding Kat's small frame standing there, her eyes filled with regret.

She rushes me, not giving me a moment to recover as her arms wind around my waist, her head falling to the center of my chest. Squeezing my eyes tightly shut, I drag a hand down her hair, trying my best to soothe my soon-to-be sister-in-law. "I'm sorry, Gi. You didn't want to talk to me, and I shouldn't have pushed you, but you need to talk to someone," she pleads with me through her apology. I feel her tears seep into my black T-shirt. I feel like a monster for making this sweet woman upset, but she's right. She *had* pushed me too far.

"Kat, I'm *okay*, I promise," I tell her, my heart doing somersaults in my chest at how easily the lie falls off my tongue, though I know I'm not fooling anyone.[1] I see it in their dull eyes every time someone asks me if I'm okay.

She unwinds her arms from my waist, straightening before she pulls away. Her amber eyes peer straight into mine, and I know she's about to deliver yet another blow to my already fragile psyche. Her bottom lip wavers as she blows out a breath. "You're getting so good at that," she tells me, her voice sounding watery. "If I didn't know you, I'd almost believe it," she says, her voice so small I barely hear her.

I take another long inhale, looking up at the ceiling as I clench my fists tightly at my sides. "I *really* can't do this, Kat," I tell her, my eyes brimming

---

1. **I'm Not Okay (I Promise) – My Chemical Romance**

with hot, unshed tears. My throat feels like it's closing in on itself, and I barely get the next words out. "I'm *begging* you not to make me," I plead with her, my throat constricting as I choke out the words.

She grasps my hand in her two smaller ones, keeping her eyes trained on me as she delivers what I fucking hope is the last bruising blow to my soul for the night. "I know you miss him, Gi, but he wouldn't want you wallowing in misery like this. He'd want you to talk to someone." She squeezes my hand tightly, my eyes dragging down to it as her words sink in. Words I know to be true, but somehow, I can't seem to let them take root just yet.

"Just give me some more time, Kat. I'm just not ready," I tell her, exhaustion seeping into me.

She gives me a small nod, her eyes glossy, and it breaks my heart. I know she wants what's best for me. I know they *all* do, but I just can't do any more than I already am right now.

Ever since the accident, it's been nearly impossible to leave my bed, let alone to rehash the entire thing to a complete stranger, over and over and over.

She pulls out of my grasp, heading downstairs to the kitchen. Dinner should be ready any minute, but I've officially lost my appetite.

Chapter Eight

Lark

Saturday, February 22, 2025

"Alright, Tiny, let's get a move on, or we're gonna be late!" Tiny trots ahead of me, his big, speckled body pulling my small frame behind him as we run toward the small gray building. Someone ahead of me sees us coming and opens the door wide for us. Tiny lacks all manners as he barrels toward the opening, catapulting us inside.

"Thank you!" I shout at the woman and direct my attention back to Tiny, scolding him as he finally slows down. "You need to calm your tits, big guy. You act as if it's the first time being here, *every time*." His droopy lids drag up his face as he glances at me from the corner of his eyes, pretending he hasn't heard me. "Such a brat," I whisper, tugging gently on one of his big, floppy ears.

My eyes scan the room for an empty seat. When I see one open, I hurry over, unfolding the mat and laying it beside me. Tiny circles it, getting himself comfortable before plopping down. "Good boy, Tiny," I whisper at the gentle giant at my feet. Okay, *usually*, he's gentle.

The woman at the door is the last to take a seat just before class starts. I turn to thank her again, and as I do, my eyes widen, and my lips part on a soft exhale.

It's Gianni's girlfriend.

"Thanks for holding the door for me," I finally manage to say, giving her an awkward smile.

If she notices, she doesn't show it because she returns my smile more warmly, extending her hand for me to shake. "I'm Katarina, but you can call me Kat. And this handsome man is Tank," she says, nodding her chin to the graying, old dog at her feet.

There's a man seated beside her who bears a striking similarity to her. He leans forward, waving at me with a wide grin spread across his handsome face. "Hey, I'm Kas, and this lovely lady is Pickles," he says, gesturing to the furry blob at his feet. She looks like she's practically melted into the floor.

I smile at him. "Yeah, I actually know Pickles. It's nice to meet you though," I explain awkwardly.

His dark brow quirks with interest, and Kat turns to him. "This is Lark. She's Gi's veterinarian," she tells him, and I feel rude, now realizing I never told them *my* name. She must've remembered from last week.

"Kas is my twin brother. Gianni couldn't make it today, so he volunteered to act as Pickles's handler," she explains, remaining unphased by my reactions.

"Ah, okay. Well, that was really kind of you." It must be nice having a brother who gets along with your boyfriend. Even if he *is* a cheating pig.

Kas says nothing, his eyes flicking to the center of the room, where he turns his attention. Stacey, the trainer for this class, goes over today's plans. My leg bounces with pent-up energy and a strange amount of frustration that's settled over me. For the first time, I just want to get this class over with.

When she finishes, we break off into groups of three, and much to my dismay, I wind up with Kat and Kas. It isn't that they don't seem nice because they absolutely do. It's just uncomfortable for me to work with them while knowing what I do about Kat's boyfriend.

"So, each one of us just takes turns holding the pool noodle up while the other coaxes the dogs underneath?" Kas asks, his hands on his hips as he stares at the blue pool noodle in my hands, his brows pinched. He's clearly still a little confused. I don't blame him. This stuff is more difficult than it seems, and we aren't just reminding ourselves what to do. There are so many moving parts, and we have to remember treats, clickers, and commands. It can definitely be overwhelming.

"I'll go first with Tiny if you guys don't mind. That way, I can give you a better idea of what to do."

"Sounds great, thanks." They say this in unison. *Must be some freaky twin thing.*

"Okay, great. So each of you will hold one end of the pool noodle. You can stay seated so you don't have to grapple with the dogs too much, though they look pretty content," I tell them, gazing down at the puddles of mush and fur melted on the ground. Both Pickles and Tank are happily snoring despite the commotion in the room.

They each do as I instructed, taking a seat and anchoring the piece of foam between themselves. "Like this?" Kat asks.

"Yep, just like that." I unleash Tiny, folding it and placing it into the back pocket of my jeans. "Stay," I instruct, stepping over the piece of foam to face Tiny, who is now standing between a seated Kat and Kas.

Extending my arm out in front of me, I place my hand palm down and motion for Tiny to lie down. He does so without a verbal command, but I explain this further. "I've had him since he actually *was* Tiny, so he tends to sense what I'm about to ask him to do before I even give him a command. You guys might need to start by having them sit, then teaching them to lie down and work on crawling later."

I wouldn't want them to feel bad if either of their dogs doesn't follow commands well. They're sweet dogs, but following these complex commands can take a lot out of them in the first several classes as their minds stretch to accommodate so much new information.

They each nod their understanding, so I continue, grasping my clicker in my right hand so I can use my dominant hand for commands. "I don't usually use a clicker unless it's a brand-new trick for him, but I'll do it this time so you can see how to use it."

"Okay, crawl." Tiny ducks his head between his front paws and army crawls his way toward me, right under the pool noodle. When he passes through, I immediately click. "Good boy!" I praise him and reach into my pocket, retrieving a treat for him. He munches it happily, slobber pooling out of his droopy lips.

"Jesus Christ, you've got the GI Joe of dogs!" Kas says excitedly, his hazel eyes lit from within as he claps for Tiny.

I laugh at that. "I promise they'll get it eventually too! This is five years in the making right here."

"You've been coming here for five years?" Kat asks.

"Yep, I rotate between which of my dogs I take with me, though Tiny comes far more often than Rex because he's kind of a spitfire and doesn't always get along well with others." I roll my eyes.

"How come you can't bring both? I thought Gi mentioned you had a boyfriend. Can't he be one of their handlers?" Kas asks me. The question sends a sour feeling to the pit of my stomach. This is one of the many sore subjects between Tyler and me.

"Yeah," I mutter. "Tyler works a lot, though, and he likes to have his weekends off." I don't mention the fact that he works from home and has never worked a weekend in his life. "Besides, they're my dogs," I tell them, doing my best to cover up the disdain I feel tingling at the tip of my tongue. I wish he'd be more involved with them. *Shouldn't he be interested in what I like?*

"Oh, sorry to hear that," Kat tells me, a hint of something lacing her words. Sympathy, maybe?

Waving her off, I walk to her side, re-leashing Tiny. "Your turn," I tell her with a tight smile.

***

By the time the hour class is over, I've actually started to really like both Kat and Kas. I think I was right about her from the beginning. She seems really sweet, and she manages to surprise me with her sense of humor.

As we head out to the parking lot, she stops me. "Hey, would you want to grab dinner or something soon?"

Smiling at her, I work to pull my cell out of my pocket. "That'd be really nice. Go ahead and give me your number, and we can plan something." I hand her the phone, watching as she meticulously inputs her information, and a moment later, she's handing me the phone back, a ping going off in her pocket.

"I sent myself a text so I'd have your number too." She smiles, but it falls from her face in a second flat. She turns abruptly toward her car, dragging Tank behind her as quickly as his arthritic legs will take him.

"Okay," I breathe out, a little confused by her sudden need to get away from me.

Kas sidles up beside me, following after his sister more idly. He chuckles as he explains, "Kat has social anxiety. She's been working on it and doing a lot better, but she probably just realized how bold a move that was to text herself and chickened out after the fact."

My lips flatten, and I draw a breath through my nose, nodding my understanding. "Ah, I know that feeling all too well," I answer honestly. "Please tell her I didn't think anything of it, really," I say, wanting to be sure this isn't something that keeps her up at night.

His full lips turn up in a broad smile. "Will do. Have a good weekend, Lark." My name rolls off his tongue, smooth like butter. God, is this woman just surrounded by sexy men? I know he's her brother, but I've also seen the rest of the De Laurentiis family in passing, and those men, hell, the women too, are all gorgeous.

***

Thankfully, Tyler's gone by the time I get home with Tiny. He didn't tell me where he was going, but I can only assume he's out with the guys and won't be returning anytime soon.

Kicking off my shoes at the front door, I pad across the worn wooden floors, grab my Kindle from the side table, and collapse onto the couch.

I've got six days to finish this book before the book club, and it's the perfect thing to help me unwind from the long week.

Pulling a blanket onto my lap, I'm about to snuggle in and get to reading when that familiar feeling of frustration settles in.

A groan slips past my lips, and I drop my head to the back of the couch when I realize I have to get up. You'd think after fourteen years of this shit, I'd be better at sticking with a schedule.

Reluctantly, I swing my legs over the side of the couch, standing and stretching my arms over my head with a low moan. I make my way into the kitchen, open the fridge, and grab the small bag with all my supplies.

I scroll through my blood sugar readings on my phone and get to work cleaning the top of the vial, drawing up the correct dose. When I'm ready, I use an alcohol prep pad to cleanse the sore, mottled skin on my abdomen.

I wince as the cold medicine sinks into my bruised, thickened skin. Truthfully, I should start injecting elsewhere because the absorption rate is likely negatively impacted by the scar tissue I've formed in my usual spots.

You should get a fucking pump, my brain screams at me. And as always, I just roll my eyes at her and move along.[1]

***

I feel a buzzing coming from my back pocket. Twisting, I pull it out and see a newly familiar name flash across the screen.

Kat
> Hey! Would you wanna do dinner tonight?

Kat
> I know it's last minute, but there's this Thai place I've been dying to try.

That's odd. Gianni must not like Thai food if she's asking me to go with her. I check the time but realize it wouldn't matter anyway since Tyler probably wouldn't even notice if I were gone.

> That actually sounds nice!

> What time?

Kat
> Meet me there at 6:00?

Kat
> It's called Mama Thai.

> Great, see you then.

---

1. **I Am Machine — Three Days Grace**

Taking a look at the time, I realize it's already after four. I've been reading for *hours*. That's not unusual, but I really hadn't been aware of the time. The book was just so good.

Typing the restaurant name into the search bar, I see that it's less than fifteen minutes away, so I have plenty of time to finish this chapter and get ready to go.

Chapter Nine

Lark

I pull up in front of the restaurant and see Kat standing on the sidewalk beside the wooden pergola that hangs over the outdoor seating. She's wearing curve-hugging light-wash jeans, a white crop top, and a cardigan. Her dark waves flutter around her in the wind, her face framed by a strand of white hair.

When she notices me pull up beside her, a huge grin slides across her face, and those light-brown eyes of hers twinkle under the café lights.

I put it in park, pocket the keys, and grab my bag from the passenger seat before exiting the car.

"Who would've thought?" She smirks, shaking her head gently.

"What?" I ask, my brow quirked.

Her smirk broadens into a wide smile. "I don't know, I guess I just hadn't pictured you driving behind the wheel of a Firebird," she prods.

Understanding zips through me. "Oh, yeah, I get that a lot." I chuckle. "I helped my dad fix this beauty up when I was in high school, and she's been mine ever since. I think in another life, I probably would've been an F1 driver," I joke.

"Well, *she* is beautiful." She laughs. "I love the dark-red interior. It looks like a perfect color match to the glossy outside."

"Thanks, it actually is," I tell her proudly. "My dad and I had the color customized so it would be exactly the same."

She appraises me quietly for a moment, a slight grin tugging at her pouty lips. "You're just full of surprises," she says, a twinkle dancing in her eyes. She nods her chin toward the door. "Well, let's head inside before we freeze our butts off."

I nod, following her in through the glass door. A bell overhead chimes at our entrance, and a short woman with dark hair approaches us from behind the counter. "Table for two?" she asks.

"Yes, please," Kat answers, and we follow behind her, taking a seat at a small booth at the back of the restaurant.

Once we're seated, she hands us the menus and asks for our drink order. "Just water for me, please," I respond.

"Me too." The woman nods, heading back to the kitchen.

"Any suggestions for what to order?" I ask her, taking in the huge menu.

"Well, I haven't been here specifically, but Thai is one of my favorite foods. I usually try the pad thai, drunken noodles, and panang curry at every Thai place so I can adequately see how they all match up against one another."

"I don't really know what drunken noodles are, but I'm up for trying literally anything you want," I tell her, setting the menu back down on the table.

"You want to do it family style and just split those three things so you can try everything?" she offers.

"Sounds like a plan." My stomach rumbles at the thought. I haven't eaten as much as I should have today.

The waitress heads toward us with two waters on her tray. "Sorry, I just need to check something real quick," I tell Kat, grabbing for my phone.

I've got a headache, and I hadn't really realized how little I've eaten today. I open up my glucose monitor app and wait for it to process the information. The number seventy-four flashes across the screen, and the dreaded arrow points down, indicating a drop in my blood glucose trend. I can't help but groan. *Can't I just get through one day without having to play this game with my blood sugars?*

Tucking my phone away, I look up at the waitress as she places the waters on our table. "I'm so sorry, but do you mind if I also get a Coke?"

Her cherry-red lips curve into a small smile. "Not at all. Would you like to place your order now as well?"

"Yeah, I think we're ready." Kat smiles warmly at the woman before listing off each item. Apparently, she gets everything with egg and extra tofu.

"You have diabetes?" she asks me after the woman saunters away toward the back.

She catches me off guard, but I answer truthfully. My stomach is unsettled as I think about her boyfriend's horrid behavior compared to how kind she's been. I really don't want to hurt her, but if I were her, I'd want to know.

I do my best to clear the thoughts away, but it doesn't ease my discomfort any. "Yeah, how'd you know?"

"You checked your phone, looked kind of worried, and decided to order a sugary beverage, so I took a look at your arms and noticed the small bump from your glucose monitor on your tricep."

My brows crease. "You're oddly perceptive, but yeah, I have type 1."

"I'm a physician assistant, so I'm used to having to take in every detail about a person to create a full picture. I also have anxiety, so I'm hyperaware of the actions of those around me." *I can tell.* A lot of her behavior strikes me as sort of odd, but it doesn't bother me at all. In a lot of ways, she reminds me of my friend Jade.

"That all makes sense, actually." I chuckle. "Do you like what you do?"

She dips her head just as the waitress delivers my drink. I thank her and take several small sips, waiting for Kat to respond.

"I love it. I love helping people, making a difference in their lives, and getting to walk them through some of the most vulnerable experiences they'll ever have, but it's physically and emotionally taxing. Some days, I have no idea how I wound up here, but then I work with a patient or get to help a family that changes my whole day, and it's easy to remember my 'why,' so to speak." It's genuinely refreshing to hear someone talk about their career the same way I do about mine.

"That's really lovely, Kat. I'm glad you've found your calling. Gianni must be really proud of you," I prod, and the way her brows cinch together makes me question whether that hit a nerve or something else entirely.

She narrows her eyes at me slightly but brushes my comment off, asking, "How about you? Do you love being a veterinarian?"

My face lights up at the change of subject to something more familiar. "I wake up every single day excited to go to work, honestly. This is all I've ever wanted to do, the only thing I've ever even considered." My hands flail around as I speak. "Even as a kid, I had a project in elementary school that required me to take a photo of myself acting out my day in my dream career," I say, beaming at her.

She smiles at me. "That's sweet. What'd you do for the project?"

"Well, my mom helped me make a book that read, '*The Day In The Life of A Veterinarian.*' I sat on the couch, holding it up as if I were reading the blank pages inside, and sat beside my old dog at the time. His name was Buddy Bear, but he was nobody's *buddy* but mine." I laugh. "He bit every person who walked by for years. He'd manage to get off his leash or his lead in the yard and go running around the neighborhood. He was hit by a car *three* different times, but somehow, he was never seriously injured." Her salt-and-pepper eyebrows shoot up her forehead.

I shake my head, rolling my eyes. "My mom wasn't great about caring for him, and Dad wasn't around a lot back then, so I honestly thought it was normal for pets to run away that often! He always came home, and he didn't pass away until we had to euthanize him at twenty-one years old. He had a brain tumor that resulted in a seizure disorder, and medication wasn't working anymore."

"I'd say I'm sorry about his seizures, but it sounds like it was more than his time." Her eyes are wide. "Sorry, that's so messed up, but god, that's an old dog!"

"It's okay. He really was rather ancient," I say with a chuckle. "Especially for a chow chow. It was pretty miraculous. My parents would joke that he was the devil's spawn and that's what was keeping him alive, but I think he was just being given a chance to make up for lost time." Her brows return to their usual spot, and her eyes soften at my words. "We adopted him from a kill shelter the day he was due to be put down. I was three when my parents let me pick out a dog, and I chose him because he looked like he needed the love the most. Then I proceeded to name him two of the only words I really knew at that time."

Kat laughs, a full-bellied one that ends in a snort, and I can feel the weightlessness I only experience when I'm with my friends. "And now, you have a dog that's twice your size, ironically named *Tiny*."

"Sure do." I beam over at her, my cheeks climbing high. *I love Rex and Tiny with all my heart.*

The waitress approaches our table, a large tray balancing on her forearm. "Can I put it in the middle?" she asks.

"Yes, please," Kat tells her, her voice light and bubbly as she helps to disperse the array of plates and bowls around the table.

"Thank you so much," I tell the waitress as she leaves.

I check my phone one more time, and luckily, the soda brought my sugar up enough that I can take my bolus insulin before eating and not have to worry about a drop before I get the carbs in.

"Sorry, just another second," I assure Kat, but she doesn't seem bothered in the least. I pull out the compact insulated bag with my insulin in it and turn the top to get the pen ready for my regular dose. I use an alcohol swab to disinfect the usual spot on my stomach before pressing the plunger, holding it down for a few seconds before putting everything back in my bag.

"Alrighty, I'm ready. What is everything?" I ask Kat, excited to finally eat an actual meal.

Kat explains what each dish is and helps me sample each one. My tastebuds are exploding with new flavors I've never explored before. The curry is slightly sweet with a coconut milk base that pairs so well with the pumpkin and the chewy texture of the stir-fried tofu. Everything's delicious, but I think the drunken noodles are my favorite. "Oh my god," I moan between mouthfuls. "This is so good!"

Kat smirks. "I told ya, I know good food. Next time, I'll have to take you to Giovanni's. It's this Italian café Aiyana and I love going to for lunch. They have the best calamari."

"That sounds great." I take another sip of my Coke before continuing. "Who's Aiyana?"

"She's my best friend and also happens to be my brother's wife now." Her smile could light up a damn arena with how bright it is at that.

"I'm sensing a story there." I lift my brow at her.

"There's *definitely* a story," she says with a chuckle. "It's one that would probably take as long to tell it as it did to unfold, but the gist is that they'd been in love for years, and there were a few very personal reasons as to why Aiyana was convinced they couldn't be together. Maybe she'll tell you about it sometime," she says with a wry smile.

I nod in understanding.

"Okay, so Gi tells me you've got a boyfriend, and you confirmed that earlier today. What gives there?" she asks, her words coming out at a breakneck speed. "I just feel like you seemed a bit uncomfortable mentioning him working and not wanting to help you with the dogs." She lifts that black-and-white eyebrow at me again. "Sorry, am I reading that all wrong?"

Her cheeks flame red, eyes widening as the wheels turn in her head. It's almost like I can visibly see the crime scene diagram she's drawing in her mind, each red piece of yarn leading her down a different path of anxiety about the possibility of offending me.

I let out a long sigh, slumping back against the booth seat. I don't particularly want to talk about my and Tyler's lackluster relationship, but it's the perfect opening for me to bring up my concerns about Gianni.

"You're not reading it wrong. Tyler and I have been together for a long time, and things have just changed between us. I think he's going to propose soon, and I hope maybe that will bridge the gap a bit, but I just don't know."

She nods slowly, her shoulders slumping slightly. "I've definitely been in similar situations, but I think you just need to trust your gut on this. Maybe you need to explore other options?" she asks, her fingers fiddling with the pendant on her neck. "Marriage isn't the only way to find happiness, and if you aren't really happy now…" She trails off. "Sorry, I'm really prying tonight, I guess. I swear, I'm not usually like this. I mind my own business and leave the meddling to Kas, but something about you tells me you have a lot on your mind."

She blows out a long breath. "I'll say this. When you're with the right person, you'll know. I found the love of my life when I least expected it. I tried to push him away, but it never worked because we were always meant to be. I think that person exists for everyone if you wait for the right time."

My appetite is officially gone. My stomach has plummeted to my toes. *This is gonna suck.*

Clearing my throat, I extend my hands across the table, reaching for hers. Her brows knit together, but she allows me to make the gesture.

"You look like someone who's about to deliver bad news," she tells me, and stress is etched into her warm complexion.

I lean forward with a stiff neck, swallowing down past the lump in my throat before saying, "Kat, I'm really, *really* sorry to tell you this. But your boyfriend isn't as great as he seems." She wrenches her hands out of my grasp, her eyes narrowing, and her head jerks back. Shock and anger are written plainly across her face.

"You don't even *know* him, so I don't appreciate the commentary. I think we're done here. I'll pay on my way out," she tells me, moving to stand. But before she can leave, I rush out the words, "He asked me out the other day, and I said no because of Tyler, but had I not seen you two together at Rocket Dog, I'd have had no idea he was trying to cheat on you. I know it's shitty of me, but I really think fate or the universe or whoever put us together so I could tell you this."

Kat gawks at me for an unsettling moment, her eyes wide as she stares at me for an uncomfortable moment before bending forward, hands on her knees as she bellows out the most unattractive bout of laughter I've ever heard. It makes me like her even more and, in the same thought, my heart clenches because this is probably the last time we'll see each other.

I sit here, grimacing at her, my head tilted to the side and my lips pursed. I feel like I might have broken her somehow. She's been laughing for so long that everyone in the busy restaurant is staring at her, dumbfounded.

She sucks in a lungful of air before righting herself and sliding back into the booth, leaning on her forearms. "Who exactly do you think my boyfriend is?" she wheezes out.

I must be looking at her like she has three heads. Who the hell else would I be talking about? "Gianni De Laurentiis..." I say it really slowly in case her brain decides to malfunction again.

She bites down on her bottom lip, trying and failing to repress another fit of laughter. Another squawk of a laugh passes her lips, but thankfully, it's over quickly.

"You don't watch hockey at all, huh?" *What the hell does hockey have to do with this?* Her brain must *really* be short-circuiting right now. If "does not compute" were a person, it'd be her.

"I prefer warm, outdoor sports over cold ones, so no, I've never watched a hockey game in my life. Though I'm not sure what that has to do with anything."

She smirks at me. "I'm beginning to think fate really *did* bring us together. But not how you seem to think."

I'm still staring at her, confused as to how this intelligent, kind woman can flip a switch to damn near unhinged in such a short time, but then I'm reminded of my mother, and the thought stabs at my heart.

"Gianni is *not* my boyfriend," she deadpans.

My eyes widen, and my thoughts freeze momentarily as I stare at her blankly.

He's *not* her boyfriend?

She remains silent, scanning my face for any sign of intelligent life within my thick skull.

As my mind unfreezes, it starts to kick up as if turning on an air conditioner that hasn't been used in years. Once it starts going, everything rushes into me at once.

The confusion when I asked about Gianni being proud of her, the lack of disappointment that he wasn't able to make it to Rocket Dog, and *the hockey.*

Oh my god, he's *NOT* her boyfriend!

My eyes are the size of saucers as I smack a hand to my mouth. The nausea clears almost instantly, and laughter bubbles over. "Oh my god," I breathe, "I'm so sorry!" She joins me, laughing the same way Kira and I used to when we'd get high in high school.

"It's really okay." She chuckles. "I'm with his oldest brother, Alessandro. He and my brother used to play for the Philly Scarlets together. Now Ale's one of the assistant coaches, and my brother still plays for the team as a defenseman. I am curious though; last year around this time, we had kind of a huge blowout with the press. How did you not hear about that?"

I mull it over. "I had just opened my clinic in the spring of last year, so I was busy and definitely wasn't watching anything sport related at the time. I grew up playing soccer, and those sports columns give me anxiety, so truthfully, I just never paid any attention to them. I'd imagine only people who are really into hockey would know what you're referring to."

"You're probably right, or at least, I hope you're right," she admits, her smile not quite as wide anymore.

"Well," I say, changing the subject, "now that I've traumatized you, maybe we should talk about something a little less morose."

Chapter Ten
Lark

Kat walks me back to my car, stopping on the sidewalk before saying, "We should do this again sometime. It was really nice."

"Definitely, without the miscommunication trope though."

She snorts at that. "Are you a reader?"

I laugh. "Most definitely, but strictly romance. Full transparency, you aren't learning all the secrets of the world in any of my books."

She muffles her laughter with a hand pressed to her mouth. "Alessandro's mom actually hosts a book club every month. She calls it 'Always Smutty In Philadelphia.'" My eyes bulge at that. If I were eating or drinking, I'd be choking right now. "Yeah, I know." She rolls her eyes. "It took some getting used to, especially when her daughter referred to her and her mother as 'smut sluts.' I thought I was hallucinating."

I release a loud snort. "That's incredible. She sounds like a freaking icon."

"Oh, she most definitely is. This is a woman who told me that if she could go back in time, she'd be the one to coin the term 'cunt.' She's made it her personal mission to 'bring back cunt,' so she uses it as often as possible.

We've considered leaving her at home, but she definitely wouldn't have that either," Kat says with a low chuckle.

"Bring back the word cunt." I breathe in disbelief. "I don't think I've ever loved anyone more than I do at this moment."

"Gloria De Laurentiis is a force to be reckoned with, but she's also the kindest person I've ever known. She'll love you. Come to book club next weekend? You don't even need to read the book. We can fill you in and try again next month."

"What day is it?" I ask, genuinely hoping I can make it.

"Saturday night. We usually start around six."

I frown. "I'd really love to, but I actually have a book club with my best friends that night."

"Any chance they'd want to combine the festivities? We could talk about both books and all start the same one next month if they're into it?"

I mull that over for a moment. I think they'd actually really like that. "You know, I'll ask. I think they might enjoy it. Plus, Madison is on her way to being the next Gloria, so she may as well learn directly from the source. They both sound like the same type of people."

She gives me a broad smile. "Perfect. Text me when you get home safely, please, and let me know about next weekend when you get a chance."

"Will do." I smile as I climb into the vintage Firebird.

***

I pull into the parking lot, turn off the engine, and search the lot. Tyler *still* isn't home, and I haven't heard a single word from him all day.

Heading inside, I shoot off a text to Kat, letting her know I got back home safely before leashing up the dogs for a walk.

When we get back inside, I flop back down on the worn beige couch, opening my texts to my group chat.

You guys remember how I told you all about Gianni De Laurentiis?

Madison
This is about to get good besties. Strap in tight!

Kira
Of course we remember. Get to the fucking punch-line bitch.

Kira
Please… hehe

Jade
Yes, we remember. New developments?

I was wrong.

About everything.

Kira
Stop speaking in riddles. Explain.

You're a real cunt, ya know that?

Madison
CUNT! Viva La Cunt Revelucion!!!

Kira
Jesus Christ, you bitches give me a damn headache. That word is revolting.

Madison
That's the point… Revolt… Revolution…

Kira

You aren't clever.

Madison

What? It's the best word in the English dictionary, and I think we should stop criminalizing it.

Kira

Moving on…

Okay, okay!

Hold on to your panties ladies!

Kira

I'm impatiently waiting…

Okay, so he is NOT dating Kat, the woman that I met at Rocket Dog.

Jade

Well, obviously not babe. That's Alessandro De Laurentiis's girlfriend. Where was I when we spoke about this?

Jade

I'm suddenly feeling rather guilty for skimming the last two weeks of messages and not actually paying attention… I have a feeling that whatever you're about to share is probably something I could've prevented… oops.

Good Lord Jade!!!

Kira

> Oh, fuck you Jade!

Madison

> JADE!!! How could you!?

>> Everyone just shut up so I can give you the details!

>> As Jade just enlightened us, she is NOT with Gianni.

>> She is, however, in a book club run by Gianni's mom and she asked if we'd join them on Saturday!

>> Apparently the group is called "Always Smutty In Philadelphia" and Gloria is single-handedly trying to bring back the word "cunt."

Madison

> This woman sounds like my new idol. I'm in.

Kira

> Sounds good to me!

Jade

> Ooh! So fun!!!

Jade

> Okay, sorry for the topic change… but are you leaving Tyler yet?

Kira

> Jade! Didn't we talk about this? When you're going to say something that may be potentially hurtful, you need to run it by one of us first.

> Jade
>
> Sorry! Neurodivergence has entered the chat.
>
> Jade
>
> Did I hurt your feelings, Lark?

Jade's inability to read the room has always been a topic of discussion among our group, but we know she genuinely doesn't mean anything by it. She just processes information differently, and that's totally okay.

Frankly, I appreciate how blunt she is. I never have to guess what she's thinking or how she's feeling. It's refreshing.

> No worries, Jade. I was just talking about this with Kat tonight, actually.
>
> Not breaking up, but I'm just processing a lot.
>
> Madison
>
> Not to be a Debbie downer, but Jade's right. You really need to leave him, babe. He's not good for you and I'm not even convinced you guys like each other anymore.

The reality of that hits home in a way I hadn't anticipated. I'm not sure when it happened, but I think if I'm honest with myself, I've been just *barely* tolerating him for quite some time now.[1]

> Madison
>
> Kira… you're awfully fucking quiet.
>
> Kira
>
> My momma told me that if I don't have anything nice to say, not to say it at all.

---

1. **Misery Business – Paramore**

I snort at that.

Madison
> You're a fucking liar, and your 'momma' is the cuntiest cunt that ever did cunt. So try again.

Kira
> Goddamn, kitty's got claws tonight, huh?

> Can we stop this already? You guys realize you're in your thirties or about to be?!?!

> I haven't figured out what I'm going to do yet, okay? But when I decide, you'll be the first to know.

Jade
> Any one of us in particular?

Madison
> Jade… She meant the group chat lol. I know damn well that you knew that. Stop being a tyrant and go to bed. I love you ladies!

Kira
> Love you, night!

Jade
> Love you, goodnight.

> Love you guys, goodnight!

God, even they want me to break up with him.

Suddenly, I've got a boulder sitting in the pit of my stomach, and I'm not sure I'm strong enough to lift it.

Chapter Eleven

Gianni

Tuesday, February 25, 2025

I somehow managed to peel my ass out of bed this morning, drop Pickles off at my parents', and make it to practice.

Now that I'm here with the dark clouds hovering over the field and the threat of rain, I'm even more miserable than I could've imagined. Soccer hasn't brought me the same joy it once did since the accident, but standing here as I stare at a man I once respected, looked up to even, as he delivers the worst news possible just heightens my feelings of disdain.

"Damien Reyes will replace Alex Casillas this upcoming season," Coach Antonio tells us.

This doesn't make any fucking sense. He's not even a goalkeeper!

"Coach, all due respect, but Reyes isn't a goalkeeper anymore, and he hasn't been for the last two seasons. How is he replacing Alex?"

Coach pins my teammate with a glare. "Gutierrez, every decision I make has a purpose. Have I steered you wrong before?" His deep baritone challenges, those dark eyes piercing Xander Gutierrez with a look that tells him to keep his mouth shut.

As usual, I'm numb.

And as fucked as this sounds, I'm actually almost *excited* to have that piece of shit in my vicinity. At least if I'm angry, I'm feeling *something*. And that's better than the numbness I've been saturated with since last September.

"As I was saying, he starts next week. Get your heads on straight because I don't want a repeat of last year," he states sternly, and this time, all eyes are on me.

Rage builds inside me at the reminder of what he'd said, but the pity on my teammates' faces makes me want to pull my goddamn hair out.

"Go get changed," he huffs finally.

I turn on my heel, not requiring the extra push to get the hell out of here, but his firm voice is at my back. "Everyone except you, De Laurentiis. Get over here."

I swear, the clouds overhead darken a shade at his words.

Steeling my spine, I turn to face him.

He approaches me, his hulking form making him eye level with me, something I'm not used to.

"We're not going to have any problems this season," he says.

"No, there won't be, Coach," I confirm, dipping my chin. Though I'm not so sure it's true.

"That wasn't a question. I'm telling you." Now, *I'm* the one being pinned with his steely gaze. "We are *not* going to have any problems this season. You're a grown-ass man, and you'll be treated like one. Last year, when you smashed his face in, I let it happen. I knew that whatever the hell he said must've been pretty bad for you to lose your temper like that," he explains, putting his hands on his hips and widening his stance. "I let it slide because the accident had happened so recently, and I know Alex was your best friend. What happened to that young man is a goddamn tragedy, but you will not be landing your ass on the bench again. You're on the same team now, and I need you to act like it."

What I *want* to do is flip him off and tell him I quit because this game doesn't bring me any fucking joy without Alex here, but I can't do that because *Alex* would be pissed. I know he's dead, but I'm rather convinced he'd come back to haunt me or at least my dreams. Not that he isn't already doing that. It's part of the reason I spend so much of my time asleep. At least then, I get to see him again, outside of the confines of pictures and old family videos.

"Yes, Coach. Can I get changed now?"

"Fine," he grunts.

I take off at a sprint, and just like that, the rain comes pouring down. My feet slap against the wet turf as I make my way to the locker rooms to change.

After I've showered, I finally check my phone. I groan, finding that ten text messages await me.

I skim through them, ignoring them all, but see that Kat's texted me. She doesn't do that often.

> Kat
>
> Hey Gi… I have a funny story to tell you that might brighten your day a bit?

> Doubtful, but I'm all ears.

At least over texts, I can be honest with her.

> Kat
>
> Well, at least you didn't lie to me this time and say you're "fine."

> Kat
>
> I went out to dinner with Lark on Saturday…

> Dr. Hughes?

Now she has my attention.

Kat

> I'm not sure how many people you know named Lark, but yes... one and the same.

Wow, snarky today.

Kat

> Just shut up and let me tell you the good news!

You're starting to sound a lot like Aiyana...

Kat

> She's reading over my shoulder like the absolute pain in my ass that she is, but she says, "thank you."

Oh, come the fuck on. These two.

Kat

> Okay, so we had dinner and SHE THOUGHT YOU AND I WERE DATING!!!

What?

Kat

> She was trying to break the news to me about my "boyfriend" cheating on me and asking her out.

Kat

> How come you didn't tell me you asked her out?

Because she said no...

And you tell my brother everything.

Kat

> Not if you ask me not to!

Kat

> Don't you think it'd make sense to have told me something like that when I was trying to piece together why she didn't seem to like you that first day?

How the hell was I supposed to know that was what you were thinking?

Kat

> Well, you never asked.

Go away.

Kat

> Wait! There's more!!!

Oh, good fucking lord. Make it quick.

Kat

> I think she's going to be breaking up with her boyfriend soon… He seems like a jerk, honestly.

Not my business. Talk later.

Kat

> You're a pain sometimes. When you're ready to fangirl about it, let me know!

Never gonna happen, but okay.

I'm not even sure what that means.

> Kat
>
> *face palm emoji*

> I'm absolutely convinced Aiyana stole your phone. You two have fun.

Now I just feel fucking twisted that I want this woman to break up with her boyfriend, but at least she really *does* have a boyfriend. She already told me *no* though. She isn't interested, so their breakup wouldn't help me any. Besides, I barely know her. Maybe she's just a pretty face.

Même moi, je ne crois pas aux mensonges que je me raconte. Even I don't believe the lies I'm telling myself.

Chapter Twelve

Lark

Friday, February 28, 2025

I was *so* looking forward to going home and getting some sleep after this shift. We've had so many emergency cases today that my heart just hurts, and my head aches.

But alas, I can't. Because, *of course,* I can't.

"No problem, Deb. I'll cover your shift tonight. I hope you feel better soon," I tell Debra over the phone.

"I'm so sorry, Lark. I know you're probably exhausted, but I just can't leave the house like this." This is the third time in two minutes she's apologized for something completely out of her control.

"It's seriously okay. I own the place, so it's my responsibility. Don't give it a second thought," I tell her, trying to calm some of her worry. She just started here last month, so I'm sure it's anxiety-inducing to have to call out already. "I'll run home and take a nap before shift change and be right as rain. Now go take care of yourself, and let me know if you need anything."

"You're seriously a doll," she says, blowing out an audible breath. "Have a good night, Lark."

"You too, Deb."

Shoving my phone in my pocket, I make my way to the front desk. "Hey Betty, Dr. Calloway won't be able to make it tonight, so I'm gonna head home for a couple of hours to nap, and I'll be back for shift change."

Her bright-blue eyes peer up to meet mine. "You sure there isn't someone else who could cover for you? You work so much, and I'm worried about you." Her sincerity crushes me, but she knows I don't pass off shifts to people unless they want the overtime.

My lips curve into a small, reassuring smile. "I promise I'll be okay. I'm just gonna skip Rocket Dog tomorrow morning and get some sleep then. I've got the futon in my office, so I'll take a few naps when it's slow."

She nods, knowing she's not going to change my mind. Her short frame slumps forward, resting on an elbow as she immerses herself back into her work.

***

As I unlock the door, I check my watch. It's just past four, so if I get in bed immediately, I'll have an hour and a half to try to nap before I've got to take Tiny and Rex for a walk and head back into work.

Hopefully, Tyler's still working in his office so he doesn't say anything about me being home early. He gets really weird about that because he finds it difficult to concentrate when I'm home, apparently. *He acts as if he pays any attention to me in the first place.*

Tossing my keys on the entryway table, I'm greeted by loud music coming from the back of the apartment.

When Tiny and Rex don't make their way over to me, my stomach starts to churn with unease. *Something's off here.*

Marching over to the office, where I hope I'll find Tyler so he can explain why the hell the dogs are locked in our room, I hear two distinct sounds hidden below the ridiculously loud electronic music.

Tiny's distinct whine comes from behind the office door, and I hear moans from our bedroom. Female moans.

What the ever-loving fuck!

As I wrench the office door open, Rex barrels through the doorway, panting as he jumps up and down with excitement at mine and Tiny's arrival. "Hi, buddy. It's okay, Momma's home," I coo, trying to settle him down a bit and mentally prepare myself for what I know I'll find behind the next door.

I take a deep breath, squeezing my eyes tightly shut before gripping the handle and pushing it open.

My spine stiffens, and my eyes widen the moment they land on Tyler.

I see red. My hands begin to shake, my nostrils flare, and adrenaline courses through my body.

My longtime boyfriend, who I've wasted the last six years of my life on, is buried balls deep inside a woman who looks like she's in pain. Her face is contorted in distress despite the moans leaving her mouth. They're clearly fake because I know for damn sure he's never made me moan like that.

I slam the door behind me, not wanting to subject my poor dogs to this image.

Tyler finally notices me standing here, my fists balled up in anger. "What the fuck, Lark!" *He* has the *audacity* to yell at *me*!

I jab a finger at him, yelling, "I should be asking you the same fucking thing, *Tyler*!" My lips pull back in a snarl. "You fucking bastard!"

"It's not what it looks like!" he shouts as he attempts to remove himself from the vice grip the woman has around his waist while she uses him as a shield, locking her ankles together behind his back.

I throw my hands up. "Oh, *I'm sorry!* So you *don't* have your dick inside some other woman? I must be fucking hallucinating or something!"

"I mean, with your crazy fucking mother's history, it's totally possible!"

My eyes flare, and I gape at him. "What did you just say?" I ask, cocking my head to the side. I feel all the blood rushing in my ears as Tyler starts to stammer before regaining some of that audacity he had just moments ago.

"You fucking heard me, Lark. And is it really cheating if you won't fuck your own boyfriend? I mean, come on! I've been trying to get you to have sex with me for months, and you won't. I have *needs,* Lark! I'm a man. Okay? I was just making sure my needs were met."

At that, the woman pushes him off her abruptly. "Meeting your needs?" she seethes. "We've been together for *two years,* Tyler! What the fuck do you mean?"

My stomach drops. *Two years? How could I not have noticed?*

The tall blonde looks at me as she rushes to get dressed. She plucks her jeans off the ground, sliding them up her long legs as she peers up at me. "I'm so sorry, girl. I honestly had no idea." She shakes her head, gathering the rest of her belongings and making a mad dash toward the front door.

If she'd have stopped to look around before jumping straight into his bed, she sure as shit would've noticed all of *my* belongings. But ignorance is bliss, I guess. For the ignorant one, anyway.

As soon as she opens the bedroom door, Tiny and Rex bolt inside. Tiny stands guard in front of me just as Rex flings his small body at Tyler.

I have no time to react as Rex bites down on Tyler's balls, eliciting a blood-curdling screech from Tyler. He's flapping his hands, his face turning beet red as he dances around the room screaming.

"Get him off! Get him off me!" he hollers, grabbing a pillow from the bed and smacking it at Rex. "You crazy fucking bitch and your crazy fucking demented-ass dog!" he yells as he spins around the room with Rex dangling between his legs, his jaw clamped shut.

I'm both horrified and *elated.*

A smile curves my lips before laughter bubbles over at the sheer absurdity. Tyler finally manages to unclamp Rex's jaws before throwing him across the bed.

My smile disappears instantly, replaced by a scowl and narrowed eyes. "What the fuck!" I yell at him as I run to Rex, who looks up at me with a lazy smile, but the moment Tyler nears, Rex growls a long, low hum of warning.

"Get your crazy-ass dogs and *leave*!" he shouts at me as if I had *any* plans to stay here.

"Fucking hell," he mutters, frantically gripping his bleeding testicles, applying pressure with a T-shirt he found on the floor—likely thrown there when he was so hurriedly fucking his *other girlfriend* while I was supposed to be at work. Debra did me a huge favor by getting sick and calling out today. If she hadn't, I might have never known that he was living a double life.

"Have fun dealing with," I wave at his bleeding scrotum, "that."

I spin on my heel, making my way to the door. I leash up Tiny and Rex and head out the door.[1]

---

1. **I Will Not Bow — Breaking Benjamin**

Chapter Thirteen
Lark

"Alright, boys, I'm just gonna get you inside, and once you're all settled in, I'll call Dad so he can help me sort this mess out." Tiny wags his tail as he enters the clinic, with Rex trotting closely behind. Both of them are blissfully unaware that our lives are about to change forever. Not that they'd care. They've always hated Tyler, and I officially see why.

How many times have they been locked in that office while he's cheated on me in our bed?

Betty's dark bob pops up over the counter at my entrance, and she rubs her chin. "Hey, weren't you going to take a nap?" She looks down at her computer, then back up at me. "You've got another hour before shift change."

"Yeah, I found Tyler cheating on me, so I'm just gonna take a nap in the office while I look for a place to stay," I say blandly.

Her brows shoot up her smooth forehead, and she stands abruptly, keeping her hands planted on her desk as she stares at me wide-eyed. "He *what*? Oh my god, Lark! Are you okay?"

"Yep, peachy keen. Honestly, the fact that I'm not more upset about it probably means I shouldn't have stuck around so long anyway." I shrug.

Seriously, is this the denial phase of grief or something?

I don't think so since I'm definitely not denying what I'd just seen, nor am I denying that my ex is a piece of shit.

"I mean, I can't disagree, but that's horrible," she says, her voice empathetic. "I'm so sorry! Let me know if I can help with anything." She pauses. "You know, you're welcome to stay with me while you find a place."

I give her a small smile. "I appreciate the offer, but you and Bran have a toddler at home. You don't need me taking up space. I'll be okay, I promise. I'll even let my dad help me out, just this once." I wink, heading in the direction of my office.

Flicking on the light, I make my way around the room, setting up the dog cot along with their toys and bowls. "I'll go get you some water, and I'll be right back, okay, boys?"

They look at me like I hung the moon, and my heart stutters to a stop. *How come these sweet little creatures can love me unconditionally, but the man I wasted six years of my life with can't even respect me enough to break up when he decides he doesn't love me anymore?*

"God, this is so fucked up." I groan, hanging my head.

Once the dogs are situated, I take a seat on the faded blue futon, slumping back and fishing my phone from my pocket to dial my dad. It rings several times before he answers. "Hey, my little bird, to what do I owe the pleasure of a call from my girl on a work night?" His soft baritone lulls through the phone, a chuckle reverberating on the other end of the line.

"Hey, Daddy-O, I have a favor to ask, and I promise I'll pay you back," I start.

"Ask me anything, and it's yours. You don't need to pay me back, Lark. Please stop with this self-sufficient crap. I *know* you're independent and can do everything without me, but you don't have to. I'm more than happy to help, and you already work so damn hard to make your dreams a reality," he assures me.

"Thanks, Dad." My voice comes out small and strained.

"You're starting to worry me. Please just tell me what's going on," he pleads.

I blow out a breath through my nose, my shoulders slumping. "I caught Tyler cheating on me, so I need to find a new apartment."

He lets out a string of cuss words on the other end of the line, and he sucks in a deep breath. "When you're ready to talk about it, I'll be here. And if you decide to burn that shitty-ass apartment down with him inside, I'll help cover that up, too, but in the meantime, I'll find you a place to live soon. Don't worry, little bird. We can work it out next week. When do you get out?"

I rub at the ache in my chest, closing my eyes as I lie flat on the futon. "I get out at six tomorrow morning. One of the vets called out, so I'm here all night."

"Okay," he mutters, taking a moment to mull that over. "I'll drop by that shithead's apartment, clear out the place, and get the dogs. You can spend the week with me if that's okay? If you'd rather be closer to the clinic, I can try to find you a hotel room or an Airbnb."

"I've got the dogs with me already, but I'd really appreciate it if you could grab my stuff. It's kind of all over the place, but I'm sure you'll know what's mine," I say, doing my best to keep my voice even. "And I'd love to stay with you. Thanks, Dad," I tell him truthfully.

"I'm glad the boys are safe with you. I'll text you when it's done. I love you."

"I love you too, Dad, and thank you again." A weight lifts off my shoulders when he doesn't pry for more information. My dad is the best and always has been. He's also never been a huge fan of Tyler's, so while I'm sure he doesn't want me to feel hurt, he's probably ecstatic.

"Anything you need, you've just got to ask. Have a good night at work. Try to get a few naps in, please. If it's not safe for you to drive in the morning, let me know, and I'll come pick you up."

"Of course. Thanks and goodnight, Dad."

"Night, little bird," he says before I hang up the call, switching to my group message.

> I don't want to talk about it right now because I have to get back to work, but I went home for a nap in between shifts and found Tyler humping some woman he's apparently been seeing for two years.

Kira
> Oh Jesus Christ, let me know if I need to burn that man's shit down!!!!

Kira's from Tennessee. She'd absolutely do it.

Madison
> Same here.

Jade
> You know, when I was in the military, they taught us how to dispose of a body… I could employ that skill here, just this once.

> I love you guys, but that's not necessary. My dad is already going to take care of it.

Kira
> Oof, Daddy Hughes for the win!

> That will never stop being weird…

Madison

> Kira… we all know you want to suck that poor man's dick, but please don't tell his daughter that shit!

> Why'd you have to go and say it like that?! I'm going back to work!!!

Jade

> You guys are gross.

Jade

> Sorry Lark, love you.

Madison isn't wrong. I'm very aware that my best friend since childhood has had a crush on my dad for practically as long as we've known each other.

I let out a laugh at the thought of them together and flip to my Dexcom app to check my sugars.

Sure enough, the stress of the night has caused my sugars to fucking skyrocket. I grab the insulin out of the mini fridge beside me and warm it in my hands before injecting and getting back to work.

Chapter Fourteen

Lark

Saturday, March 1, 2025

My lids are so heavy I can barely keep them open by the time I get the front door open. "Dad! I'm home," I shout into the oversized house, the sound echoing around me.

His footsteps boom as he makes his way down the metal winding staircase in the center of the room. Dad's bright-blue eyes meet mine, and a wide grin stretches across his face when he sees me. "Hey, little bird, how was work?"

I unleash the boys and toe my shoes off before heading toward him. "Exhausting, but it's over, and I get the next two days off, thankfully."

"Head up to the guest room, and I'll bring you something to eat. We can talk after you've gotten some rest," he tells me with a warm smile that shows off his dimples.

"Thanks, Dad, but I've been snacking all night. I think I'm just gonna knock out. I honestly don't have the energy to eat right now," I say, my shoulders slumped. I'm ready to crawl into bed.

"I gotcha. You head to bed and leave the boys to me. Just please make sure your sugar is fine before knocking out, okay? I'll take the boys on a walk and get their breakfast ready." I'm so damn tired and starved for affection that my dad doing the most normal things for me makes my eyes well with tears.

He closes the distance between us, wrapping his arms tightly around me and resting his chin on the top of my head. "Everything is going to be okay, I promise," he whispers as he squeezes me in a crushing hug. "Now head up for a nap, and I'll see you in a few hours, and we can talk about dinner plans," he says, releasing me before he can manage to squeeze all of the air out of my lungs with his vice grip.

"Oh shit." I clap a hand to my forehead. "I forgot about book club tonight. I guess I'll have to cancel that." I shake my head, knowing the girls will be disappointed but won't give me grief for it, considering the circumstances.

Dad flattens his lips, waving me off. "I'll watch Rex, and you go out. It'll be good to see your friends. Besides, there's nothing for you to do but sit around and wallow in misery," he says, and his lips curve up in a lopsided smirk. "Though I'm sure you're not that miserable. Tyler never deserved you, and I think you were finally coming to terms with that anyway."

I nod, sighing dejectedly. "You're right. Alright, if you really don't mind watching him for me?"

He rolls his eyes with a wry grin. "Of course I don't. Now, get to bed; you look like you'll drop at any second."

Smiling at that, I jog up the stairs, entering the only room in this house that doesn't look cold. The walls are painted a pale pink with white bedding, but art covers nearly every surface in some way. Mostly with paintings my mother drew for me growing up.

After cleaning up in the bathroom and checking my blood sugar, I practically collapse on the bed, falling asleep in a matter of seconds.

***

"And you're *sure* you don't mind watching him for the night?" I ask him, just making absolutely certain he didn't have plans.

"When have I ever given you the impression that doing something for my *daughter* felt like an obligation?" he asks, a dark brow quirked at me.

"Never, but you don't need to be a brat about it." I chuckle.

"Have fun, and promise to either stay the night or call me to get you if you're too tired to drive or if you drink." He envelops me in a quick hug, pressing a kiss to the top of my head before releasing me to leave.

"I promise. See you in a few hours," I tell him, waving as I head out.

***

I park along the street, a little nervous about leaving my baby, affectionately named Cherry, out here, but at least I know I'm in the right place. Familiar cars belonging to my best friends line the narrow road.

I walk up the paved pathway with Tiny glued to my side, and the moment I step on the porch, the door bursts open, startling me. My heart pounds inside my chest as I jump backward, but the monster of a man before me juts out his hand, wrapping it around my lower back and steadying me before I can fall backward and crack my head open.

My eyes widen when I realize who it is. "Gianni." I breathe.

His aquamarine eyes bore straight into me, the dark circles under them making him look even more haunted than the last time I'd seen him. "Dr. Hughes." He nods, releasing me once I'm steady on my feet. He makes his way around me, rushing to his car like a madman, and it isn't until he's at the vehicle that I realize Pickles is trailing behind him, her fluffy tail happily swishing as she waits for him to open the trunk for her.

I watch as he opens it and see that the trunk is filled with pink fluffy blankets. Pickles jumps in, circling around the center of the blankets and nudging them into the right position with her nose before finally deciding to plop down.

Gianni's eyes dart up, boring holes into me when he notices me still standing here. I feel a flush creep across my skin, so I duck my head, and I enter the house, hoping the open door was an invitation.

I head down the thin limestone-walled corridor with peeling wallpaper on the top half. The entryway opens up into a larger living space with the kitchen to the right, and a room of smiling faces greets me. "Lark! You made it!" Kira shouts as she bolts out of her seat and runs toward me, dragging me by my bicep over to the group of women.

"Hi, everyone." I smile sheepishly, feeling a little out of place.

"Lark! God, no wonder my baby Gi has the hots for you! You're gorgeous," the older woman sitting in the wheelchair beside Kat tells me. My eyes widen, and I feel my cheeks flush with heat.

The room fills with everyone shouting "Gloria!" and "Mom!" as if they're used to her making outlandish statements.

A busty redhead is seated on the floor in front of a woman with pastel-pink hair. She smiles brightly at me, her eyes gleaming with excitement. "Gloria has a way with words," she says with a laugh, her voice taking on a light quality reminiscent of a fairy. "Kat filled us in on your dinner the other night, and Kira filled in the rest of the details. Don't worry, Gi isn't here pining after you." She winks at me. "Though we hear you just had a breakup, so if you want him to be—" She doesn't finish her sentence as the pink-haired woman behind her smacks her over her pretty head with a pillow.

"You guys are insufferable," Kat says, still smiling, her words laced with affection. She pats the seat on the worn floral couch beside her. "Come sit by me, and I'll introduce you to all the tyrants in the room."

That makes me chuckle, and I'm hit with a wave of longing as I notice Gloria smiling so fondly at Kat as if they were cut from the same cloth. *I wish my mother were still around.*

Shaking the thought from my mind, I take a seat beside her. She leans forward, pointing at each person, starting with Gloria. "This is my mother-in-law or soon to be, I hope," she laughs, "and as you already know, her name is Gloria."

"I could be your future mother-in-law too, sweet cheeks." The older woman winks at me, her blue eyes shining with mischief.

"Ignore her," another woman says. "I'm Charlie, and this is my wife, Rose."

Rose waves and smiles at me but doesn't say anything. "This troublemaker is Arielle. She's Rose's best friend and my brother's wife." Arielle blows me an exaggerated kiss from her spot on the floor.

I already know the other women as they're *my* troublemakers, but just when I thought the introductions were over, a tiny woman with glowing tawny skin comes barreling into the room. Her long black hair is strewn around her head in a knotted mess. "Sorry!" she shouts as she rushes to take her seat on the floor in front of Kat. "I was, uh…" Her eyes dart around the room as her hands fly to her hair, trying to flatten it. "Really busy at work," she explains, grimacing at her own lie.

"I call bullshit. We literally work together, Aiyana. I sign your damn time cards," Rose deadpans.

"She was getting railed into the mattress." Charlie chuckles, which makes Kat lean forward, making a retching sound.

"Gross! You do realize she's married to my *brother,* right? Boundaries, please!" Kat practically begs.

"Have you met these women? There *are no* boundaries in this house," the woman mumbles before turning toward me, extending her hand for a shake. "Hi! You must be the veterinarian, Lark. Nice to meet you." She smiles. "I'm Aiyana."

"It's nice to meet you too, and uh, good for you," I say with a smirk, a chuckle passing my lips. The room erupts in a fit of laughter.

"I think you'll fit right in," Gloria says, smiling broadly.

Kira looks toward Madison and Jade, wearing an expectant look on her face. "Can we move in and never leave?" she asks jokingly.

"You're all welcome anytime," Gloria tells her. "Now, are you ladies ready to talk smut?"[1]

Kira smiles widely at her, but the gleam in her eyes tells me whatever's about to leave her mouth should have me worried. "Gloria!" she says in her singsong voice. "Is that a freaking custom 'smut slut' T-shirt?"

Oh, for fuck's sake.

Gloria's bright eyes light up, her pearly white teeth glowing in the warm lighting. "It absolutely is! Do you ladies want one? I've got tons in my room. I tried to open an Etsy shop, but..." Her eyes swing around the room, glaring at the women I now recognize as Charlie, Rose, and Arielle. "*Some people* wouldn't help me set it up because they were embarrassed of me! Can't an old woman have her fun?"

"Mom, you're not even old enough to qualify for a discounted meal at IHOP. You aren't old, and you know it." Charlie groans from across the room. "And it's not the T-shirt selling we were embarrassed by, and you know that too! It's the fact that you wanted the *entire family* to wear the shirts in a group photo for you to advertise on social media."

"And it wasn't just the shirts either." Arielle rolls her eyes. "The freaking underwear and men's briefs with tiny glow-in-the-dark stick figures hunching. Like, *come on*, Gloria." She snorts. "That's just strange, even for you."

"It's not like I wanted you to wear the underwear in the photos!" Gloria shouts, exasperated, rolling her eyes.

---

1. **Animal – Neon Trees**

"Yes. Yes you did," Rose says in a no-nonsense tone.

This family is so fucking weird, and I love it.

"Fine, maybe I did. Moving on!" she says, tossing her arms up and leaning back into her chair with an eye roll that has me worried they might just pop out of her head.

Kat peers over at my friends, wearing a small smirk. Her fingers fiddle with the zipper of her olive-green jacket before sliding it down, revealing a hot-pink shirt with a white print that says "STFUATTDLAGG" across the chest.

Kira and Madison squeal, "Oh my god! Is that from Gloria too?"

"Yep," Kat answers. Gloria leans forward to peer at what they're staring at as Charlie runs a ragged hand over her face, releasing a loud groan.

"She got to you too, huh, Kat?" Charlie grumbles.

Aiyana smiles up at Kat, then pulls her hoodie off over her head, revealing her own custom "Hot girls read smut" shirt.

Gloria claps her hands enthusiastically. "Ah! See? Someone appreciates my genius!"

"You bitches staged a damn coup, didn't you?" Arielle asks, her bright smile still intact as she says the words with no bite.

"Absolutely. Now let's talk about this book I never managed to read." Aiyana smiles brightly.

"That's okay. We all know you only come for the snacks anyway." Kat laughs.

Turning her gaze on my friends and me, Kat asks, "Did you guys get a chance to finish reading it? It's okay if not; we usually have the whole month."

"Absolutely. I read it in one sitting. It was so good! I hear the author is releasing the next one pretty soon, and I seriously couldn't be more excited!" Madison explains.

"I was actually an ARC reader for it, and I'd give just about anything to be able to experience reading it for the first time all over again. Ryder was so swoony, and Lola was the spicy badass we needed in a cowboy romance!" Kira says.

"Ryder was a little rough around the edges." Kat chuckles. "But that dance class he took her to had me kicking my feet and giggling the whole time."

Arielle laughs, leaning forward as her eyes twinkle. "I went my whole life having no idea that the one thing I'd been missing this entire time was a beefy cowboy taking pole fitness lessons," she says, bringing her fingers to her mouth and letting out a loud whistle.

"Yes!" I shout, bouncing in my seat. "That was so hot! And the freaking lap dance? I almost passed out," I say, laying my hand on my forehead, my body swaying as I pretend to faint.

Tiny rests his big head on my knee, gazing up at me in question. I pat his head, smoothing his big wrinkled brow, and he sags against my side.

Gloria nods fervently at my assessment, chuckling as she does. "Wholeheartedly agree, and I *loved* the tropes! Second chance, Latin dancer, cowboy, an unhinged best friend, runaway bride, oh my!" she says, fanning herself.

We spend the next hour and a half talking about this month's book and everyone's individual takes on each thing, making it pretty easy to relate to who they are as people. So far, I really like them all, and they've accepted my friends and me as if they've known us our whole lives.

***

The front door opens, and several tall men saunter in, each of them carrying a sort of swagger that would turn heads. Even the older gentleman, who I have to assume is Angelo based on everything Gloria's told me about him tonight.

"Hey, Ma!" The man with dark waves and heterochromatic eyes shouts as he enters, bending down to kiss Gloria on the cheek. I've definitely seen all of these men before at soccer matches, but seeing them all up close and in person is a little startling. They're so damn tall and even more gorgeous than should be humanly possible.

"Hi, trouble," Gloria says, smiling up at him, his one blue eye a perfect match to hers. "How was bowling?" she asks with a knowing smirk.

"It would've been great if Luca hadn't insisted on using the fucking plastic dinosaur they give the *children*," one of the dark-haired men grunts out.

One of the guys, who I now know to be Alessandro, rolls his eyes and says, "He was trying to impress a table full of women bowling beside us by being a goof. Newsflash, it didn't work. Their boyfriends all showed up, and that was the end of that, but he was committed to the bit."

Gloria grins and looks over to where Gianni is leaning against the back of the love seat Charlie and Rose are sitting on. "And, Gi, did you need the bumpers up this time, or were you able to score like a big boy without them?" she asks.

"Oh shit, shots fired," Kira says with a laugh.

My cheeks burn red hot at his clear embarrassment. He cups the hair at the base of his neck before meeting my eyes.

"I didn't score, even with the bumpers," he says, and my mind gets caught on what I think might be an innuendo but really couldn't be. This is Gianni we're talking about. The guy is pretty somber. He doesn't strike me as someone to make sexual references, especially not around his family. That apple fell pretty far from the smutty tree.

I finally break eye contact with him, but my skin tingles as if I'm being watched. I swing my eyes around the room, and sure enough, several of the women have theirs glued to me.

Gloria clears her throat and tells him, "That's alright. You always sucked at bowling." She gives him a smile that crinkles the corner of her eyes. "You can't be good at everything, and considering the magic you make with all those instruments, I'd say you have more than your fair share of talent," she says, turning her attention to me with a wink.

All of the air is sucked out of my lungs, and I feel like I might faint. Despite how unabashedly she works to make everyone in the room laugh, usually at the expense of others, it seems like she has her comforting moments too. Almost like she changes her parenting style to meet the needs of her children, even in adulthood.

Aside from her little wink at the end, what she said was actually really sweet, and frankly, it intrigues me even more. I had no idea he played any instruments. Where does he find the time with his busy soccer schedule?

"Thanks, Mom," he says quietly, ducking his chin and heading into the kitchen.

"I hate to break up the party, but Kat and I should probably get home to take Tank out," Alessandro says.

After lots of hugs and goodbyes, my friends and I agree to come back for next month's book club. It's definitely an improvement from our monthly rotation between our tiny apartments, and, of course, I have not a single fucking clue where I'll be living come next week.

Chapter Fifteen

Gianni

Sunday, March 2, 2025

This woman has somehow managed to invade my brain in a matter of weeks. No, *minutes*.

Everything about her makes me feel like a live wire lying over a car on the road. My body hums with apprehension when I'm around her, knowing she's in a relationship but seemingly unable to stop me from fantasizing about her. I'm volatile. When a power line falls on your car, you stay in your goddamn vehicle.

And if I were to try to act on these feelings? That would just end poorly because she's not interested. *She's taken.*

I repeat that mantra over and over until I no longer feel like the electric line lying on the road, waiting to singe anyone who dares to get out of the safety of their grounded vehicle. Because ultimately, that's something that I most definitely am not. *Grounded.*

I haven't felt tethered to this planet since September thirteenth, when my life went to hell. Or further than it already was, at least.

Ever since the accident, I haven't been able to take a full fucking breath. I'm constantly on edge, just waiting for something else to go wrong.

When Dr. Hughes didn't show up to class on Saturday, I felt sick to my fucking stomach. I barely even know her, but every time someone becomes some form of a constant in my life, and I don't know where they are when they should be with *me,* I lose my mind with worry. I've lost too many important people to reckless drivers. It's honestly a wonder how I'm still able to even manage driving myself around.

Letting out a shaky breath, I work to calm my racing mind. I feel Pickles's soft fur glide across my cheek as she nudges me, moving to lay her bulk across my chest like she does most mornings.

She's a big girl, but she doesn't seem to think so. I swear the damn dog thinks she's a teacup Yorkie with the way she demands to lie in my lap and crawl on my chest for hugs.

I wrap my arms around her fluffy bulk as she settles in with her chin resting on my shoulder. I'm unable to work my puffy eyes open just yet, so I take in my surroundings instead, focusing on my senses just like Alex used to coax me.

"*When you're feeling anxious, just close your eyes and focus on what you can feel and smell. It works. Just trust me.*" I can hear his voice, clear as day in the back of my mind, still coaching me out of my own thoughts. My heart squeezes in my chest at the memory and the realization that that's all it'll ever be now. *Memories.*

I run my hands up and down Pickles's long, soft fur, taking in the feeling of it beneath my calloused hands. I focus on the scent of her fur, an earthy one from the dirt she rolled in on her walk last night.

The faint scent of bleach permeates through the air, leftover from the kind woman who cleaned my apartment yesterday after I had had enough of living in squalor. Alex would have been pissed to see me letting myself fall into such misery without him around.

That's the only thought that made me get on that app and find someone who could come by.

The woman, Lucia, was really nice, willing to work on a weekend as long as she could bring her daughter since she couldn't afford a sitter. She primarily spoke Spanish, so that's how I conversed with her, not wanting to force her to communicate in broken English when I could speak to her in her native tongue. Her daughter sat on my couch, watching a children's movie about a special family who each had some form of power, like the daughter who was extremely strong, the other who was beautiful with the voice of an angel, and then the youngest daughter who seemingly had no gift at all. After she left, I sat on the couch with Pickles and watched the movie by myself.

I won't lie. The music was good, and the message was sweet.

Lucia told me all about how she immigrated to the US two years ago and all the people who've shown her kindness along the way. She doesn't know me, doesn't know that I have demons fighting to make their way into my every thought, and yet, she was kind to me. She treated me like a normal person and never once made me feel like the sad sack that I've become, nor did she make me feel bad about my disgusting apartment.

She just cleaned and spoke to me.

I can't imagine how difficult it was for her to make that move, especially with how downright horrible people can be to those who are different from them. She's strong. I hope to find just an ounce of her strength to carry me through as I continue to grieve.

Lucia said she'll return each week to clean for me to ensure I have a safe space to be myself.

I felt something pull at my heartstrings when she offered, and I can't say I'm not excited to speak to her again. *She reminded me a bit of my mom.* I don't have my own memories of her, but from the home videos I've watched countless times, she was kind and strong. A force to be reckoned with.

Once my breathing has calmed some, I crack my eyes open, blinking several times to adjust to the still-dark room. The blackout curtains give nothing away.

Peering over to my nightstand, 10:31 stares back at me in red.

I groan, planting a kiss to the side of Pickles's head. "Good morning, pretty girl. You ready for a walk?"

She stands abruptly, trampling over me with a punch to the gut before jumping out of the bed. She does a full-body wiggle of excitement as she paces the floor, waiting for me.

I roll out of bed, settling my feet on the gray carpet. It feels a lot softer after Lucia came to clean, and my heart squeezes again.

"Alright, get up," I urge myself as I push up and make my way to the bathroom.

***

Unleashing Pickles after our walk, I pad across the vinyl floors, heading for the coffee machine.

Once the machine is cued up, I wait, scrolling through the myriad of missed messages, skipping over all but two.

Kassian Narvaez

> Hey man, I won't be able to bring Pickles to class next weekend if you can't make it. I've got an away game.

Kassian Narvaez

> Oh, and the redhead? She's newly single, according to my sister. Just giving you a heads up.

She's single.

Oh hell. Cupping the back of my neck, I cuss under my breath. The only thing keeping me away from that woman right now is Kas's ability to take Pickles to her classes *and* her boyfriend.

Now I have neither.

> **Thanks for letting me know.**

Kassian Narvaez

> **Anytime.**

I flip to the next message.

Kat

> **Lark is single, but don't make a move just yet. It's not my business and I have no interest in breaking her trust, but I just wanted you to know so you don't make any mistakes. Her boyfriend cheated on her, so give her some time.**

> **I barely know the woman, but that sucks. Sorry to hear that.**

While it's true that I barely know her, hearing that her boyfriend, no, *ex-boyfriend*, cheated on her pisses me off to no end. My blood simmers with anger, and a desire to take a swing at him lights up inside me.

Just like I had with Damien. The things he'd said after Alex's death were deplorable, and frankly, his death was too raw. I couldn't help but react poorly at the time. *And I can't say I regret it.*

Though I'm glad she's at least okay physically. The breakup must be why she wasn't there yesterday.

Kat

> **You know better than to do that with me, Gi.**

Kat

> Last night, you literally couldn't keep your eyes off of her. Take it from my experience. Sometimes that kind of instant attraction is just fate.

I don't warrant that with a response. I agree that she and Alessandro being together was by some great cosmic being; truly, I have to. They're so clearly madly in love, but that isn't what's going on with Dr. Hughes and me.

She said no to me once, and even if she were interested, she'd find out what a wreck I am and flee for the hills.

And I wouldn't blame her one bit.

Chapter Sixteen

Lark

Sunday, March 2, 2025

"I'm so sorry I can't make it to look at apartments with you today, little bird," Dad tells me, looking genuinely disappointed.

"Honestly, it's okay, Dad. I promise. It's probably a good thing you won't be there." I snicker. "You'll just tell me nothing's good enough, and I'll never find anything."

He rolls his eyes at me playfully. "You're probably right, but I'm still bummed about it. Dinner together tonight though?"

A smile stretches across my lips. "Of course, Daddy-O. Now let me get out of here before the agent cancels on me for being late!"

I rush out of the door, planting a quick peck on his cheek as I launch myself down the driveway and into my Firebird.

The engine hums to life, familiar lyrics trickling through the speakers as I make my way to the first apartment.[1]

---

1. **Drive – Incubus**

***

"I'm really sorry, Lark, but this is the last one I have to show you that's in the budget you set. I know you don't want to have your dad help with the cost, but if you don't like it, you really may have to consider it," Shay says, her voice pleading as lines gather on her forehead. "I know Tiny's a good boy, but unfortunately, most of the rentals in this area only allow one dog," she reminds me regretfully for the third time today.

"It's okay, Shay. I have a good feeling about this one anyway, and believe me, I've lived in so much worse before. My apartment with Tyler was super small, and I only got into that place because Tiny's my service dog."

She huffs, taking long strides toward the entry of the apartment building. "I know, and I really tried to sell that piece of info too, but rather *conveniently,* all the normal places I'd suggest for dog owners are suddenly not allowing dogs, and since Rex isn't a service animal, those places are a no-go." Her sharp eyes convey the message that this wasn't merely a coincidence. Tiny trails alongside us, blissfully unaware of our current housing situation.

My shoulders slump involuntarily despite how positive I'm trying to be right now. The circumstances surrounding this move may not be great, but I'm feeling optimistic. "I get it. Let's just go see how this place is before we go down that rabbit hole," I tell her because there's really no use in whining about it. It won't change anything.

The building is tall, probably about five stories, so not anything super huge, which is convenient for when I need to let the dogs out to potty. The parking lot is located just across from the building with what looks like plenty of parking spaces available, so I can feel comfortable keeping my car parked here.

We enter the lobby and wave at the concierge, who's sitting at the desk, reading a golfing magazine.

Once we've made it up the elevator to the second floor, we make our way down to unit thirty-six. *Two thirty-six.* That's a good number. Even numbers are lucky for me.

She enters the door code, and there's a click as the light flashes green. She twists the handle, pushing it open and revealing the perfect space.

My heart flutters and soars in my chest, and I feel breathless as my lips stretch into a wide grin.

I knew that number was lucky.

"I'll take it," I tell her the moment we step inside.

She cocks her head to the side in question, raising a perfectly manicured brow at me. "You haven't even seen the place yet," she deadpans.

I roll my eyes playfully, resisting the urge to skip into the living room, an overly energized feeling thrumming through me. "I can see that everything's up to date and mostly furnished, so it'll be a lot less work and money than other places," I say, beaming at her. "Besides, there are two rooms, so it's a huge improvement from the studio apartment I was anticipating needing to have."

She takes a deep breath, placing her hands on her hips. "Alright, well, let's just properly tour the place for a few minutes so your father doesn't kill me for letting you make a rash decision."

I chuckle at that. Shay doesn't seem to realize this yet, but the reason he's stayed so loyal to her, always having her work as his agent for any and every investment, is that he has a crush on her.

And over the years, it's become pretty apparent that she feels the same.

Her round hips swish from side to side, hugged by the fabric of her navy pencil skirt as she leads me from room to room.

Her heels click across the vinyl floors, but as we enter the bedroom, the sound is muffled by the gray carpeting. An idea sparks, and I decide to throw her a bone. "When you tell my dad that I want this place, you can let him know that we'll need to see about swapping the carpet out for hard floors because the dog hair will be difficult to keep up with otherwise. That way, he'll know we both gave it ample thought," I say, waggling my brows at her.

A small smirk quirks at the corners of her bronze lipstick, the apples of her smooth mahogany skin flush just the slightest bit as she averts her gaze to the ground. "Sounds perfect. Thanks, Lark."

She claps her hands together gently. "Now, how about we go sign a lease?" she asks me, her voice jumping to a higher octave.

"Let's do it." I wink, following her.

Chapter Seventeen

Gianni

Tuesday, March 4, 2025

The sun is high in the sky, and it feels like it's blazing hot out here, and for no good fucking reason. It's almost never this hot this time of year.

My shirt sticks to my sweaty chest, and I can't take it anymore. The friction is practically rubbing my nipples raw.

I clutch the soaked fabric behind my neck and yank it over my head, tossing it to the side of the field, just out of bounds.

A breeze whips past me, drying some of the salty sweat that feels heavy on my skin.

I hear Damien shouting at someone from his goalpost, and it riles me up even further. He just got here, and he's already starting shit with every player on the team.

It's almost as if he doesn't realize we're not excited to have him here, and frankly, *fuck him*. He's taking over a position he hasn't played in two years, which means he sure as shit doesn't have the right to correct any of us.

I turn on my heel, ready to run toward the sound of Gutierrez arguing with him, but Coach's death glare from across the field snags my attention, and I find myself running back to my position with my tail tucked between my legs.

Seriously, fuck this guy. Shouldn't we have a say in who replaces our fucking *dead* goalie? Wouldn't that make more sense than selecting someone our coach already knows most of us have a problem with?

Apparently not though.

I make my way back to the center of the field, waiting for the next practice round to start, and when Gutierrez finally flips Damien off and rushes back onto the field, it's go time.

We each punt the ball away from the players wearing green vests, indicating them as our practice opponents.

I run full speed ahead at my teammate, knowing he's about to miss his shot. I save it by kicking it out from under him and take it as quickly as my legs will carry me to the goal. I pass it to one of the newer guys on the team, and he successfully makes it past Damien, further pissing him off. It's the first thing to bring a smile to my face all day. [1]

---

1. **One Step Closer – Linkin Park**

Chapter Eighteen

Lark

Friday, March 7, 2025

"Alright, boys," I huff out, slouching over the side of the couch. "The last box is all sorted, and do you know what that means?" I ask, peering over at where Rex and Tiny are standing by the coffee table, staring at me with a slow blink. "We're officially home!" I tell them, trying to sound as excited as possible, and my newfound energy has Tiny's whole body wiggling.

As happy as I am to have this step over with, truthfully, I'm exhausted, and I just want to spend my weekend off in my new apartment, reading a good book and cuddling with Tiny and Rex. This is how I wound up moving all of my belongings into my new apartment on a Friday afternoon… alone.

Everyone that I know who could help me was working. My dad let it be known how annoying that was for him, but he eventually let it go after trying to hire a moving company for me. I know he would pay for it, but I didn't want him to, and why would I hire movers when I could do it myself?

But it's all done now.

A smile lights my face as I take in the eight-hundred-square-foot apartment with its dark wooden fixtures and gray walls, now splattered in color from all of my belongings.

Photos of the dogs, my friends, and my dad line the walls with an array of memories, and my colorful boho throw rug brightens the whole place up.

I love it. And it's all *mine*.

Unlike when I lived with Tyler. I hadn't realized it quite to the extent that I do now, but he was so controlling about everything. Always reminded me that the lease was in *his* name.

Nothing ever looked or felt like my own, and I think a part of me knew that, and it may have factored into why I was always working, covering extra shifts to avoid being there in the first place.

The more I've had time away from him to consider the details of our relationship, the more glad I am that we broke up.

He was honestly the freaking worst, and truthfully, if I'd cared more about our relationship, I probably would've noticed something was off while he was out cheating on me for *two years*.

I guess I was just comfortable being uncomfortable since he's all I've ever known. He wasn't my first kiss, but he was my first for *everything* else.

This is a good thing—a positive change, and it'll be a little scary, but I need this chance for self-discovery. I remind myself of this before swinging my legs over the side of the couch and heading out to take the dogs on their first walk around our new complex.

***

My phone buzzing beside me drags me out of my book. I rest it on my lap and grab for my cell, answering when I see who's calling.

"Hey there, hot stuff. How's the new apartment?" Kira asks, her voice projecting over the blow-dryers running in the background.

"Are you still at work?" I ask.

"I just got done here but figured I'd give you a call. I'm gonna get the Bluetooth set up as soon as I get in the car."

I wait patiently as I listen to the heavy back door of her salon slam shut, followed by her car door. "Alrighty, I'm all set. Tell me about the place!" she says, her voice sounding high-pitched and bubbly.

I tell her all about it for the next couple of minutes, making sure she knows just how excited I am for this new change. I hope to settle the worry I know my three closest friends have been fighting with since finding out about the breakup.

"And what are you going to do as your first show of freedom?"

"What does that even mean?" I ask, my voice breaking into a laugh.

"You just got out of a six-year relationship and moved into your own apartment. You should celebrate. Do something for yourself to commemorate this moment," she says, and I can hear the way her voice picks up speed with each word. "Your hair is too pretty to dye, and I don't have the time to get a new tattoo with you, but you should do something for yourself.".

I think on this for a moment, but my mind is drawing up blanks. "I don't really think there's anything I want to do that I couldn't while I was with Tyler, so I'm not really sure."

She releases a puff of air, sounding exasperated. "Babe, you haven't had an orgasm in *how long?* You should explore that!"

My cheeks turn ruddy as my mind is flooded with the images of Gianni that had brought me to my most recent, albeit self-induced, orgasm. "Kira, are you seriously suggesting I go out and have a bunch of one-night stands?"

"I said *orgasms,* not *sex,* but you could totally do that too if you wanted. There's literally nothing stopping you. Come on, isn't there something you've wanted to do or try that you couldn't with Tyler? Whatever *that is, do it*!"

My shoulders tense with the memories of all the times I'd make a suggestion, only to be shot down by Tyler for it being "dirty, disgusting, depraved." Though now I've come to realize that none of those things were true. There's nothing wrong with exploration as long as everyone involved is consenting, but it comes as no surprise since Tyler was his own version of that triple D. Dishonest. Disloyal. Douchebag.

"I mean, there's a lot of stuff I wanted to do sexually but couldn't, but I'm not sure I'm ready to start dating or looking for people to sleep with just yet," I answer honestly, even though the thought of being intimate with a stranger makes my skin crawl a little.

"Well then, buy a toy or two, and maybe make a list of things you want to try. That way, when you *are* comfortable, you know what you want."

"Are you telling me to make a fuck-it list?" I laugh.

"I mean, I wasn't, but now I am! Fuck yeah, Lark, make a fuck-it list!" she says, her voice growing louder with each excited word. "Come on, let's think. What kind of stuff would you put on there?"

With almost anyone else, this conversation would be weird, but with Kira, it's borderline *tame*.

"Oh, and pull up a notes app on your phone so you can type it out while we talk about this. That way, you won't forget anything."

Strangely, I do as she suggests and put her on speaker.

"Alright, I only have one vibrator, and it's a tiny bullet. It does the job, but it's not great by any means, so I'd like to get a new one, maybe a few, to see what I like."

"Perfect. Consider it a belated birthday gift or, *no,* a breakup gift. I'll send you a few of my favorites, all new, don't worry," she clarifies, chuckling.

"Thanks." I snort, knowing she isn't going to let me turn her down, so it's easier just to accept the gift.

We spend the entirety of her drive writing down a list of all the things I've ever wanted to try that Tyler always made me feel bad for even having an interest in. The list includes everything from types of dirty talk and positions to role-play and everything in between.

"Ooh, I have the best idea!" *Oh, fucking great.* "How about you download that erotic audio app I keep telling you about so you can try out some of these things from the comfort and safety of your own home? It's good to explore your own body, and if you don't like any of this stuff by yourself, then you know not to bother trying it with a partner, at least not one you're super comfortable with."

"That's—" I stutter. "Alright, that *is* sort of a good idea. I know damn well you have a referral code for that app, so go ahead and text it to me," I tell her.

"That's my girl," she says, and I can practically hear the wide grin that I'm sure is spread across her face. "Okay, I just parked, so I'm gonna head in and feed the cats. I'll order you some fun new toys when I get done!"

"Thank you. I love you. Tell Harry and Percy I love them too!"

"I will! I'll give them some good belly rubs and an extra treat from you too. Goodnight, and love you!" she tells me before hanging up.

I look down at the long note written on my phone and realize I definitely need to save this to the "my eyes only" section, just in case.

Once I've done so, I set my phone down and bury my face back in my book.

Chapter Nineteen

Lark

Saturday, March 8, 2025

After blow-drying my hair and getting changed, I get Tiny leashed up for his class at Rocket Dog.

An unfamiliar heat sears through me as I think about the cagey blue-eyed man I'm actually *looking forward* to seeing this morning.

As I make my way outside, the cool breeze whips my red strands around my face, and I catch a glimpse of a familiar pair. As if summoned by my thoughts alone, Gianni and Pickles trot ahead of me in the same direction Tiny and I are headed.

On a whim, I start to jog ahead, trying to catch up with them. "Hey! Gianni, wait up!"

His hulking frame nearly shrieks to a stop with Pickles at his side, quickly dropping to her butt at his silent command. Gianni turns slowly to face me. Those same dark circles surround his beautiful blue eyes, making them appear even more strikingly pale.

"Dr. Hughes." He nods, his lips pressed in a thin line as I sidle up beside him. Pickles stands quickly at our approach, she and Tiny taking turns sniffing one another.

"You know, you can call me Lark," I tease, giving him a wide smile.

His dark brow lifts, but he says nothing for a long moment. "We should, uh, we should probably get going if we don't want to be late," he says, clearing his throat. It's possible that I'm imagining things, but *I swear* I see a pink hue creeping up his neck as he averts his gaze.

"Yeah, we should," I answer, starting to walk ahead. I can't help myself, though, as questions nag at the periphery of my mind with each step we take. "Do you live near The Groves?"

He stops in his tracks again, those piercing eyes sweeping across my face. "I live *at* The Groves," he responds.

My eyes go wide at that. "Oh," is all I manage, but the unfamiliar feeling of butterflies fluttering in my stomach takes hold of me, and now *I'm* the one dislodging the frog in my throat. "I do too, well, now I do anyway. We just moved in yesterday, actually."

He continues walking again, this time not facing me, as he asks, "You and your boyfriend?"

My lips tilt in a grin. Something about the way he asks this makes me think that Kat might've spilled the beans about my breakup. "No, we actually broke up, but something tells me you already knew that," I challenge, intrigued by his line of questioning.

"I did," he says with a nod, refusing to meet my eyes. "But you said 'we,' so I just wanted to be sure," he responds as we approach the building we're headed to.

"I meant myself and the dogs," I explain with a chuckle.

"Oh, you have another dog?" His voice is filled with genuine interest, and our conversation flows better than I had anticipated for a man of such few words.

"I do. His name is Rex; he's a really pissy Chihuahua-shih tzu mix," I say, peering up at him with a grin. "Worst attitude ever." I shake my head with a laugh. "But he loves me dearly, and he's eventually warmed up to my friends and my dad, at least."

That makes him chuckle, a sound I'm not used to hearing from such a surly man. Those butterflies from moments ago flap around violently in my gut, and my head spins as my pulse begins to speed up.

"Well, I look forward to meeting Rex, assuming he doesn't try to bite my balls off."

I guffaw at that, eyes wide with shock. I hadn't told anyone about that, but then laughter bubbles out of me so abruptly it's a surprise, even to me. Gianni stares wide-eyed as the laughter turns to borderline hysteria. The memory of Rex's little jaws latched onto Tyler's nether region will be fully ingrained in my brain till the end of time. *I hope he can't have children after that. Men like him don't deserve to procreate.*

Something like a smile, but not quite, twists Gianni's lips. "What's so funny?" he finally asks, amusement lilting his voice.

I snort, and he rewards me with an even brighter version of his almost smile. "I actually caught Tyler in the *act*," I say with a giggle.

But his expression doesn't match my own. His face goes hard, almost feral at my words, and it sends a tendril of something unfamiliar through me, so I rush to continue. "Rex ran in the room, latched onto his testicles, and I'm pretty sure he won't be able to reproduce." I explain the reason for my sudden outburst of laughter.

"Jesus Christ," Gianni mutters, gripping the back of his neck. "Well, I can't say he didn't deserve worse for what he did, but I'll be sure to keep *my* balls far away from Rex."

I smile at that. "Believe me, Rex isn't really violent. He's usually all bark and no bite, but not this time." I snort again, an unattractive sound that I haven't been able to stop from happening despite my repeated efforts over the years.

His eyes turn soft, one side of his lip curving up a fraction. "Are you okay, Lark?" he asks me seriously, concern lacing his melodic voice.

That's the first time he's called me by my first name. It sounds so pretty when he says it. Almost like a poem.

I give him a broad, reassuring smile. "I promise, I'm really okay. Better than okay, actually. I feel like the weight of never being good enough for him has lifted off my shoulders, and I'm just so damn excited to not have to be around his negativity anymore."

"Good," is all he says in reply before holding the door to Rocket Dog open for me to pass through with Tiny.

Chapter Twenty

Gianni

Sunday, March 9, 2025

Who in the hell would cheat on this gorgeous fucking gem of a woman?

I've known her for practically no time at all, and she's already been more kind to me than half of my teammates since Alex's passing. More than that, she's opened up to me and been vulnerable despite my reluctance to give her the same in return.

She just bares her soul to me as if it isn't a precious gift, a piece of herself that she could choose to keep locked away for safekeeping.

Her smile manages to burrow itself into my gut and practically warms me from the inside out; it's a feeling I'm unfamiliar with.

Lark.

It's the name of a woman who deserves to have songs written about her. Sonnets written and published in her honor as a declaration of love and devotion.

That is *not* the name of a woman who's tossed to the side and treated like she's less than by a waste of space who thinks he could find better.

Unclenching my balled fists, I do my best to calm my racing mind, taking in my surroundings just like Alex had instructed time and time again.

As I near the last wave of emotions, Pickles jumps up on the window ledge, peering out through the blinds. She releases a shrill whine, begging for something.

I make my way to the window, and when I part the blinds, I find the fiery-haired goddess I've begun pining after walking with Tiny and who I assume to be Rex.

Shaking my head, I pet Pickles's soft, golden fur. "Not yet, pretty girl. I don't want to give Lark the impression that we're stalking her, okay? I'll take you out in a bit."

Pickles ducks her head in understanding and slowly moseys away from the window, looking unbelievably glum as she does.

Taking a seat on the edge of the couch, I scroll through social media and land on a post by a local musician.[1] The post reads, "Do something today that makes you happy, even if you're afraid of it."

That sounds eerily similar to something Alex said on a daily basis. "Do something today that brings you joy, even if it scares you," he would say. A lot of the time, it grated at my nerves because I'm not so sure I've ever *truly* felt joy.

I miss music. I miss playing and singing and writing, but those were all things I did with my best friend. And now? I'm terrified to dredge them up or sully my memories with my shit mood, but something tells me this is what I need. I've got to start allowing myself to feel things again and, more than anything, *enjoy* things.

Heading into my closet, where my instruments have been tucked away for months, I pull out the electric keyboard and stand, setting it up and plugging it into the wall beside the couch.

---

1. **Zombie – Bad Wolves**

I take a seat, letting my fingers flit over the keys to re-familiarize myself with them. I take a deep inhale, holding it for four seconds before blowing it out, a technique Alessandro once taught me.

Feeling more steady, I begin to play a song that leaves me speechless each and every time I play it. As "golden hour" by JVKE trickles through the room, my heart stutters and clenches with every stroke of the keys.[2]

I feel myself start to relax into it, my posture less rigid now.

Images flit behind my closed lids, my fingers still dancing around, not needing to see what I'm doing. This is second nature and something I've deprived myself of for months now, only adding to my pain.

A new song starts to play as the pain I've been consumed by begins to ease just the smallest bit. Though a familiar throb still sits dead center in my chest.

Memories of my parents, not Gloria and Angelo, but my biological parents, flit through my mind. My mother's long, dark curls swept up in a bun, paint splattered on her clothing and streaked across her face as she stood in front of the massive canvas she was painting on my birthday, the year that they died.

My father's relentless need to smother each of us in crushing hugs before he'd leave the house. A need I now understand.

Neither memory is my own, as I was too young when they died to remember, but Dante did his best to remind Charlie and me of whatever memories he could recall at just five years old. Gloria and Angelo did their best to keep us in contact with our other family and ensured we had piles of photos to fill in the blanks.

The next song tugs at my chest. *Alex's favorite.*[3]

---

2. **Golden Hour – JVKE**

3. **Use Somebody – Kings of Leon**

I can picture his spikey blond hair as he knocked on the door shortly after we started kindergarten, standing on the porch with a black-and-white soccer ball, asking Gloria if I could play with him.

We were in the same class that year, and we became inseparable from the first day. He taught me how to play soccer and helped me develop my love for it as I navigated my first experience with grief. The loss of my parents crushed me as a child with no real concept of why it had to be *them*.

I hadn't realized how much I was missing out on until I was old enough to understand that my siblings and I were adopted. That new knowledge had sunk in my gut like a rock. The lack of authentic memories haunted me as I became old enough to grasp what had really happened.

I play song after song, the weight lifting a little more with each one, and when Pickles rests her head on my thigh, I don't have to ground myself before opening my eyes.

"Hi, pretty girl," I coo, petting her head. "You ready to go on a walk?"

Chapter Twenty-One

Lark

*F*uck. Fuck, fuck, fuck!

I stare into the dark, *warm* fridge filled with now rotting food and *my insulin.*

"Goddamn it," I groan, working to pull the fridge out from the wall, thankful that it isn't heavier.

Hanging just barely out of the wall is the plug. The plug that apparently decided the connection between itself and the wall was *not* strong enough to hold on any longer. *Much like mine and Tyler's. What an unfortunate yet fitting metaphor.*

Amidst my mental breakdown, my phone pings with a text.

Daddy-O

> You still coming to the game today, little bird?

> Yeah, just some technical difficulties, but I'll be there just as soon as I stop at the office! Love you, see you soon.

Daddy-O
> Alright… Let me know if you need me, okay?

> Always.

Apparently, we're lying today, Lark? Maybe he's right. *Maybe* I really do need to quit with my unrelenting need for independence.

Daddy-O
> Love you, kid.

Alright, the clinic isn't too far from here, but it's in the opposite direction of the stadium. Though I don't really have much choice, do I?

"Come on, Tiny. We've gotta get going," I tell him, waving at Rex before we make the run to my car.

As soon as we pull into the parking lot of Toute la Famille, I hop out, leaving the car running for Tiny, who's blissfully unaware of my internal panic as I make a mad dash inside.

"Hey, Lark! You don't work today, do you?" Betty asks me from behind the counter.

"No, I'm on my way to meet my dad at the game, but my new fridge wasn't plugged in properly, so my insulin went bad overnight." I groan loudly.

Her face twists. "I'm sorry, Lark. Is there anything I can do to help?"

"No, don't worry about it. I was just gonna grab my backup stash from the fridge in my office," I explain as I rush back there.

Popping the door to the small fridge open, I grab for the only vial in here, and my heart sinks to my stomach at the sight. I've fucked up. *Again.*

There's *maybe* half a dose left in this tiny vial of short-acting insulin, but it'll have to do.

You need to get a fucking pump, Lark.

There's a pounding in my temples. *I should've just used the warm insulin.* It might not be as effective, but I'd have been able to get a full dose. Hindsight's twenty-twenty though.

At least I hadn't eaten anything yet. Of course this would happen on a Sunday when I'm due to change my damn continuous glucose monitor anyway, and of course, I forgot to put a new one on when I took the other off. My dead fridge has officially thrown off my entire day.

"No use in whining about it now. I'll just inject what I've got and call the pharmacy on the way to the game," I whisper to myself, preparing the syringe.

After disposing of the sharp, I run back to the front, waving at Betty as I go.

"Alright, Tiny, we're cookin' with gas here!" Her big, speckled head peers up from her seat in the back before she settles back in for the drive.

***

We rush along the side of the field, heading toward the bench my dad is always hovering by. He may own the team, but he's far more involved than most of these executives. He genuinely loves soccer and adores this team. And as it turns out, the coach is his best friend.

When he spots me, his arms open wide for me to step into him. He presses a kiss to my head. "Hey, little bird. What were those technical difficulties you speak of?"

He crouches down beside Tiny, giving him scratches behind the ears and pressing a kiss between his eyes.

"The fridge wasn't plugged all the way in, apparently, so my insulin got warm." His eyes flash up to meet mine, worry etched into his thick brows. "Don't worry. I stopped by the clinic and injected what I had left. I've already called the pharmacy, too, so it should be ready for me to pick up on the way home from here."

"You worry your old man, you know that?" he asks, groaning.

I shake my head, giving him a sly smile. "You are definitely not old." I roll my eyes, steering the conversation away from my lack of insulin.

"Maybe not, but some days, I think you age me." He chuckles, mussing my hair as if nothing's changed since I was a child.

"Oh, hush. Focus on the game," I tell him. Tiny and I arrived about twenty minutes into it, so the Divine Flyers are up by one goal.

Tiny stands by my side, his eyes tracking the men rushing behind the ball across the field. The sun is high in the sky, but the light breeze makes this the perfect weather for game day.

It's been a long time since I've had the chance to attend one, but I'm glad to be here, and not just because of my new neighbor.

My eyes zero in on the man I've been thinking about a lot lately. *Too much*, in fact.

Gianni De Laurentiis rushes the field; his particular style of play as a striker has always been of interest to me. He doesn't play the position as a center-forward like most opt to. Instead, he acts as a target, allowing the sheer strength of his muscular legs to carry him across the field with ease, luring the other players away from their goal, and when the moment comes, he *strikes*. Literally.

His lithe body dashes back and forth as if he isn't using any energy at all. He's so fast that I almost find it hard to track him, but my body feels honed into him. Gianni has the speed of a jaguar and the stealth of one too. He's mesmerizing, strategic, and everything it takes to be an incredible player on the field.

His sinewy muscles drip with sweat, and just as soon as he gives Angel a silent instruction, the ball is being passed to him and driven right into the net. His teammates cheer, rushing to him on the field, slapping him on the shoulder, and dancing with excitement. Gianni pants with his hands on his hips, regaining control of his breathing as he returns their excitement with a guarded smile.

Dad watches me out of the corner of his eye, a brow quirked in question. "He gets better every day, doesn't he?" Dad asks from beside me, curious eyes still assessing me.

"Uh, yeah, I guess," I grunt, flushing with embarrassment, and thankfully, he lets it go.

***

The game is nearing the end, with the Divine Flyers in the lead.

My attention is still focused on Gianni as I'm seemingly unable to take my eyes off that gorgeous man, but Tiny stands abruptly at my side, staring me down, and what I'd thought was just a response to heat suddenly feels like so much more.

A heaviness settles in my chest, and my pulse begins to race.

Dad's eyes grow with worry as he takes this in. "Lark, did you eat anything after you took your insulin at the clinic this morning?"

"No." I groan, fully aware of why he's so concerned. I start to feel lightheaded, the edges of my periphery blurring.

Tiny places a paw steadily on my thigh, continuing to stare at me expectantly. "I'll be right back. I'll grab an electrolyte drink, just please, sit the hell down," Dad pleads with me, turning to run up the sideline.

Nodding my head, I move to take a seat on the turf, knowing that if I sit on the bench, I could pass out and hurt myself or someone around me, but as I do, my legs feel weak, and my vision goes black.

Chapter Twenty-Two
Gianni

From the first moment Lark arrived at the stadium—running along the side of the field to meet up with the owner of our team, who I can only assume is related to her in some way given their last names—I haven't been able to keep my eyes off her.

I've been stealing glances at her the entire game, and each time I look in her direction, her eyes are already on me, and a strange feeling tugs in my gut. She seemingly never looks away, a permanent smile spread across her bowed lips as she watches my every move.

That's why, when I spare a glance in her direction and I don't see her, my eyes automatically search the area, finding her limp body being gently lowered to the ground by her Great Dane, Tiny.

My breaths come out in short pants as panic sears through me. My legs move of their own accord, taking off in a sprint toward her, her father also running in from the other direction.

We both reach her at the same time, falling to our knees beside her. I pull her across my lap as if on instinct. Dereck gives me a curious look but says nothing as he ditches the sports drink beside him, grabbing something from Lark's fanny pack.

A small crowd has gathered around us, the on-site medics hurrying toward us.

"Is she going to be okay?" I ask Dereck. My words sound jumbled together, but I'm not even a little concerned about how my rushing over here will look to others.

"She'll be fine, Gianni. Just keep your head down and wipe that look off your face, or you'll wind my daughter up in a tabloid," he whispers so quietly I almost don't hear him. He pushes the plunger on the syringe, and the liquid transfers into a small vial with a white powder. He detaches the needle, shaking the vial before reinserting the needle, and finishes pulling up the fluid from the small orange case before glancing up at me briefly. *Jesus, that seemed like a process.* "Hold her very still for me, please."

I do as he says and watch as he meticulously administers the fluid-filled needle into her delicate, porcelain skin. His hand shakes with an almost imperceivable tremor, but it's enough that I notice, and my heart plummets even further in my gut.

The medics stand by, waiting to see if they're needed, and a moment passes by before her lashes are fluttering open, the big hazel orbs staring up at me. I see the very moment she recognizes whose arms she's in because her cheeks turn pink instantaneously as she tries to move out of my lap, but I hold her to me.

"Just..." another deep breath in, "just wait another moment, okay? You just came to. Please just chill out for a second before you go flying out of here."

She gives me a small nod and Tiny stands from his position at her side, watching his owner, ensuring she's okay.

A hand snaps to her head, rubbing her temples as she groans, her eyes cinching shut. She drags in several shaky breaths, and for each one she takes, I swear, I mirror the action.

I reach over Lark, scratching the massive dog behind his speckled ears. "You're a good boy, huh? Your mommy's lucky to have you," I tell him, my voice wavering and my chin trembling.

When I peer back down at her, those supple lips of hers are open the smallest bit, and I have to fight the urge to duck my head and take a taste.

Her dad clears his throat. "You ready to give this whole standing thing a go?"

She nods her head, reaching for his hand as he pulls her up out of my lap. She stands on shaky legs, and the medics move in, ready to take over.

Those around us cheer, and Lark takes a seat beside her dad, taking small sips of the sports drink he brought over for her.

As I make my way back to the field, I see Damien standing to the side, a smirk spreading his lips. Unease trickles into my stomach, but I brush the thought away, trying to focus on the game as the paramedics help Lark over to the ambulance, pulling away a few minutes later.

We finish the game, winning three to zero. I drag my exhausted body across the field, hoping to shower and head home to take Pickles out before Sunday dinner at my parents' house, but as I enter the locker room, Damien is leaning against my locker.

"Move," I tell him, shouldering past him to grab the duffle I left on the bench.

He leans into me, gripping my forearm tightly, and says, "It turns out your little boyfriend *can* be replaced, huh?" Alex was never my *boyfriend*, but that doesn't matter. Because now he's going after Lark too.

"I don't feel like getting into it with you. Just get the fuck out of my way. Steer clear, and we won't have any problems," I say through gritted teeth.

"Hah, tell that to the fucking plastic surgeon who had to fix my pretty face back up after the job you did on it," he growls like a fucking deranged animal.

I shouldn't warrant that with a response, but I do anyway. "You should be glad that's all I did. If anyone on this team knew the shit you spewed to get your face wrecked, you wouldn't be here at all."

Grabbing my things, I leave him there, not caring for whatever slow-ass reply he's cooking up in that Neanderthal brain of his.

***

In all the years I've called these people my family, I've never once missed a Sunday dinner unless it was for an away game, but today, I'm just fucking exhausted.

I want to go home, hang out with Pickles, and see if I can somehow check in on Lark. From what I gathered, she has type 1 diabetes, so she probably had low blood sugar, but I'd like to know *why*.

If I'm being honest with myself, I'd like to know every damn thing about that woman.

> Mom, I'm really sorry, but I'm exhausted. I just want to go home and sleep.

Almost immediately, as if she were waiting for this text, she replies.

Momma
> Mi bambino, go rest. We'll see you soon <3

> Thank you. I love you.

Momma
> I love you more, my sweet boy.

***

Once back in from my walk with Pickles, arms filled with the biggest bouquet of red and pink flowers that I could find from one of the street vendors in the park, I pull out my phone. I figure I'll text Kat to see if she happens to know Lark's unit number.

I pluck a flower from the bouquet as I wait for a reply, placing it in a tall glass cup with water. This way, when they're getting close to dying, I'll know when to replace them.

Assuming she even wants me to be in her vicinity. I'm not exactly a very "fun" person to be around, so I wouldn't blame her if she didn't.

She responds a few nerve-wracking minutes later.

Kat

> 236

Kat

> But you didn't hear it from me.

Kat

> Kidding, I had to text her for the door number and told her you'd be over soon. Go get the girl Gi.

> Thanks Kat. You're the best.

Though she's got no business lodging that little bit of hope in my chest the way she does.

"Hey, pretty girl, I'll be back in a bit, okay? I don't want Lark's doggies getting upset about you being in their space."

Her head bobs in understanding, but her ears are on high alert from my mention of Lark's name. She's even got my dog falling all over her.

I rush out, making my way to her floor, and the moment I'm at her door, my feet won't move any farther, unable to take the extra step forward to knock. *Should I leave? Is this too awkward?*

"What would Alex tell me to do?" I ask myself quietly, considering this. With a huff, I rap my knuckles against the door, and as if she were waiting for me, her door bursts open. Her cheeks are flushed, her glossy hair splayed out around her shoulders.

God, she's gorgeous. It takes everything in me not to groan at the sight of her.

"Hey, Gianni. Uh, come in." She waves me inside.

Taking a step into her apartment and removing my shoes, I peer around the room. It's exactly what I pictured from someone as vibrant as her. She has splashes of color all over and seemingly hundreds of photos framed and hung on every surface. It's both overwhelming and chaotically beautiful.

"Sorry, I would've cleaned up, but I wasn't expecting visitors," she rushes to tell me, and the moment her eyes zero in on the massive bouquet of pink and red peonies, her eyes go wide, that round bottom lip jutting out. She redirects her eyes on me. "They're beautiful," she says, sounding breathless.

Apparently, I'm all in on this because the next words to leave my mouth leave us *both* stunned. "Beautiful flowers for a beautiful woman." Her lips part, eyes dilating as she stares at me. My heart hammers in my chest, and I fight the need to cringe inwardly.[1]

I busy myself, heading into her kitchen to look for a vase as I leave her gaping at me in the living room. I find a dark-red one with a deep base and work to fill it up, then trim the ends of the stems. When I'm finished, I look over to see her seated on the countertop of the kitchen island behind me, watching my every movement.

---

1. **Cupid's Chokehold – Gym Class Heroes**

It appears her normal spunk has reappeared. "And what brings you here, Mr. De Laurentiis?" She smirks at me.

"I came to make sure you were okay." My words feel thick in my mouth as flashes of earlier play through my mind. I approach her, my hands resting on either side of her hips on the counter.

I watch as her pupils dilate, reacting to my proximity. The reaction has my dick hardening, and it seems she's the only person to have that effect on me. It's nice to know my dick *even works*.

As she continues her blatant perusal of me, I take the time to do the same to her, no longer stealing glances but outright staring this time. She has a dusting of freckles over the bridge of her nose, and her eyes are like pools of rust, emeralds, and liquid gold swimming together. My gaze dips down her neck, her breasts full as they make an effort to burst from her white tank top, but before I can make my way farther down, she clears her throat, causing my eyes to snap back to hers.

"See something you like, Mr. De Laurentiis?" she asks, her tone light and flirty. But that's not why I came here, so I take a step back. One of the most difficult steps of my life, might I add.

"I always see something I like when you're in a room with me, but you still haven't answered my question."

"That's because you never actually asked a question." She snorts, the sound sending a shiver of pleasure down my spine. "It seems you were too *distracted* by something to finish your thought."

I feel heat climb up my neck. "Apparently, that happens more often than not where you're concerned." I groan, gripping the back of my neck. "Why did you pass out today?"

"I had an episode of hypoglycemic unawareness." She shrugs. "It's when my blood sugar drops too low, but I don't realize it's happening because I don't get the normal symptoms that others experience, which would alert them to the problem. I just, kind of, drop." She shrugs. "Which is why I've got Tiny around to warn me and make sure I make it to the ground safely."

"And that shot your dad gave you, that was something to raise your blood sugar?"

She nods. "It was." Assessing me, she says, "How'd you know that was my dad? Have you known he owns your team this whole time?"

"I knew he owned the team, but I had no idea that you were related. I'd never seen you at any of our games before; I'd have remembered if I had." I duck my face for a moment, embarrassed by my sudden boldness. "What happened that made it drop so low, do you know?"

Her face contorts in a look of guilt. "Yeah." She groans. "The cord to my fridge wasn't plugged in all the way, so somehow it slipped out during the night, and I woke up with bad insulin. I used up what I had left from my stash at the clinic, but then I forgot to eat."

"Are you okay now? Do you have enough?" If she didn't, I'd make sure she did. I'm certain that between Rose, Kat, and Aiyana, they could get her whatever she needs, or I'd figure out another way.

"I do. I wasn't expecting the next three weeks of medication to go bad, but I stopped at the pharmacy on the way home from the hospital. They also gave me a small supply when I got discharged, and I replaced my glucagon."

I consider this, but I am not a fan of how sensitive this medication seems to be. "Would you want to keep a vial or however it works at my place? That way, if something happens to yours here, you know I'm just a stone's throw away." *A stone's throw?* Who am I, a ninety-year-old?

Her eyes widen, and her lips part. "That's, wow, that's actually a super sweet offer. I mean, if you wouldn't mind, that would honestly give me a lot of peace of mind. My dad, too, I'd imagine," she says.

I nod, leaning back against the counter again and crossing my arms. "Alright, then it's settled. Do you have a piece of paper I could write my door code down on for you? That way, you can grab it if you need it, even if I'm not home."

Her light brows knit together. "You'd trust me with your door code?"

"No offense, but I'm not too worried about you beating me up. Honestly, I'd probably like it." I smirk as heat creeps up her neck at my words.

She hops off the counter at that, scrambling around until she finds a hot-pink pack of sticky notes in the drawer. She groans, looking up at me in an expression I can't quite decipher before she hands them to me with a pen.

As I peer down at the paper, a laugh *almost* escapes me, but I manage to muffle the strange snorting sound. "Are these what I think they are?"

She covers her face with both hands, dragging them down slowly. "Mama De Laurentiis book club merch? Absolutely."

I suck my lips between my teeth, having to physically hold them shut to prevent the laughter threatening to escape me. These sticky notes are shaped like penises, and with that, there's a faint shadow of cum dripping out of the tip. "Jesus Christ," I breathe out. "Why is my mother like this?"

"I don't know, but I kind of love it. You know, if it weren't for her, her incredibly sexy son wouldn't be standing in my kitchen staring down at my penis sticky notes."

My lip turns up at that. "You think I'm sexy?" *Where did this sudden playfulness come from? I've never been this frank with anyone in my entire life.*

"You *know* you're sexy," she says, rolling her eyes, strolling out of the kitchen and toward the dogs lounging lazily in the living room. I jot the door code down quickly, leaving it on the kitchen counter before joining her.

As I approach the dogs, I peer over at her. "I don't know; he doesn't seem too vicious," I joke.

"You know, he doesn't usually let people in the house, and he definitely doesn't let them cage me in on the kitchen counter, so he must sense that you're not a threat or something. Though it took him months to warm up to my dad, and he's the best person I know." She shakes her head, her wavy hair flying around her face.

"I'm glad I get the Rex seal of approval. Here's to hoping this isn't just his attempt to make me feel comfortable before a sneak attack." I chuckle, the sound foreign to my own ears.

Lark's head is tilted as she takes me in, a look of wonder on her face as if she's not sure what to think of me. She runs the palms of her freckled hands down her bare, porcelain thighs nervously. "Wanna watch a movie? If you don't have other plans, that is?"

A movie? When was the last time I watched a movie with someone outside of my family? No better time than the present, I suppose. "Sure, that sounds nice."

I follow her to the couch, taking a seat on the opposite end of the light-gray sofa. "What kind of movies do you like?" I ask her, hoping she'll suggest a rom-com or a Disney movie so I don't have to. They've always been my favorite, but that's kind of hard to admit to a woman I'm so desperately attracted to.

"I watch a little of everything, honestly. I love thrillers, horror, romantic comedies, cartoons, and I *love* anything with fast cars!"

"Horror, really?" I'm not going to lie, horror fucking terrifies me. I've got enough demons in my own mind. I don't need them on a screen too.

"Yeah, but let's skip that actually. I can't sleep alone after watching one and, well, you know." What she doesn't say is the part about her newly *having to* sleep alone. And I can't even begin to dissect the reason why I'm so damn thrilled about that. Plus, it's the perfect excuse to not have to watch a fucking scary movie.

"How about a rom-com, then?" I ask, doing my best to hide the hope in my words.

"Hmm," she hums, assessing me. "I gave you all those options, and you *still* chose a romance, didn't you? Like mother like son." She laughs, and my cheeks flush as she grabs the remote off the wooden coffee table.

Heat climbs up my neck. *This fucking woman.*

The way she's able to read me already has me unnerved.

"I don't mind them," I tell her, doing my best to sound indifferent.

She rolls her eyes as she scrolls through movies before landing on *Made of Honor*. "This'll do," she says as she lounges back against the cushions, propping her feet up on the coffee table and pressing play.

Having her feet on the table drives me a little insane. I'm starting to think that I might have some form of undiagnosed obsessive-compulsive disorder. But it's another thing I'm not willing to talk about just yet, so I reach over, grab her perfectly manicured little feet, and lay them over my lap. Her toenails are painted teal, and she has a gold toe ring wrapped around her second toe on the left foot.

"Was something bothering you, Gianni?" she asks me, her voice light and airy as she holds in a laugh.

"Not at all." I do my best to keep my voice smooth and controlled. "Just giving you a more comfortable place for them."

"Ah, I see." She sucks her lips into her mouth, shoulders quaking with uncontained laughter as I become nauseous with worry at what she could possibly be about to say. She makes me feel bare.

And I can't stand it.

I feel unhinged around her. Like every thought and secret I hold locked inside of the Pandora's box within the carefully crafted shell of a person that I've become has been broken open for her, and her alone. She reads me like an open book. Every page written just for her eyes.

The next words out of her mouth break me out of my spiraling thoughts.

"You," she points at my chest, "Gianni 'whatever your middle name is' De Laurentiis, have a foot fetish," she tells me with a mischievous smile.

It's so bright and beautiful that it takes me far longer than it should to process the words she's just spoken.

A... a foot fetish? A fucking foot fetish? *Goddamn this woman.*

Everything about her leaves me reeling, so instead of answering her, I do something neither of us expects.

Chapter Twenty-Three
Lark

Jesus Christ Almighty. Maybe *I'm* the one with the foot fetish?

This delicious fucking man surprises me at every turn, and right now? He's popping my big toe out of his mouth after licking it like a lollipop.

His hot mouth, combined with the swirl of his tongue and that gigantic, calloused hand of his scraping up my calf, has my body feeling like jelly. I have to bite my bottom lip to keep the traitorous whimper begging to release itself from breaking free. And as if nothing ever happened, he rests my leg back down in his lap, turning his attention back on the screen.

"Patrick Dempsey's a stud. Good pick," he says, and my racing mind can't keep up.

Patrick Dempsey? I follow the path of his eyes and remember the *movie* that we're *supposed* to be watching, but instead? I'm just begging my body to cool down and stop responding to every word out of this man's mouth.

I grab a strawberry lollipop from the glass container on the small table beside me, unwrapping it. "Oh, yeah, he is," I finally get out, sucking the lollipop in my mouth. I set my eyes back on the screen, practically gluing them there as it seems to be the only safe place for them.

Ten minutes go by, and my body is finally starting to relax, but he breaks the silence, never looking away from the screen as he says, "It's Elisio, by the way."

I frown, unsure of what he's talking about. Was something said in the movie? "I'm sorry, what?" I stutter.

He peers over at me, studying my face in that controlled way of his. "My middle name—it's Elisio."

"Gianni Elisio De Laurentiis." I hum in approval. "I like it."

"My full name is really Gianni Elisio Amato-De Laurentiis. Gloria and Angelo are my adopted parents. They let us keep our last name, hyphenating De Laurentiis for ease with schools and other documentation."

"Oh," I say in surprise. "I didn't know you were adopted. Why don't you go by Amato-De Laurentiis at your games then?"

He chuckles, a low and sudden sound that makes my insides turn to mush. "Because Gianni Amato-De Laurentiis is a really long-ass name," he tells me, his voice light.

"You've got me there." I grin.

"Your turn."

"My turn?" *My turn for what?*

"Your middle name; what is it?" he asks, wearing a small smirk as he enjoys watching me flounder around him.

"Amalie."

"Lark Amalie Hughes," he muses, whispering in a hushed tone so quiet I almost miss it. "*Beautiful.*"

My whole body flushes at that.

Turning on my side to watch the movie I've officially lost interest in with who's sitting beside me, I pull the green blanket from the back of the sofa, lay it over myself as best as I can, and tuck a throw pillow beneath my head.

I set the stick of my lollipop on the coffee table and settle farther into the couch.

I feel Gianni's hand slide up my calf, tugging on the end of the blanket and pulling it over my legs to cover me up. He rests his hand on my feet, squeezing them periodically as if unable to control the movement. I fight the exhaustion weighing my lids down for as long as I can, but darkness takes me soon after.

Chapter Twenty-Four

Gianni

As the closing captions scroll by, I take in Lark's sleeping form beside me. She snores in her sleep, and it sounds like a kitten purring. Everything about her is adorable as hell, and it's nerve-wracking.

Looking behind the couch, I see the dogs starting to stir now that the movie's stopped. I click the TV off and lift her legs from my lap gently as I stand.

Rex runs over, his eyes squinting at me as if trying to look menacing. He sniffs my ankles as I stand still, allowing him to make his decision. He lets out a little huff and putters away toward the door.

They likely have to go out, but she looks so damn peaceful, and from the sounds of it, she works a lot. This is probably the first time she's allowed herself to nap in a while.

I head to the kitchen, looking around until I notice a small set of hooks by the door that her keys dangle from. Here's to hoping she doesn't wake up to find her dogs missing. *This is probably a horrendous idea.*

"Come on, guys," I mutter to them quietly. They meet me at the door expectantly as I harness and leash them, pocketing her keys before I go.

When I return a half hour later, she's still sound asleep on the couch, blissfully unaware of her surroundings. Contentedness and frustration war inside me. On the one hand, I'm glad she slept. On the other? I'm annoyed that she's so peaceful as she lies on her couch, sleeping when anyone could break in and harm her.

I recognize that I was already here, and if I had broken in, she'd likely have awoken, but it doesn't settle the beast inside me.

Shaking the rampant thoughts away, I place the keys back on the ring once the dogs are all settled and check their food and water bowls. I fill the water bowls and grab the food from the fridge that reads each of their names, perfectly portioned. Once the bowls are filled and water refreshed, I watch as they eat. I'm not sure if they ever have problems with food aggression, but the last thing I want is Lark to wake up to her dogs fighting. I wait for them to finish eating as I write a note to her.[1]

Lark,

I didn't want to wake you, so I took the dogs for a walk. I fed them and gave them water. I hope you don't mind.

Sleep well,

Gianni

---

1. **Tear In My Heart — Twenty One Pilots**

After cleaning the dogs' food bowls and leaving them to dry on a dish towel, I grab a vial of insulin from the fridge and ensure the door locks before heading back to my apartment for the night.

Chapter Twenty-Five

Lark

Monday, March 10, 2025

Yawning, I stretch my arms over my head, cracking my eyes open. I'm groggy, but not enough to have forgotten where I am or who *should* be sitting beside me.

I glance around me, confirming what I already know. Gianni's gone.

I head to the kitchen and see that the stove clock says it's just after midnight. *Shit.*

Frantically looking for the boys, I see them cuddled together on the bed in the living room. Two pink, phallic-shaped notes are stuck to my counters. One reads the door code to Gianni's place, and the other is a note letting me know that he *walked the boys, fed and watered them.*

Oh, my fucking heart.

This man, this gorgeous, haunted man, is going to be the absolute death of me.

I know very little about him, and yet, he's somehow managed to show me more kindness in a few short weeks than my ex did in six years.

***

I crawl under my covers, ready to pass out, when my cell vibrates on the nightstand beside me.

Madison
> Not me getting an arrest warrant from an expired parking meter in October 2023.

Madison
> AN ARREST WARRANT!

>> You've got to be shitting me.

Kira
> NO WAY

Kira
> How much is the reward if someone calls and tells them where you're at?

Kira
> Asking for a friend…

>> I'm the friend.

Madison
> I'm literally cracking up. This county is just really quiet I guess.

Madison

I'll ask them. Maybe if I turn myself in, it's free?

Kira

You'll look good in orange.

Agreed, it'll really complement your eyes.

Madison

I loved Orange Is The New Black!

Madison

image of official envelope

Madison

image of official summons

THE COMMONWEALTH OF PENNSYLVANIA VS MADISON HARTLEY!!!

Kira

What do we do now?

Madison

It feels very official…

That's probably because it is…

Are we all going? I feel like this would be a good party story. Can I go with you?

Madison

It's $160. I'll just pay it and hopefully keep my license.

> Do you have a GoFundMe? I'll donate $10.

Kira
> Same here.

Kira
> Ask Daddy Hughes for a donation!

> Please never call him that again.

Madison
> Jesus Christ

Jade
> *fire emoji, US flag emoji, fire emoji*

Madison
> I want to live in a lawless society.

Jade
> That's exactly what a criminal would say ☒

Madison
> This is just the start for me.

Madison
> Money laundering is next.

> You guys are out of control…

QUAKE

Madison

I mean, if I'm gonna commit a crime, it's going to be for my financial gain. NOT because I didn't move my car when I went to get a bagel.

Kira

Is James prepared to be an empty nester?

Madison

We will arrange conjugal visits I guess.

Jade

You are hereby CANCELED by the commonwealth for toxic parking and ghosting.

Kira

Man, I can't believe Mads is getting arrested...

Kira

insert photo of custom made navy shirts reading "The Commonwealth of Pennsylvania V. Madison Hartley"

Kira

I'm accepting pre-orders, ladies!

I'll take three! One for me and each of the dogs!

Kira

Coming right up!

Jade

Jackie and I will take two, thanks.

Madison

You think they'll let me wear that instead of the jumpsuit?

Unlikely, but we'll give it a shot.

Madison

Deal. Alright, I'm going to sleep. Gotta get my beauty rest before my red and blue chariot arrives for me.

Kira

Wee woo, wee woo… Goodnight! Love you guys!

Jade

Yep, need that beauty sleep for your mugshot. Love you.

Madison

Love you guys! I'll use my one call on Lark since I know she'll be most likely to answer.

Goodnight, love you guys!

I love these women, but god, they are not fucking normal.

Chapter Twenty-Six

Lark

Tuesday, March 11, 2025

The dogs head into the kitchen to drink some water after our walk, and I grab a knife from the butcher block to tear into the box left at the front desk for me.

As soon as the top is opened, I know exactly what's inside and who it's from.

There are six boxes inside this one, each with a different picture of a toy on the outside. There's a clitoral sucker, a larger-looking bullet vibe, one that I think is meant to just sit on my clit hands-free during penetration, a thrusting dildo with a clit vibrator, something remote-controlled, and the last one looks like it does a bit of *everything*.

Well, shit. How much did this all cost her?

I'd like to think there was a good-ass sale, but who knows?

I look over at the dogs, who are now passed out in their bed beside the couch, and figure, *what the hell?*

I head to my room, dumping the contents of the packages onto the bed and plugging each one into the outlets around my room.

The sight makes me giggle. It looks like a swingers club in here.

I flop down on the bed and open my texts from Kira.

> Just got your gifts. Thank you!!! You wild, wild woman LOL

> Also… Send me that referral link.

Kira
> Hell yeah! One sec!

Not even thirty seconds later, my messages ping with the link. I open it up and set up an account with a free trial.

My jaw drops when I start browsing the app. "Holy fucking shit," I murmur to myself. There are literally *thousands* of these recordings voiced by hundreds of different voice actors.

I'm starting to feel giddy the more I scroll, the titles for some of these turning me on. Another text pops up from Kira.

Kira
> Click on the three dots by each title and select "See Audio Details." It'll give you a whole list of what's in store for that recording.

I do as she says and settle on a male-for-female, direct-to-listener audio that features guided masturbation, finger sucking, oral, and pillow humping.

I'm not so sure I'll be into the pillow humping, but who the hell knows until I try it, right?

Bolting out of bed, I gather a couple of the toys that have a glowing red light, indicating they've finished charging, and head to the bathroom to clean them off before grabbing my headphones and crawling under my covers.

I relax into the firm mattress, slide my shorts down my thighs along with my panties, and kick them to the end of the bed.

Turning the audio on, I listen as the deep voice tells me exactly how I'm about to come, and I can't deny that it's hot as hell.

"I want you to start picturing I'm lying beside you, running my hand up the inside of your slick thighs." I do as he says, but instead of picturing whoever this guy is, my mind automatically fills in the blanks with Gianni.

I can practically feel his long fingers trailing up the inside of my thigh, and my own hand slips between them, stroking up my wet center.

My toes curl as the man keeps going. "Now, kitten, be a good girl and take your favorite toy and hold it to your clit until you're squirming."

I take hold of the light-pink clit sucker and turn it onto the first setting, then press it to my clit. My back arches off the bed, and my body tingles with arousal. "Oh god." I moan, clicking the button to the next setting.

It thumps and sucks faster, dragging another moan out of me that leaves me breathless.

"Just like that. Keep fucking that perfect needy clit, just how I know you want it," he commands.

I feel like I'm flying. My skin is buzzing with need, and my thighs are clenching so tightly I'm not sure how much more I can take.

I pull the suction off, setting the sucker aside and grabbing for the thrusting wand.

"Now, I want you to roll over and stuff your pillow between your legs. Ride it like you'd ride my face, angel."

Instead of riding the wand like I'd planned, I do as I'm told because I'm suddenly *very* compelled to take this homework assignment seriously.

I shove the extra pillow between my thighs and clench my eyes shut, imagining Gianni lying on his back in my bed. My earbuds fill with the sound of this man slurping and sucking on god knows what, but the sound is so erotic it spurs me on further. I rub myself against the pillow, shifting my weight until I'm in a good spot where my clit is getting the attention it needs too.

"Are you ready to slide my dick between those plump little pussy lips?" he asks. At this point, I feel wild as if I can't control my body's responses to his words, the sounds he's making, the images flashing behind my eyes from my own imagination, and the high of finally having a fucking orgasm from something other than my hand in my shower.

"Lie on your back and let your knees fall to the sides so I can bury myself in you."

I do exactly as he instructs and open my eyes just long enough to turn the thrusting wand on, making sure to also turn the clit attachment on before placing the head at my entrance.

"I'm sliding in, nice and slow," he says. "Now don't be greedy, angel," he chides. "Oh, you want more?"

I can't help myself when the word "Yes" leaves my lips in a breathy moan.

"Well, alright. I'll give my sweet angel what she wants."

He relays exactly how I'm supposed to imagine being fucked, and again, Gianni is on top of me, thrusting deep inside as I bury my toy in me.

I buck up off the bed with each thrust, my core clenching tighter and tighter as I deep dive off of the cliff of my release. It wracks through my body, knocking the breath out of me as I collapse farther into my mattress, completely spent.

I turn the toy off and stop the recording. "Okay." I blow out a breath. "Evidently, *that* is something I'm fully into."

Several minutes pass before I'm able to leave my bed. I finally work my heavy legs over the side of my mattress and make my way into the bathroom. I clean up the messes I made and change my pillowcase, not even a little embarrassed by the puddle of cum I left behind. Why be embarrassed when it's cool as hell that my body can do *that*? I mean, seriously, Tyler nearly had me convinced that it was *me* that was the problem, but it turns out, it was just him and his lacking skill set. [1]

---

1. **What You Need – The Weeknd**

Chapter Twenty-Seven

Gianni

Saturday, March 15, 2025

P utting my guitar away and leashing up Pickles, I head to the door. Just as I open it, Lucia is standing there, arms full of cleaning supplies, as her daughter, Josie, stands at her side.

"*Hola señoras, lo siento, olvidé que vendrían temprano hoy. ¿Te importa si me voy hoy mientras limpias? Tengo que llevar a Pickles a su clase.*" *Hey ladies, I'm sorry I forgot you were coming early today. Do you mind if I leave today while you clean up? I have to take Pickles to her class.*

"*¡Oh, por supuesto! Nos iremos en una hora. Me aseguraré de cerrar.*" *Oh, sure! We'll be leaving in an hour. I'll be sure to lock up.* Her tan skin wrinkles around her eyes as she smiles up at me.

"*Gracias, Lucía. Hay bocadillos para Josie en la despensa. Llévate lo que quieras.*" *Thanks, Lucia. There are snacks for Josie in the pantry. Take whatever you want,* I tell her as I head out, ruffling the little girl's chestnut-brown curls. She looks up at me, her crooked grin with only a few teeth left hanging on pulls a genuine smile out of me as I head downstairs, hoping to see Lark on her way to class.

It's really started to warm up out here. A sheen of sweat is already starting to coat my skin as I stand in the sun, waiting to see if Lark will make it down the stairs before I absolutely have to leave to get there on time.

As if I'd called her, she rushes through the doors toward me, her red waves a mess behind her as she pants. "Gianni, hi!" she shouts at me, sounding out of breath.

"Good morning, Dr. Hughes. What's got you so out of breath this morning?" I ask, realizing too late that my words sound suggestive.

She doesn't seem to notice as she answers, still breathless. "I had to stay at work late last night, and I missed my alarm this morning, so I'm a bit of a mess today. Hopefully, nobody cares too much since we'll all be getting covered in dog hair, anyway." She flashes me a smile.

I take in her flushed face, wild hair, and smudged mascara, presumably left over from yesterday. "You're beautiful," I tell her, more by accident than anything else. She's not the only one who's breathless here. Even looking like an absolute mess, she still manages to make me hum with the need to devour her mouth.

She peers up at me through thick lashes, a smile curving her lips, but says nothing as we continue in the direction of Rocket Dog.

When we reach the building, I hold the door open for her, letting her and Tiny pass us.

Chapter Twenty-Eight
Lark

As we make it inside our building, I feel a little sad at the thought of not seeing Gianni for the rest of the day. He is guarded, and rightfully so, considering everything my dad's told me about what happened to his best friend, Alex Casillas, who was the Divine Flyers goalkeeper until his passing. And since my dad is the owner of the team, it's his job to know every detail about his players to avoid scandals.

But while he's absolutely got a dark cloud looming over him, he's been nothing but gentle and kind with me. He says things that make my heart flutter in my chest, so I can't help but ask, "Wanna come over for a bit?"

"Yes," he says immediately, icy-blue eyes widening and cheeks flaming as he realizes his mistake. Gianni Elisio Amato-De Laurentiis *likes* me, and he wants to spend time with me.

God, this feels like a high school crush, but I haven't felt so desired in my entire life, so I have no qualms about leaning into this feeling. May as well bask in the glory of it while he's still willing to give it.

"Great," I tell him, leading us upstairs.

"Mind if Pickles comes too? I don't like leaving her home alone if I can help it."

"Oh, absolutely. The boys love Pickles," I say, shooting him a reassuring smile over my shoulder.

"Thanks, um." He pauses. "I've gotta drop by my place real quick," he says, and he blushes again, averting his gaze.

"No problem. Just meet me back at mine when you're ready."

A few minutes later, I'm back in my apartment, thankful for the moment away from Gianni as I now realize my place is a wreck.

I rush around, tossing the plates left in the sink into the dishwasher, throwing a hamper of clothing into the wash, and making my bed. I'm not sure why I prioritize that part of my home, as I have no intention of taking us there. I mean, not unless something rather big changes.

I hear Gianni's soft knock at the door, and I rush to open it.

He's standing there in black skinny jeans and a black T-shirt that hugs his muscular chest so perfectly. He's holding a pink stuffed animal in one hand and Pickles's hot-pink leash in the other. He unleashes her and passes the toy to her, which she grabs so gently by the big floppy ear of the stuffed rabbit's head as she heads over to where Tiny and Rex are lying in their beds together. She curls up beside them, suckling on the stuffed toy, presumably worn out from their class this morning.

He clears his throat, appraising me as I stand here, gawking at him.

"Uh, sorry, want something to eat?" I ask, picking at the hem of my shorts.

His eyes flare with heat, and under his breath, he says, *"Je le fais maintenant."* *I do now.* He works on a swallow, and my mouth suddenly feels dry. He blinks a few times as if he just had an out-of-body experience and didn't mean to speak at all. Gianni turns, heading into the kitchen and adds, "Sure, I'll make us something." He says it as if he hadn't just insinuated he wants to eat *me*.

Opening the fridge, his biceps bulge as he grabs ingredients, laying them out on the counter.

It takes a little while, but my brain *does* eventually catch up. "Gianni, it's my house, and I asked if *you* wanted anything to eat. I can cook for us, really. It's not a problem."

"Lark, mind if you just let me busy myself and do something for *you* for once? I get the feeling you don't let that happen often," he tells me as he continues opening cabinets and grabbing items out.

"Well, alrighty then." I huff, blowing out a long breath. It's uncanny how he's already figured that out, but something tells me he has that exact same habit.

***

I finish loading the dishes into the washer as Gianni passes them to me from the sink. Not only is he sexy as hell, but he can cook too.

While I enjoy cooking, I don't often have the time to do so, and it's become just another thing to do when I get home, already exhausted from work.

"Want to watch a movie or something? Unless you've got plans, of course," I ask, hoping like hell he stays.

"I don't," is all he says as he heads over to the couch.

Gianni takes a seat on the same end he sat on the other day, except now he's reaching under his ass for something.

My heart drops to my toes, and my skin feels flushed when I realize what's happening.

My vibrator!

He holds it up. The blush-pink silicone looks so small in his massive, tattooed hands.

His expression is concrete as he stares at it, rolling it around in his hand to inspect it. My pulse races as his thumb glides over the power button, and before he can press it, I'm jumping into action.

I rush over to him, snatch it out of his hand, and sprint toward my bedroom. Sweat beads on my brow as panic and embarrassment seize me. I'm not sure what my plan is, but hiding in my room until he leaves sounds like a definite option.

Maybe even the best option.

I finally toss the toy in my nightstand, slamming it shut. Apparently, I'd forgotten it in my orgasm-induced bliss after getting home late from work last night. One hand drops to the top of the nightstand, and I lean over it, smacking my other hand over my face, sucking in a ragged breath.

Get it together, Lark. That man is still out there. You've gotta own this.

I spin around to deal with the embarrassment but find him leaning against my doorframe.

I REPEAT.

The man is leaning against my fucking doorframe.

Does he know just how fucking sexy he looks? Is he purposefully trying to get me to spread my legs for him right here and now? Because I've got to be honest, I'm losing any ounce of the little willpower I had left to keep him at arm's length. I mean, I don't really have a good reason to push him away, and frankly, I have no desire to. The only thing that maybe *should* stop me would be the fact that I don't really know him very well and that I just broke up with my longtime boyfriend.

But as it seems, I didn't know *him* very well either.

"I'm sorry," he tells me, leaving me a little confused for a moment until a smile quirks either end of his lips into an *almost* full smile. He looks fucking delicious.

"Sorry for what?" I ask, dazed as my whole body flushes with warmth.

"For breaking up your solo party. Did I come back too soon?" His brows climb his forehead in question.

Oh, so he *does* have a sense of humor?

I'm not so sure I like it as much when it's directed at me.

I match his smirk and roll my eyes, deciding to take back some of the power in this dynamic. I approach him, planting my hands on his chest, and the cocky look on his face instantly disappears. His jaw twitches, and those icy-blue eyes warm. They look like turquoise waters from some hidden gem in the tropics, and instead of wanting to swim away in them, *I want to drown in them.*

I try not to think about the hard muscles beneath my fingers as I put on a mask of confidence. Confidence that I most certainly do not feel in this particular moment, but I've gone this far, so may as well take it one step further. Standing up on my tippy toes, I lean as far into him as I can, but he still has to duck his head for me to get anywhere near his ear. Thankfully, he seems to feel the same pull to be near me as I do him, so he lowers his head until I'm able to run my lips across the shell of his ear. I revel in the way his body quakes at the feeling before whispering, "It doesn't have to be a solo party with you here."

I fully expect him to pull away from me or tell me to stop messing around, or at least, that's what my intention was. I had no plans to follow through with the statement, but when this man runs those huge hands of his around my hips, clutching my ass to him, my intentions officially change.

I roll my hips the best I can while still on my tiptoes, and he groans so low that I feel it vibrate through his chest and against mine.

Heat floods my core as he hovers his lips over mine, just a breath away. My eyes start to flutter closed, but he snakes a hand back up my body, over my shoulder. The rough pads of his fingers cup my jaw, and my eyes meet his. "If this is what you want, you're gonna have to take it because I'm willing to give you whatever it is you need, but I've gotta see those pretty eyes in return," he says, and all the air has officially left my lungs.

"Okay?" he asks when I still haven't responded, but my lips part as my brain *very slowly* starts to catch up. I nod, and his lip quirks, giving me a peek at one of his cute dimples.

"Words, sweetheart," he says, his voice rough.

"Yes," I answer, moving my hands up his chest to grip his shoulders. "I want you."

His tongue darts out to lick his lips, and I watch intently as his Adam's apple bobs against the tattooed skin of his throat. Gianni's eyes clench shut, and when they open again, *he looks ravenous*. His hands find my ass, gripping me firmly as he hoists me up his body.

My legs wind around his hips, and I feel his thick length hardening under me. An involuntary moan slips past my lips. Gianni holds me up, kicking the door closed behind him as he saunters over to my bed, taking a seat on the edge. He holds me in his lap, his grip never loosening as he burrows his face in my neck, sucking in a sharp inhale.

The dusting of a five-o'clock shadow along his jaw teases my overheated skin, and I find myself clutching him to me, rocking my hips against his lap as I seek the friction I can't help but want.

"God, woman." His hands move to my hips, fingers digging into my skin almost painfully. The bite of pressure causes heat to coil inside me. "I want to make it known that this is *not* what I came here for," he grits out.

I loosen my grip on him, pulling away to look him in the face as I tease him. "I know, silly. I was the one that asked *you* to come over." But I realize my mistake the moment his lips press tightly together and his shoulders slump. I rush to correct his assumption, never wanting him to feel used or unwanted in any capacity.

Tyler made me feel like that for the majority of our relationship, and I'd never knowingly do that to someone else.

"I didn't invite you over for this either, by the way. I just wanted to hang out with you," I tell him, keeping my eyes locked on his so he, *hopefully*, knows I mean it.

He breaks the eye contact, his neck flushing as frustration flashes across his face, his brows notching together.

Running a hand over his neck and up to cup his cheek, I watch as his body responds to my touch. My eyes flit across his face, taking in the softening of each of his features as my words start to sink in past the armor he's put up. "But," I run my thumb across his full bottom lip, "I really do like you, and I haven't got much experience, but if you'd like to have some fun with me, I'd be interested in that."

"If you're okay with it, of course," I add as nerves ripple through my stomach.

His eyes flare with heat, but his next words stun me. "What do you mean you haven't got much experience? Weren't you with that dickhead for *six years*?"

My cheeks heat with embarrassment, and now it's *me* who's averting my gaze. "Yeah, but he didn't want me, and I'm not sure when it happened, but eventually, I stopped wanting him too. Besides..." I frown at the memories this conversation is dredging up. "There's a lot that he refused to try. He said the things I suggested were too dirty, and, well, I stopped asking after a while. My ego can only take so much."

Like talking about my lack of experience and how undesirable my ex found me with the sexiest man on the planet. That is most definitely at the top of the list of things that have hurt my ego in the last decade.

He lifts his hand, running his thumb across my cheekbone in a featherlight caress that sends goosebumps through me. "I haven't been with anyone in years, haven't had any desire to, but you? I find you invading my every thought. So, if you'd like to explore some of these 'dirty' acts you speak of, I'd be more than happy to act as your distraction. And for my sake, I hope they're positively *filthy*."

I suck my lower lip between my teeth, unaware that my body has started rocking over him again, until his hands grind my movements to a shrieking halt.

As much as his words turn me on, they also tear me in two. *He thinks I'd only want him as a distraction?* Maybe this really is too soon after my breakup, but I may never get this opportunity again. Gianni's the kind of person who withdraws when they feel unwanted, and that became clear when I turned him down the first time.

I'm definitely not torn up about the end of my relationship, so there's very little stopping me from taking what I want. Hell, I'm not even that angry about what happened with Tyler. Everything seems to be picking up for me, and I may as well grab life by the balls, so to speak.

"Okay," I finally answer, apprehension lacing my next words. "But if there's anything I suggest that you find too," my cheeks heat furiously, "um, just too much, let me know."

His lips curve in a small smirk. "Does this mean we get to pick a safe word?" he asks, one full brow quirked.

I'm seeing a side of this man that I'm nearly certain he doesn't show anyone, and not only is that hot as hell, but I feel *honored*.

"Sure. Your pick."

He tsks at me. "Your kinks we're fulfilling here, darling, *your* safe word."

The way the word "darling" rolls off his tongue sends a shiver down my spine.

I think on this for a moment, and when the word comes to me, it's like a fucking lightbulb goes off in my head! "I have it!"

"Do tell." A smile tugs at his lips.

"Meatball."

He releases a choked laugh that lights a blazing path through my chest. "Well, I sincerely fucking hope you won't be calling that out in bed," he says, shaking his head with a slight smile that wrinkles the corners of his mouth.

"Well, isn't that kind of the point? You only say it when absolutely necessary." I roll my eyes playfully, as if I've ever used a safe word, let alone had one.

My heart rate picks up as the realization starts to sink in that this may actually be happening. This man who's become the star of every one of my recent fantasies may actually be about to help me live some of them out.

"Fair. Well, now that we have that settled." He stands after depositing me into the middle of the bed. Pulling his shirt over his head, I'm graced with his smooth skin, a trail of dark hair scattered below his navel. Not for the first time, I have a full view of his incredible body covered in tattoos that skate up his neck, the black ink contrasting with his light skin and crystal-clear eyes.

He crawls over top of me like a predator, dipping his head to press a wet, open-mouthed kiss to my collarbone that has my nipples pebbling.

"What's on your list?" he asks me in a sultry tone, lowering his melodious voice to an octave so low it reverberates through my chest, making me tingle all over.

"How'd you know I have a list?" I ask, suddenly breathless as he continues with his kisses, this time licking up the length of my neck so slowly that I can't help but arch my back into him, holding back a whimper.

"Well, you mentioned wanting to try things, so I just assumed there was a list. If not, feel free to make one." Another kiss. "I'll be glad to play along for each and every one. I'm just a floor away," he reminds me. I'm not sure if he's joking or if he's really offering what I think he is, but my body is coming alive under his touch.

"*Little red*, you haven't answered me. What exactly are we doing here?" My mind short-circuits at that.

"If I'm little red, does that make you the big bad wolf?" I tease, biting on my bottom lip as I fight to hold back a smile. [1]

---

1. **The Kill – Thirty Seconds To Mars**

He releases a low chuckle, mouth popping open after sucking on the sensitive skin at the base of my throat. "It does if you want me to be," he rasps.

God, that was *not* on my list, but it might be now.

"I'm not sure what to, uh, start with. Tyler wouldn't do anything other than missionary." I *know* I now have an entire list written, and frankly, right now would be an ideal time to procure that, but I'm too stunned to think, let alone form words.

Is this really happening, or have I been imagining this man while listening to those audios too many times this week?

Gianni lifts up to stare into my eyes. His brows knit together, moist lips pursed. "First rule, *never* say his name. Preferably ever, but definitely not while I've got big plans to bury my tongue deep inside your pretty cunt."

I open my mouth to respond, but he presses a finger to my lips, my eyes going wide. "And since you can't seem to make up your mind, I'll give you two choices to start out with. Pick wisely, little red."

He lifts the finger from my lips and says, "Option one, I dominate and praise you." I suck in a breath at his words. "Option two, I submit to you and do whatever you ask of me."

Oh, fuck me.

My thighs press together, trying to tamp down the ache settled between them.

Both of those options are *definitely* on my list, but I really don't think being the one in control is something I'm ready for just yet. "Dominate me," I whisper.

Without another word, he dips his head, sucking my nipple into his mouth through the thin fabric of my shirt. My hands wind around his neck, twisting into the hair at the base of his skull.

He bites down hard, and a jolt of pain sears through me. His hand cups my other breast, twisting and teasing the nipple. "C'est un très bon choix, mon petite rouge. Je te ferai ma sale petite salope de sperme aujourd'hui."

Such a good choice, my little red. I plan to make you my dirty little cum slut today.

Oh, for the love of all that is holy, does he know I speak French, or is this his internal monologue making an appearance when he thinks I can't understand? In either regard, I don't plan to call him out on it just yet.

"If at any time you're uncomfortable, let me know, and I'll stop immediately," he tells me sternly, his face still buried between my breasts. When I don't answer, his piercing blue eyes gaze up at me. "Answer me, little red, or this stops right now."

I nod, squeaking out my response. "Yes, okay."

"Good, now strip for me." He sits back on his shins, watching me as I shimmy my shorts and panties down my thighs before my fingers make their way to the hem of my top.

I hesitate, blowing out a breath.

His brows pinch. "Something wrong?" he asks, his voice barely above a whisper as he assesses me.

I swallow thickly. "I just—" I stammer, my hands feel clammy under his gaze. He waits, allowing me the time I need to find my words. "We can't get too carried away," I say, my voice quieting with each word. "My blood sugar drops with exercise, so I just have to be conscious of that and listen out for my phone alerting me to it, and—"

He nods, urging me to finish. "I just don't want you to freak out," I tell him, and he turns his head to the side like a puppy dog trying to understand what's being said. I blow out another breath through my nose. "I haven't gotten a pump yet, and I have a lot of extra bruises on my stomach because of it." Once I've managed to get the words out of my mouth, he shifts his weight to hover closer to me, gripping my cheeks in his palms as he searches my eyes.

"Never, *ever* feel embarrassed for something that's keeping you *alive*, Lark."

I can feel hot tears pooling behind my eyes, but they don't fall. Gianni senses what I need, so he places his hands over mine, helping me work my shirt up and over my head.

He releases a low groan, clutching the back of his neck as he squeezes his eyes shut so tightly I think he might be in pain. "I'm going to absolutely wreck you, and I'll enjoy every second of it. *You fucking unhinge me.*"

"Um, I'm sorry?" I say, unsure of whether I'm supposed to respond.

"Don't apologize. Just scoot to the edge of the bed and lie on your back," he instructs.

Once I'm bare and spread for him, Gianni collapses to his knees, running his large hands up my thighs. He leans over me, caressing the bruises on my abdomen with the pads of his thumbs before pressing a kiss to each of the several spots. The desire never leaves his eyes the more he watches me, and it's all the encouragement I need to feel safe and, for the first time, *comfortable* with whatever might happen in the bedroom.

He places each one of my thighs over his shoulders, sinking his fingers into my flesh as he pulls me into his face.

I feel his nose as it dips between my wetness, and the unfamiliar sensation of having someone down there, with his face so close to such an intimate part of my body, unnerves me. My senses are in overdrive as I battle my warring emotions. The feel of his skin against mine, the touch of his nose as it nears my clit, sends jolt after jolt of pleasure zinging through me. Then, on the other hand, I'm bared to him in a way that would've made my skin crawl if I were with Tyler. But with Gianni, I feel *safe* and attractive.

I've never felt so exposed to anyone in my life.

Gianni's tongue swipes out, delving inside me, and I can't help but squeeze my thighs around his head, my hands gripping for purchase into the silky sheets surrounding me.

My core vibrates around a low moan as Gianni makes it clear that this is for his pleasure too. The thought eases that insecurity, begging to tear free, but as the thoughts begin to calm, he looks up at me through hooded lids and thick lashes. His tongue is still working me to the edge so quickly that I think I may levitate off this damn bed. I do my best to hold his eye contact, but when those crystal-clear irises stare at me for a moment too long, I break the contact, throwing my forearm over my face with a groan.

The moment I do, he stops, wrenching my arm away as he stares so deeply into my eyes that I fear he can literally see my thoughts.

"You're going to look me in the eye as I bring you over the edge. Do you understand? I need to know how you're feeling, and your eyes are the best way to do that," he tells me as he climbs onto the bed, his mouth hovering over mine just an inch away.

My lips part on an inhale as I aim to steady myself, but he takes that as an opportunity. He strikes.

His tongue dives into my mouth, the salty sweetness of my own arousal igniting a fire inside me. My skin is both too hot and too cold at the same time.

His lips scald me, seeking out whatever it is he wants. Fingers twining into his hair, I pull at his roots, overcome by sensation. "You seem to have a problem with forming answers tonight, little red," he groans out against my lips.

"O-okay, I'll keep my eyes open," I stammer.

"Eyes on me," he whispers as he makes his way back down my body, pushing my legs apart as he settles between them. He laps at my slickness, teasing and tasting, diving his tongue deeply inside me, and just when I think I can't take anymore, he stands abruptly.

"Get on your knees, *mon petite rouge.*" I sink to the ground from the edge of the bed, turning to face him as he loosens his belt buckle. Gianni runs his thumb along my bottom lip before plunging it into my mouth. "Suck."

I do as I'm told, sucking his thumb into my mouth and swirling my tongue around it as if it were his dick, which I can now see trying to break free of his pants. "Bite," he tells me sternly.

My eyes widen at his command, but I do as I'm told. Wet heat drips down my thighs the more he commands me. "Such a good little slut," he says with approval that tenses my muscles as he pulls his thumb from my mouth, working his zipper down. "You're going to suck my cock until you choke on it, and when you can't take anymore, I'm going to come all over that pretty face of yours."

I whimper, so turned on I might come without touching myself.

Gianni keeps his eyes on mine, shaking his head the smallest bit as he says, "You're going to look so damn pretty with a pearl necklace."

Another whimper escapes me, and he bites his bottom lip at the sound... so hard he draws the smallest drop of blood, but I don't have time to think about licking it off when he smacks my cheek with his dick.

My eyes widen, and my mouth gapes. "Open wide, little red."

Pushing the head of his swollen cock against my parted lips, he smears his precum across my mouth, and my tongue darts out, tasting him. My hand slides down my abdomen, reaching for my aching clit, but he tsks at me. "I said open your fucking mouth, or your hair won't be the only thing that's red."

Obediently, my mouth opens wide as he presses the tip inside. He's so big that I start to panic. My eyes open wider as I tap on his leg to stop him when the sheer size of him obscures my breathing. He shakes his head. "Calm your breathing, close your eyes, and relax your jaw. Breathe through your nose and adjust to my size." His voice is soft, a distinct contrast to the demanding tone he'd just used moments prior. It soothes me, and I'm able to regain control of my breathing. When ready, I open my eyes to look up at him, his hard cock still in my mouth.

"If you want to stop, *really* want to stop, tap on my thigh three times. And if somehow I'm not able to see past the haze of how goddamn perfect your mouth feels around me, fucking bite me. I'd rather lose my dick than hurt you," he explains, and my heart flutters in my chest, but that same rush of arousal courses through me.

I *want* to please this man. More than anything. I want to make him feel as good and as wanted as he's making me feel, so I take a deep breath in through my nose, slide my hand up to cup the base, and take him as far into my throat as I can without gagging. Hollowing my cheeks, I bob my head, sucking on the hard shaft as his fingers sink into my scalp, pulling on my hair. The burn sends a shiver down my spine.

He tosses his head back in ecstasy, pushing me farther down around him as he grunts out, "You can take it. Open that throat for me, baby." I do my best to relax my throat, but when he pushes even farther into me, I have to grip his hips with both of my hands, struggling just to stay upright.

He moans, bucking his hips into my face. "Fucking hell," he says, his fingers tightening in my roots.

I feel him stiffen, and his movements become more erratic as he groans.

"Lark," he practically whimpers, and his muscles strain against my fingers as he pulls out of my mouth. "Stick your tongue out," he rushes to say.

I listen obediently, sticking my tongue all the way out and exposing as much of my neck as I can to him before he spills his cum all over my face and chest. Once his eyes are back on me, I swallow what made its way into my mouth.

His nostrils flare as he watches me lick my lips, and it emboldens me to swipe a finger through the cum on my chest, bringing it to my mouth. I suck, moaning as his arousal coats my tongue.

"Get up," he says once he's recovered, his dick still hard and bobbing against his chiseled abdomen. Once I'm standing, he spins me, pushing my chest into the bed, my ass exposed to him. "Now, I'm gonna spank this tight little ass, and if you scream, I'm fucking it with my cock."

My core clenches, and my eyes nearly roll back.

He positions himself behind me, running the head of his cock through my folds and up my ass before taking a step back. I fight another whimper as it climbs up my throat.

One hand is on my right ass cheek, rubbing circles across it as he bends forward, biting down on the skin of my left cheek. My body tenses, pain and pleasure mixing into one deliriously euphoric concoction.

"This tattoo, it'll be the fucking death of me, you know," he grinds out, referring to the tiny pink heart tattooed in the center of my left ass cheek.

"I'm sorry." I moan, unsure as to whether or not he wants me to answer.

"What did I say about apologizing?" he asks me, but there's no bite to his tone. His massive hand makes contact, a loud smack erupting as I fall even farther forward from the force. The pain radiates to my needy center, feeling so much better than I'd have anticipated. He works the skin with his fingers, soothing it.

He delivers several more deliberate blows, and when my ass is on fire, actual, genuine pain searing through me, he lifts my hips and tosses me into the center of the bed. Gianni climbs over me, running his nose up the length of my neck, my sore ass feeling raw against my bed, but I'm still so turned on I could cry. When his lips make it to the shell of my ear, I shudder. "I got a little carried away," he murmurs. "So I'll give you the choice because I'm feeling generous."

My thighs clench with anticipation. "Either I can fuck you into this mattress with no regard for your aching ass, or..." He draws out the word. "I can lay back and let you slide your pretty pussy up and down my shaft while I choke you until you're coming undone on my cock. Choose wisely, sweetheart."

How is this man real?

It's like he's taken a drive down memory lane of every one of my fantasies and somehow managed to bring them to life, bigger and better than even my imagination could render them.

"I want to ride you," I tell him, trying to sound confident and assured. Truthfully though? I'm terrified that he'll split me in half. His dick is nearly the length of my forearm and almost just as thick. But maybe my eyes are deceiving me.

He rolls off me, lying back against my pillows with an arm behind his head, but his eyes flit to where my phone sits on the nightstand. He sits up, grabs it and hands it to me. "Check your sugar," he says before saying, "please."

I ignore the need to rub the heel of my palm over my heart where it aches in my chest.

Nodding, I open the app for my CGM, and when I see a reassuring number, I turn it for him to see. He stares at the screen before his eyes flick to mine. "One forty-one is good, right? So your blood sugars don't drop too low?"

A small smile stretches my lips, and I nod. "That's right," I confirm, and I hear the little breath he releases. I lock the screen, set the phone back down, and crawl closer to him.

His cock is now standing straight up, waiting for me. Clearly, he's recovered from his orgasm just a few minutes ago.

Everything about that fact makes me feel desired in a way I hadn't known possible, but as my mouth starts to salivate with need, I'm struck with a realization that threatens to dampen the heat searing through me.

"I don't have a condom," I tell him with wide eyes.

"I haven't slept with anyone in over five years. It's up to you, but I don't have one either. This isn't why I came over today." He adds the last sentence softly, reminding me that he's not using me or expecting more from me than I can give in return.

"Tyler and I haven't had sex in probably a year, and I always made him wear a condom."

I lift my leg to straddle him, doing my best to hover just over his tip without sinking down just yet. "God, you have no idea what that does to me." He groans.

"Huh?" I ask, confused.

"You've known me for just a few short weeks, and you already trust me more than that pig." He breathes. "It fucking delights me." His eyes flare as he grips his shaft, rubbing the head against my entrance and urging me to lower myself onto him.

"God," I cry out as the first inch stretches me wide.

He groans, biting his lip again. "I prefer Gi, but god will do," he pants out.

"I'd smack you if I weren't so caught up trying to keep from splitting in two," I grit out at him, almost frustrated at his ability to make a joke right now.

"And I'd smack you right back, princess. Like I said, you can take it, so spread those pretty lips for me and take my cock like the good little slut I know you are." His fingers wrap around the base of my throat, squeezing almost gently at first. But as his thumb shifts to my windpipe, he presses down with so much force that I'm unable to squeak out the scream I feel clawing up my throat as his hips drive up into me.

His fingers loosen, giving me a false sense of relief before increasing the pressure once again. He continues this game, toying with me until I have him fully buried inside me, almost to the hilt, as I rock against him, seeking pressure on my clit.

My nipples are so hard, they're screaming to be touched. My skin is on fire as pleasure strikes white-hot up my spine, the growing ache between my legs building and building. I'm on the precipice as his rough hand glides down my breasts, grazing my sensitive nipples and down to my clit. His thumb presses against me, and I see stars.

My heart rate climbs, and my breaths come out in short bursts.

"That's it, little red. Take what you want," he urges, rubbing circles over my swollen clit.

Tingles spread down my thighs, and I feel myself begin to spasm around him. He sits up to tug my nipple into his mouth, and I go off like a bomb.

My toes curl as my back arches into him.

"Gianni." I moan over and over again as I collapse against his chest, and just when I think I can finally see straight, he adjusts his fingers, pinching my clit between his thumb and forefinger as he spills his hot cum inside me.

An overload of sensations fills me, and I can't help but be satisfied with the sounds he's making as he comes for the second time.

When we've both had enough, he lifts me off him, my mind hazy as I float, barely aware of my surroundings.

My chest is heaving, slightly able to take in enough air.

Did that really just happen?

That was incredible, and what shocks me most is the lack of guilt I feel. I was just in a relationship for six years, and yet I feel nothing but ecstasy at finally having my needs met.

Gianni lies beside me, panting alongside me as we try to get our bearings.

That was incredible.

My racing heart begins to settle, and I feel the edge of the bed dip as Gianni leaves.

I hear running water, and moments later, a warm, moist cloth is wiping my face, my chest, and, finally, the spent and overly sensitive place between my legs. I feel Gianni run another dry cloth over me, covering my body with a blanket before leaving me again.

Just as panic begins to take hold of me, he squeezes my hand. "I'll be right back. I just need to clean myself up."

Moments that feel like lifetimes pass before he's turned off the lights, the sun peeking through my blinds, the only thing illuminating my room. I feel his large, warm body wrap around mine, another blanket covering us both as he nuzzles his face into the place between my neck and shoulder.

I swear I hear him sigh as I relax into his embrace and drift into a restful sleep.

Chapter Twenty-Nine
Gianni

I grab her phone, turning the volume all the way up to make sure I don't miss any alarms that might go off if her blood sugar drops or spikes. I put it back on the table, face down, and turn my attention back to Lark.

Possibly the most fucked-up part of this whole thing is that *I know* how undeserving I am of this woman's attention, let alone for her to share such private information with me. And yet, I just couldn't help myself from offering to live out her fantasies with her.

I'm afraid I'll crave her touch.

Be desperate to drag out every moan she has left in that beautiful body.

And when she finds someone else, someone better and more worthy of meeting *every* need she has, I'll be twice as broken as I am now. Because ultimately, that day will come when she leaves. *Because everyone leaves eventually*, even if not of their own will.

But I haven't felt this decent in months, maybe even *years,* so I plan to ride this wave as long as she'll let me.

I watch as she takes small, peaceful breaths, her chest rising and falling methodically.

Tucking her hair behind her ear and running the pad of my thumb over her cheek, I feel the softness of her skin as my own glides over it. Thirty-six.

Thirty-six freckles dust the bridge of her nose and cheeks, with one rampant one taking place in the center of her bottom lip. *That one's my favorite.*

She begins to stir, her lids fluttering open, and a smile spreads across her face as I come into view. Her immediate reaction to seeing me makes my heart clench inside my chest. Somehow, I had anticipated regret at seeing me when she woke up. I even considered leaving when she fell asleep to avoid that but couldn't drag myself away from her.

"Hi," she says, her voice soft, almost a whisper, but her smile remains.

"Hi," I repeat, an unfamiliar lilt to my voice.

"How long was I asleep?"

Checking my phone on the nightstand, I tell her, "Only about an hour."

"Really?" she asks, eyes widening in surprise. "I feel like I was asleep for twelve hours."

"I can take care of the dogs and let you keep sleeping if you want," I offer, wanting to give this beautiful woman anything she desires in exchange for the weight she's somehow lifted off my shoulders.

"It's okay, but can we just, uh, talk?" Her words send panic racing through me, my body tensing with fear. *Does she want me to leave? Is she already done with me?*

"Of course," I tell her, worry evident in my tone, and my brows pinch together. *Did I hurt her? Go too far?* "Did I hurt you?" I finally ask.

"What?" She looks at me with wide hazel eyes. "Oh my gosh, no," she says, waving a hand through the space between us. "No, you definitely did *not* hurt me. That was honestly the best sex of my life," she admits, her cheeks flushing.

"Oh," is all I manage as my tongue sits thickly in my mouth.

"Yeah, I just want to get to know you better, if that's okay?"

I consider this, deciding I'd like to know everything about her, and I know how this works. It's a trade. "Sure," I respond, voice strained.

"Okay, good," she says, rolling over to lie on her back with her hands crossed over her stomach. I do the same, staring up at her ceiling. "What's your favorite color?"

"Well, it *was* light blue, like my eyes." I answer her honestly, deciding to give her some additional context as it's one of the safest questions she could have asked, and I appreciate her going easy on me. "As a child, I was fascinated with mirrors. How they worked, how the different angles and shapes changed our perception. How lighting could have such an impact on the way our pupils constricted, or what color our irises appeared."

"That's actually really sweet, but you said it 'was' your favorite color. How about now?" she asks, a light-auburn brow raised at me.

"Emerald green," I tell her on impulse. The unspoken part is that it's only recently become my favorite color. More specifically, emerald green and rust. *Just like her eyes.*

She hums beside me before finally breaking her silence. "Mine is pink, and no, I don't have a sweet reason for it like you." She chuckles. "I just really like pink. Your turn."

I'm certain that I could ask her anything, and she'd answer me, but I know she'll make me respond, too, so it has to be something that isn't too personal. "Okay, I've got one. When's your birthday?"

"It's January twenty-sixth. I'm an Aquarius," she says with a lazy smile.

"Happy belated birthday," I tease.

She laughs at that, the small sound sending tingles through me. "It's been almost two months," she says, and my eyes flit back to her to catch the way she playfully rolls her eyes at me. I love how expressive she is. I never have to guess with her. It's a freeing feeling. "Your birthday?"

"March twentieth," I admit.

She hums. "You're a Pisces." I feel the bed shake with her silent laughter before she says, "That makes entirely too much sense now."

Before I get to ask her what she means by that, she sits up straight, peering down at me with wide eyes. "Your birthday is in *five days,* and you haven't mentioned it before? What are we doing?"

My brow wrinkles in confusion. "It's not a big deal, Lark. I don't really celebrate my birthdays. I don't like big parties or loud atmospheres, so I just have Sunday dinner with my family, and my mom makes my favorite dessert."

She settles down, understanding calming her confusion. She lies back down slowly, reaching out her tiny hand to grasp mine. I can't help myself as I lift it to my lips, running them across her knuckles before placing a kiss to the center of her palm.

"What's your favorite dessert?" she whispers.

"Carrot cake," I answer, but before I get to ask her the same, she rolls over, partially on top of me.

"Can we at least watch a movie for your birthday? Here or at your place? Just something quiet and relaxed." Her eyes look almost pleading as she chews on her lip, keeping that tiny freckle just out of view.

My lungs expand, but I'm unable to blow out the breath just yet as I hold it in, waiting for the moment she changes her mind. When she just continues patiently waiting for my response, I release the breath in a low huff, squeezing her hand quickly. "I'd like that."

"Good," she says more cheerfully. "Then it's settled. Now, do you have a favorite tattoo?"

A deep chuckle vibrates through my chest before I answer. I watch as her eyes turn bright with interest at my response to her question.

"Yeah…" I reach under the covers and pull off my left sock, exposing my foot to her.

Her mouth forms a perfect "O", and her eyes widen, auburn brows climbing up her face.

"Gianni," she breathes out. "Is that—"

"A tiny penis with angel wings and a crown? Why yes, yes, it is." I smirk.

She sits up again, trailing a finger over it and taking a better look at it. "Why the hell is this one your favorite?" she asks, laughter bubbling out of her.

My lips curve into an easy smile as I think about that day. "Alex and I had an ongoing bet while we were in undergrad. At the end of every semester, the one with the lowest grades had to do whatever the other wanted. I almost always won, but there was one semester I'd been struggling to care about school at all, and things had gotten away from me."

She hums beside me, encouraging me to keep speaking. "I lost, and that fucker dragged me down to the tattoo shop to get this little gem. The artist said he based the penis off his very own." I groan.

A burst of laughter fills the room, and it feels good as hell to speak freely about dumb shit like this.

I haven't really let myself be this at ease with anyone since Alex's passing.

"I kind of love that." She laughs.

"It was also my first tattoo," I admit.

Her hand shoots out to cover her mouth. "Oh my god! He made you get a dick tattoo for your *first one*?"

"Yep, he thought he was so fucking funny," I grumble, trying to sound annoyed. "Turns out he actually was."

She laughs at my expense but curls her body around mine, resting her head on my chest.

We continue like this for probably the next hour, talking about anything, and everything but keeping the conversation light. It's nice, actually. Getting to speak to someone about things that aren't particularly heavy but still gives them the smallest glimpse into the inner workings of my mind. Maybe if therapy were like this, more people would go. Though I'm not sure how helpful that would be.

"Okay, one last one, and then we need to take the dogs for a walk." I nod, allowing her to pick the last question. "Did you mean it? What you said about helping me fulfill my fantasies? Did you mean that?"

"Yes," I grunt out immediately, no additional thought necessary. Hell, I'll probably be doing a whole lot of thinking about those fantasies in all my spare time.

"Why would you do that for me?" she asks in a soft tone.

"That's two questions, little red. You only get one."

"Fine." She sighs, rolling onto her side and swinging a leg over me. "Can we do that again, then? Not now. I'm thoroughly wrecked, to be honest, but some other time? I'd like to keep seeing you." Her voice is so honest, but she doesn't really know me. Doesn't know just how many demons I hide from the world, but I'm willing to give her as much of me as she wants until she finally *does* come to the conclusion everyone always does. *I'm too broken and emotionally stunted for a romantic relationship.*

"I'd like that too." My voice almost cracks, but I hold back the emotion bleeding into the forefront of my mind.

She peers up at me, holding my gaze with her own, and I watch as her lips spread into a wide grin. "I know I don't have any questions left, but..." She trails off, chewing on her bottom lip. "Would you have *really* been my sub if I'd chosen that?"

Rolling my eyes at her, I grab her hips, pulling her farther on top of me. She plants her hands on my chest, straddling me. "I'd gladly submit to you any day." Her hazel eyes widen in delight, but that smile still remains. My dick twitches, and she obviously notices.

Lark rocks her hips against me, heat coursing through me, but she jumps off, giggling as she works to get changed. "We've gotta walk the dogs!"

"I hate it when you're right," I groan out under my breath.

Chapter Thirty

Gianni

Thursday, March 20, 2025

I know it's my birthday, and she'll probably give me shit for it, but the flower on my counter is finally starting to look a little droopy. So here I am, nervously standing on her doorstep with a bouquet that's twice as large as the last as I wait for her to open the door.

"Coming!" I hear her yell from inside, and my dick twitches automatically, wishing she meant something else entirely.

The door opens wide a moment later, and there she is, wearing a pair of snug, light-wash jeans and a white cropped band tee. She looks like the best goddamn birthday gift I could've ever asked for, and it takes more effort than I'd like to admit to keep my jaw from scraping the ground.

"Hi!" she greets me cheerily, her lips glossy and even more kissable than usual as she smiles up at me expectantly. Her eyes widen as she takes in the flowers in my arms. "Gi! It's *your* birthday. You didn't need to get me anything!"

She called me Gi. Only my closest friends and family call me that. I kind of love hearing it from her.

"I know, but you're hosting, so it's only right, little red." I give her a small smile, hoping she lets it go.

Rolling her eyes and waving me in, it appears she's decided to have mercy on me.

"Okay, so I didn't have time to cook or anything, and I forgot to ask if you have any allergies or if there's anything you don't like, but there's this restaurant down the road that has *everything*. I mean, literally everything. Latin, Mexican, Italian, Polish, French, and some random things like burgers. So I got us an assortment." She ushers me into the kitchen, Tiny and Rex already standing in there staring at the trays of food with stars in their eyes. "Oh, gross! Tiny, get out of the kitchen and wash your face or something!" she jokingly shouts at him, drool pooling from the sides of his jowls.

The sight makes me chuckle. "That sounds perfect. And full transparency—even if I *were* allergic to everything you got, I'd probably still eat it and hope an epinephrine pen and antihistamine would be nearby."

She smacks my chest. "Stop it! I don't need you dying over here. Now grab a plate." She pushes one into my hands, then begins piling food on her own. I like that she isn't afraid to eat in front of me, and I like it even more that she isn't afraid to take charge and go first, avoiding the awkward "You first, no, you first" situation that I dread. I take the time to swap out her flowers, washing and refilling the vase as she finishes making her plate.

Once satisfied with her loot, she digs in, leaning her hip against the counter as she watches me. "Okay, what movie are we watching?" she asks once I'm ready to take a seat.

"Anything you want, except for horror. Unless, of course, you want me sleeping over the next few weeks while you recover."

Her cheeks heat as she looks up at me sheepishly from the end of the couch where she is now seated. "As much as I'd actually really like that, I'll have to pass. You know, considering it's your birthday, and I know damn well you're afraid of scary movies." She chuckles at herself.

"Wow, way to call me out, little red." She isn't even remotely wrong, but it feels good to hear that she'd like me here every night with her. I'd like that more than I care to admit.

"Your eyes were the size of saucers when I mentioned liking horror films. It was easy to tell." She grins, but her expression turns somber. "You know, you aren't hiding as much as you think you are behind that stoic expression."

A weight sinks into my stomach.

"But it's okay. We don't have to talk about it." She reaches over to me, squeezing my thigh gently before readjusting back in her seat. "I'll be here to talk if you ever want to though." She smiles gently at me.

I give her a brisk nod, trying to keep from releasing the deep sigh fighting its way from my lungs. Lark scrolls through a seemingly endless stream of movies, finally landing on one. "Oh my gosh! Have you seen this yet? It looks so cute!"

On the screen is a movie called *Puppy Love* featuring Lucy Hale and Grant Gustin. The picture is of them lying in the grass with their dogs. "Looks good; let's go for it."

"Yes!" she says excitedly as she presses play, setting her empty plate on the side table beside her.

Several minutes later, I've finished my food, and it takes her no time at all before she's in my lap with her arms wrapped around my neck. The change in demeanor is almost startling to me, but I relax into her touch as she brings her lips to mine, pressing soft kisses to them.

My hands slide down her ribs, gripping her waist as she breaks our kiss, whispering gently in my ear. "I didn't get you a present, but I'd let you unwrap me," she says with a soft laugh.

I pull her more tightly to my chest, reveling in the feel of her body flush against mine. "Can I just..." I stop for a moment, fear that she'll be disappointed seeping into me, but decide it's better to know now if she isn't okay with *just* hanging out. I'll give her anything she wants, but I at least need to know.

"Just what, Gi?"

"Can I just hold you tonight?"

Her lips break out into the most beautiful smile, her white teeth gleaming at me before she presses a sloppy, open-mouthed kiss to my cheek, pulling another laugh out of me as I wipe my cheek dry. "Nasty girl," I scold jokingly.

Lark readjusts herself, scooting around to lie along the couch with her head in my lap now, ignoring my comment.

"Why didn't you bring Pickles over?" she asks a few minutes later.

"Kat took her for the night. She said Tank needed another playdate, but I think she's just decided to break her 'no meddling' rule."

"What does that mean? A 'no meddling' rule?" *I shouldn't have mentioned that.*

"My family and Kat's brother, Kas, tend to play matchmaker, but not Kat. She avoids getting involved in other people's business, but it seems she's recently started. In Kat's perfect world, she'd be completely off-grid where it's quiet and low-key."

"That sounds pretty nice," she answers. "But I can't deny that I also love the loud, probably annoying things that quiet people don't enjoy."

That piques my interest. "Like what?"

"Well," she hums, "I love live concerts, raves, comedy shows, parades, fairs, festivals, all of it. Basically anything with music, art, or roller coasters."

"What kind of music do you like?"

"Everything." She laughs. "I have an eclectic taste, to put it plainly. I'd say my favorites are anything two thousands, electropop, and death metal."

"Death metal?" I breathe in disbelief.

"Yep." She snorts. "I love a good headbanger."

God, this woman.

"Your turn."

"I also like just about everything, aside from country music anyway. But I'm really into rock of all genres."

"Very good answer. You've officially won additional brownie points." She smirks up at me before turning her attention back to the screen.

***

Hours go by as we watch movie after movie, only taking a break to put the food away and let the dogs out before bed.

"Hey, birthday boy," Lark says with her arms wrapped around my neck as I stand by the front door, trying to convince myself to leave.

"Yes, little red?"

Her eyes look glassy with exhaustion, but she wears a small, pleased smile. "Sleep over tonight?"

"You don't have to ask me twice," I admit, lifting her into my arms and backing her into her room, pressing a kiss to her jaw.

She hands me a new toothbrush from a pack under her sink when we get to the bathroom, and we brush our teeth together, getting ready for bed. It feels so... *domestic?* I'm not sure since I've never actually been in a relationship, but I imagine this is what it's like. Doing normal, everyday things together that just feel like *more*.

Once we're in bed together, the dogs happily snore at the end. I tuck Lark under my arm, drawing her into me and pressing a kiss to her temple.

"Goodnight, birthday boy," she says sleepily.

"Goodnight, *mon petite rouge*."

Chapter Thirty-One

Lark

Friday, March 21, 2025

A large, warm arm is draped across my abdomen, drawing me into Gianni's hard chest. That isn't the *only* thing about him that's hard though.

His cock is pressing into my lower back, and I can't help but wiggle my ass into it. He grunts, sliding his hand down my abdomen and cupping me through my sleep shorts. "If you keep moving like that, I'll need you to do something about it, little red."

Placing my hand over his to urge him on, a moan slips past my lips as he pushes my shorts aside and slides a finger through my folds. From the end of the bed, I see Rex lift his head, squinting his eyes to glare at us. I reluctantly push Gianni's hand away. "The dogs are in here," I grumble, upset by that reality.

He slides out of bed, yanking me out from under the covers and tossing me over his shoulder. I hang so low on his back that his ass is directly in my face. He grunts as I pinch his ass cheek while he hauls me into the kitchen, setting me down on the countertop.

"You," he points a long finger at my chest, "are a fucking menace."

"Well, it was in my face! I couldn't help it. Besides, I'm hungry. You should be glad I didn't try to take a bite out of all that cake you've got back there!"

"Good news for you then because I'm *starving*, and I plan to have a bite of *you* for breakfast."

Heat spreads down my body as he steps into me, grabbing the waistband of my shorts and sliding them down my legs, dropping them at his side. He lowers to his knees, parting my thighs and tossing them over his shoulders. His tongue darts out, licking the exposed flesh and settling on that sensitive bundle of nerves.

"You taste so damn sweet." He groans, lapping at me. My body is on fire.

Tingles of pleasure ripple through me, my nipples peaking at the sensations lighting me up. He draws back, nipping at my inner thighs and my pussy lips before diving back in to feast on me.

My fingers tangle in his hair, holding him to me. "Gi," I moan between gasps of air.

The hard counter beneath me is a cold contrast to the heat of his tongue as it delves inside me. "If I could have this for breakfast every day, I'd be a happy man," he says with a moan.

Something about that both lights me up and saddens me.

He is so *clearly* not a happy person in his day-to-day life, but when we're together? He seems content, and that's enough for me. *For now.*

His thumb presses against my clit, bringing me out of my thoughts. "Is this enough for you, or do you want my fingers too?"

"Everything." I gasp. "Give me everything."

"I'll give you a single finger, and you'll like it," he grits out. "If I give you *everything,* you won't make it into work today because the next time my dick is buried inside this sweet cunt, I fully plan on breaking your goddamn legs."

One thick, long finger slides into me, my pussy walls clamping down around him as he sucks on my clit, alternating movements that drive me wild. The tension is too heavy, coiling inside me like a taut spring. I'm seconds from climax as he sucks my clit into his mouth, dragging it lightly between his teeth and slipping a second finger inside me.

I go off like a bomb. My hips buck against him, my chest heaving as I moan his name. "Gi, oh god, yes!"

"So good, *mon petite rouge*. Just so damn good," he mumbles into my core.

***

Pressing a kiss to his chin, I walk Gianni out. "You sure you can't stay for me to return the favor?"

He shakes his head adamantly. "I'm not keeping track here, Lark, but if I were, I fully anticipate you to be in the lead. And honestly? That'd make me the real winner." He smirks, leaning down to close the distance between us. My arms wrap around his neck, pulling him closer to me as he claims my mouth in a feverish kiss before heading back to his apartment.

Once he's gone, I lean against my door, looking down at Tiny and Rex as they watch me from the living room. "What am I going to do about this, you guys?" I ask them, knowing they won't answer.

Chapter Thirty-Two
Gianni

It only takes a minute for me to get back to my apartment, and as soon as I do, I'm greeted by an overly excited Kat unlocking my door. Pickles notices me first, lunging toward me.

"Pickles, what the heck!" Kat says to her, but she sees me, and her excitement from moments ago returns in full force.

Pickles rams her head into my thigh, demanding scratches. "Hey there, pretty girl. Were you good for Aunt Kat?"

"As always, she was the perfect girl," she answers, opening my apartment wide for us to step into.

"Glad to hear it."

"So." She waggles her eyebrows at me suggestively. "You spent the night?"

"Yes, Kat. I spent the night." I roll my eyes at her but can't help the small smile that breaks free.

She jumps up and down excitedly before saying, "I'm so happy for you, Gi, seriously. You deserve the best things in this world, and I really think Lark is good for you. She's a good person."

"She is a good person, but she's also dealing with a breakup, and it's not like we're dating. I have no clue what we're doing, but I wouldn't get too excited if I were you."

"Alright, I'm going to let you simmer in that for however long you need. Let me know if you need me to watch Pickles again in the future." She smiles, leaning in for a quick hug before leaving.

Chapter Thirty-Three

Gianni

Saturday, March 29, 2025

My chest heaves, panting as I work to calm my ragged breath. "How does it get better every time?" Lark whispers.

"Practice makes perfect," I joke.

"Yeah, well, that was enough practice for tonight. I swear, you're going to break me."

"And that would be a bad thing?" I tease.

"No," is all she says.

Well, alright then.

I roll out of her bed, gathering everything I need to clean her up. When I'm done, she's lying on her back, eyes closed, with a content smile spread across her swollen lips.

"Alright, you start," she says.

"Start what?" I ask in confusion.

"Pick a question."

The fact that she wants to get to know me further thrills me and worries me all at once, but I won't look a gift horse in the mouth. "Favorite animal?"

"That's fucked up, Gianni," she says in outrage. "I'm a *veterinarian*. I can't pick just one!"

"Yes," I say with a chuckle, "you can. No skipping questions."

"This is really cruel," she mumbles. I hear her hum thoughtfully before finally answering, "Dogs. I know, *I know*, so boring, but they're just so unique. So many sizes, color variations, unique features, and personality traits. They express themselves in such interesting ways, and I just adore how unconditionally they give their affection. If more people were like them, the world would be a better place."

"That's a solid answer, actually. I'll accept dogs," I tell her with a nod of approval.

"Your turn."

"For pets, dogs are my favorite. But for wildlife, I think the titi monkey is pretty cool. They're super loving but also display jealousy, and they mate for life. Something about that just seems so simple and easy to understand."

She snorts. "There's also the fact that their name sounds like titties. That alone makes them pretty great."

"Agreed." I chuckle.

"Okay, what about your family? Tell me something about your siblings."

I allow the question, assuming she won't make me speak too much about this. "I'm the second youngest of five. My oldest brother is Alessandro, Dante and Luca are the same age, and then my sister, Charlie, is the youngest."

"You said you're adopted, right?"

I swallow around the lump forming in my throat and keep this short and sweet, attempting to avoid further questioning. "Yep. Dante, Charlie, and I were adopted when I was two. Our parents passed away in a motor vehicle accident." I decide to provide this detail, knowing if I don't, she'll probably ask eventually, anyway.

Her hand snakes out, wrapping around mine and squeezing gently.

"I'm sorry," she tells me softly.

We lie in silence for a few moments, the weight of the conversation settling over me.

She speaks first. "My mom left when I was twelve, so it's just my dad and me. He's the best, though, and I don't know what I'd do without him."

Pulling her hand up to my mouth, I press kisses over her knuckles.

"Favorite hobby?" I ask her.

She perks up at this, rolling over on her side and twining her leg between mine. "I like to read, as you already know. Oh, and I paint sometimes. I haven't in a while, mostly because I haven't really had time, but also…" She bites her bottom lip, hesitating.

"Also, what?"

"He who shall not be named… He didn't like my art supplies being out, so I didn't have anywhere to set it up, and since I've moved in, I just haven't had the time yet."

Understanding dawns on me. It wasn't just sexual exploration and orgasms that he was withholding and unwilling to compromise with. It was *everything*. The most important, seemingly insignificant parts of her that brought her joy. He didn't want any of it. He thought it was clutter. A nuisance to him. *I'm so damn glad they broke up.* She deserves someone who can make her feel comfortable being her most authentic self and who encourages her, even if it messes with their neat and tidy space.

It's the annoyance building inside me that makes the next words slip out. "My mom was a painter."

"Gloria?"

"My biological mom, Antonella."

She spares me yet again. "We should paint together sometime." She smiles up at me.

Tilting my chin, I press a kiss to her temple. "Anytime you want."

She doesn't let the silence last long. "Okay, last one and then I'm gonna need you to do that thing with your tongue again," she says, giggling and nipping at my jaw.

I groan, desperate to do anything she wants me to. "Okay, your turn."

"You never told me your hobbies, but I'll let it go." She grins. "Favorite TV show?"

"Oh, that's easy. You can't laugh, though, okay?" I ask her, though I don't really care if she laughs. *I love the sound.*

"I pinky promise," she says, sticking out her little finger for me. I clasp mine with hers and tell her, "*Jane the Virgin.*"

"Really?" She smiles wide.

"Yep. I love Gina Rodriguez. She's hilarious, and that show has so many twists and turns, you can't get bored. Besides, the whole premise is fucking incredible."

"Alright, then it's settled. We're watching *Jane the Virgin* tonight. Assuming you're staying over again?"

I nod, kissing the top of her head. "Sounds like a plan."

"Okay, but once we finish that show, we're moving on to *Gilmore Girls*. It's my comfort show."

"You realize there are over a hundred episodes, right?"

She gives me a small smirk, and her next words make my heart flutter in my chest. "I think we've got time," she tells me in a soft tone before widening her smirk. "*Now,* how about that tongue?"

Chapter Thirty-Four

Lark

Tuesday, April 1, 2025

> **Jade**
> On my way, need me to pick anything up?

"You guys need anything? Jade's on her way over."

"Nope, I think we have a sufficient spread," Kira says, taking in my kitchen counter covered in trays of food.

"Yeah, just tell her to drive safe, please."

I nod, doing just that.

Twenty minutes later, Jade's at the door. "Hey, sorry I was late. I can't ever seem to get out of that place on time." She groans.

"It's totally fine," I tell her, grabbing her duffle bag and setting it in the guest room where she and Mads will be staying tonight.

"Hey, Jade!" Madison shouts, patting the seat beside her. "Come sit with me."

Once we're all seated on the couch, the venting begins.

"Alright, Jade, you start first since you got here last."

She lets out a huff. "Well, you know how I keep saying that there's a strange number of transphobic people working at my hospital? You know, considering we're literally a hospital for queer healthcare? Like, I *literally* work in gender-affirming surgery."

We all nod, worried about where this is going. Over the years, we've heard a lot about the downright fucked-up things some of Jade's coworkers say about patients.

"Well, today, the anesthesiologist on one of my cases said, 'Why the fuck would you want to cut off your dick? I'd rather kill myself!'"

I suck in a breath. "Jesus Christ, Jade. Is he usually part of your care team there, or have you not worked with him before?"

"Well, the surgeries aren't done at our facility. They're done at the hospital. The surgeon basically just rents the OR for these surgeries, and the anesthesiologist comes with. But it doesn't matter what the surgery is for. Respect the fact that these patients are putting their literal lives in your hands and trusting you to respect them while they're out!"

"I'm so sorry, Jade. That's horrendous. Really, truly fucking despicable," Madison says, shaking her head.

"I can't even imagine how difficult that must be for you, Jade, just in general because you care about your patients but also as someone who's endured this transphobic behavior firsthand," Kira tells her.

"It's terrifying, honestly. Aside from the lengthy recovery time and the cost, it's comments like those that make me so damn worried about my own bottom surgery."

My heart clenches at the way her voice breaks. I worry about this all the time. I want her to be happy in her own body and recognize herself when she looks in the mirror. But the more I hear about how casually people seem to throw around transphobic commentary, even in a place that's supposed to be accepting and safe, the more it terrifies me to think of her as one of those patients. "Your surgery is with Dr. Delgado, right?"

"Yes, she normally wouldn't agree to perform surgery on a member of her own staff, but she understands my concerns. I'm just too scared to go in there without knowing anyone, so I'm incredibly thankful that she's willing to do this for me."

"Does that mean you guys have set an official surgery date?" Kira asks excitedly, trying to brighten the mood a tad.

"Yep, six more months! Dr. Delgado has a vacation lined up then, so we agreed to do it a couple of weeks before so that some of my downtime could overlap with her vacation."

"That's amazing, Jade! Let me know the official timeline, and I'll take a week off to stay with you and nurse you back to health," I tell her.

"I'll take the week after her," Madison jumps in.

"And I'll take the week after that." Kira chuckles. "By then, you hopefully won't need as much actual 'nursing' help because, as we all know, I am essentially useless in that department."

"Don't we know it?" I roll my eyes, thinking of the time I tripped and scraped my knee. Kira ran over to help me up but passed out when she saw the blood. Not much has changed in the last decade.

"Alright, Madison next," I say, laughing.

"I don't have a whole lot to share or bitch about, honestly. The kids are all back in school, and it's warming up outside, so we don't have as many people coming into the library to stay warm or keep their kids occupied. Overall, things are pretty quiet," she explains.

"Quiet is good! It might sound boring, but it's good, I think," Kira tells her.

"Agreed. I wish I had more quiet time." I groan.

"You're kind of to blame for that, though, Lark. Your dad would gladly hire several other veterinarians and staff, but you *choose* to work wild hours. I know you love it, but have you ever considered taking a step back now that things are running smoothly?" Madison asks me.

"I have, but the clinic is my baby. I don't think I'm ready to part with it."

Kira rolls her big brown eyes. "No one's asking you to part with anything. We're just suggesting you maybe work a normal fucking schedule."

"That's fair," Jade chimes in.

"I'll consider it, but I like to stay busy."

"Speaking of staying busy. How are things with Gianni going?" Kira asks, her ashen brows dancing across her forehead.

"Well, we've um…" I nervously pick at my nails, not looking forward to the attention I'm about to get.

"You *what*?" Kira's shrill, eager tone fills the small space.

"We've had sex, actually. Twice. Well, twice, plus he ate me out the other day too."

"And you're just now telling us this?" Madison nearly screeches with excitement.

As usual, Jade is the peacekeeper. "She's an adult and is not obligated to share the details of her relationships with us." Then she turns to me. "I'm really happy for you, though, Lark. Even if this isn't a long-term thing, you deserve someone who makes you feel good."

"Thanks, Jade," I whisper. Feeling good isn't something I've felt for a very long time, especially not while I was with Tyler. With Gianni, though? It seems his only purpose in life is just that. *To make me feel good.*

"Okay, now that you've made her sad, let's talk about me," Kira pipes in, sounding narcissistic, but I know what she's doing. Steering the attention off me.

"Ah, yes, queen bee. How's the salon?" Madison asks her.

"Mon Cheri is doing really well! I've officially gotten all seats rented out to stylists, and my client list is growing," she tells us excitedly.

She's been working on opening her own salon for the last two years and finally opened hers last month.

"Proud of you, babe," Madison tells her affectionately.

"I'll have to come by soon to get a trim. I haven't had my hair cut in over a year."

"Any time you want, you know my chair is always open to you," she tells me.

"Can I actually book a color appointment with you for the first week of April? My roots are long as hell. Someone really should've warned me about how frequently I'd need to get this shit done to keep up with bleach-blonde hair for someone with natural black hair," Jade grumbles, twisting a lock of her hair. The roots have grown out about three inches.

Kira swats her shoulder playfully. "I *did* tell you that, dumbass."

"Okay, no more attacking Jade. She's delicate." I chuckle, joking because she's the least fragile person I've ever known. She's been through hell and back and still maintains a candid humor and positive outlook that I could only hope to have an ounce of.

***

"Alright, I've got my alarms set, so none of us sleeps through them. I don't want a repeat of the last time we decided to throw our grown selves a slumber party on a work night." Madison groans.

"It won't happen again. Now get some sleep. Love you guys."

Kira follows me to bed, Madison and Jade taking the air mattress in the guest room.

After using the restroom and climbing in with the dogs, she turns on her side to face me. Her voice is soft as she asks, "How are you *really* feeling about things with Gianni? It seemed like there was more there than just sex."

While Kira may come across as a harsh asshole with a dirty sense of humor and a complete lack of a filter, deep down, she's the most caring person you'll ever meet. And I feel blessed to have her as my best friend. Especially in moments like this.

"Honestly? I've become strangely attached to him over the last month. He opens up to me more than I think he does anyone else, but at the same time, it still feels surface-level. Does that make sense?"

"Almost as if he *wants* to tell you more but isn't quite sure how?" she asks.

"I'm not sure if it's that. I kind of think that maybe he's taking baby steps with me in a way. Like maybe he thinks he'll scare me away with his particular brand of unstable."

She snorts at that. "Well, if that's how you feel, you *obviously* haven't told him about your mom."

"I have, just not in detail. I'm not ashamed of what happened to her. She was struggling with a mental illness that was out of her control. Do I wish she had taken her medication and gone to therapy? Of course I do, but that doesn't make her crazy."

"I never said it did," she whispers. "I just meant that if he thinks you're going to be scared off by whatever demons he's supposedly got tucked away in that handsome head of his, he's seriously misguided. Though I am curious how your mom came up at all."

"I feel a little confused. I'm developing feelings for him that feel so much deeper than they should, and we aren't even dating."

"I've got a couple of questions to hopefully unpack that a bit," she says, almost hesitantly.

"I'm ready when you are. Unpack away." I chuckle.

"Alright, first question. If you aren't dating, what exactly *are* you doing?"

"Not entirely sure, actually. We've never discussed it, really. We've been sleeping together, and he's helping me try things on my kink list that Tyler made me feel guilty for even thinking about, but it feels like more than sex. For me, anyway. I can't ever be too sure where his head is at."

"So maybe start there? Try to clear that up so you're both on the same page?"

"I'm not so sure about that just yet. It may be a little too soon to discuss dating, and I don't want to scare him off. If I'm right, and he really is opening up to me, I want to be that safe space for him for as long as I can be."

"I think that maybe you can be a safe space for each other. I have a good feeling about him," she tells me softly.

"I do too," I say into the dark room. She squeezes my hand before rolling over and stealing most of the covers.[1]

---

1. **All The Small Things – blink-182**

Chapter Thirty-Five
Lark

Wednesday, April 2, 2025

"We're still going to Gloria's for book club, right?" I ask my best friends as they head off to work.

"Yep, I love Gloria! I want her to be my new mommy, honestly." Kira laughs.

"Same, she's incredible. She and I have actually been working on some new merch designs for the last couple of weeks," Madison pipes up.

"Ah, I see you're digging those old graphic design skills out of the depths of your brain," I tease.

"I am, and I kind of love it, honestly."

"That's great, Mads. I'm glad you're picking that up again. You were also so good at it," Jade encourages.

"Thanks, Jade," she tells her, then turns to face Kira and me. "We should head out though. I can't be late since it's just me today."

I walk them out, my heart feeling full from the night spent with some of my favorite people.

***

"Hey, Daddy-O, are you free for dinner tonight?" I ask my dad as I head out of the clinic. For once, I'm actually getting out early.

"For you? Always, little bird. Takeout or do you wanna meet somewhere?" he asks me, sounding excited for some quality time together.

"Mind if I grab the dogs and head to your place? We can do dinner at the house with whatever you want," I tell him as I get into my car, buckling my seatbelt.

"Sounds like a plan. See you soon, and Lark?"

"Yeah, Dad?"

"I love you, kiddo," he tells me, and it fills my heart to the brim. *I have the best dad.*

"I love you too, Daddy-O. I'll be there soon."

***

"Okay, *that* was so not fair!" I shout at my dad, tossing a fry at his face. He catches it, popping it into his mouth as he chuckles beside me on the couch. Tiny watches us with rapt attention, hoping for a morsel to drop on the floor for him.

"Hey, last I checked, you didn't mind watching the Divine Flyers play! Besides, I've seen how you stare at De Laurentiis's ass the whole game." My wide eyes meet his, and I'm full of surprise that he not only noticed, but called me out on it. Though I shouldn't be, he's always been perceptive of every move I make.

"Dad," I whine, covering my face with my hands. "Why'd you have to make it awkward?" I say, slouching back against the couch cushions.

He leans back beside me, his body vibrating with a laugh. "I'm just calling it like I see it. And ever since you passed out on my field? That surly man has been a hell of a lot happier when you're on the sidelines. That's for sure. I'm actually pretty certain I've never seen a genuine smile out of the guy until now."

I roll my eyes at that. I've been watching the Divine Flyers games since I was a kid. I wasn't able to attend the games while away for school, of course, and since opening the clinic, it's been nearly impossible. Though, I'll admit that I've been making more of an effort to actually go these days, and yes, that's largely because of Gianni, but I wouldn't say *I've* had any impact on him. "You're seeing what you wanna see." I scoff, mostly joking.

"Lark," he says in a more serious tone that drags my attention to him. "That man is signing autographs and staying late, almost missing our buses after every away game just to make sure he gets to every single kid in the stands. Something's changed for the better, and I wouldn't be upset if it were you."

His words hit me like a ton of bricks. *Gianni's been staying behind to interact with his fans?*

"Well," I say, my eyes cast downward to my lap, where I'm picking at my cuticles. "I don't think it'd be a bad thing either."

When I look up to meet his eyes, he has a small smile spread across his face. "From what I know of that family, they're good people, and I think Gianni's a good person too. He seems to have a lot of demons he's battling, but so did your mom, and she was the love of my life."

A wave of sadness washes over us. I scoot closer to him, wrapping my arms around his shoulders, and he envelops me in a hug. "She was the best person I knew, but she didn't know how to be better for herself. Everything she did was for us. I don't say that to deter you, but just be careful, okay? I think you could be good for him, and maybe he could be the kind of man who puts you first, but if things don't work out, I don't want you to blame yourself if he does something—" He chokes out the last words. "If he does something to hurt himself."

My heart sinks to my toes, even considering the possibility of that happening. He releases me from the vice grip he had on me. "I'll be careful, Dad," I promise him.

"I'm proud of you, my little bird." He turns his attention back to the screen. "Maybe tonight's an *Encanto* night instead?"

His words have the desired effect, and a laugh bubbles out of me. *This man loves Encanto.* "Sounds like a plan," I tell him, pulling Rex into my lap and turning my attention to the TV.

Chapter Thirty-Six

Gianni

Thursday, April 3, 2025

I get up from the couch, put my guitar back in its case, and slide it into the closet before heading to the kitchen for a glass of water.

I hear a light knock at my door that has my brows drawing together in confusion.

I put my glass down, wiping the water from my lips, and head to the door. I peer through the peephole, and standing outside my door in a cropped band tee and tiny jean shorts is Lark.

As I unlock the door and wrench it open, her face lights up when she sees me. "You free tonight?" she asks, sounding overly cheerful.

"Uh, I am," I tell her, moving out of the way to let her in.

She looks around my apartment, taking it in quickly before meeting my eyes again. "Go get changed. I have a surprise for you," she tells me.

I don't particularly like surprises, but for this woman? I wouldn't dare tell her that and risk ruining that gorgeous smile of hers.

"Okay?" I say, the word coming out like a question. I grab a black T-shirt and black jeans before heading to my bathroom to get changed. When I'm finished, I see Lark curled up on my couch with Pickles, looking right at home. *This woman is going to be the death of me.*

When she leaves, I'm afraid the crater-sized hole she'll leave won't be easily repaired.

She hears my footsteps and turns to look over at me, a smirk spreading across those cute, bowed lips of hers. She brings her fingers to her mouth, releasing a loud whistle. "Look at you, hot stuff." She winks. Lark kisses the top of Pickles's head and practically bounces off the couch and to the front door. "We've gotta grab Tiny, and then we can get going," she tells me.

I follow after her, and once we're in my SUV with Tiny in Pickles's usual spot, Lark sets up the GPS, refusing to tell me where we're going.

Thankfully, whatever it is, it's only ten minutes away.

I back out of the parking space and onto the main road, following the directions all the way to my worst fucking nightmare.

"Lark." I look over to her, frantic. "What is this?"

She rolls her eyes, placing a calming hand on my thigh. "It's a *carnival*, you goober."

My heart rate picks up as I follow the line of cars into the dirt parking area. "I can see that," I tell her, my voice strained. *I hate crowds.*

"Gi," she tells me softly once we've parked. "I know you don't like crowded places, so I figured we could take it kind of slow, okay? It's Thursday, and kids are in school, so there shouldn't be nearly as many people as there are on the weekends. And if you're overwhelmed, we can leave at any time, okay?"

It's not like I have some sort of PTSD from crowds or anything. Hell, I play for stadiums filled with thousands of fans several times a week. It's just that places like this are loud and uncomfortable for me. I just feel entirely too overstimulated, so even as a kid, I never really enjoyed them.

But I'll give it a shot *for her*.

"Okay." I nod. "We'll try it out." I finally turn to look at her, and those silky auburn waves are just begging for me to run my hands through them.

I rake my fingers through her hair, tugging at her roots and dragging her lips into mine for a chaste kiss. When I release her, she slumps back into her seat, her soft lips gently parted and her eyes hooded.

"That good, huh?" I joke, feeling better already.

She bounces back quickly, a sly grin across her face. "If you're a good boy, maybe I'll give you a taste of some other things on the Ferris wheel." She wiggles her eyebrows before hopping out of the car to grab Tiny from the trunk.

God, my dick is already getting hard.

We make our way through the lines, and once inside, I realize this might not be that bad. There aren't huge crowds of people at every corner, and with the sun still up, the lights from the rides aren't so aggressive.

Lark grabs my hand, rushing us in the direction of a cotton candy stand. "Pink or blue?" she asks me.

"Blue, but…" I hesitate.

"What is it?" she asks, worry lacing her words.

"Is it safe for you to eat that much sugar?" I ask, hating that I sound so worried. I just want to make sure she's safe, but I also trust that she knows her body and condition far better than I do.

"I've got my CGM on, my notifications set to high, and my fanny pack has everything I need in case I eat too much." She stands on her toes, pressing a kiss to my cheek that warms the deepest parts of me. "But it's cute that you worry about me," she says.

A blush creeps across my face, and I have to look away. *How is she so fucking adorable all the time?*

The guy making the cotton candy gives her one twice the size of her head. She takes it from him and leads us over to a picnic table where a live band is playing.[1]

---

1. **R U Mine? – Arctic Monkeys**

"I *love* cotton candy," she says, taking a bite. I pull off a piece, stuffing it in my mouth and nearly moaning at the sugary taste melting on my tongue. Lark watches intently as I swallow, leaning into me to bring her lips to mine. She dips her tongue inside my mouth, and mine tangles with hers. The taste of her is so much sweeter than this sticky candy.

Tiny whines from beside us, drawing our attention back to the here and now.

She scratches behind his ears and lets him lick her sugar-tipped fingers before standing. "Alright, now it's time for you to win me a stuffed animal," she tells me.

I toss the cone of the cotton candy in the nearest trash bin and find a food truck with a giant pump bottle of hand sanitizer. I dispense way too much into my hands on purpose and head over to her. "Hands, little lady," I say, and she extends them in front of her. I douse them in the alcohol, rubbing our hands together to distribute it evenly.

I follow after her, and for a few minutes, she takes in each game, shaking her head after every one until she gets to one called "The Strong Man." As the name implies, it's one of those games where you hit the metal plate as hard as you can, and if the bell rings, you win a prize.

"What am I winning you from over here?" I ask, and immediately, she points to a massive green-and-purple stuffed dinosaur. "Well, okay then."

I hand over my tickets and pick up the oversized mallet, judging the distance before swinging it over my head. The bell rings loudly, and the teen working behind the counter rolls her eyes. "Which one?" she asks.

Lark tells her which one she wants, and a bright smile beams across her face as she carries it over to me, with Tiny trotting beside her, leashed to her waistband. "Thanks," she tells me, cuffing her arm through mine.

We're about to turn away, but I see a little boy take a swing, to no avail. *These games are rigged.*

Lark turns her attention to him, watching as he gets more and more frustrated, using several of his tickets to try to win the game. "You good here for a second?" I ask her. She gives me a nod of approval, and I crouch down beside the little boy.

"Hey, bud, it looks like you're really working those big, strong muscles of yours to win something up there." I use my chin to direct his attention to the net above our heads, holding hundreds of stuffed toys.

"I think I just used all my energy at baseball practice yesterday," he tells me, his voice small. He couldn't be more than six years old. I see his parents standing a few feet away, and the dad gives me a small, thanks-filled smile.

"Well, that's not your fault. You've gotta put all your muscle into the game, isn't that right?"

"Yeah!" he shouts into my face, still seeming exasperated by his inability to win the prize.

"You wanna borrow some of my strength so you can win one of those toys tonight? It's only fair with how hard you've been working at practice," I tell him.

"Sure!" he says enthusiastically, picking up the discarded mallet.

"Alright, buddy," I tell him, positioning his hands on the mallet and closing my hands over his. "On three."

We count down together, and on three, we hit it out of the park, so to speak.

He jumps up and down excitedly, shouting at his parents to see how strong he is before running over to the counter to pick out his prize. I wave goodbye to him and his parents before rejoining Lark, who's standing with Tiny, looking every bit as infatuated with me as I feel about her.

I wrap an arm around her waist, resting my hand on her hip and pressing a kiss to the top of her head. "Just when I thought you couldn't get any hotter," she jokes.

"Come on, trouble. I have a date with a teacup, and I'm not willing to reschedule," I tell her as we head toward the spinning cup ride. [2]

2. **All My Life – Foo Fighters**

Chapter Thirty-Seven

Lark

Thursday, April 3, 2025

"Okay, one last ride and then we can go home and watch *Jane the Virgin*," I say, smiling up at Gianni. He's been a good sport about this whole night, and I think he *may* even have actually enjoyed himself.

"Alright, one more ride. What will it be?" he asks as if he doesn't already know the answer.

I drag him over to the Ferris wheel, excitement buzzing through me. The sun is about to set, so the lights are bright, and the view from the top should be pretty incredible, overlooking the skyline. "Where is Tiny gonna go?" he asks me, genuinely seeming concerned.

"I'm sure the guy taking the tickets won't mind watching him." I wink up at him, pulling out a wad of bills I've been saving for just this moment. Absolutely nothing is going to stop me from getting my perfect kiss at the top of the ride tonight.

Besides, Tiny would stay put wherever I tell him to, but I really prefer for someone to have a hold on him just in case.

When the last round of people get off the ride, we're up next. I pass our tickets and the twenty dollars in ones to the guy taking the tickets. "Would you mind watching my service dog, Tiny, for us while we're on the ride?" I ask, batting my lashes at the young man in the ticket booth.

"Uh, sure," he says, accepting the money and opening the gate to let us through. I tie Tiny's lead to the metal bar and tell him to stay put.

Grabbing Gianni's hand, I pull him toward the two-person seat waiting for us. We close the gate, ensuring it's firmly shut, and a minute later, someone comes by to do the same. When everyone's locked in, they pull the lever, and we're off. Gianni grips my hand as we make our way slowly to the top.

His hooded gaze is practically burning a hole in my mouth. "Was I a good boy tonight, little red?" he asks.

"A *very* good boy," I tell him, trying to say it how he had, the words dripping sex but failing miserably because, frankly, I'm kind of an awkward person.

He lets out a low chuckle, dipping his head close to mine and nipping my bottom lip. He releases my hand, dropping it to my lap and raking his middle finger over the seam of my jean shorts. His chest rumbles with a sound of approval. "You're already soaked for me, and I've barely touched you," he says, continuing to stroke me through the thick fabric.

I look around, frantic, to make sure no one can see us, but we're almost at the top. Just as I'd thought, the view is incredible, and yet, the only thing I want to look at is the man sitting beside me.

His hand cups the back of my head, dragging my mouth to his. He sucks my lip into his mouth, releasing it with a pop and dipping his tongue inside to taste me. The hand on my lap shifts, and I hear my zipper lower before the weight of his calloused hand slides in under my lace thong.

He puts pressure on my clit, and I'm squirming beneath him, ready to burst with one simple touch. I grip his hand, pulling it closer to where

I need it most, and *finally,* he slips two fingers inside me. I roll my hips, unable to keep still despite the wobbling bucket we're swaying in.

"Toujours aussi belle. Surtout sous ces lumières quand tu te baises sur ma main." *Always so beautiful. Especially under these lights, fucking my hand.*

He removes his hand, zipping my shorts back up and fixing the top button. When he pulls his face from mine just as we're nearing the bottom, he slides those fingers that had just been inside me into his mouth, sucking me off them. "Definitely better than cotton candy." He smirks, and it sends fireworks shooting through me.

How is he so damn sexy?

***

"I'd have sued, one hundred percent. Jane is too freaking nice!" I shout at Gianni as he lounges on the couch, idly rubbing my feet.

"It's a TV show, little red. I'd like to think that Gina Rodriguez herself would have sued if this were real life. Now just keep watching," he tells me, shaking his head.

I settle back into the couch, enjoying just how normal this feels. Tyler refused to just watch TV with me and relax. He'd throw a fit when I just wanted to cuddle or do pretty much anything, just the two of us.

I know that Gianni and I aren't really a couple, and as much as I want to just ask him about it, I'm not ready to give whatever this is up if he isn't interested in more. So, for now, I plan to just enjoy it and keep doing my best to make him feel as happy and content as he makes me in the hopes that this could last.

We spend the next several hours cuddling on the couch with the dogs at our feet until Pickles finally climbs over me to lie between Gianni and me.

She's such a little cuddle bug. I love it.

"Do you guys wanna spend the night?" he asks me, and I feel like I could float away.

"We'd love to, right, boys?" I ask them jokingly, neither of them even looking in our direction. They're both completely passed out at our feet.

"I'll take that as a yes." He chuckles, maneuvering Pickles into his arms before carrying her to her bed and setting her stuffy beside her.

"Me next?" I ask, lifting my arms in front of me, only half kidding. He stands in front of me, gripping my waist, and slings me over his shoulder, carrying me to his bed.

He crawls in beside me, pulling my hips firmly into his and snuggling against my back. He buries his face in my hair, taking a deep inhale and letting it go on a long sigh. "*Fuck,* this is nice." He groans.

A smile tugs at my lips, hearing how at ease he is with me. It fills me up in ways I hadn't known possible. "It is," I whisper into the dark room.

Gianni trails kisses along my neck, pressing the last one between my shoulder blades. "Goodnight, my little red."

"Goodnight, Gianni," I tell him before drifting into the most relaxing dreamless sleep.

Chapter Thirty-Eight

Gianni

Saturday, April 12, 2025

Pickles and I head inside, arriving uncharacteristically early for our monthly guys' night with my brothers and dad.

My mom wheels herself through the kitchen, a huge smile spread across her tan face. "You're here early," she says, eyeing me quizzically.

"Yep, figured I'd see if you needed anything around here," I tell her.

"Mhmm, well, the girls should be here soon if you'd like to help me set the food up in the living room."

"Sure thing, Mom," I say as I bend to give her a hug and a kiss on either cheek. "New eyeshadow?"

"I'm working with a cosmetic chemist that Rose set me up with! It'll be a part of my book club merch line, so I figured it was only fitting to try it out tonight." She beams up at me, her sparkly silver lids shining under the kitchen lights.

"It looks very nice, Mom," I say, smiling at her.

"Is that..." She trails off, her eyes beginning to glisten. "A smile?" She finally finishes, and it makes me realize just how long I've been depressed and how much it's impacted my family.

Shame fills me, but before I can dwell on it, the door bursts open. Dante's booming voice fills the foyer. "Hey, Mom," he calls.

"I'll grab the food." I rush out.

***

"You're here awfully early today," Dante notes, his brow quirked at me.

"Just wanted to see if Mom needed help setting up."

He hums before replying, "Right, and it wouldn't have anything at all to do with the pretty redhead coming over tonight?"

"Nope, I like Arielle and all, but I'm not showing up early for her." I know damn well he wasn't talking about his wife.

He laughs. The sound is a deep boom that fills the living room. "Look at you being a smartass," he says, smirking.

I ignore him, but a moment later, there's a knock at the door. "I'll get it," I say, heading to the door as quickly as I can. I hear Dante attempting to muffle his laughter behind me, but he's literally a therapist. There's not much I can hide from him.

Gripping the door handle and wrenching it open, I'm fucking elated when I see the group of women on the doorstep. One of which being Lark.

"Hey, come on in." I wave them through the entryway but grab Lark's forearm before she can walk through, pulling her out onto the porch and closing the door behind me.

"Hi." She beams up at me. The setting sun makes the orange in her eyes appear even brighter.

"I missed you today," I tell her, then second-guess myself. "I mean like I missed the class. I had a game today, not that you don't already know that," I add nervously, gripping the back of my neck.

She rolls her eyes at me and steps into my embrace, sliding her hands up my chest. "You can say you missed me and just leave it at that," she tells me, her voice sounding breathless.

Nuzzling my face into her hair, I whisper, "I missed you, *mon petite rouge.*"

I can feel her hot breath dance across my neck, sending goosebumps erupting all over. "I missed you too, *mon ciel étoilé.*"

My brows pinch together in confusion. "My starry sky?" *And she speaks French?*

She gazes up at me, but just as she opens her mouth to answer, a car pulls up.

Chapter Thirty-Nine
Lark

Before I can answer him, Luca comes sauntering up the driveway toward us.

I called him *mon ciel étoilé*. He's right that it means "my starry sky," but *someday, I'll have to tell him why.*

"Well, hello there." He greets us with a cocky grin.

I pull away from Gianni and move to head inside. "Hi, Luca," I tell him as I pass Gi, entering the doorway.

My friends are sitting in the living room, each of them wearing a look that tells me exactly what they're thinking.

I roll my eyes at them and take a seat next to Jade because she's the least likely to poke fun at me. Gloria wheels out into the living room with a huge box in her lap.

"Okay, ladies! I've got some new merch I've been cookin' up."

"Ooh, gimme gimme!" Kira tells her excitedly, grabbing the box from her lap and digging through it. "Oh my god! Gloria!" she shouts, delighted.

Kira pulls a tiny pen out of the box, holding it up for everyone to see. On the top is a tiny, squishy penis with a little smile painted on it. It's the cutest pen I've ever seen.

"Jesus Christ, Mother!" Charlie shrieks as she rushes into the living room, snatching the pen from Kira's hand. Her eyes widen, but a slow smile spreads across her face. "Alright, fuck it. I'm all in. This is actually really cute. I think I'll get over the embarrassment once we've made our millions from your merch line."

"No." Gloria huffs, folding her arms across her chest.

"No?" Charlie asks her, confusion lacing the word.

"You're a hater. So see you later, alligator! You aren't profiting off my good ideas. Not till I die and leave you my millions, anyway." She chuckles, though, and her expression gives her away.

"I'm sorry I didn't support your ideas, Mom." She rolls her eyes. "These are really cute, though, and I think you'll make a killing, so let me know how I can support you."

"Could you help me set up my website?"

"Of course I can, and I'm sure Rose will be happy to help too." She smiles lovingly at her wife, who's now sitting on the love seat across from me, a small smirk dancing across her lips.

"She already is," Gloria deadpans.

"What are you on about?" Charlie asks.

"Rose is helping me already. She set me up with a cosmetic chemist, and we're working on these gorgeous eyeshadows," she tells us as she flutters her lashes.

Charlie spins to face her wife. "Rose!"

She raises her hands, palms up. "Hey, if you can't beat 'em, join them. And after being married to you for almost a decade, I can genuinely say that *no one* beats Gloria De Laurentiis."

"You'd think I'd know better," Charlie grumbles, taking a seat beside Rose. She lifts her legs up into her lap and rubs small circles along her calves.

Kat and Arielle arrive a few minutes later, and once we're all here, the guys start to head out.

"You know what? I'm kind of curious about what goes on in these book clubs. Maybe we should skip guys' night and join the ladies," Luca pipes up just as they're almost through the front door.

"Why would you want to hear your mother talk about books with sex?" Angelo grumbles, with his hands on his hips.

"You know, I've always been curious too," Alessandro adds, a grin playing across his lips.

Gianni's eyes dart to mine, holding my gaze as Dante calls to Gloria. "Hey, Mom, would you mind if we intrude on your girls' night, just this once? *Feel free to tell us to leave,*" he adds almost pleadingly.

"Not at all, honey. Come on over." She waves the men back over but looks around the room. "That okay with you, ladies?"

"Absolutely," Kira says. Everyone else nods their agreement, each of them giving me a peculiar look that fills me with anxiety.

Gianni pulls a chair up next to Kat, sitting directly across from me. I'm regretting not sitting somewhere with space for Gi to sit beside me.

Over the next hour, we discuss this month's novel and take a vote on what next month's read will be.

"I vote for *Shiver* because we haven't read a hockey romance in a while, and the tropes are top-tier in this one!" Charlie suggests.

"Yes! We love a single-father romance!" Kira agrees.

"And the FMC sounds super promising. I think we're all really going to like her. She sounds like a badass lawyer," Arielle points out.

"Completely agreed," Jade chimes in.

"Alright, I think it's settled then." Kat chuckles. "*Shiver* it is!"

Kat's sitting on Alessandro's lap with his arms wrapped around her waist, his head on her shoulder. They're the epitome of relaxed when together, and I can't believe I ever thought she and Gianni were dating. Just the thought makes me squirm.

I have no idea what Gianni and I are actually doing, but I know I don't want him with anyone else. *Ever.*

***

We continue chatting, with Gloria telling us about all of her fun merchandise until the night winds down. As soon as I'm in my car, my cell goes off with tons of messages flooding in.

Kira
> OMG! That man wants to eat you right the hell up!

Madison
> He sure does!

Madison
> All I want is a man who looks at me like Gianni does Lark. *Swoon*

Jade
> As much as it pains me to agree with anything either of these two says… I agree. Wholeheartedly.

Jade
> That man wants to take a bite out of you.

> He does not. You're all over-exaggerating.

> **Kira**
> You, my friend, are BLIND!
>
> **Madison**
> Please tell me how exactly you didn't feel those piercing blue eyes searing into you? I don't think he so much as looked away from you for even a split second.
>
> **Jade**
> Again, painful, but… True. Sorry chica.

My cheeks heat. I absolutely did feel him staring at me. His gaze on me feels like a delicious caress, and I can't say I mind it even a bit. Though, if they all noticed, his family absolutely did too. I hope that doesn't make things awkward for him.

> You guys are ridiculous. Drive safe. Love you.
>
> **Jade**
> Love you too.
>
> **Kira**
> LOVE YOU!!!
>
> **Madison**
> Love you guys!

On my drive home, I can't help but think of Gianni and the way he makes me feel. Like my skin is on fire, my heart is beating too damn fast, and I'm somehow always turned on around him. It's the perfect mix of desire and emotions that I never felt with Tyler.

Chapter Forty

Gianni

As soon as Lark and her friends made their way outside, I hurried to my car to follow behind her.

There's a parking spot right beside her, so I pull in and jump out, running around to the back to grab Pickles before Lark can even turn off her engine. I make my way to her door, opening it for her. She smiles up at me. "Didn't want to stay for movies with your family?"

"Not when I could spend time with you. If that's okay," I add.

"I'd like that," she says. Her eyes dart to her feet, looking away sheepishly. An idea strikes me.

"Hey, would you want to go on a drive with me?"

"Now?" she asks, sounding surprised.

"If that's okay," I say, my shoulders sagging with the possibility that she might say no.

"That sounds nice, but I've got to let the dogs out first."

***

Once all three dogs are snuggled up at Lark's apartment, we head out to the parking lot.

"You mind if we take my car?" she asks, and my stomach churns.

I don't answer for a moment too long and watch as her smile falters.

"I—" I swallow thickly. "I don't feel comfortable with other people driving, and I'm not a huge fan of anything smaller or less durable than my Jeep," I admit.

Understanding dawns on her, and she nods, grabbing for my hand. She squeezes it as we continue to walk.

"That makes sense," she says, shooting me a reassuring smile. "So, where are we going?"

My legs feel unsteady as they carry me to my car. "There's an overlook about thirty minutes from here. Almost no one is ever there. It's just somewhere I feel like I can think."

We drive there with my favorite playlist trickling through the speakers and my hand on her thigh the entire ride.[1]

I pull up, parking right in the middle of the dirt spaces for the best view.

It's dark, so there isn't much to see besides the trees surrounding us and the stars in the sky. They're so bright out here, away from some of the light pollution in the city.

"It's gorgeous." She gapes. "How'd you find this place? I've lived here my whole life, and I've never heard of it!"

"Alex used to bring me out here when I was getting too in my head. He always had a way of knowing when I was dwelling on or overthinking

---

1. **Tongue Tied – GROUPLOVE**

things," I tell her, and for the first time, I feel like I'm able to speak freely about Alex without grief gnawing at my chest.

"He sounds like he was a really great person." She smiles up at me. Her hand wraps around mine, still lying on her thigh, and she gives it a reassuring squeeze.

"He was. Sometimes, I felt like he was the only person who truly understood me."

She averts her gaze before speaking her next words. Her voice is choked as she says, "Do you ever think that maybe people don't understand you because you don't open up to them?"

Her words don't hurt me though. I *know* I don't open up to people, and that's my fault. It's just another reason I feel guilty. "I know that's the reason. Genuinely, I do. But I don't want to burden anyone, and I know my family is incredible. Absolutely wild but incredible nonetheless. I just haven't worked through those insecurities, and everyone in my family has their own things going on. I know they'd never feel like I was a burden, but I still can't shake that feeling."

"Your family *is* incredible, and they'll love you no matter what, but maybe it'd be easier if you tried opening up to just one person first?"

I quirk a brow at her. "Are you asking to be that person?"

"I mean, I'd love to be, but it doesn't have to be me. It could be anyone you feel comfortable with." She sounds so honest, and it gives me the courage to actually agree to let her be that person.

I want her to be that person for me.

"Okay."

"Okay?" she asks, sounding shocked.

I nod. "You've never given me a reason not to trust you." Besides, I've already decided that she deserves someone better. And since I'm entirely too selfish to ever see her with someone else, I'm taking on the task of bettering myself. Not just for her but for *us*.

"Thank you," she says quietly.

I lean back in my seat, closing my eyes as I prepare to speak the words that no one has ever heard me admit.

My heart clenches in my chest, nausea roiling through me.

Lark squeezes my hand again, and my next words leave my mouth through gritted teeth.

"I think I have depression."

That weight begins lifting off my chest the moment I've spoken the words into the quiet space of this car.

Lark's thumb begins rubbing small circles across the back of my hand.

She allows me the time I need to continue speaking, not rushing to fill the silence with affirmations. Just letting me *feel*.

"I don't think it's a secret that I'm depressed. I think anyone within a mile of me would have to be blind to not see it despite how hard I've tried to hide it, but it's never something I've put a name to. I've never actually labeled it and verbally spoken those words before."[2]

She leans forward, resting her head on my shoulder.

"I'm not *ashamed* that I'm depressed though. I'm embarrassed that I have such a privileged life with such supportive people surrounding me from every direction, and my brain is still finding ways to make me feel unappreciative. I don't want to burden anyone. My mom and Ale have MS, Dante and Arielle are dealing with my nephew's OCD, Rose and Charlie have to navigate male-predominant careers as lesbians, and here I am, a fucking musical prodigy with a kick-ass career playing a sport I *used* to love, and I can't seem to dig myself out of my own thoughts."

I take a deep breath in, filling my lungs and pushing it out through my nose to calm myself. "I'm not capable of just talking my feelings out and letting them go. I react so strongly to every fucking thing. Like when Alex came out and he was being bullied, it took everything in me not to pummel

---

2. **Sweater Weather – The Neighbourhood**

every person who so much as looked in his direction. He'd just shrug it off, perfectly content with himself, but I couldn't do that, and with how much stigma there is in the sports community, it made it that much harder to ignore the comments."

She kisses my shoulder and reaches forward, gripping my cheek in her palm and pulling my lips toward hers. Lark presses a soft kiss to my mouth and rests her forehead against mine. "I'm so proud of you, *mon ciel étoilé*."

Her words tear me apart inside. *There's nothing to be proud of.*

"Your mental health is *important*, Gianni. Yes, everyone has something to worry about, something that makes their life difficult in some way, but that is just *life*. It doesn't make your struggles any less real, and it's no one else's business. But it sounds like it's something that's been eating you up inside, and I'm here to talk about it anytime you want."

A heaviness settles on my chest. "Before he died, he was coaching me through just that. Talking about my feelings. Alex was a wealth of wisdom. He knew me better than anyone and somehow always managed to get through to me when I was getting stuck in my own head."

"I know it's not the same, but I can be there for you if you decide you want that."

Her soft-spoken words tie me up in knots. Her support means more to me than she may ever know.

"Thank you," I choke out. A single tear falls down my cheek. She swipes it away with the pad of her thumb and kisses me again before leaning back in her seat.

"Alright, you've shown me yours, so I'll show you mine." She sighs. "The reason my mom left was because she quit taking her medication. She was diagnosed with bipolar disorder and would have manic episodes. As long as she took her medication, she was mostly fine, but sometimes, she'd get overwhelmed with life and forget a few doses, and things would spiral."

My stomach drops. "I'm so sorry. Do you know what happened to her?"

"No, we don't." She shakes her head. "One day, we got home, and she was just gone. No note or anything. My dad hired a private investigator, but he wasn't able to track her down. After five years of searching, he finally had to call it quits. Wherever she is, I just hope she's gotten the help she needed and she's living happily."

"That sounds like a lot for a twelve-year-old to handle. How'd you manage?" I've been seemingly falling apart my entire life, so I'm genuinely curious how she was able to process her circumstances so well.

She smiles at me. "My dad insisted I start therapy. He said he wanted to give me the tools I needed to handle stressful situations and to find outlets for my feelings. It's actually why I started painting."

Therapy. How come that always seems to be the answer for everyone?

"In high school, when I was dealing with more changes than my coping mechanisms alone could help me with, I started taking an antidepressant that helps with my anxiety too. I've been on it for years now, and it's improved my quality of life more than I can express. My mom was always embarrassed about her diagnosis, so the times she'd stop taking her meds were usually surrounding girls' trips or nights away with friends because she didn't want them to know she struggled with mental illness." She pauses for a moment, squeezing my hand before she continues. "My dad says she was afraid people would judge her or think she was a horrible person, but that's just not true. When she was all there, she was the best mom I could have ever asked for. She was a *good* person, and being bipolar or struggling with any other mental health condition doesn't make someone a bad person. We all have struggles, and they manifest in different ways, but there is no shame in asking for help. Whether that be with medication, therapy, just talking things out with friends, or a combination of it all."

She speaks so freely about the things that have plagued me for years. These are the same things Dante tries to preach to me, but he works as a mental health professional. His opinions are biased, but hearing it from

Lark eases some of my worries. Maybe it *is* time that I at least try some things she's suggesting.

"How long were you seeing a therapist before you felt like it helped?"

"I'd say the very first session was helpful. I won't lie and say everything was butterflies and roses immediately after an hour-long session, but I left with a few new techniques to manage things. Every week after that, we worked on whatever was bothering me. We changed gears as we went because sometimes we found one thing would work better than another, or I'd have a different set of stressors, but it was easier to navigate. After the first year, I was able to see her twice a month instead of every week, and now I still speak with a therapist once a month. It's mostly just for a mental health check to ensure I'm taking care of myself and what I need to do, but it's reassuring to have someone there who knows my history but has no biases surrounding what I tell them. I get to say anything I want and know it won't be used against me or brought up later outside of our video call."

That piques my interest. "You do your therapy sessions over a video call?"

"Yep. I used to do them in person, but my schedule is so hectic these days that the video calls make it easier to fit in."

The words bubble over. "Can you help me find a therapist like that? One who does calls over the phone or something?"

A small smile spreads across her bowed lips. That little freckle is staring right at me, begging me to kiss it.

"I'd be happy to."

***

"Okay, so your dad calls you little bird, you've spoken French your whole life because your mom spoke it in the house, your favorite meal is anything with grease, Ghostface turns you on, and you prefer soccer over hockey, but you like hockey romances better?" I ask, raising a brow at her, confirming I've memorized each and every detail she's shared with me while we've sat here.

She smiles brightly at me. "Yep, that sums it up."

"I've got a burning question for you that's been bothering me for weeks."

She shifts in her seat. "Shoot."

"What exactly *is* on that list of kinky things you want to do? I'm just trying to gauge how much of that list I've actually crossed off." I smirk at her.

She rolls her eyes, huffing out a small breath. "Fine, if you're gonna keep asking, I'll list them off, but *only* if you tell me some of yours too."

"Deal."

"Okay, well, obviously being submissive and dominant. And clearly, you've crossed one of those off." She wiggles her cell out of her pocket and stares down at the screen for a few moments.

"Noted. Do you keep a list on your phone or something?"

Her freckled cheeks turn pink. "It's something I made recently, but yeah." She giggles. "There's a lot of usual stuff on here, too, and like I said, I absolutely have a Ghostface kink, so I'd like to explore that at least once and find out if it's really something I like."

I know what I'll be buying online when I get home.

"Go on," I urge.

"I'd like to try bondage, but I'm not interested in ball gags or those leather masks that spread your mouth open." She giggles, and the sound goes straight to my cock.

"No ball gags or mouth spreaders. Got it. Aside from my dick in your mouth, of course," I say with a wink and revel in the way her cheeks flush.

She nods, confirming what I've said with a wry grin. "Exhibitionism is something I'm into in theory, but not really sure I want to risk *actually* getting caught."

Well, isn't that interesting?

"I think that could be arranged..." I trail off, but my cock is already swelling in my jeans. Gripping her jaw, I pull her mouth to mine roughly, planting a sloppy kiss on her lips. "No one gets to see my woman's pretty pink pussy besides me." I trail kisses down her slender throat. "But out here, if someone pulls up, they might see us together. Would that suffice?" *I love that she didn't object to being called "my woman."*

Her body quakes under my grip, goosebumps lining her skin. "Y-yes." She moans.

Pulling out my wallet, I extract the condom I put in there just for Lark. I sure as shit hadn't needed it before.

Opening it with my teeth, I pull out the lubricated condom. "Lean back in your seat, little red."

Her brows pinch in confusion, but she does as I say. I work the condom over the gearshift, and her jaw *literally* drops. "Wh-what is going on?"

"You'll see. Do as I say, and I'll have you coming so hard, you won't see straight for a week."

Her eyes are wide, but her shoulders relax. "Okay," she whispers.

"Slide your tights and panties off."

She does as I say, sitting beside me in her flowy black skirt and band tee. I slip my hand over her thigh and dip a finger through her slick heat. "You're so goddamn wet." I groan.

"Mhmm," she squeaks out.

"Does this turn you on, *mon petite rouge*? To know you could get caught out here? You could be seen *begging* for release, riding my hand."

She releases another moan as I slip two fingers inside her. She's absolutely soaked.

Chapter Forty-One
Lark

I'm dripping all over Gianni's leather seats, heat coiling in my abdomen. "God, yes," I cry out as he pumps his fingers inside me.

"Alright, Lark, now's your time to shine, baby." He smirks as he pulls his fingers out of me. The loss of them inside me leaves me wanting to pout in annoyance, but he puts them in his mouth and sucks my juices off.

"Straddle the gearshift," he instructs.[1]

I have no idea how he thinks I'm going to do that, but I adjust myself, moving to toss my right leg over it, but he stops me. "Face the windshield."

Oh hell.

I huff but throw my left leg over to the driver's side, angling my knee between Gianni's thighs and hovering above the sheathed handle.

He slides his hand up the back of my thigh, lifting my skirt and tucking the bottom into my waistband so he can bare my ass to him. "This little tattoo," he says, almost sounding pained. Leaning forward, I feel him bite the tender skin, more heat pooling at my core.

---

1. **Dirty Little Secret – The All-American Rejects**

Gianni slips his fingers over my center and spreads my folds. "Sink down on it, *mon petite rouge*."

I do as he says, moving slowly to adjust to the feel of it as it stretches me wide. I'm barely on it, and I feel like I could burst.

"That's it, just go slow. It gets more narrow the farther you go. You like being stretched, and this isn't much thicker than my cock."

He's not wrong.

I sink down a bit more, and just as he said, it's narrower at the base. My walls clamp down around it, and once the initial sting has subsided, I'm so ready for my release.

"Put your hands on the dash and ride it. Let me see your ass bounce as you fuck anything you can get inside your needy little cunt."

I'm struggling to keep myself upright as Gianni's hand slides up my thigh, his knuckles grazing my clit. A shudder wracks through my body, and I fall forward. My eyes widen as headlights shine up the dirt path toward us. "Oh my god," I cry.

He runs a finger over my clit, rubbing quick circles, and I can't help but buck my hips at the movement. Heat coils inside me, my orgasm nearing and sweat forming at the base of my spine. "If you don't want to get caught, you'll come for me right now."

I see stars at his command, my body reacting exactly as he hopes it will. I bite my lower lip, doing my best to muffle my cries as the orgasm rolls through my body, my core clenching around the hardness inside me.[2]

His fingers bite into the skin of my hips, lifting me off and back into my seat just in time. He slides the condom off the gearshift and tucks it into his pocket as someone shines a flashlight into the window. Gianni rests a settling hand on my thigh. "Everything's okay, little red."

---

2. **Whore – In This Moment**

He rolls down the window, and a tall police officer with kind brown eyes and dark skin is looking in at me, wearing a small smile. "I drove by and saw a car parked here. Figured I'd let you both know that this park is technically closed at sundown."

My cheeks heat further, nausea clawing through me.

"I'm so sorry, officer. I hadn't realized there was a specific time we had to be gone by. My girlfriend and I were just enjoying the stars, but we'll head out now." Gianni speaks to the officer with such a calmness about him, you'd never believe what he just had me doing less than two minutes ago.

"That's alright, I just didn't want you getting in trouble if someone else came across you here. Have a good night and drive safely," he tells us, tipping his head at me and widening his smile before turning and heading back to his car.

The moment Gianni rolls the window back up, I slump back in my seat, releasing a breath.

"That was terrifying," I complain.

He chuckles. "You did fine, little red. Let's get you home." He pats my thigh and pulls out of the space, heading back toward our apartment.

Chapter Forty-Two

Lark

Sunday, April 13, 2025

Gianni's head is resting on my chest, his massive arm draped over my abdomen as I watch his chest rise and fall. He looks content like this. The usual worry he carries around is absent as he sleeps.

I run my fingers through his silky strands, pressing a kiss to the top of his head.

Last night was so much to digest that I hadn't processed what he'd told the police officer. He'd called me his *girlfriend*.

Was he just saying that because it was the easiest way to explain what we are? Or does he assume that's what we are? I'd love nothing more than for this man to claim me. To really be mine, and not just in the sexual sense.

I want to know everything about him. The parts he loves, and the ones he despises. The incredible memories and the ones that haunt him. I want every piece of him to be woven with mine because with Gianni De Laurentiis, I feel more myself than I ever have.

And I think he needs someone there to tell him that the things he's feeling are valid, but there *are* ways to lessen the burden they hold over him. I can be that person for him. I desperately *want* to be that person for him.

He stirs above me, his dark lashes fluttering as he opens his eyes. Those crystal-clear baby blues stare up at me, and the edges of his lips spread into a smile as soon as his eyes meet mine.

"Good morning, *mon petite rouge*."

"Good morning, *mon ciel étoilé*." I smile at him, realizing this is the first time since we met that he doesn't have dark circles.

"What time is it?" he asks me.

I grab my phone and see the screen light up with a text from my dad.

"It's 7:44," I tell him before opening the chat to respond.

Daddy-O

> Hey little bird, still meeting me at the game today?

> Wouldn't miss it :)

Daddy-O

> Perfect, see you soon.

Gianni kisses my cheek and rolls off me. "I've got to start getting ready for today's game. You coming?"

I nod. "Yeah, I'm meeting my dad there."

"Good." He smirks. "I just hope you can walk straight today."

My eyes widen. "Asshole!" I shout playfully, smacking his chest, but he grabs my wrists. He brings my hands to his lips and kisses the inside of each wrist.

The tender gesture makes my heart clench in my chest, butterflies taking flight in my stomach.

"I'll see you there," he tells me, pressing a chaste kiss to my lips and heading to the bathroom.

Chapter Forty-Three
Gianni

Sweat is dripping into my eyes, the saltiness burning.

My muscles are heaving with the effort it takes to run the ball down the pitch, but for once, it feels good. I'm finally *enjoying* soccer again. For the first time since Alex's death, I'm feeling almost optimistic.

The opposing team's offense is fast but not fast enough.

They can't keep up, and it shows. I see their goalie readying himself at my approach, but just before his teammate side-checks me, I send the ball flying.

He jostles me, nearly sending me to the ground with the force of the hit, but it doesn't matter. *Because we won.*

The ball flew straight into the corner of the net, with the goalie missing it by less than an inch.

I collapse to the moist grass, hands clasped over my abdomen. I'm panting, but a smile spreads across my lips. The sun's rays warm a part of me that felt cold and dead for so long. Or maybe that's just *Lark*.

My teammates rush to me, cheering me on, and one of them puts his hand out to help me up. I take it, and surprise flits across his tan features before quickly smoothing out.

Once upright, my eyes search for Lark, who should be standing beside her dad.

I find her quickly, her auburn waves now braided down her back. My stomach churns as I notice who she's standing beside.

Damien.

My feet carry me over to them, but the sound of her giggle stops me in my tracks. She's wearing a bright smile and doesn't look uncomfortable at all. *She's allowed to speak to other men. She isn't your goddamn property. Calm the fuck down.*

I turn on my heel, heading to the locker room and try to cool my racing thoughts. I know that, rationally, Damien is just trying to get under my skin. But the jealousy coursing through my blood is *not rational*.

After showering and changing, I head out to the parking lot and find Damien leaning against the side of my SUV.

I ignore him, walking around to the driver's side. I toss my duffle bag into the passenger seat, and as I move to get in, he grips my shoulder, forcing me to face him.

"Who would've thought your lover boy would die and you'd move on so soon? She's got a sweet little mouth on her though. I'd like to take it for a spin." He says the words with such nonchalance that it takes a moment for them to register with me.

My fists clench, nails digging into the palms of my hands.

I close my eyes, counting down from ten. When that doesn't work, and I realize he's started speaking again, I do my best to think of what Alex would tell me to do in this situation. *"Don't waste your breath or your career on this guy. He's picking on you because he's insecure. Get in the fucking vehicle and drive away."*

That does it. Popping my eyes open, I wrench his hand off my shoulder, hoisting myself inside and slamming the door in his face. I start the ignition and back out, not bothering to check how close he's standing. If he doesn't move, that's his problem.

***

"Uncle Gi! We have another soccer game on Tuesday. Will you come?" Benny asks me from his seat at the children's table.

"Don't say yes unless you mean it," I hear Dante growl from beside me, just loud enough for my ears alone. His tone sends a shiver through me. I know I've disappointed them before, but I'm going to be better. For all of them.

I give him a small nod before turning back to see Benny's shining brown eyes. "I'll be there, Benny. Six p.m., right?"

"Yeah!" he shouts excitedly before turning his gaze to Dante. "That's right, isn't it, Dad?"

"Yep, six sharp." I know he added that last part for my benefit.

His need to protect his children is valid, especially when I've repeatedly disappointed them, but I won't anymore. I'm going to do better. I *want* to do better.

Chapter Forty-Four

Lark

Tuesday, April 29, 2025

I hear a knock at my door minutes after showering and changing into my pajamas.

I look through the peephole and see Gianni standing there with Pickles, both of them decked out in sports gear for a team I don't recognize.

The moment I open the door, Gianni's arm thrusts forward. He pushes a purple shirt into my hands. "Are you doing anything tonight? I promised I'd go to my nephew's soccer game, and I want you to go with me if you're free?"

That makes my heart soar. He wants to hang out with me and include me in his family time?

"I'd love to. When do we have to leave?"

His smile lights his whole face up. "Ten minutes."

"I'll be ready in five," I tell him, rushing to my room to change.

***

We walk toward the grass field and make our way over to where Dante and Arielle are standing along the sidelines. Arielle waves her arms over her head excitedly as soon as she spots us, and Dante whips around at the commotion. A grin plasters itself on his handsome face, and I hear Gianni release a content sigh.

Opening my arms wide, I embrace Arielle, and she squeezes me so tightly to her chest that I'm afraid I'll pop. "Thank you so much for coming," she whispers before releasing me.

Dante is nothing like what I'd expect if I just saw him in passing and had never met him before. He's covered in dark tattoos, his dark eyes and hair creating an almost dangerous quality to his look, but he's all smiles and sweet words. He wraps his hulking frame around me and presses a kiss to either of my cheeks.

"The boys will be ecstatic that you both made it," he tells us. "Mom and Dad are over there." He points behind us to where Gloria and Angelo are seated beside the bleachers.

I know from the news reports I read about their family that Gloria and Alessandro both have multiple sclerosis, and Gianni confirmed it the other night. I just hope that modern medicine keeps Alessandro out of a wheelchair.

"The others should be here soon, but Kat got caught up with a patient, so they might be a little late." Gianni nods, placing his large hand at the base of my spine and leading me over to his parents.

***

"Yes! That's my little man!" Gloria shouts from beside me, her hands turning red from the amount of clapping she's been doing since the game started.

Sammy and Benny throw us wide smiles each time they pass us on the field, and it's clear how much actually showing up for them means to not only them, but Gianni and his entire family too.

The boys are racing up the field, showing off for their Uncle Gi, and frankly, I'm impressed. These two have some moves on them.

Gianni's finally letting loose, just enough that when Sammy scores the winning goal, he jumps up from his seat, dropping my hand in my lap as he hollers out to him, "Heck yeah, Sammy! Show 'em how it's done!"

I can't help the grin I'm wearing as I take it all in. It must be such a privilege to have a family so invested in your success.

***

"Uncle Gi! Uncle Gi! You made it!" Two little boys come running toward the stands after their winning game.

The smaller one, Benny, catapults himself into Gianni's arms. He holds him close, ruffling his hair. "Good game, Benny."

Sammy sidles up to us. "Thanks for coming," he says, much more timid than his brother.

Gianni gives him a smile in response, and the whole family congratulates them, tossing the boys around for hugs. They invite me to get ice cream with them, but I have to pick up an early shift, so I have to decline.

***

"Thanks for tagging along," Gianni tells me as he drives us back to our apartment building. His hand grips my thigh tightly at every red light but returns to the steering wheel the moment the light is green.

"Anytime," I answer truthfully. I'll go anywhere this man takes me.

"Do you need a snack before we get back? I don't want your blood sugar to drop," he tells me, and his thoughtfulness warms my heart.

"I'm okay. I just checked my continuous glucose monitor before we got in the car," I tell him with a small smile.

He eyes me speculatively. "Would you mind explaining how that works to me? I've looked into it, and it seems like it's just kind of always checking your sugars, but there were so many brands, and even within the brand that you use, there were a few different kinds."

Heat creeps up my chest. "You were researching diabetes?"

He clears his throat. "Uh, yeah. I just want to make sure you're safe."

This man.

"The CGM I have checks my sugar constantly, just like any other continuous glucose monitor, but each company has its own devices. Mine can connect to a receiver, a watch, or an app on my phone, which is my preference," I explain. "It's got a wire-thin filament that stays in my skin, and I wear it all day, in the shower or wherever. I change it once a week, but some people change theirs every ten days. I just know I won't remember to change mine unless it's always on the same day of the week. It checks my sugar levels all day and uploads the data to an app on my phone." I open the app so I can show him what the interface looks like. "I have mine set so that if my sugar falls below seventy, an alarm will go off through the app, so I know to drink some juice or get anything high carb in my body. On days when my sugar gets too high, I feel crappy for hours, even after I've corrected it. It's a constant battle to reach some semblance of homeostasis."

"So the day you had that episode, why didn't an alarm go off?" he asks, his brows pinching together.

"Because I had already taken my CGM off, thinking I was going to change it out, but then I realized I didn't have any insulin and forgot to put another CGM on. It was just a string of bad luck that day."

He hums beside me. "Is there a certain brand of that glucagon I should get? I'd just like to have it in case something like that happens again."

My throat feels thick as tears prick my eyes. We pull into the parking lot. "Anything will do, thank you," I tell him, holding back the tears that are threatening to spill over.

Chapter Forty-Five

Gianni

Wednesday, April 30, 2025

I'm sitting at my laptop, staring at the screen. My heart is pounding inside my chest with the growing unease wrestling inside me.

I'm really doing this. I'm actually speaking to a psychiatrist.

The loading symbol in the center of the video call finally stops, replaced by a smiling middle-aged man sitting in front of a cherrywood bookshelf.

"Good afternoon, I'm Dr. Slader. Would you mind confirming your name and date of birth before we get started?"

Once I do, we get into it, and slowly, the nausea starts to subside. "So I see you filled out the forms I sent ahead of time. I appreciate that because it allows us more time to get into what you've written and allows us to discuss a plan that works best for you and your schedule and meets you where you're at right now."

I like that this is a discussion and not just him telling me what *he* thinks I need to do to get better. "Do you mind if I ask you some questions about that form?"

"Of course not. Go right ahead," he urges me.

"Okay, so the PHQ-9 is a screening tool for depression, right?"

"Yes, it allows us to look objectively at what you've been going through without allowing subjective opinions to muddle your diagnosis. But at the end of the day, whether we diagnose you with one thing versus another doesn't matter as much as working through what it is that *you* want to overcome."

"That makes sense, I guess. So, where do we go from here?" I ask, feeling better about this whole situation. I like that I can just shut my laptop if this becomes too overwhelming for me, and the fact that I've never met this person in the real world is also really helpful.

"Well, let's start by discussing some answers you filled out on the form and determine from there. Sound like a plan?"

I nod, and that's exactly what we do. We spend the next forty-five minutes going over all of my answers, and at the end, unsurprising to anyone, I'm diagnosed with persistent and major depressive disorder. I met the criteria of PDD as a result of the length of time I've felt this way and MDD because of the situations that exacerbated it.

"It sounds like at one point you hadn't been open to speaking with a therapist, but you might be more open to that now, is that right?" I really appreciate that he doesn't put words in my mouth and clarifies the things I've said. That's been a huge fear of mine going into this.

"That's right. I think I'd benefit from just getting some things off my chest, but I'm also open to learning some healthier coping mechanisms rather than just sleeping the day away," I say, sucking in a breath through my nose as I try to steady my breathing before speaking the next words. "I also think it's time to try medication too."

"That's really great, Gianni. It's clear that you've come a long way from your initial feelings toward your mental health to where you are now, and I'm truly so excited to see where you go from here with the right support. I have a colleague in my office who can see you as early as this Friday for your first therapy session. Does that work?"

We get it scheduled, and when we're done, we discuss medication. "So there are a lot of medications that work very well for depression, but I'd like to start you off with what we consider 'first-line' therapy. That would be a medication called an SSRI or selective serotonin reuptake inhibitor, which essentially means that this medication blocks your body from getting rid of the serotonin you produce naturally and allows you to maintain more of that. Serotonin is a neurotransmitter or hormone produced in the brain that regulates mood and allows you to experience emotions, such as happiness. It plays a huge role in regulating your mind and body, but as with any medication, there are potential side effects."

He spends the next couple of minutes going over those with me. "The most common side effect we see with these medications is sexual dysfunction. Now, some people would say that if they had to choose between not being depressed and having a quality sex life, they'd rather not have depression, but I'm here to tell you that you don't have to choose. I find all too often that people get help, take these medications, and see tremendous improvements. But they also experience sexual side effects, and rather than saying something, they remain quiet. There's no reason to do so though. Yes, it's true that it can be very scary to find something that works for you and then potentially have to stop it and try something else because of a side effect that may not be hindering your well-being *too* drastically, but there *are* other options. And again, you may not experience these side effects at all. It doesn't happen to everyone, but I just want you to be fully aware that if they do, just let me know, and we'll try something else. Medicine has come such a long way in the last several decades. If you have any concerns at all, please don't hesitate to reach out."

I'm not exactly thrilled at the idea of my libido suddenly tanking, especially knowing that Lark felt so undesirable in her last relationship. But the fact that he's making sure I know that it's a possibility ahead of time makes me feel a lot better.

"I won't. Seriously, thank you for going over all of that with me. I just have one last question before I let you go."

He nods, urging me to go on. "How long does this sort of thing take to work?"

"It's different for everyone, but typically, you'll start to see an improvement in your mood after about two weeks, but it reaches its peak efficacy at around four to six weeks. So give it about a month or two and if you don't see much improvement, we'll try something else out. There's no reason to suffer in silence," he assures me.

There's no reason to suffer in silence.

That's something Lark has told me in her own way many times now, and I think I'm finally starting to understand the truth behind that statement.

"Thank you, Dr. Slader. I appreciate your time, and I look forward to following up next week," I tell him sincerely.

"You're very welcome, Gianni. It was great getting to meet you, and I'm excited to hear about your progress next week. Have a great rest of your day," he tells me before ending the call.

Now that I've taken some time for myself, it's time to show my girl just how dedicated I am to *her* happiness.

Chapter Forty-Six

Gianni

Thursday, May 1, 2025

L ark has to work late tonight, so it's the perfect day to finish my surprise for her.

Luckily, my mom has been seeing Lark's best friend, Kira, for her hair ever since they first combined their book clubs. I was able to contact her about helping me with this plan for Lark.

> **Kira**
> She's going to love it! I'll text you when she's on her way home from work.

> You're the best. Thanks.

> **Kira**
> Anything for Lark.

I enter the door code, heading in per Kira's instructions.

Rex pops his head up to glare at me but quickly curls back up on his bed sleepily. Kira said she was already over during her lunch break to take him on a walk, so he should be okay for a while.

I toss out her old flowers, replacing them with the new ones I got today before heading into the guest room.

The room is bare, with nothing but an easel, a single box of paints and brushes, and an air mattress in the center of the room, half deflated.

I make several trips to my car and back, bringing up all the supplies I got this morning. I may have gone a bit overboard, but there's nothing I wouldn't do to make this woman smile. She deserves a space to relax and enjoy the things that bring her peace.

Kira said she prefers oil paints and watercolors but dabbles in a little of everything, so that's what I got. *Everything*.

I have all the boxes stacked in the living room, bringing them in one by one as I unbox the furniture and build each piece. When I'm finished, two of the four walls are lined with interconnected shelving and tables to give her space for her projects to dry, a place to draw, and lots of room for her brushes and other supplies.

I insert the little organizers, separating everything by type and color, and then move on to the brushes. I place the canvases in their holders, with the largest ones in the back.

This is a rental, and while I'll gladly replace the carpet before she leaves, I don't want her to feel she needs to hold back in here.

After unrolling the massive paint splatter rug, I set up her easel, placing a small stool I painted with little red songbirds and pink and yellow flowers up the legs in front of the easel. I put the finishing touches on the room, setting up the hooks along the sides of the furniture for her paint smocks to hang and plugging in the essential oil diffuser and Bluetooth speaker.

I step out of the room to view it all put together. It's perfect, just like her.

It'll look even better once she hangs some of her artwork on the walls, but it should have everything she needs, and the huge window should provide the perfect amount of lighting.

My phone vibrates in my pocket.

Kira
> She's on her way home. Should be about 25 mins.

> Just finished, thanks.

I snap a picture and send it to Kira before gathering all the boxes and trash, hauling that down to the dumpster. I grab Pickles from my apartment and take her on a walk, waiting for Lark's arrival.

Mon Petite Rouge
> I'll be home in ten. Wanna come over for dinner? I'm thinking tacos.

> I'd love to. See you soon.

Chapter Forty-Seven
Lark

I step into my apartment, with Tiny trotting behind me.

He sticks his nose in the air, sniffing around. Something feels different, but I'm not sure what it is.

Gianni
> Tacos ordered for delivery. I'll be up in twenty so you can shower.

Gianni
> Unless you need help with that, of course.

I roll my eyes at that. He's certainly gotten more outspoken since we first met.

"Alright, Rex, let's go on a walk before Gianni gets here."

***

Gianni's fingers tangle in my damp strands, drawing my mouth to his. His tongue swipes into my mouth, and a zing of pleasure shoots to my center. A moan slips past my lips.

There's a loud knock at the door.

He chuckles, pulling back from me. "Must be the tacos," he says, heading to answer the door.

When he returns, he's got a huge paper bag in his arms, but he makes no effort to bring them to the couch. "Can I show you something before we eat?"

My brows pinch, but I stand. "Sure, what is it?"

He takes my hand in his, the bag of food still in one arm. "Close your eyes, and let me guide you."

My suspicion is building, but I have no idea what he could be up to.

I do as he asks and let him guide me across the hard floor. The soft click of a door opening is the only sound until he says, "Open your eyes, little red."

My lids jolt open at the command, and shock steals the breath from my lungs.

My barren, sad guest room with nothing more than an air mattress is now the art studio of my dreams.

There are rows of white cabinets with supplies on top, and my easel is set up with the sweetest stool tucked under it.

Tears prick my eyes. "How?" My voice cracks on the word.

He wraps his arm around me, pulling my body into his side. "My mom sees Kira for her hair appointments, so I got her information, and she offered to help me out." He tells me this like it's no big deal.

He went out of his way to find my best friend's contact info just so he could do something so unbelievably sweet for me. And he thinks it's *nothing*.

Gianni guides me farther into the room, taking a seat in the middle of the vibrant rug. "Take a look around, and we can eat on the floor in here." He chuckles.

Making my way through the room, I scour through the drawers and organizers, gaping at it all as Gianni sits patiently on the floor with our food laid out in front of him.

When the initial shock wears off, I rush to him and fall into his lap. Wrapping my arms around his neck, I press kisses to his cheeks, his forehead, and the tip of his nose. Hot tears leak from my eyes, falling silently down my cheeks. *This man is so fucking sweet.* I want to shrink him down and put him in my pocket to carry around every day for the rest of my life.

Gianni rubs reassuring circles down my spine, and his eyes glimmer. "I had my first psychiatry appointment yesterday," he admits.

I'm taken aback by his statement, but pride fills me. "That's incredible, Gi. How'd it go?"

He takes a moment before answering. "Really well, I think. He and I spoke about my history a bit, and he explained that he thinks that while I have a lot of trauma that hasn't helped the situation, it's also clear that I have a chemical imbalance causing a lot of these feelings. We discussed medication a bit, and I decided that I'd like to give it a try. So he helped me schedule another appointment with him for next Friday as well as one with a colleague in his clinic for tomorrow. So on Friday, I'll start seeing the psychologist for therapy as well."

I pull him into me, burying my face in his hair. "I'm so fucking proud of you, Gi."

"Thank you," he whispers. "If it weren't for you," he chokes out, "I'm not sure I'd have ever gotten here."

I burrow myself farther into him. "Yes, yes, you would have," I tell him firmly.

"I appreciate the confidence, little red, but I'm really not so sure I'd..." He doesn't finish his sentence, which alarms me. My heart is clenching in my chest as the room fills with an eerie fullness that tugs me under its cloud of darkness.

I pull away just enough to look up into those haunted blue eyes. "What do you mean, *mon ciel étoilé*?"

His eyes are brimming with tears, the red, puffy skin making them appear an even brighter blue. "When we met, I was in the deepest depths of my depression. It was nearly impossible to get up and out of bed, and most days, I just didn't, aside from taking care of Pickles. And even then, I did the bare minimum. I've never been the happiest person, but after Alex died, it was like I had died too. A lot of the time, I felt like I wished I had and..." He looks away from me, sucking in a deep breath before meeting my eyes again. My heart is pounding at an erratic rhythm in my chest with every word he speaks. "For a while, there were very few days where I hadn't contemplated taking my life just to make it stop. To make the guilt and the agony just *stop*. And then there was you," he says with a small smile that makes my heart soar. "You showed me kindness and patience, and you didn't treat me like I was broken. You weren't afraid to joke with me, poke fun at me, or be one hundred percent yourself with me, and it made me realize that maybe if I showed myself just an ounce of that kindness, I could start to feel things too. I'm not saying you've cured me, but even if I were to never see you again after today, I'd be thankful for the moments I've had with you."

Tears continue to spill down my face; the words I want to say are lodged in my throat as he swipes the pads of his thumbs over the tears. Gianni pulls me back into his lap, pressing kisses to the crown of my head, mumbling words that I can't completely make out.

We sit in each other's embrace for so long that the sun starts to set outside of the large window. When our tears have dried and some of that dark fog has lifted from the room, Gianni tugs my earlobe between his teeth. He chuckles deeply when I flip around in his lap, straddling him.

A wide smile tugs at my lips when I'm greeted by the most beautiful smile on his face. And I can't help myself.

I lean forward abruptly, pushing him onto the ground and wiggling my fingers under his arms, tickling him. His eyes go wide with surprise, but his smile turns mischievous as he flips us over, mercilessly tickling my sides.

"Stop! Stop!" I shout between giggles, but he's relentless.

"You started this." He laughs, with no sign of giving up.

"Please, stop! It's too much!" I shriek, and he nuzzles his face into my neck, his fingers finally stopping their onslaught.

"The only thing that's going to be too much is when I fuck you into your mattress tonight, and I won't stop until I hear you scream just like you did moments ago," he tells me. Heat sears through me, and I can't stop my thighs from clenching at the thought. *I can't wait.*

Chapter Forty-Eight
Lark

I crawl into bed, my whole body wrapped in that warm feeling I always have when I'm with Gi.

When he comes out of the bathroom, I expect to see him ready for bed, but instead, he enters the dark room with the lights off, and I'm momentarily blinded.

A chill shivers down my spine as I hear his next words.

"Little red," he chides, his voice filled with a mocking quality that both infuriates me and turns me on in equal measure. I blink rapidly, my eyes adjusting to the dark room, and when I see him looming over me, it clicks.

Ghostface.

"I've been waiting all day for this... Watching your every move, taking in the gorgeous curve of your ass, and imagining how those lovely bowed lips of yours would look curled around my cock as you choke on it within an inch of your life." He chuckles darkly, further encroaching on my space.

Through the mesh and plastic of the mask, his voice is even deeper, reaching a bravado so uncharacteristic of him. The sound rushes straight to my core, where I clench involuntarily.[1]

He crowds my space, his hands settling on either side of my hips as he brings his face to my ear. "Is this okay?" he asks me, his voice barely above a whisper as he reminds me exactly who's underneath that mask.

I nod instinctually, fully aware that I'm safe with him—*with Gianni.*

He hums beside me, unmoving as he waits for my answer, and I realize he can't see me or my nod of approval. "Yes," I croak out past my trepidation.

"Such a good girl," he tells me. "I bet you're absolutely soaked for me, *mon petite rouge.*"

Who is this man kidding? I'm *always* soaked for him. And no mask is about to change that. *Especially* since this is exactly what I'd asked for.

He stands, pulling away from me abruptly, and the loss of his body heat sends a tendril of ice racing down my spine.

"Get on your knees and prove just how excited you are to *scream* for me tonight," he tells me, his voice so deep it reverberates through the room around me.

I slide off the edge of the bed and to my knees, obeying as he steps out of his briefs, completely bare for me. Except for the mask, of course.

He grips my roots roughly, and I open my mouth on a gasp. He uses the opportunity to plunge deep inside my throat, my eyes watering as I gasp and gag around him. My hands shoot out, clinging to his muscular thighs, the hair rough beneath my fingertips.

"That's right," he taunts. "*Fucking choke on it.*"

He fucks my throat, my head bobbing up and down his thick length as he relentlessly uses me for his pleasure. I'm dripping wet as my lips repeatedly meet his hips, and he abruptly pulls me from his shaft.

---

1. **Animal I Have Become — Three Days Grace**

I collapse, my hands sliding to the ground to hold myself up as I heave, sucking air into my lungs.

He flicks the bathroom light on and illuminates the bedroom through the bottom of the door. It's just enough to make him out in all his glory.

"Get up," he grunts as he slowly strokes himself. When my brain takes too long to catch up to his demands, his head tilts slowly, almost menacingly, as he assesses me. He grips my face tightly, squeezing my cheeks together as he stares down at me. "I said—" He tugs on my face, not hard enough to hurt me, but enough to will my body to follow his earlier command. "Get. *Up*."

My cheeks burn as his hand remains clamped down on them, but my thighs are so slick I wouldn't dare lie and say I'm not thoroughly enjoying myself.

"Remember your safe word, little red," he tells me, angling himself over me, crowding me, and suddenly, all of the air has officially left my lungs.

He whispers his next words, and my limbs feel weak, unable to hold me up much longer as my core tightens. "Because tonight, I'm coming for your screams." When he drops his hand, he drags his masked face over the bridge of my nose.

"Now *run*."

My eyes widen, and a moment passes before my brain reconnects with my legs, and I take off. I yank the door open, knowing full well if he wanted to catch me immediately, he already would have. I run across the living room, my head whipping from left to right as I try to decide where the fuck to run to in this godforsaken tiny-ass apartment.

The dogs are lying in their bed, and embarrassment at being caught like this by our fucking *dogs* rushes through me, but Rex practically rolls his damn eyes and tucks his face back into Tiny's side.

Suddenly, the lights go out around me, and I realize I'm stuck. "Fuck," I whisper.

I rush to the bay window, and I'm so damn glad I put up both blinds *and* curtains. I crawl up onto the ledge, perching myself there and hoping like hell he didn't see me.

I don't know why I'm trying so hard to hide in the first place. Hell, I *want* to be found.

I'd love nothing more than to find out exactly what my punishment is.

I hear him tsking as he strolls through the room. "I can hear you breathing, little red. You aren't very good at this game we're playing now, are you?"

Sucking in a deep breath of air, I hold it, letting it out slowly as I consider my next move, but his words float through the room again, a deep, gravelly sound that makes me crawl out of my skin in the most delicious way.

"Are you wet for me?"

A moment later, "That's okay. You don't have to answer because I know you are positively *soaked* for my cock. And I can't fucking wait to dole out your punishment when I find you."

I inhale sharply, and I see his head snap in my direction. He prowls over here but keeps his distance. "Come out, come out wherever you are," he says, chuckling darkly.

Trepidation sparks up the base of my spine, and his next words sear through me. He stops just two feet from me as I hide behind these curtains.

"Are you scared, little red?" he whispers, his voice so low that if he weren't right in front of me, I would never have heard him.

"If not, *you should be*," he says, his hands jolting forward and gripping me through the curtain.

I release a loud yelp and hear Rex release a single warning bark that makes Gianni chuckle lightly.

Using that as a distraction, I push him off me, throwing myself off the ledge of the windowsill and running around to the back of the couch.

"Let me make myself abundantly clear," he says, staring right at me through the dark room. "When I find you, *I fuck you*. And you'll be begging for my mercy."

Before I can move, he's running toward me, jumping over the front of the couch and landing behind me. A scream leaves my lungs, but an arm snakes around me, pulling my back to his chest as he brings his palm to my mouth, effectively muffling my screams.

"It's time to pay up," he tells me, his voice gruff, brushing against my skin like sandpaper. "Hold your screams for when you're coming undone around my cock."

I feel his dick nestling between my ass cheeks as he thrusts his hips against me, showing me exactly how much this turns him on.

When I start to relax into his touch, he releases his grip on me, but only long enough to swing me over his shoulder and drag me back to bed.

He throws me down into the center of the bed, and I scoot away, moving toward the wall as he crawls toward me from the end of the bed.

"There's no escaping now. Take those panties off."

My fingertips graze the edges of the white lace, and slowly, I slide them down my thighs, but before I can toss them to the side, he snatches them from my hand and pushes me flat against the bed, a hand on my chest.

My eyes go wide as I realize what he's doing a moment too late.

He stuffs the panties in my mouth, gagging me as he says, "Taste yourself, *mon petite rouge*. Taste how fucking drenched and needy you are for my cock. How goddamn much you *love* the idea of being chased. Of being *punished*."

I squeeze my thighs together, doing anything in my power to chase the friction I so desperately need.

"Absolutely not. When I finally let you come tonight, it'll be because of *me*. Now be a good little songbird and spread those thighs nice and wide for Daddy Ghostface," he demands, his words holding a humorous quality while also remaining dead serious.

This is fucking torture. Need is practically weeping from my pores.
Why did I ask for this again?

Oh, right... Because sometimes, I just want to be fucked like a dirty little slut, and Gi makes me feel safe to explore that.

When I don't obey in the split second he expects me to, he wrenches my thighs open, his fingertips digging into my flesh as he pulls my body down the bed. I don't have a single second to regain control of my breathing as he lines the head of his swollen, dripping cock up with me and plunges in.

A shudder wracks my body, quaking through me as his hips meet mine in one swift movement. I can barely breathe.

Grabbing the lace panties from my mouth, I toss them to the side, and luckily, he's so lost in the feel of me spasming around him that he doesn't seem to notice. Or at least, he doesn't seem to care enough to punish me for it. Not yet, anyway.

It was a fleeting thought because as soon as the words fly through my head, his hand darts out just as quickly, wrapping around my throat. His thumb digs into the soft skin at the base of my neck, pressing down with so much force that my vision is narrowing. Before I can lose myself to the darkness, he releases his hold on me.

He grips my calves, bringing them up to rest on his shoulders as he takes me even deeper. My mind is spinning, my body floating higher and higher as heat licks up my spine. A moan leaves me, followed by a plea that sounds so unfamiliar to my own ears.

"Gi, *please*, let me come," I beg.

"I don't know who *Gi* is, but tonight, the only name that'll be grazing that twisted little tongue is *mine*."

My eyes widen, and the pad of his rough, calloused thumb glides over my clit. My body bucks off the bed, my calves tightening around his head and neck as my hands grapple for purchase in the sheets.

I'm about to come; I'm seconds away as he plucks his thumb away, leaving me wanton and aching. "Oh god," I cry. "Please, *Ghost*, let me come!" I scream, begging for my release.

"What a good little slut." He chuckles darkly, returning his thumb to my clit. It swirls the sensitive bundle of nerves, my body writhing and quaking as I shatter around him.

I see stars, my vision blurry as I come hurtling back down to earth, my core clenching as he comes with me. "Oh fuck," he groans out. "Such a tight, sweet little cunt. I could fill you up all goddamn night," he tells me, and the words both sound like a promise... and a *threat.*

My breathing finally starts to settle, and as it does, I'm finally able to open my eyes. Gianni rips the mask off, tossing it over the side of the bed, and reaches for the lamp on the nightstand, flicking it on before returning his gaze to me.

His bright-blue eyes are dancing as he smirks at me. "As much as I loved every second of that, *mon petite rouge*, it turns out that I'm not even a little bit okay with another man *or ghost's* name leaving your mouth."

Gi slides up the length of my body, never removing himself from inside me as he claims my mouth with his.

His tongue swipes across the seam of my lips, begging for entrance. My lips part, allowing his tongue to tangle with mine. He sucks my lower lip between his teeth, nipping the swollen skin as he releases my mouth and sits back on his haunches, finally gliding himself out of me, still mostly hard.

Just as I think we're done for the night, he slides down my body, burying his face between my legs.

He breathes me in, licking a hot trail up my seam and spreading me wide with his fingers.

"You're fucking gorgeous," he praises me. His hot breath coasts over my clit, and he dips his chin, sucking it into his mouth and swirling his tongue, sliding down my center as he laps at me.

My body is spent, and yet, it behaves exactly as he wants it to, coaxing me to the edge of another orgasm.

Before I know it, my thighs are crushing his head, his scruff tickling my sensitive skin as he drives his tongue inside me, unabashed at the combination of our arousal. He licks and slurps at my skin, electricity shooting through me.

My hand jolts out, gripping his roots as I call out, my hips jerking against his mouth. "Yes! Yes, Gi, oh god." I moan.

I ride the wave, coming down from the high of my second orgasm.

My eyes flutter closed when he removes his mouth from my overly sensitive core.

My eyes burst open as his mouth returns, shock rocking through me.

"Stop! Stop, stop, stop! It's too much!" I shout, repeating what I'd said earlier this afternoon. Gianni's tongue slides through me one last time, causing me to buck off the bed.

"Just like that." He chuckles. "*That's* exactly how I wanted you to sound."

My body is buzzing with that familiar feeling of happiness. It sings through my blood every time I'm with this man.

He kisses the insides of my thighs, trailing up my abdomen, paying special attention to the bruises where I inject my insulin and then to the CGM on my deltoid. He kisses that, too, and looks up to meet my gaze. "Why don't you get an insulin pump so you don't have to keep jabbing yourself all the time?"

A sly smile grazes my lips. "How is it that you can go from 'Daddy Ghostface,'" I say, using air quotes as I chuckle, "to being concerned about my insulin?" I lift a brow at him as he repositions himself beside me, pressing a chaste kiss to my cheek.

"Because I'm a multifaceted man. What can I say?" He winks. "Now, please, answer the question, *mon petite rouge.*"

"I've thought about it, and frankly, it'd be a good idea to do with how busy my schedule can get, but they're just expensive, and the last time I really considered one, I was a lot more self-conscious about my body. So that played a role in my decision not to get one at the time too. I think I've just gotten so used to doing it this way that I haven't put much thought into changing it up."

He hums softly, then props himself up on his elbow beside me. "I know your father would give you the world," he tells me, and I can't disagree. "So why would money be an issue, then?"

I lean farther into my pillows, tugging the sheet over my body and rolling onto my side to face him.

"Ever since my mom left, my dad has done everything for me. He's given me a life most people could never even dream up. I owe *everything* to him, and yet he wants nothing in return. He's just so content as long as I'm happy. Did you know that most veterinarians, at least in the US, will spend most of their careers trying to pay back their student loans?"

His brows crease, confusion clear on his face from the turn in conversation. He shakes his head but remains quiet.

"Well, most do, but I never had to worry about that because I *always* knew that I had my dad to fall back on. So when he asked me what I wanted to do with my degree, I told him about my plans for the clinic and made it clear that I wanted to have it be donation based. I never wanted to turn someone away because they couldn't afford our services," I tell him, and the way his eyes soften makes my heart feel like mush.

"All too often, I see people searching for advice online, and there are always nasty comments ridiculing these people for not just taking their pet to the vet. But that's just such a privileged way of thinking about it," I say, my hands now flailing as I become more and more passionate about the conversation.

"Yes, if your pet is sick, you should take them to get help like you would your children, but not everyone has the means. And then there are the people who say if you can't afford to care for your pet properly, why have one at all? Who's to say these people have always been living in the current circumstances?"

Gianni clamps a hand on my thigh, squeezing it as he listens, seemingly enraptured by every detail. "Maybe they just lost their job or their home to a natural disaster or literally any number of things that could change a person's life to make something as simple as a vet visit nearly impossible. So, that's where Toute la Famille pet clinic started," I say, smiling brightly.

"I wanted to offer around-the-clock veterinary care to those who need it while only accepting the bare minimum payment from those who can afford it, and those who can't, well, they're supported by donations from people who visit our website and on occasion, from my dad when I come crawling to him for the money. He has literally never cared, but I try my best to support myself, so he knows that one day when he's not around, I'll be okay." I give him a small smile, squeezing my hands together, suddenly feeling shy. "Sorry, that was a lot more detail than you probably needed."

He cups my jaw, dragging it up so I can see his face more clearly. "I want every detail you're willing to give me," he says, pressing a tender kiss to my forehead, and more butterflies flap around in my gut.

"So, you don't want to bother him with the cost of a pump? I've been reading up on the different kinds offered, and some of them are covered by insurance too. Though there are a couple at the top of my list due to reliability, so if those aren't covered, I'd like to just buy one for you as a gift," he tells me. "The one I'd really like you to get is called a tubeless insulin pump or something. It's compatible with your CGM and it uses an automated insulin delivery system that determines when and how much insulin you need based on the numbers recorded by your CGM." *He's been researching insulin pumps for me?*

Tears prick the corners of my eyes, and not for the first time tonight. *Where did I find this man?* He's so much better than I could've thought up, even in my wildest dreams.

"I've also read that the majority of people your age with type 1 diabetes have had a pump most of their lives since they're more reliable and easier than jabbing a kid multiple times a day. Why didn't you get one as a kid?" he asks. Nothing in his tone is judgemental; he's just curious.

"Type 1 diabetes is usually diagnosed in childhood, and there are two common age ranges when it first becomes apparent. That's ages four to six years and ten to fourteen years, though it's diagnosed in babies and everyone in between too. I was diagnosed at fourteen, and since I played contact sports, I refused to get one even though my dad pleaded with me. He was always big on autonomy as long as I wasn't doing anything that could hurt myself or others. So when I explained that not only was I embarrassed about wearing a pump, but that I'd read that the tubing gets tangled and causes the possibility of injury, he let me continue with the injections."

"How'd you make it through veterinary school having to manage your insulin without a pump?"

"I had been doing it like I am now for so many years that it's just become second nature, like brushing your teeth or showering. And like I said, I haven't really thought about it recently, but I'll look into my insurance and see what it covers," I assure him. "I think it could be nice to not have to worry about dosing myself or running out of insulin. I just have to make sure to refill the pump, but it'll remind me. Most new ones will."

"And what about if your insurance doesn't cover it? Will you please tell me?"

I nod, knowing he won't let this go even if I ask him to. He cares, and that's more than can be said for my ex.

"I'll tell you if it doesn't. Unfortunately, the thing about running a clinic that's as close to nonprofit as possible is that I don't really make any money at all, and I still have to pay my employees, so I don't have a whole lot of savings, but I'm lucky. I still have more than I need."

"Well, if there's anything you *want* or *need,* you just say the word, and it's yours, okay? I have far more than *I* need, and I'm happy to spend it on my girl." His words swirl around inside me. There he goes again, being the most incredible person I know and making me feel like maybe he feels the same about me too. *My girl.*

Before I can ask him the question that's sitting at the tip of my tongue, he says, "Will you tell me more about your mom?"

"What do you wanna know?" I ask.

"Anything you want to tell me," he says. His features are relaxed as he pulls me closer to his chest, waiting for my response.

"Well, she was always the brightest person in any room. Figuratively and literally." I chuckle.

"She wore these bright-colored sundresses everywhere and always looked like she was moments from heading to the beach on any given day. She had this way of understanding exactly what you were going through without saying as much and just letting you be so you could simmer in it. I always knew I could work through anything that was bothering me so long as she was by my side."

The memories that stir inside me warm me to my core as I'm brought back to the months before she'd left. "She taught me to paint, and for my birthday, she would take me anywhere I wanted to go so we could collect an item for each year of my life and turn it into art so we could hold onto those memories forever."

Sadness threatens to take hold as I think of that twelfth birthday. We'd never made it to that one. "She was the best person I knew, second only to my dad," I joke. Truthfully, they were always equals. "Even when she'd have bad days or weeks and wouldn't take her medication, she was always in there somewhere. Her bold ideas were just larger and all-consuming during those times, but she was still at the forefront of them."

Gianni sits in silence, taking in my words and allowing me to sit with the heavy feeling, not trying to use humor to break through the shift in the air surrounding us. Much like my mom, he acts as a calming presence to just let me feel.

"From what Dante remembers of our mom and the family videos we grew up watching, it sounds like our moms were a lot alike," he says, his voice quiet and thoughtful.

"I like to think they'd be proud of us," I tell him, my voice small. He pulls me into his chest, and I bury my face into his comforting embrace.

"Do you know why I call you my starry sky?" I finally ask, my voice barely above a whisper, and I'm hoping he's had some time to finally work this out for himself.

"No," he tells me simply. "But I'd like to understand." Gianni presses a kiss on the top of my head. Who'd have thought that something so simple could be the most comforting thing I've ever experienced?

I peek up at him, and wait until his eyes meet mine. "I call you my starry sky because even through all of that darkness swirling around in your head, you still manage to act as a bright star for those around you." I feel my cheeks heat, and the way his lips part convinces me to keep speaking. "As corny as it sounds, it's like you're the North Star, leading your loved ones home, even when you yourself have been led astray. I don't think you even realize the impact you have on the people around you." I whisper the last words. "I've only known you for such a short time, and you've brightened my life in nearly every moment of that time," I admit.

He runs a hand down the back of my head, pressing my cheek against his before he whispers against my ear, "*Thank you*."

Two simple words that mean so little when spoken from the mouth of someone else, but they weigh more than the entire universe when breathed past the lips of this incredible man.

Chapter Forty-Nine

Gianni

Friday, May 2, 2025

I can tell it's still early because the sun isn't up just yet, but then why is Lark not in bed? In her place is Rex, who has his scraggly ass pressed up against her pillow. I roll my eyes at him when he looks over his shoulder at me, one lip caught on his snaggletooth. I do my best to maneuver out of the bed, which is now filled with all three dogs, taking up every inch of moveable space.

I make my way into the empty living room and pad across the hard floors to where the door to her new art studio is cracked open.

The sight before me nearly takes my breath away.

Lark is sitting on the stool with a paintbrush in hand, and even though I know whatever she's painting on that massive canvas has got to be breathtaking in itself, I can't look away from her.

Her soft, auburn waves cascade over her slim shoulders. The sun is starting to rise through the window, and she's engulfed in their rays. *She looks beyond stunning,* and I can't take my eyes off her.

She must feel my eyes on her because she spins in her stool, her eyes wide when she sees me, but a slow smile turns her lips. "Good morning, handsome," she tells me, and I'll be damned if that doesn't make my heart rate pick up.

"Good morning, gorgeous," I say. My feet carry me to her, and she plops her brush down onto her palette before winding her arms around my neck. *I could wake up every day to this beautiful woman in my arms and die a happy man.*

"I'm sorry I interrupted."

She kisses the side of my neck, leaving warmth trailing down from that spot and into my heart below it.

"It's for the best. I've gotta get to work soon, and you," she says with a smile, pointing the tip of her finger into my chest, "have an appointment soon."

My brows raise in confusion, but I quickly remember what *appointment* she's referring to. I expected to be nervous thinking about this again, but instead, I'm excited? I'm not really sure if that's the right word for what I'm feeling, but I'm not torn up inside about it. I'm sort of looking forward to talking about the things that have bothered me for so long and seeing if there really is something I can do on my own to keep from letting these emotions drag me down.

This reminds me that I should take my medication soon. I picked it up yesterday and took my first dose in the morning. Thankfully, I didn't experience a headache or nausea like Dr. Slader said I might after the first few doses, so hopefully, that remains the same. As far as the sexual dysfunction, that hasn't been a problem yet, but I appreciate that Dr. Slader made me aware and went over options for changing medications if that does arise, though I imagine that side effect might take a while to rear its ugly head.

"Well then, we should both get going," I say with a laugh, picking her up. Her legs wind around my waist, and I carry her into her bathroom, depositing her on the counter.

***

"Unless I can get someone else to cover for me, I think I'll have to come back here to sleep for a few hours and then work the night shift into tomorrow morning too," she tells me. Disappointment fills me, but I recognize that I can't have her with me all the time. As much as I'd love that, I also know that being content with my own company is just as important as enjoying the company of those around me.

"That's okay. I'll miss you," I tell her honestly, "but I'll see you tomorrow, right? And then I can tell you all about how my appointment went."

She smiles brightly at that. "I can't wait," she replies, standing on her tiptoes to press a warm kiss to my mouth. We lock up, and the dogs trot in front of us as we make our way to the elevator.

***

"I wouldn't say I really experience feelings of panic or anxiety so much as dread?" I say it like a question.

"Are you asking me or telling me? I'm not being flippant, by the way. I truly just want to know if you're struggling to put a name to the emotion or if you've already figured it out," Dr. Fasano says.

I take a moment to think about this before speaking. "I think the feeling is dread. It's not been so bad recently, but I worry that if I didn't have Lark around to remind me of the good things, I might find it easy to slip back into my usual way of thinking. I'm absolutely certain that I'm not projecting my feelings or using her as a distraction, but I think it's important for me to get my mind healthy with or without her."

Dr. Fasano gives me a small smile and says, "That's very insightful, Gianni, and I couldn't agree more. From everything you've explained so far, it seems this woman has had a positive impact on your life, likely because of her own ability to process her emotions in a healthy way. So I feel that she's been a good influence on you, but I don't believe you're trying to better yourself for her alone, which would be my concern. It seems pretty clear to me that you genuinely want to be better for *yourself* and that any self-improvement that might better her life as a result would just be the cherry on top, so to speak. Is that right?"

There's no doubt in my mind as I answer him. "Yes, that's right. I want to experience every emotion, but in ways and amounts, for lack of a better way of explaining that, that are considered normal, I guess. I don't want to be happy all the time or sad all the time. I just want to have better control of my emotions and feel the right things at the right times."

"And a lot of that will come with time as you and Dr. Slader work out your medications. Much of what you're feeling is a result of a chemical imbalance, but we can absolutely work toward handling your grief in a healthy way. Now that we've gone over a lot of your history, would you like to discuss a coping mechanism and maybe some homework to try out for the week?" he asks me. His desire to only go as in-depth as I'm comfortable with makes me feel even better than I had at the start of our conversation. So far, this seems to be going well.

"That sounds good," I agree.

"You mentioned on your intake questionnaire under hobbies that you play several instruments. Is this something you do because you find it enjoyable or because someone told you that you were good at it, and you felt you had to, or something similar?"

Without hesitation, I tell him, "I love music. I loved playing and singing and teaching myself how to play a new instrument."

His face lights up. "You said you 'loved' those things. What's changed?"

I have to fight the groan making its way up my throat. "I've been playing more recently, but not nearly as much as I used to. It was something Alex and I used to do together, mostly, and since he's been gone, it just doesn't feel as enjoyable."

"Is that because that emotion you describe as dread comes creeping in?" he asks with a heavy nod, gaining me the confidence I need to tackle this topic.

"Yeah, I guess it just makes me think a lot about Alex and all the memories we shared and the ones we'll never get to make," I answer, but a frog is lodged in my throat. I don't feel quite as sick talking about this as I'd expected to, but it definitely doesn't feel *good*.

"How about this, then? This week, I want you to play or sing whatever you want, and when you start to feel that dread creep in, I want you to just play past it. Maybe include your partner in the activity so you can start to develop new, happier memories. Then, when we meet next week, I want to discuss how it made you feel. If you think you can handle it, maybe jot down a few sentences about how you felt afterward so we can discuss it."

"That sounds like..." I hesitate. "Like a lot," I answer as panic threatens to seize me. I clench my eyes shut, dragging in a breath for four seconds, holding it for four, and breathing it out for four before opening my eyes. "But I'm willing to try." [1]

Dr. Fasano's lips curve into a smile. "That was very impressive, Gianni. The way you were able to sense your emotions trying to get the better of you, and then you were able to do something about it even with someone else watching. That was excellent," he praises. "And giving it a try is all I ask. Not every technique is going to work the same for everyone. If this doesn't work for you, we'll just try something new. Give it a shot, and if it

---

1. **Welcome to the Black Parade – My Chemical Romance**

proves to be too much, we'll reconsider what you might be ready for next week. Don't hesitate to call my office if you feel you need to speak with me sooner, okay?"

We finish up our conversation and end the call after scheduling another appointment right before my follow-up with Dr. Slader next week so it doesn't interfere too much with my soccer schedule.

Speaking of which, I have a game in a few hours that I need to get ready for.

Chapter Fifty

Lark

Saturday, May 3, 2025

"I'm hungry," I whine as we head back to our apartment building.

Gianni places his hand on my lower back, grinning at me as he turns me around to walk in the opposite direction. "Let's get lunch then."

"Ooh, I know just the place! It's close, and they're dog-friendly as long as we're out on the patio," I tell him, and a little squeal passes my lips.

His bright eyes crinkle at the corners as he extends his arm in front of us. "Lead the way, *mon petite rouge*."

A few minutes later, we're standing outside of the Rusty Dog Saloon, which has nothing to do with any of the above. It doesn't even have a Western theme, but they have the best live performers.

The hostess seats us at one of the metal tables along the sidewalk, the dark-green umbrella guarding our eyes from the sun.

Pickles and Tiny lie down under the table as Gianni and I take our seats across from one another.

After we order our food, I relax into the seat, letting the warm sun's rays soak into my skin.

"What's that smile for?" Gianni asks with a lilt in his voice.

"Oh, nothing," I tease. "I'm just with a really hot guy at one of my favorite burger spots on a beautiful day, and I'm enjoying it."

"You think I'm really hot?" he asks with a wink. He chuckles, already knowing the answer.

"Oh, for sure. *The hottest,*" I assure him, always wanting to feed his ego when I have the chance.

"Well, you, little red, are the most magnificent, gorgeous, breathtakingly stunning person to ever live. And you have a really fantastic ass." He smiles brightly, and his white teeth glimmer in the sun.

My heart stammers. No one has ever said anything remotely that kind to me. It was almost *poetic*?

"Gi, do you write music?" I ask, my brow lifting in question as I nibble on my bottom lip, waiting for the inevitable blush to climb up his neck.

His eyes cast downward, and his cheeks pinken, supplying the answer without speaking the words.

"You do! I knew it!" I shout, my smile beaming at him.

When those baby blues find my eyes, he asks, "How could you have known that?"

I shake my head and shoot him a little eye roll before explaining. "Sometimes, the things you say sound like song lyrics. They don't sound like the words of a thirty-two-year-old man, but I like them. And your voice sounds so melodious and smooth as if you're singing every word without actually doing so."

His dark brows crinkle. "I've never noticed."

"I don't think you would. It is *your* voice. You've lived with it your whole life."

He rolls his eyes playfully, bending to scratch Pickles and Tiny from under the table.

The live band has been setting up behind us, and it looks like they're finally ready to play.

"Hey, everyone, thanks for coming out today. I'm Jack Shadow, and we're The Ghosties."

They start off with a remix of some of my favorite nineties and early two-thousands punk-rock songs.

I stare at Gianni as he watches the band play, unknowingly bobbing his head and tapping his foot just the smallest bit. The waiter delivers our food, drawing his attention back to me.

"Why don't you do something like that? You love music, and it would be a good change of pace, I think. Besides, I bet your voice is incredible."

"No, I couldn't," he says, shaking his head dismissively. "I play for myself more than anything else." He brushes me off.

"*I* want to hear you sing and whatever else it is you like to do. You never told me—what instruments do you play?"

He finishes chewing and takes a sip of water before responding. "I play the guitar, piano, drums, harp, accordion, harmonica, clarinet, trumpet, French horn, violin, bass, and one year I went to Cuba to visit Alex's family, and his uncle taught me how to play the guiro and the batá drums."

A startled laugh nearly chokes me. "I probably should've asked what instruments *don't* you play, good lord," I tell him. "I tried to learn the violin in middle school, but I was so bad that the teacher had to call my dad and beg him to convince me to try just about anything else. That's how I started playing soccer."

His eyes widen. "How did I not know you play soccer?"

I laugh at that. "My father *owns* a soccer team. I figured that it went without saying. Besides, you know more about me after the last two months than my ex did after six years."

He slides his hand across the table, taking mine and bringing it to his lips. He presses a tender kiss to the inside of my wrist, then my knuckles. "Your *ex* wasn't worthy of any of your secrets, and neither am I. But I'll work toward earning them every day, regardless."

There he goes again, sending my heart fluttering in my chest.

I stare at our intertwined hands, and his words remind me that I never asked about his appointment yesterday. "How did your session go yesterday?"

His cheeks pinken, and it's just about the cutest fucking thing. "It went really well, actually. Dr. Fasano and I discussed a homework assignment for this week that I think you'll be interested in," he tells me with a small smile.

"Do tell," I say, leaning forward on my elbows.

"Well, he said for me to start playing music again, and if it feels right, to have you with me so I can start to associate it with making new, happy memories instead of thinking of it as something that just dredges up old memories of Alex and me."

He was talking about me with his therapist? God, this man.

"I'd love that if you think it's a good idea," I tell him honestly.

"Maybe when we get home after lunch?"

"Sounds like the perfect day," I answer. *The perfect day with the perfect person.*

Chapter Fifty-One
Gianni

"You are just such a good boy, Tiny!" Lark tells the massive Great Dane, scratching affectionately behind his ears.

"You wanna head to bed when we get inside and call *me* a good boy?" I grin, my filter wearing thin around her.

She halts her steps, staring at me, slack-jawed. "You'd actually be *okay* with that? I didn't necessarily think you were joking, but I wasn't sure you'd really be *this* willing when you offered to be," she lowers her voice to a whisper, leaning into me, "my sub."

I have to work to hold in the laughter threatening to spill from my lungs at how absurd it is that we're even having this conversation, but also at the fact that she's whispering on the sidewalk as if anyone else is actually around.

I bend down dramatically, brushing my lips along the shell of her ear. "With you? I'm serious about everything." I figure why not, right? I may as well keep voicing the shit in my head. It's what Alex had always told me to do, and before he died, I was actually starting to do just that. He'd be disappointed as hell that my progress took a deep dive after his death, but this? Speaking my mind and getting the girl? *This he'd be proud of.*

When I straighten, her eyes are wide, but a sly smirk fixes itself across her face. She reaches out with her freckled hand, grabbing mine firmly and dragging us toward our building.

Looking over her shoulder at me, she giggles. "I'm not sure if this is about to be your luckiest day or your most unfortunate, but I'm excited to find out."

The moment we're inside her apartment, she kicks the door closed, hurrying to unleash the dogs.

Her excitement is bubbling over, and it makes me a little nervous, but mostly, I just feel fucking euphoric that I'm capable of making her this happy for any reason at all.

Grabbing her by the waist, I carry her over my shoulder, slamming the door behind me and depositing her in the middle of her bed.

"I can walk, you know." She rolls her eyes at me, but there's no bite to her words.

"Let me see your phone," I say, extending my hand expectantly. She presses it against my palm, and I go to the app to check her sugars. The number's reassuring, so I turn her notification volume up before setting her phone down on the nightstand. "Alright, little red. No more playing around. What do *you* want?" She's got quite the list for us to cross off, and it's about time I start having her pick for herself.

She sucks her bottom lip between her teeth, fingers toying with the hem of her sleeve.

"Don't get shy with me now," I tell her playfully. "What happened to it being my lucky day?"

"Or your most unfortunate." She chuckles, repeating what she'd said not long ago. "Alright, I'll play along. Just turn off the lights because I can't be that bold with the lights on."

I shake my head. "Nope. If you're going to dominate me, little red, you're going to get a full view of exactly what you do to me."

She climbs off the bed, standing in front of me. She bites her bottom lip nervously but says, "Strip for me, and do it slowly."

She moves to sit on the edge of the bed, leaning back on her hands as she watches me with a small smirk spread across her lips.

I resist the urge to talk back, biting my own lip as I grip the collar of my shirt from the back, pulling it over my head and tossing it playfully at her. Running my hands down my chest and slowly over my abs, I see her breasts heave against the material of her V-neck top. My cock twitches against my zipper.

My fingers wrap around the belt buckle, unfastening it. I tug it out of the loops in one smooth motion. She falls back against the bed, swinging her arm over her face as she squeals. "Oh my god, you didn't! That was so hot!"

I laugh, dropping my pants and briefs to the ground, kicking them off. When she uncovers her eyes, I'm standing before her with my dick fully erect, bobbing against my abdomen. Her plump lips pop open, eyes dilating as she takes me in.

"It looks like you're ready to play," she tells me.

"For you? Always," I say.

She lifts a brow at me. "Then beg for it," she says, her voice dropping an octave.

I drop to my knees as if on instinct. "Crawl to me," she instructs.

Placing my palms on the ground, I make my way to her and set my chin on her knee. "What a good boy." She grins.

"Can I *please* eat your pretty pussy until you come all over my tongue?" I plead, and my cock twitches against my abdomen as she parts her thighs a millimeter, fully unaware of her body's response.

"I don't know, *can* you?" Her eyebrows climb her forehead as she stares down at me.

Fuck me, this is hot.

"*May I please* eat your gorgeous cunt?" I ask, my tone pleading.

"Better," she remarks. "*You may.*"

My fingers hook into her waistband, tugging her pants down her legs along with her panties. I toss them to the side, but she squeezes her thighs closed. Leaning forward, she whispers in my ear, "Fold them like a good boy, or you'll starve."

I'm practically salivating for her, but I reach for the clothing. I fold them both meticulously as she pulls her top and bra off over her head, tossing them into my face.

She watches as I fold them, placing them delicately on the edge of the bed beside her. "Is this how you like them?"

"It'll do," she tells me flippantly, but her grin gives her away. Lark opens her thighs wide, placing one on each of my shoulders.

"Eat," is all she says. *One word, and I obey.*

My tongue darts out, circling her clit with the tip. A moan slips past my lips as her sweetness lights my tastebuds. My cock feels engorged, precum dripping from the tip. Her fingers slip into my hair, tugging my face into her. I lap her up as she moans my name, but it doesn't last long.

She pulls my face away, tugging on my roots. I look up at her, concerned that I may have hurt her, but she says, "I said *beg*."

I groan. "I want to taste you and feel you come around my tongue. Will you please let me make you come? I'll do *anything* to watch you come on my tongue."

She responds by pressing my face back into her. I wrap my hands around her thighs for purchase, my fingertips digging into her creamy flesh. She's bucking against my face, riding out her pleasure as her cum drips down my chin. I swirl my tongue inside of her, feeling her walls clench around me.

God, she's fucking perfect. I'd do just about anything to stay right here for the rest of time.

Chapter Fifty-Two
Lark

My thighs are clenching around his face as I buck against him, unable to stop myself as his tongue delves inside me. My skin is on fire, and the sheets beneath me feel rough against my overly sensitive skin.

He drags his teeth along the inside of my lips, alternating between nipping and sucking on the tingling flesh.

It's almost more than I can handle, and just as I'm about to beg him to stop, I topple over the edge. My orgasm crashes through me as I shatter around him, panting with exhaustion from the way my body reacts to him.

When I'm finished, he sits up on his heels, smiling up at me, his eyes dancing. He's clearly amused by how much I enjoyed myself.

"What would you like me to do next?" he asks, clearly eager to provide anything I might think up.

Unfortunately, I hadn't really gotten this far in the fantasy. I'd planned to boss him around, but since I've never actually done that before, coming up with what to tell him to do is sort of difficult.

"Don't overthink it," he tells me gently.

"Okay, lie on your back," I tell him, scooting over to the side of the bed for him to join me.

He does as I say, staring at me eagerly. I grab the clit sucker from my nightstand and maneuver myself over him, straddling his waist.

Before I start, his gold chain catches my eye, and I'm not sure why, but it brings me a huge amount of joy to do this one little thing. "Take your chain off and clip it around my neck," I instruct him, pulling my hair up so it doesn't get caught.

He eyes me speculatively, his brow quirked, but he does as I say. The warm metal slings around my throat and, with it, the smallest hint of his usual cologne. Another flood of wet heat pools in my core with the idea of having something of his pressed against my skin as I do whatever I want with him.

I drop my hands back to his hard chest, letting my hair fall around my shoulders as I reach for the toy. I rub my hips back and forth along his length and watch with satisfaction as his fingertips twitch to touch me.

"Can I *please* touch you, any part of you?" he begs, and I smirk, shaking my head *no*.

I balance myself over the top of him with my right hand and bring my left between us, pressing the toy to my clit. My head snaps back with the intensity, and I feel his hands land on my hips.

My eyes reach his, and a guilty look greets me. "Did I say you could touch me?"

"You didn't," he admits, his voice soft as if he's truly in trouble for something.

"Now, what am I going to do with you? You can't even follow a simple command," I tell him, doing my fucking best not to let a laugh slip free. I might be enjoying this a bit too much, and not even for the reasons we're trying to explore. *This is fucking fun.*

He casts his gaze downward to where my hand is still firmly pressed against my core, the suction driving me wild, but it's not quite as distracting as the man beneath me. "I think I deserve to be punished," he tells me, sounding shy. "You should smack me for being disobedient, but I have to warn you," he says, his crystal-clear eyes crinkling at the corners. "I might *really* like it."

Oh fuck.

I practically collapse onto his chest, but the idea of smacking this man across the face is both hilarious and fucking sexy as hell.

Before I can respond, he says, "*Please, mon petite rouge,* I'm begging you to discipline me so I can be worthy of your sweet cunt."

My hand rears back almost of its own accord. *Well, I guess I've made that decision.* Gianni's amused expression tells me everything I need to know. *He was dead serious.* He's going to like this.

My palm flies across his cheek, making contact with a quick "thwack," and I instantly feel his hard length twitch beneath me as his gaze smolders, and he lets out a low moan. The red palm print I left acts as a reminder of just how filthy this man likes it in the bedroom, and I can fully say *I've been missing out.*

I see his belt hanging on the back of the chair beside my desk. I climb off him and grab it, tying it around his wrists and securing him to my headboard. "Much better." I smirk as I climb back on top of him. "Now you can't touch me until I tell you to."

Gianni groans loudly, clenching his eyes shut as if he's in pain, and I revel in the way this man wants me.

I continue to pleasure myself with the toy as he watches, his full bottom lip paying the price of our little game here as he bites his lip so hard he's drawing blood.

My core is clenching tightly with every passing moment, and I can't take it anymore. I want him inside me.

"Are you ready to fuck me?" I ask, and his teeth finally leave his lip. His tongue darts out, licking the blood away before he replies.

"Please, god, please let me fuck you. *It's all I want.*" He moans out his plea.

"Well, alright. I guess you've been a good boy," I tell him, placing the toy beside us and leaning across him to undo the belt buckle. My breasts are hovering over his face, and I'm deliberately slow as I remove his restraints, his mouth inching closer to my pebbled nipples.

"See something you like?" I ask.

He nods with vigor. "Can I suck on your gorgeous nipples? I just want a taste," he whines.

I nod, allowing him to because I want it arguably far more than he does.

He drags a nipple into his mouth, moaning as he sucks and swirls his tongue around the sensitive bud. I feel the head of his dick pressing against my center, and it takes every ounce of self-control for me not to just bounce onto it.

I have a plan, I remind myself, finishing unfastening him from the headboard. I lie down beside him as he rolls his wrists, shaking them out and renewing blood flow.

"What next?" he asks.

"Simple missionary..." I taunt. "With a twist." I smile up at him and watch as he positions himself between my legs.

"Do I get to bury myself inside you now?"

I nod. "I suppose," I joke.

He wastes no time sinking himself deep inside me. I stretch around him, trying to relax my muscles to let him all the way in. He's just too fucking big.

I'll admit, it's a pleasant problem to have though.

"Ask nicely, and I'll let you make me come." I smile brightly.

His eyes flare with heat as he plows into me, my body shifting with every rapid thrust of his hips. His hand snakes between us, and he takes my clit between his fingers, circling and tugging on it.

My eyes roll to the back of my head, my toes curling and core clenching with every thrust. *I'm so close.*

I'm moments from coming apart around him, but one last idea hits me. I hoist my leg up as high as I can get it, the change in angle allowing him to drive even deeper into me, which I hadn't thought possible before.

I bring my toes to his mouth, and with a smirk, I tell him, "If you want to make us come together, suck."

With the hand that isn't currently occupied, he grips the arch of my foot, dragging my toes to his mouth and wrapping those full lips around them. He sucks as he continues pounding into me, and I damn near lose my mind.

I come apart around him, pulsating and writhing against him, calling out his name so many times I lose count.

"Fuck," he grinds out. "That's it, baby. Give me everything you've got."

He lengthens inside me, and I feel his hot cum filling me to the brim before he finally collapses on top of me, our chests drawn together, heaving.

***

"Okay, I've thought of another thing I want," I tell him, peering over at him.

Gianni rolls his head to the side to look at me, and he's wearing a slight smirk. "You wore me out already. Role play is over, so you don't call the shots anymore."

"I *always* call the shots," I tell him, winking so he knows I'm kidding. *We're equals.*

"You're not wrong. Where I'm concerned, you certainly do," he tells me. "What would make that pretty smile of yours stay in place, hmm?" he asks.

"I want you to play a song for me," I tell him.

He rolls his eyes, wearing a silly grin. "Done, but you know what that means, right?" he asks, and I have *no idea*.

I shake my head, and he says, "We'll have to actually get dressed because I need to grab some instruments from my place."

I groan. "You mean you can't just walk around naked all the time for my viewing pleasure?" I ask, my voice full of mirth.

He shakes his head, his unruly dark waves sticking to his damp forehead. "Unfortunately not. I mean, I'd do just about anything to make you happy, but it wouldn't last long because I'd wind up in prison for indecent exposure." He laughs.

I groan, resigned, as I sit up, dragging the sheet with me. "Fair enough. I suppose I'll allow it in that case."

He shifts beside me, sitting up and grabbing his clothes to get dressed.

It's hard not to pout about it when he puts his clothing back on. It should be illegal to cover all of *that*.

Once dressed, he bends forward, pressing a kiss to my forehead. "I'll be back in a few."

***

Gianni has quite the setup here. We're sitting on the couch with his keyboard sitting on a stand, a guitar, and a tambourine.

"Okay, what would you like me to play first?" he asks.

I'm at a loss. I think I've had to make entirely *too many* decisions today. "Just play whatever will make *you* feel good," I tell him.

His shoulders relax as he scoots to the edge of the couch and sets his hands on the keys. I see him close his eyes, seemingly lost in thought, and then it happens.

The most beautiful thing I've ever witnessed in my life.

He lets go of every warring emotion running rampant in his mind and just lets himself enjoy this with no qualms. My apartment fills with an unfamiliar melody that sounds so breathtakingly haunted, but it twists into something lighter and more upbeat.[1]

His body sways with the rhythm, eyes still shut as he trusts that he knows exactly where the keys are, and judging by the sound of it, he definitely does.

Tears prick my eyes as I slink back in my seat, listening as he takes us on a rollercoaster of emotions.[2] My heart seemingly speeds up and slows down as the music does, and I simply ride the wave with him.

He goes on like this for probably fifteen minutes or more, and when he's finished, my heart feels like it could explode. He leans back against the couch cushions with a small, contented smile that has butterflies fluttering around in my stomach.

Gianni De Laurentiis is *always* beautiful, but there is nothing more stunning than this man when he's content.

"That was incredible," I choke out. He wraps his arms around me, pulling me into him and holding me tight against his side.

"*You* are incredible, *mon petite rouge*. It's because of you that I can replace the dread I felt about playing with more of these happy memories. So *thank you* for that." His words settle something inside me, and over the next hour, he continues to swap back and forth between the piano and guitar. I officially know how he's so skilled with those fingers of his.

"Why the tambourine?" I finally ask because, truthfully, it seems like a strange choice.

---

1. **I Found – Amber Run**

2. **Fuck it I love you – Lana Del Rey**

"Just because you were terrible at the violin in middle school doesn't mean you can't at least play *something*," he tells me with a smirk.

"Here, I'll show you how it's done," he says. He spends a few minutes instructing me on how to hold it and which way is best to gain speed or change the sound, and when I feel sort of ready, he chooses a Latin playlist from his phone.

We laugh the entire time as I do my best to match his motions, but ultimately, I'm speeding up when I should be slowing down, and I think the fact that I'm left-handed makes it even more difficult for me to copy his movements. He tries to show me with his left hand instead, but that proves to be a waste of time.

Not because *he* doesn't figure it out, but because, apparently, my middle school orchestra teacher was *right*.

I may not have mastered a new instrument today, but I got to spend it with one of my newfound favorite people, and that makes my heart soar beyond the clouds.

Gianni pulls me into his arms, laying us across the couch as he buries his face in my hair. I have no desire to be anywhere but here. Having Gianni in my life makes even the most mundane things seem groundbreaking, and a peace I've never known until now settles into my chest.

I thought I'd known what love felt like, but I'm sure that I hadn't. *Until now.*

Chapter Fifty-Three

Gianni

Friday, May 16, 2025

I'm seated at the end of the long dinner table, waiting for Dante to bring out the birthday cake for Dad.

As he enters the room, Ale turns down the lights, and we all start singing, "Tanti Auguri a Te."

Even in the dim light, I can see Dad's cheeks turning pink. We do this every year, and yet, he still seems embarrassed by something as simple as his family singing "Happy Birthday" to him.

He's the epitome of not wanting to be the center of attention, and I guess that's one of many reasons he and Mom are so good together. They share the same values, but their personalities contrast in ways that just seem to work.

Much like Lark and me.

Where I like to remain inside, watching reruns and doing something low-key, she likes to be out and about, exploring the world and just enjoying all that life has to offer. Knowing that I play some part in helping her slow down, relax, and enjoy what can be found in moments of stillness has warmth flowing freely through me. In contrast, she makes me feel alive and encourages me to enjoy adventure, even if I'm uncomfortable at first.

Dad leans over to Mom's chair, planting a kiss on her cheek and whispering in her ear before turning his attention back to the rest of us. "Thank you, everyone," he says sheepishly.

***

When the kids are all tucked into bed, having their weekly sleepover a couple of days early, we're all seated in the living room.

Mom turns her attention to me, and a wary feeling creeps in at the look of mischief playing across her face.

"Alright, sweet boy. Go ahead and tell us about your plans to make things with Lark official." As she says this, my gaze catches on my dad's. He shoots me a sly smirk, sinking back into his armchair with his arms crossed over his stomach. He's looking entirely too damn happy that the attention is no longer on him.

Unfortunately, I don't share the sentiment.

Everyone is watching me and waiting excitedly.

I shift uncomfortably in my seat. "I don't know what you want me to say," I tell them, my breath accelerating, and it feels difficult to sit still.

"We want you to own up to the fact that you fucking love her, you doofus, and then tell *her* that so we can all stop talking about you in the group chat," Luca informs me.

My eyes shoot up to his. "What the hell do you mean? I'm in the damn group chat." I grunt. Hell, I wish I weren't though. With the way my family talks all damn day, you'd think we never saw each other.

"Not this one," he says and smirks.

"What is going on?" I groan, wanting to get this sorted so I can go home with Pickles.

"You're clearly in love with her, and frankly, we've never seen you so happy, Gi." Kat fills me in, her expression soft.

"All we want is for you to be happy, and *clearly*, you are with Lark. We don't want you to wait so long to tell her that you waste precious time with her," Charlie explains.

I nod, slowly taking in what they're trying to get across. "I want to tell her, but it's only been a few months since we met, and I don't want to scare her off."

Being this vulnerable about my feelings is extremely new to me, but I'm sure Dr. Fasano will be proud as hell when I tell him during next week's appointment.

"No offense, but you'd have to be blind not to see the way that woman looks at you. She feels the same as you do; I'm absolutely certain of it," Ale says. His words fill me with a kind of hope that I can't help but fear because when there's hope, it's that much easier to be crushed if the outcome isn't what you want.

I avert my gaze, not wanting to look at any of them, as I mutter, "I'll tell her soon. I just need a little more time to convince myself she isn't going to run for the hills."

***

I can't sleep as I lie in bed, my family's words flitting through my mind.

What if she doesn't feel the same? The thought sinks to the pit of my stomach, but a new one quickly follows it.

But what if she does?

That's all it takes for me to decide. I'm going to tell her how I feel, *and soon.*

Chapter Fifty-Four

Lark

"Be good today, Rex; Gianni's gonna stop by to take you on a walk later," I tell him and blow him a kiss. As usual, he glares over his shoulder at me and goes back to napping like his usual grumpy self.

I lock the door and head downstairs with Tiny. My phone vibrates in my pocket as we make our way to the parking lot so we can head to work.

"Hey, Dad," I say as I open the back door for Tiny to climb inside.

"Hey, do you have any plans for tonight?"

"Uh, yeah. Sorry, I do, actually. It's Kira's birthday, so I'm going out to dinner with the girls."

"You think Kira and the girls would mind if I tagged along?" It takes all of my restraint not to burst out laughing. He has known since we were in high school that Kira would *never* mind having him around.

"I don't think that'll be a problem. I'll send you the name of the restaurant when I get to work."

"Sounds good, little bird. I can't wait to see you and the girls. Have a good day at work," he tells me.

"You too, Dad. Love you."

"Love you more," he says before hanging up.

***

We're seated on the patio of a restaurant Kira's uncle owns, and the sun is starting to set, creating the most beautiful halo around us.

"I'm surprised Daddy Hughes asked to join us tonight," Kira muses beside Madison and Jade, knowing damn well it annoys me when she calls him that. She also knows that it's her birthday, and I won't say anything for that reason alone.

"Speak of the devil," Madison whispers across from me as she peers over my shoulder to where the parking lot is. "And it seems he isn't alone." She laughs quietly.

That gains my attention. I turn to figure out what she could be talking about, and sure enough, Shay is walking hand in hand with my dad.

Finally.

I knew they had a thing for one another.

Dad and Shay approach our table, Shay's bronze cheeks literally glowing in the sun with the massive smile she's wearing.

He releases her hand just long enough to shoot me a wink and bend down to hug Kira. "Hey there, birthday girl. Thanks for letting me crash your party," he tells her, planting a kiss on her cheek and handing her the massive balloon bouquet he has tied to a small black-and-white gift bag.

"For you?" she asks, waving him off. "Anything." She turns her attention over to Shay. "And Shay, my favorite realtor! How are you?"

"Happy Birthday, Kira. I'm doing really great," she tells her, taking a seat beside my dad, who plants himself to my right. Shay worked with Kira to find the salon she now owns.

"I bet you are," Kira hums suggestively. My cheeks heat, but I roll my eyes, ignoring her antics.

Jade interjects, always acting as the peacekeeper. "Hey, Dereck. I'm glad you made it. I feel like we haven't seen you in forever."

He meets Jade's round eyes with a warm smile. "Unfortunately, that's because you haven't. We really need to bring back the days of trash-talking soccer players and binge eating junk food at the house." He chuckles.

"I'm pretty sure we haven't done that since undergrad," Madison chimes in. "But I agree, it was my favorite part of the sport."

"You wound me!" Dad says, clutching his chest. As the owner of a soccer team, he takes it rather seriously.

The waiter comes out moments later, bringing out waters and taking everyone's drink and appetizer orders.

As soon as he heads back inside, Kira turns her attention to my dad. "Alright, Dereck. Let's get to business. What's this all about?" she asks, jutting her chin out toward where Shay and Dad have their hands interlocked under the table.

Dad's smile spreads, and he turns to look at me. "Shay and I are in a relationship," he tells me.

I roll my eyes, smirking as I say, "Obviously."

"I considered talking to you about it since she's the first woman I've dated since your mom left, but Shay convinced me that you'd just roll your eyes at me and tell me I was being ridiculous. It turns out, she knows you pretty well." He laughs.

Shay leans across him. "To be fair, I told him he absolutely could have a private conversation with you about it, but I really thought you'd think that was absurd, so I guess I was banking on it."

A smile spreads across my face, and my chest feels like it's expanding. "Well, you were definitely right. I'm really happy for you both," I tell them, honestly.

"Good," Kira says, leaning back in her chair. The waiter cuts her train of thought short as he delivers our drinks.

"As I was saying," she starts the moment he's left. "I'm glad Dereck's found love." She winks at him. "And our Larky has too." She leans forward on her elbows, cupping her cheeks in a cartoonish display.

"She has, has she?" Dad questions, his voice light as if he's holding in a laugh.

"Isn't it Kira's birthday? Shouldn't we be talking about her favorite subject?"

"Herself!" Madison finishes for me.

The whole table erupts in laughter, but Kira takes her fork and gently taps it against her wineglass to get our attention.

"Ha ha ha, very funny. As it turns out, my favorite subject is *actually* the latest gossip. So spill the beans, Larky."

"Yeah, little bird. Tell us all about you and Gianni De Laurentiis," Dad goads me.

Of course he'd have figured it out. Not that I was trying to hide it.

My cheeks turn pink as I'm suddenly reminded of all the things I've done with and *to* that gorgeous man.

"What *exactly* do you want to know?" I ask, stalling as I prepare myself to let out all the things I've been thinking for months now.

"Oh, you know better than that, little bird. We want to know everything, but *please* save the sex talk for when I'm not around," Dad explains.

I lean back in my chair and feel a chill quake through me now that the sun has officially set. Shifting my body so my back is to the patio heater, I get started from the beginning.

Several minutes pass as they all eat, watching me intently and hanging onto my every word as I tell them about Gianni, how selfless he is, and how he immediately came to check on me the day I passed out on the field. I tell them about how he's purchased himself several diabetic rescue kits that he keeps in his car, backpack, and apartment.

They're floored by the time I get to the art studio he made me and how incredibly perfect it was. Kira begs to see pictures now that I've had a chance to hang up some of my art. She's particularly invested since she's been holding that secret close to her chest for a little while now, as she was the one who helped him with it.

"It's perfect," she says in a hushed tone. "Absolutely beautiful."

Madison grabs the phone from her, taking it all in, and I see the moment her eyes snag on the painted stool. Jade leans over her shoulder, and a smile turns her lips up.

"My turn," Dad says when he can't wait any longer. He snatches it out of Madison's hand, causing her to giggle.

He and Shay take it all in as I wait in silence. His eyes finally look up to meet mine. "Lark, this is…" His words get cut off as he chokes back emotion. "That man loves you," he says, his tone reverent.

And at precisely that moment, I realize the truth behind his words. As if hearing someone else point them out was just what I needed to get them through my thick skull. More than that, I realize I feel the same.

I've fallen for this man. So deeply that I don't know how I'd ever dig myself out of the valley of my despair if I had to go back to living in a world without him.

Sudden sadness starts to seep in, the feeling crushing me as I think about how my dad must've felt to lose the love of his life. I look over his shoulder to see how relaxed Shay is with him, her hip connected with his and her eyes filled with all the love she's been holding back all these years as they fought their emotions.

"I'm so glad you two finally gave in to each other," I tell them, my voice sounding strange to my own ears as I hold in the tears clawing their way up my throat.

Dad looks over to Shay, squeezes her hand and kisses the top of her head. "I am too," he admits. "And it looks like my little girl has found the one who makes her heart happy too. And that absolutely thrills me," he tells me. "Even if he *is* one of my players," he jokes with a wink to lighten the mood.

The next couple of hours are a lot lighter as we eat dinner, bullshit with each other, and eat tons of dessert.

Once we've walked Kira and her mountain of gifts to her car, Madison and Jade leave with her. Unfortunately, I have to head to work for the night, so I won't get to join them for movies and a sleepover.

Once they've pulled out of the parking lot, Dad brings Shay to his car, opening the door for her and buckling her seatbelt.

It's nice to see him happier than usual and, of course, always the gentleman.

Once her door is closed, he rounds the car to start it for her, calling over his shoulder at me, "Just one minute, little bird!"

"Take your time, Daddy-O," I tell him.

He walks me over to my car, stopping to open the door of my Firebird for me. He pulls me in for a tight hug before I get in, but instead of releasing me right away, he tells me, "Gianni is a good guy, and he clearly makes you happy. I'm not sure what's holding you back, but based on the way he's come out of his shell for you, I think it's safe to say he feels the same. Maybe it's time you make a move, just like Shay did." He chuckles.

That surprises the hell out of me because Shay has always been the quiet type. My eyes bug out of my head, and I pull back to see his shit-eating grin. "There's no point in waiting when it feels so damn good to finally claim them as yours. Find those big-girl panties of yours and put 'em on, little bird. I'm pretty confident in saying that you won't regret it."

"Thanks, Dad. I'll figure it out soon," I promise.

"Glad to hear it, little bird," he says, releasing me. I bend down to get into my car and buckle my seatbelt. Before he closes the door, he says, "One last thing before I head out."

My brow lifts in interest. "You work too damn much, and you shouldn't be missing girls' nights with your friends because you don't have the staff available to cover a shift for someone else. I'm paying to hire two new docs, and don't worry, you can hold all the interviews."

I start to interject, but he holds up his palm to stop me. "Please, Lark, just let me do this for you. It's a literal drop in the bucket for me, and it would make me feel better to know you aren't working all hours of the night and missing out on life."

I give him a smile, resigning to this because it *would* be nice to not constantly have to turn down plans with my friends or Gianni.

"Okay, fine. Thank you," I tell him.

He goes to close the door, but a mischievous smile quirks his lips before he does. "Oh, and I fired Val. Betty called me to complain, and you know I can't say no to that woman. Besides, Val needs to get her head out of her ass."

That makes me burst out laughing as he slams the door shut, heading back to his car with Shay waiting inside.

***

It's late, and there's no one in the waiting room, so I should sleep, but I can't stop thinking about what my dad said before he left.

As usual, he knows exactly what he's talking about.

Gianni is the most thoughtful person I've ever met. The constant stream of red and pink peonies on my counter, which he miraculously refreshes just before they start to get droopy, is just one of the seemingly insignificant reminders of just how *good* he is. To his core, Gianni is a *good man*.

Everything about being with him feels so *right*.

I feel more comfortable with him than I ever have in my life, and I can actually see a future with him. I can picture us eloping, surrounded by no one except our closest friends and our immediate family members. I can see us having children, one way or another, and I can *definitely* picture all the ways in which we'd try to get pregnant.

These are all things I'd never thought about with Tyler. I always played it day by day with him, and I guess that's because, deep down, I never had any plans for a future with him.

The soul-crushing, gnawing feeling I get in my gut at imagining going back to a life without Gianni is reason enough to tell him exactly how I feel.

"I'm in love with Gianni Elisio Amato-De Laurentiis," I whisper into my dark office.

And I want him to know it.

Chapter Fifty-Five

Gianni

Monday, May 19, 2025

It's been two weeks since Lark agreed to look into whether or not her insurance covers that damn insulin pump. Something you'd really fucking think would be covered, considering their existence drives down the rates of people with diabetes ending up in the emergency room due to a hyperglycemic episode or, worse, diabetic ketoacidosis.

But of course, the insurance companies aren't thinking about the future. They just want to do anything they can to save a buck in the here and now.

Fuckers.

Rather than bug Lark about it because I'm sure she'd just forgotten with how busy things have been at the clinic, I figure I may as well take it off her plate and give myself, and maybe even her dad, some peace of mind.

I watch as the delivery service app moves across my screen, counting down how many stops away the package is. When he finally gets to my door, I greet the young guy, thank him, and take the package inside to figure out how the fuck to assemble this thing.

Chapter Fifty-Six
Lark

I text Gianni as soon as I'm home, and his response has my stomach twisting in knots.

> Gianni
>
> Hey, little red. I'm sorry I missed you. I have an away game tomorrow and we left about an hour ago. I left a gift for you on the kitchen counter and took Rex for a walk. I hope you don't mind. Xo, Gi.

I enter my apartment with Tiny, surveilling the space for any sign of Rex. He doesn't come running and barking out from his bed like he normally does, but when I see him curled up in the corner of the couch, I realize exactly why.

I head over to him, scratching behind his ears as I take in the sight of my once-seemingly feral dog, now using Gianni's sweatshirt as a cushion under his tiny ass.

I shake my head as I walk to the kitchen, and a small box awaits me. I open the package up, and what greets me has salty tears pooling in my eyes.

An insulin pump.

Not just any insulin pump, but the automatic delivery system that syncs with my Dexcom.

Goddamn this man. He's too sweet for my own good.

> Have I ever told you that you're the sweetest man alive?

Gianni
> Not recently, but I accept <3

Gianni
> Goodnight, mon petite rouge. I'll see you tomorrow night.

And when he does, I'll finally tell him I'm in love with him.

Chapter Fifty-Seven

Gianni

Wednesday, May 21, 2025

I wanted nothing more than to get home after my game and run to Lark so I could *finally* tell her how I'd been feeling all this time.

But instead, someone called out of work sick, and she had to cover their shift.

And now, I have to wait two more days to see her because I've got another away game.

I take a deep breath in, trying to steady myself.

All I want is to *finally* tell her how madly in love with her I am.

Chapter Fifty-Eight

Lark

Saturday, May 24, 2025

This week is *so* not going as I'd hoped it would.

Instead of finally getting to admit to the man of my dreams how much I love him and hoping like hell he feels the same, which I'm pretty goddamn confident he is, I keep having to cover shifts for my employees because their kids have all managed to infect them with some horrid stomach bug.

On the one hand, I'm glad I don't have kids right now to make me sick. On the other, at least if I were home sick, I'd get to see Gi.

God, I miss him.

Chapter Fifty-Nine

Gianni

> Please tell me you'll be at the game tomorrow.

Mon Petite Rouge

> Yes! I won't miss it! Everyone seems to have recovered from that bug, and I'll finally have the whole day off. I can't wait to see you.

> Can I drive you there? You'd have to be early as hell since I have to be, but I want to see you.

Mon Petite Rouge

> I can't :(I'm still at work right now and don't get off till an hour before your game starts, but I WILL BE THERE! I promise <3

> I wish you were here right now, in my arms. I miss you, little red.

Mon Petite Rouge

> I miss you too, mon ciel étoilé. More than you know.

Little does *she* know just how much I miss her.

How much I love her.

Chapter Sixty

Gianni

Sunday, May 25, 2025

I see Lark on the sidelines as I rush onto the field with my team. Her smile is beaming as her eyes meet mine, and my heart revs up, clenching tightly in my chest.

She waves at me and lifts the hem of her shirt, pointing to the device now stuck to the skin just above the waist of her shorts.

I tap a loose fist against my heart, and my throat feels tight as I return her bright smile.

Fuck, she's beautiful. And in just a few excruciatingly long hours, I'll have her in my arms.

***

Knowing that Lark now has an insulin pump as an extra measure to keep her safe helps me focus on the game, but regardless, it doesn't seem to matter today.

We have three minutes to score another goal and win this game. My muscles ache as I rush down the field, holding onto a fucking prayer that I'll make it there in time.

Chavez kicks the ball in my direction, but the opposing team's offense toes it in the opposite direction before I can get to it. My fists clench at my sides as I pump my arms quicker, frustration taking hold of me.

Sweat is dripping into my eyes, burning like hell. The salty wetness floods my mouth as I run toward the goal. I see their striker gain speed, his foot making contact with the ball and soaring right past Damien's outstretched hands.

We lose.

My jaw clenches, anger ripping through me. *What the fuck was he doing? He should have caught that.*

I fight the overwhelming urge to stomp my feet like a petulant child, but I'm blinded by rage when I notice Damien makes a beeline for Lark. She gives him a small wave, but her expression is visibly uncomfortable as she subconsciously angles her body away from him.

At my approach, Damien eyes me from over his shoulder, placing his hand at the small of her back. Her eyes widen, but before she can move, I'm gripping her waist, shoulder checking him out of my way. I spin us out of his reach, ignoring his existence entirely as I place her back on the ground. Her eyes flare, lips pursing with annoyance.

"What, Gi? Are you gonna lick me and call dibs on me like a child with a piece of candy?" she asks, her head cocked to the side in question. Her lips tip upward, challenging me in that playful way of hers so I know she isn't actually upset with me.

My lips curve into a smirk. "Lick you? *Hell no.* I'll do more than that." I run my hands up her arms, lowering my mouth to hover beside her ear. "I'll fucking spit in your mouth if it reminds you and everyone around you what's happening between us."

"And what, exactly, *is* happening?" She quirks her brow, arms crossed over her chest in defiance, but that tiny grin stays plastered across her face.

"Isn't it clear?" I ask her, my voice a strange mix of confusion and disbelief. "You," I say, loosely gripping her chin between my fingers, "are *mine*. And I'll be damned if you forget it."

Tugging her lips to mine, I claim her mouth.

My tongue slips inside, tangling with hers in a mix of salt and the strawberry lollipops she's always eating. Her hands snake up my chest, wrapping around my neck to pull me closer, and just when I'm ready to drag her up my body, I feel a large hand grip my shoulder, wrenching me out of her grip.

I reluctantly remove myself from Lark's embrace, and when I turn to find Damien wearing a sadistic smile, my blood runs cold. "Well, isn't this fucking adorable? Do you think your boyfriend would approve?" He taps his chin, making a show of this entire display of his. "Oh, that's right. *He's dead.*"

My fists clench tightly at my sides as rage overtakes me. Not for the first time, I want to slam my fist into this guy's face until he no longer resembles a person at all.

"Be the bigger person, Gi. Walk away. He's baiting you, and you know it." Alex's voice comes trickling into my mind, and as my fists begin to loosen, I'm hit with a wave of guilt. *No. He's right. You are dead, and someone's gotta teach this fucker to keep his goddamn mouth shut.*

I straighten my spine, encroaching on his space, and feel when his hot breath invades my lungs. He takes a step back, his eyes turning frantic, almost wild, as I follow him, allowing him no room to escape me without *literally* running. "This has gone on long enough, Damien. So it's now or never. Tell me what the fuck your problem is, or deal with it in silence. I don't care either way, but what you *aren't* going to do is talk shit about my best friend. *My dead best friend,* as you've just pointed out."

Instead of a snide remark, he straightens his spine, readying himself for the fight he's been practically begging for since he got here.

"What, cat's got your tongue?" I goad him.

"You know exactly what my problem is. You and Alex used to walk around like you were such hot shit, always acting as if he practically walked on fucking water with how goddamn nice you both tricked everyone into thinking he was. And now that he's gone, you're out here sucking face with the daughter of the man who owns our fucking team. So maybe ask yourself this, what the fuck is *your* problem?" he says, getting into my face.

I can feel more than see a crowd starting to form around us. Damien turns his head to look around for just a split second, but it's long enough to allow me to push my palms flat against his chest, knocking him several feet back.

"You think this is a game?" I say. The anger I felt just moments ago is renewed.

"Gianni, please just walk away from him. He's not worth it." Those words sound so familiar, and yet they aren't coming from Alex this time. Lark is standing beside me, her cheeks pink with emotion.

Damien takes the opportunity to shove me in the chest, but I grab his hands, wrenching them off me, and throw a punch that clips his jaw, the crunch of bone reverberating under my knuckles. *That's gonna leave a mark.*

His eyes blaze as they meet mine.

"Enlighten me, Damien. Not only did you take my best friend from me, but you tried to fucking *replace* him too. What's next? *What more do you want?*" I shout, my voice growing louder with every word.

"You're fucking crazier than I'd thought," he spits, blood-tinged saliva pooling out of his mouth. "He's the one who played me."

"What the hell are you talking about?" I scoff, shifting my position to angle myself in front of Lark. She doesn't think I notice her moving subtly closer to me, but she's wrong. *I notice everything about her.*

His face drops, hands falling slack to his sides. "He never texted me back," he breathes out. "And then he died."

It hits me then. *He really didn't know.*

Remorse dawns on Damien's face, his split lower lip hanging as he stares at me, glassy-eyed.

I realize what's happening a second too late. He collapses to the ground, a sob wracking his body, and guilt floods all of my senses.

Shit.

"*I told you to walk away, didn't I?*" I hear Alex's snarky voice invade my thoughts once more.

Reporters start to crowd our space, and panic seizes my lungs. I drop to my knees beside him, lowering my mouth to his ear as I say, "I'm not sure what the fuck is going on, but you don't want to do this here. Get the hell up." I practically plead for him not to involve my family in yet another scandal. His limp body makes no effort to move.

I groan, annoyance whispering through me as I make a split-second decision to actually *help* this douchebag.

"*That's more like it,*" Alex snarks from the recesses of my mind. *Oh, you fucking shut it. Even from wherever the hell you wound up, you still manage to be a royal pain in my ass.*

I tug Damien up, my arms supporting his weight from under his armpits as I drag him across the field toward the locker rooms.

The glare I shoot the guys at our entry is more than enough to send them all running out of the locker room to give us some privacy.

Once I let him go, he slouches down onto the bench, his shoulders slumped forward. I crouch down in front of him, snapping my fingers in his face, and he shows no sign that he notices.

"Hey, you've gotta tell me what the hell is going on," I demand, feeling clueless.

His brown eyes slowly make their ascent to meet mine, but instead of being fueled with his normal bad attitude and snark, they're filled with sadness.

"I..." He chokes on another sob. "I did this," he finishes.

"Did what?" I ask, confused, but quickly remember the words I'd just recently spoken to him out of anger and spite.

"I'm the reason he's dead," he says. His head hangs limply against his chest, his body shaking with the effort it takes him to suck in enough air to keep himself afloat.

"Listen," I say, doing my absolute best to sound comforting and not like a massive prick. "You had nothing to do with his death. I just..." I grip the hair at the nape of my neck in frustration. "I said those things out of anger. It doesn't make them true, but I'm really gonna need you to fill me in here. I barely even know you, and the only interactions we've had have been filled with nothing but homophobic slurs and lies. Alex was my best friend, but I wasn't his lover. And even if I were, what the hell does it matter to you?" I ask, unable to hide how much his words have bothered me over the last few months.

"I know you weren't," he says, his voice so small it's barely a whisper. "*Because I was.*"

It takes my mind several seconds to catch up, and when it finally does, my world comes crashing down around me in waves of frustration and understanding. "You and Alex." I breathe, and he nods his head to confirm it.

"That's why he was so adamant about picking you up," I say, more for myself than for him. "Why didn't he ever tell me?" I ask, not sure that I really want the answer.

"Because I begged him not to tell you. He *hated* hiding it from you, but I can't come out. I can't have people knowing I'm gay," he explains. "People are bad enough as it is, but in the world of men's sports? It carries a stigma far heavier than I'm able to bear. I just couldn't handle it. I don't want to put a target on my back, and when I texted Alex, he said you guys would come get me but that he was done hiding our relationship and that we'd have to, at a minimum, tell you. *I thought I was ready.*" He whispers that last sentence. Silent tears drain down his cheeks now. "He said he'd text me when he was on his way, but the text never came, so I thought he'd changed his mind about being with me," he cries, sucking in a breath.

"I don't know how I never realized it before," he sobs, his emotions ebbing and flowing with each passing moment. "*I'm the reason he's gone.*"

"No," I tell him firmly, my hands gripping his shoulders. "I was the one driving that car, and even *I* wasn't responsible for his death. For the longest time, I blamed myself. And then I blamed you," I admit, but quickly explain as his tortured expression meets mine. "But we could have gone for a drive for any number of reasons that night. And it wasn't my fault because while I was driving, I wasn't the one who was drunk. I wasn't the one who lost control of my vehicle. The *only* person at fault here is the man who made the decision to drink and drive that night, and he's paying for it by rotting in prison for the rest of his life."

"Such a small price to pay for the loss of someone so special," Damien says so quietly that I almost miss it.

I hear booming footsteps coming from behind us. "Gloria! You can't be in the men's locker room!" I hear Coach shout at my mom.

I can practically hear the eye roll she gives him before wheeling herself farther inside. "Cover up your jimmies, boys, 'cause Mama De Laurentiis is comin' in!"

"Jimmies?" Damien asks me in confusion, his head tilting to the side.

"Who the hell knows?" I grumble.

My mom wheels into the room, plugging her nose dramatically. "God, it reeks in here! This is *so* not how they describe it in the books."

"Books?" he asks, even more confused. This time, I just ignore him.

As my mom wheels herself beside us, she smiles at me, grabbing my hand and squeezing it tightly. "Care to explain what's going on in here?"

I look hesitantly to Damien before opening my mouth about any of this. She's my mother, the second most important woman in my life, but this isn't my story to tell.

Damien gives me a small nod, seemingly resigning to it. It seems he's learned pretty quickly that my mom isn't someone you say no to.

For the next several very tense minutes, I relay the entire explanation to my mom and watch as a parade of emotions flit across her tan face.

When I'm finished, Damien looks even more exhausted than he had. Mom pins him with her blue eyes, and a familiar softness fills them. She doesn't pity him. She empathizes with him.

That's potentially her best quality. Her ability to be aware that she doesn't understand what you've lived through, but to not cast judgment or try to tell you about a time she's lived through something similar. No, she just lets you feel what you need to feel and makes it known that she's there when you're ready to talk about it.

She places her hand gently against his cheek, drawing his attention to her the same way she has with all of her children on one occasion or another.

His sad eyes are brimming with tears, and it takes everything in me to not let the guilt I feel creeping in take over entirely.

He *was* a dick. I reacted based on the information I was presented with, and there was no way for me to have guessed any of this. I shouldn't blame myself for that. *I can't blame myself for that.*

"Damien, I don't know you well, and if I were a betting woman..." She chuckles at that. "Hell, who am I kidding? I *am* a betting woman. Who doesn't love a good casino?" She shakes her head when she sees his confusion and decides to move on, clearing her throat. "As I was saying, I'd bet that what we've seen of you, what you've shown us anyway, is not all there is, and much of it isn't even the truth. Is that right?"

He nods solemnly, giving in to this impromptu intervention of sorts.

"Good because I sincerely hope that you'll take this as a life lesson in authenticity. People will love and support you for who you are, Damien.

The *right* people. And I hope that I get to see more of who you are and get to meet the side of you that Alex knew. Because aside from my own children, that young man was the kindest person I'd ever known." Her eyes are glassy, and her voice chokes on her next words. "Which is how I know that he must've seen so much good in you. He was such an incredible man," she finishes, and my heart feels like it's being wrenched out of my chest.

I've never seen my mom openly fall apart before. She's always been the building blocks, holding my family up time and time again. I've never thought about all the times she must have mourned in private, protecting us from her own emotions.

She moves her hand from his cheek to his hand, squeezing reassuringly. Tears slide down both of their cheeks, and my stomach twists in knots. God, I fucking miss him. Before Lark, I had no idea how the hell I'd possibly make it without him. Some days, I still don't.

"I'm so sorry," he cries, his voice watery and strangled.

"Sweetheart, what happened to that young man is not your fault. I've known Alex almost all his life, and I can say with absolute confidence that he wouldn't have changed a single thing. He was always thinking ten steps ahead of everyone else, and if he'd known what would happen that night, I guarantee he'd still want to make sure you got home safely."

Damien nearly shatters, losing all of his resolve, and he practically falls into my mother's lap. She clutches him to her chest, gently patting his back as he crumbles.

"How can I ever make it up to him now that he's gone?" he asks, sounding earnest.

"I think the best thing you can do is to live your life for *you*. Be your most authentic self, just like Alex always had," she tells him.

An awkward feeling cloaks me, making me realize I haven't spoken a word during this entire exchange.

"Love is love is love, Damien. You'll always have the support of my family if and *when* you decide to allow yourself the joy of living as you truly are," she assures him.

He straightens, squeezing her knee gently, and his eyes flash to mine. "I'm sorry, Gianni." Before I can interrupt him to stop him from apologizing again, he continues. "Genuinely, I'm so damn sorry for the things I've said about you and about *him*. I was bitter and, if I'm honest, jealous. God, I was so damn jealous of the time you'd gotten to spend with him over the years, even just as friends. My rage was misplaced and, frankly, misguided. I don't expect you to forgive me, but I hope you know I'll spend every day, for the rest of my life, trying to make up for it and doing my best to honor his memory."

I clap him on the shoulder and peer down at him. "Consider it forgiven. If there's one thing Alex was good at, it was his exhausting ability to forgive at the drop of a hat." I give him a small smile, all of my rage from earlier effectively running dry.

He stands, looking between my mom and me. "Thank you, both," he tells us, his voice small but sure, and he heads out of the locker room.

"Alright, Gi. Now that that's settled, go get the girl because I'm getting tired of waiting on you to make things official with that sweet woman." She smirks, wheeling herself out of the locker room.

Shaking my head, I push what just happened to the side, deciding to reflect on it later, preferably with my psychologist and not another person in this smelly-ass locker room. My mind races, immediately traveling to Lark, who I'd just left confused as hell outside after some half-ass profession of love.

She deserves so much better than whatever that toxic masculine bullshit I just gave her was.

My feet hit the ground running as I make my way out of the locker room. My team is standing outside of the tunnel, waiting for the go-ahead, and as soon as they see me, they run inside, eager to get showered, changed, and home for the night.

My eyes scan the field, hoping like hell she's still out here and hasn't gone home with her dad already.

The moment I see her fiery hair shining in the bright sun, I'm at a full sprint toward her.

She sees me moments before I'm on her, her bowed lips curving up in a playful smile as I rush her. One of my hands curls around the nape of her neck, dragging her mouth to mine as the other digs into her hip, pulling her even more tightly against me.

Her lips part, and my tongue delves in, tangling with hers. She gasps as I drag her body up mine, and her legs wrap around my waist. Her hands clutch my jersey, returning the need I feel pouring through me.

I vaguely hear a throat clearing beside me, but it isn't until Lark is gently pushing me off her, her legs unwinding from me, that I release my hold on her.

I don't know who I expect, but Dereck Hughes, the owner of my team and Lark's father, is not it. And he doesn't look upset.

His arms are crossed over his chest, Tiny standing at his side obediently as he takes us in. One side of his lip is quirked in a strange grin. "You coming to dinner with us?" he asks me as if it's the most normal question in the world.

"Sir?" I ask, my head cocked in confusion.

He pats me on the shoulder before turning to head down the field, calling back toward us, "I'll see you both at six."

My brows pinch as I look back to Lark, who's wearing a content smile. "He never invited Tyler for dinner. He hated him," she says, shaking her head.

Pride rushes through me. "Really?"

"Yep." She reaches up on her tiptoes and presses a kiss to my cheek. "So what exactly does this make us?"

"I'll be anything you want me to, *mon petite rouge*," I tell her honestly.

She cups my cheek in her hand. "I just want *you* to be *you, mon ciel étoilé*. Because you are the most incredible person I know, and you light me up inside. I've loved nothing more than getting to know every piece of you, and I want nothing more than to continue."

My cheeks heat at her admission. "You know, I've never been in a relationship," I admit.

She smiles up at me, pressing another kiss to my cheek before whispering against the shell of my ear. "Then I look forward to being your *first* and your *last*."

I rest my hands over hers, staring down into her glimmering eyes. "Nothing would make me happier," I tell her. "Lark," I say, keeping my eyes trained on her so I don't miss any part of this moment. "I think I've known it for a while now but wasn't able to accurately put a word to it until more recently…"

The way her lips part and my heart starts pounding in my chest causes the words to get stuck in my throat for a moment. "I love you." I breathe, and she sucks in a sharp inhale, her eyes softening and pooling with tears. "Ever since we met, it's felt like you've been the thread, actively sewing together the shredded fibers of my soul. You're not just my muse. You don't just inspire me to work on myself for you or anyone else. You make me feel whole in a way I'm absolutely certain I've never experienced and will never be able to accurately describe. Being with you is my every desire encapsulated into one," I tell her, my voice cracking as a tear breaks free.

She clenches her eyes shut, tears streaming down her pink cheeks as she releases a sob. Her bottom lip quivers, and her hands drag down my neck. I hold them to my chest, waiting for her to look at me again, and when she does, all the air is sucked from my lungs.

The red puffiness surrounding her hazel eyes makes them look like the deepest swirl of calming green. "Gianni," she says with a sob, and the tears in my eyes flow freely now.

I don't care who's around to see. Lark isn't just my girlfriend. She's my partner. The love of my life. My other half. My reason for being, for existing, for working to better myself, for sticking around at all.

She's my everything.

"I love you so much," she finally says when the sobs have stopped wracking through her. Warmth radiates throughout my body, and my heartbeat continues to race as pure elation fills my chest. "I don't know how you manage to come up with all of the poetic stuff, and just like the violin *and the tambourine*," she says, groaning. "I'm not going to do it justice if I try. Instead, I just want you to know how special you are to me and everyone in your life. I know you may not see it, but *you are so damn special.*"

She stands on her tiptoes and presses a chaste kiss to my lips before wrapping her arms around my neck. "You've managed to heal years of wounds I hadn't even known I had," she says softly. "You're thoughtful beyond words, and your selflessness truly astounds me. I just want to spend every day, for the rest of our lives, in your arms."

My heart bursts open as I collect her in my arms, burying my face in her hair as her head rests above my heart.

Alex's voice creeps into my mind. *"Just like I've always said, you deserve the absolute best, and now you have her."*

And the only thing that could make it better would be you, I think to myself, wishing that Alex really were here to see this.

But who knows? *Maybe he is.*

Epilogue: Part One - Gianni

Thursday, December 18, 2025

I'm not sure I've ever been as happy as I am in this moment, though I'm nearly certain the feeling I'm about to experience in just a few minutes will be twice as good as this.

Butterflies are flying rampant in my stomach today as I lead the love of my life into a quiet bookstore. A bookstore I've managed to rent out for the evening.

As we enter, the owner waves at us from behind her desk but quickly disappears after greeting us.

Lark looks like she's moments from taking off down the aisles like a woman on a mission, and her giddy excitement fills me up inside.

"Calm down," I joke gently. "It's just a bookstore." *It's anything but.*

Her mouth drops in shock. "*Just* a bookstore?! Are you kidding? There's no such thing! Besides, *this* bookstore only sells romance, which automatically brings it to the top of my list."

I remember not so long ago, a time when there was an entirely different kind of list she was adding items to. And we haven't stopped since we crossed off all that she started with. Now *that* is my favorite kind of list.

She tugs on my hand, leading me toward an aisle I'm keenly familiar with after this morning. "Not so fast, little red. I have a surprise for you," I tell her.

Her wide eyes meet mine, and a smile tugs at her lips. "I love surprises!" she shouts. Once upon a time, I hated them, but seeing how goddamn excited she gets about them has easily changed my mind.

Not that that's a surprise to anyone.

I lead her toward a pile of books in the center of the room and grab the first one on the stack of orange illustrated books, handing it to her. She stares at it for a moment, and finally, she opens it up to the first page, where a note is handwritten inside for her.

She reads it aloud.

"Dans l'ascenseur que nous montons,

Appuyez le bouton, démarrez la tendance.

Où les repas sont préparés et les cœurs se réjouissent,

Suivez-moi dans une chambre si brillante.

> *Pas à pas, nous glissons à travers les portes,*
>
> *Vers un espace où la chaleur réside.*
>
> *Écoutez bien, la bouilloire chante,*
>
> *Trouvez l'endroit où le confort s'accroche."*

In the elevator, we go up,
Press the button, start the trend.
Where meals are prepared, and hearts rejoice,
Follow me into such a bright room.
Step by step, through the doors we slide,
Toward a space where warmth resides.
Listen carefully, the kettle is singing,
Find the place where comfort clings.

"Okay," she says. "Well, this book is *Elevator Pitch* and the riddle is talking about an elevator and a kitchen. So maybe the next book is about cooking?" she asks me.

I smile at her, extending my arm forward. "Lead the way."

She rolls her eyes, dragging me along down the aisles. She spots a doorway with dark wooden trim that leads us into another part of the store. She pulls us through it, similar to what the riddle had suggested. As soon as she sees the tall floor lamp lit up in the corner with a table and another stack of books beneath it, she sprints over to it. She grabs the book *Desserts for Stressed People* and opens it up, quickly reading the next poem.

"IN PAGES SWEET, WHERE SUGAR WEAVES,

A TALE OF LOVE IN FROSTING LEAVES,

A HIDDEN PATH BEGINS TO SHOW,

TO FIELDS WHERE PASSIONS FREELY FLOW.

FROM CAKES AND PIES, A LOVE DIVINE,

TO WHERE THE HEART AND SPORT ENTWINE,

FIND THE ROMANCE, KICK AND SCORE,

WHERE LOVE AND SOCCER MEET ONCE MORE."

Her eyes meet mine. "A soccer romance?" I nod, and she pulls me to the sports romance section. I watch as she trails her fingers along the spines of the books. They stop the moment she sees it.

A paper crane sits on top of a book called *Scoring Wilder*. She flips through the pages, and instead of a poem, a *Hockey Smut Book Club* bookmark falls out from the center of the pages. It's from someone my mom met online who runs her own smutty book club. Hopefully, this one will be pretty self-explanatory.

"A hockey book..." she says, trailing off. She turns around, looking through the hockey section and snags a book off the shelf with a maroon cover that looks sort of out of place amongst all of the blue, purple, and pink books.

"*Quiver?*" she asks, opening it up and finding another message written inside the cover, this time in Spanish. This one she stares at but doesn't read aloud. "You're gonna have to help me out here. I can't read this."

I chuckle. "Oh, come on. Lucia and Josie have been teaching you Spanish for months now."

She rolls her eyes at me. "Yeah, *months* not *years*. I've got something about goals being scored and hearts. That doesn't really help me."

I take the book from her, reading it in Spanish first and quickly translate it to English for her.

"IN THE GAME OF ICE AND FLEETING CHANCE,

WHERE HEARTS MAY GLIDE, AND SPARKS CAN DANCE,

A LOVE STORY STARTS WHERE GOALS ARE SCORED,

BUT SHIFTS TO DREAMS OF A STAR ADORED.

FROM SKATES AND STICKS TO GUITAR PICKS,

A second chance in life's grand mix,

Where a rock star's tune calls hearts to play,

Find your love On The Rocks today."

Her eyes go wide, and my favorite smile spreads across her lips. "I know that one!" she shouts, running toward a display labeled "Rock Star Romance."

She picks up the first book in the display, *On The Rocks,* a second-chance romance. This one simply reads, "Find the one that makes you *Quake* with need and emotion."

And again, she's off, sprinting back down the sports romance aisle. When she gets there, she can't seem to find it. Her frustration seems to grow, as does how goddamn adorable she is.

She lets out a huff. "I don't see it," she tells me. That's because this one has the spine turned toward the shelf.

"Look again," I tell her, nodding my head toward the end of the shelf where the book can be found.

Finally, she realizes which one it is.

This is it.

She pulls it from the shelf and grips it tightly to her chest as she spins around to meet my gaze, but I'm already on my knee beside her.

Faint music trickles in around us, and my whole world stops.

Her plump bottom lip juts out in shock as she takes me in, and the moment she sees the ring tethered to the bookmark inside *Quake,* she falls to her knees in front of me.

I can't help the laugh that rumbles through my chest at her completely ass-backward reaction to this.

"Lark, baby, what are you doing?" I ask.

Her eyes shimmer with moisture. "We're equals. We should be eye level for this," she squeaks out.

I shake my head gently, taking the book from her grasp and dislodging the ring. "Whatever you say, *mon petite rouge*."

I set the book aside, and the moment I do, she scoots into my lap, her face just inches from mine. I have to fight hard to keep the laughter from my words as I profess my undying love to this woman for what's probably the ten thousandth time since May.

"Before I met you, I never quite understood what it was like to love someone with every ounce of your being. To feel so connected to another person that it seems absolutely ridiculous to be apart for even a moment."

Her eyes are already welling with tears. *My sensitive girl.*

"I've been surrounded by people who love not only me but each other my entire life. I'd thought I had at least some grasp on what it all means," I say with a chuckle. "But god, I was so *wrong*."

"You came into my life when I least expected it, and while it definitely wasn't on an elevator, I can wholeheartedly say that your moving into my apartment building was divine intervention. As strange as this sounds, I kind of have myself convinced that Alex may have told that crow to toss Pickles that bone just so I could meet you," I tell her, and her lips crack into a smile. "And when that didn't work, he made sure you moved in so close to me that we couldn't escape this invisible string tethering us together."

She kisses the tip of my nose, laughing lightly on a watery half sob. "And then, that day when you invited me over and actually let me cook for you, I should've known right then that I was a goner," I say, shaking my head. "As much as I've always enjoyed soccer, I'm so fucking thankful that it brought you even further into my life, as did my mom's love of hockey romance and her ridiculous smutty book club." Lark snorts at that.

"And finally, when you became such an essential part of my day, allowing me to enjoy music again and encouraging me to be better for myself rather than for anyone else. That was really when I knew I'd gone too far. There's no turning back for me now, little red. I love you so much; it feels like I've lived every lifetime with you, and if there is an afterlife, I wouldn't want to explore it with anyone else. And hell, if there's not and we get reincarnated, something tells me we'll be together then too." I smile.

"But..." She snorts. "What if we're slugs or something?" she asks, and it only widens my smile.

"Then I'll love every moment of being a disgusting, slimy slug with you, *mon petite rouge*. Though, I sincerely hope that slugs live *very* short lives so we can get back to being human again," I tell her, my chest shaking with laughter.

She hums against me, wrapping her arms around my neck and bringing her lips to mine, pressing a soft kiss to them.

"Lark?" I ask softly, her body officially melted into mine.

"Hmm?" she says, completely content to just sit here with me on the floor of this bookstore.

"Lark, baby, are you gonna marry me or what?" I finally ask.

Her eyes snap up to mine, and *finally,* she pulls my mouth to hers for a kiss that has my soul skyrocketing with joy. "Yes! In every lifetime and on every planet, yes. I love you more than words could ever express," she tells me, those beautiful hazel eyes swimming with so many emotions as she meets my gaze.

"And I love you more than any song or poem could ever convey," I tell her earnestly as I take her hand in mine, pressing a kiss to her knuckles before placing the ring on her finger, *exactly where it belongs.*

Epilogue: Part Two - Lark

Saturday, September 16, 2028

When I head back downstairs, following the sound of the piano drifting through the house, my heart swells. Just like it does every time I see this man.

Lucia and Josie are seated on the couch, light smiles grazing their lips as they watch Gianni and Sammy sit side by side, their fingers sliding over the keys together.

Sammy's come out of his shell over the years, as has Gi. They've formed a bond that has helped Gianni reignite his love for music while allowing Sammy an outlet for his creativity.

Once upon a time, that creativity had been dragging him around by the neck as he struggled with his OCD, but now, he uses it as a healthy outlet for those big feelings he doesn't always seem to understand.

It's something that Arielle, Dante, Gianni, and I have discussed at length and have loved experiencing.

And now, I can't wait for Jeremy to experience it, too, when he's old enough. For now, he and Gi enjoy spending a lot of time plucking away at plastic guitars and toddler-sized pianos.

The music stops as the song comes to a wistful end. Sammy's bright eyes shoot up to meet mine. "Aunt Lark! I think I'm ready!"

A wide smile overtakes my face, my body lighting up with excitement. "You totally are! You're gonna crush it, little man!" I agree excitedly, approaching him and Gi. I ruffle his hair playfully as he passes me to plop down on the couch beside Benny and Josie.

Gi's arms wind around my hips, tugging me to him. I stand, tucked between his thighs, and my arms wind around his neck.

Those blue eyes shine up at me, and a small smile plays across his lips. "Wanna play a song with me, little red?"

My cheeks still occasionally flush when all of his attention is on me, and right now is no different.

I nod, sitting beside him. He brushes a strand of my hair behind my ear, the back of his knuckles lightly grazing my cheek as he does.

"How did I get so lucky?" he asks me quietly.

"I ask myself that question every day," I whisper back, pressing a kiss to his stubble-covered cheek and then another to the top of his hand where a red lark bird is etched into his skin.

He turns his attention back to the piano, his fingers nimbly gliding along the keys as he starts a song that I find so familiar. And... the only song I know how to play.[1]

My fingers move alongside his, missing a key here and there. My throat tightens, the feeling of excitement starting to well over.

Gianni kisses me softly when the music is finished and slides off the bench. He heads into the living room, sweeping Jeremy into his arms. Our little guy giggles; those big blue eyes, the same as his father's, nearly glow at the sight of his daddy.

1.

The doorbell rings, and momentarily, my thoughts are cut short as I shout, "I'll get it!"

Gi smiles at me and looks over to Sammy and Benny. "Your parents must be here to get you a little early," he tells them, and it takes everything in me not to blurt out the truth.

When I pull the door open, the whole family is standing outside, looks of confusion greeting me.

I had invited them all over tonight but didn't want them to get any ideas about why, so I had sent the messages individually.

My dad and Shay enter first, followed by Kira, Madison, and Jade, as well as the entire De Laurentiis crew.

They head into the living room, sitting anywhere they can find the space, and they all watch me expectantly. I can already see the gears turning, and of course, the moment my eyes meet Gloria's, I know she's already figured me out. When I look to her right, I see Angelo's small smirk, and he shoots me a fleeting wink. He's easily the most quiet one in the entire family, but where he lacks in words, he makes up for in perceptiveness.

Much like his wife, Angelo always knows what's going on with each of us, and I have a sneaking suspicion that he may actually be the one who feeds Gloria all of the hot gossip.

I send him a little wink back and turn my attention to Gi.

"Little red, do you care to tell us what's going on?" he asks me with a raised brow.

The whole room fills with chatter, everyone complaining about having to wait to find out about what's going on, so instead of answering, I race to the other room, grabbing the small gift bag I'd hidden.

I pull Gianni to the center of the room and plop down on the rug before handing him the bag.

He takes it tentatively, peering inside. He pulls the tissue paper out and then the tiny folded garment.

He unfolds it, and as he reads it, his eyes go wide before snapping to mine. A wide smile plays over his lips as he pulls me into his lap, crushing his mouth to mine and knocking the air out of my lungs.

The room erupts in cheers, and when we finally part, I see that Luca couldn't wait. He's standing, holding the onesie up for everyone to see the graphic: "Player #4... Loading."

Everyone buzzes with excitement, and my joy skyrockets again.

Epilogue: Part Two - Gianni

I'm still beaming from the news.

We're having another baby.

My arm is wrapped around her hips, my face still lined up with Lark's stomach as I litter her abdomen with kisses, paying special attention to the skin above her insulin pump.

Her fingers tangle in my hair, and she releases a contented sigh. "What will you do when we're old and gray and my legs stop working?" she muses.

I peer up to meet her gaze, a small smile playing on my lips. "I'll wheel you around, obviously."

She rolls her eyes gently. "And what about if you can't walk either?"

"Well, then I'll hire somebody to push us both at the same time, side by side, so we never have to part," I tell her, knowing there's absolutely nothing that could stop me from fulfilling that promise to her. Not even divine intervention.

"You seem so sure of yourself," she says, smiling down at me.

I press a final kiss to her belly, sliding farther up the bed to capture her lips with mine. She melts easily into me, sprawling on top of my body.

When we part, my lips graze the shell of her ear. "I've never been more sure of anything in my life. You're my end, and my beginning, and everything in between. We're made for each other," I whisper, pressing a kiss to that sensitive spot just below her ear. Her body shudders against me.

"I love you, *mon ciel étoilé.*"

"And I love you, *mon petite rouge.*"

The end.

Bonus Scene: Gianni

Saturday, June 8, 2030

Mom is seated in her wheelchair at the center of the aisle. As the final part of the ceremony comes to an end, my mom excitedly shouts, "You may now kiss the grooms!"

Damien and Aaron wind their arms around one another's necks, their lips locking in a passionate kiss. As they pull apart, the whole crowd hoots and hollers, waving tiny rainbow flags with big smiles plastered across their faces.

Several of Aaron's friends shoot off rainbow confetti cannons as the happy couple dances their way down the aisle and off to their reception.

Lark blows me a kiss, which I catch, pressing it into my chest just over my heart.

She shoots me a wink and heads off toward the reception area, realizing I need a moment alone with my mom.

Mom's eyes meet mine, and I reach out my hand for hers. She squeezes it, pressing a kiss to the top.

"Alex would be so proud," she tells me quietly.

I smile, knowing for certain that, as usual, she's right.

"Yes, yes, he would," I whisper.

Afterword

Quake is a work of fiction, but Gianni's depression resembles the real-life experiences of an estimated 280 million people worldwide. If you or someone you love is struggling with your mental health, please reach out for help. You are worthy of happiness, and I promise *it does get better*. But you'll never know that if you don't stick around to find out.

My DMs are always open, and I've included a link to a site that allows you to search for a crisis line in your country. This is not all-encompassing, unfortunately, but I hope it helps at least someone.

https://www.helpguide.org/find-help.htm

Please remember that you are worthy of joy, and your story is still being written. Don't type a period when a semicolon is just above it.

;

All my love,
Giuliana Victoria <3

***

If you'd like to see more of Luca, hold tight for his and Samara's book! You'll also get to *finally* see Kat & Ale's wedding <3

Acknowledgments

To the real life Dr. Hughes, thank you for listening to me and not making me feel like a neglectful dog parent when I swore something was wrong. My sweet Wiggly baby is back to her old self thanks to you and I literally could not thank you enough for that. So, the best I could do was write a smutty book about a really sweet, redheaded veterinarian. I hope you enjoy it <3

As always, my books not only require but deserve the use of sensitivity readers. **Quake** is no different, and I'm unbelievably blessed and thankful to each and every single one of the nearly fifty sensitivity readers who helped make this book as accurate and representative of as many people and their lived experiences with each of these conditions as possible. So thank you to each of you, with an extra special thanks to Zephyr, who answered far more of my questions than any one person should ever be subjected to.

Thank you to each of my readers, who have given my books a chance and have shown them all the love in the world. I actually can't believe I'm here, writing this acknowledgment, and about to release my fourth book in less than a year, so thank you for being here. I hope you stick around. <3

Evelyn Leigh (go read her books), thank you for always being here, reminding me that I'm a badass with a good ass, who writes stories that need to be shared. Thank you for lifting me up when I find myself crumpling under the immense pressure that comes with writing full-time, going to school full-time, and now work, and all other aspects of the author life and just life in general. I can't wait to see what kind of magic we continue to make! All my love to Cynthia and Kath (who each have incredible books you need to read!), and a special thank you to Kait for dealing with me every day, putting the hyperlinks in this book, and making sure I stay off of social media as much as possible!

To Sabrina for proofing this copy so random things weren't bolded or out of order, and Delaney for reading this early and helping me figure out where the hell to put some of these songs that I refused to take off of the list!

And, of course, to my husband, who is so incredibly supportive of every one of my ideas and reminds me that there's nothing I could possibly do to change that. You're the most amazing person, and I look forward to endless lifetimes spent loving you. If that's all I ever accomplish, it'll always be enough.

Xoxo,

Giuliana <3

About the Author

Giuliana Victoria is an author based in Pennsylvania who shares her readers' deep love of all things romance. She's a full-time physician assistant whose passion lies in being there for her patients during their most vulnerable moments and lifting their spirits to make a shitty situation a bit less lonely.

When Giuliana isn't writing swoon-worthy book boyfriends, she can be found delivering babies, hiking with her three large breed rescue dogs, and, of course, curled up with a good book beside her husband.

She hopes you'll love **Quake** as much as she enjoyed writing it, and she looks forward to sharing all of her future works with her incredible readers.

Books & Book Clubs Mentioned In Quake:

Elevator Pitch by Evelyn Leigh
    Desserts for Stressed People by Letizia Lorini
    Scoring Wilder by R.S. Grey
    Quiver by Giuliana Victoria (Me)
    On The Rocks by Marja Graham
    Always Smutty In Philadelphia Book Club
    Hockey Smut Book Club

Made in the USA
Columbia, SC
07 January 2025

01025cf2-2ed2-4b48-8622-945e9341fa21R01